the SONG of David

of David

NEW YORK TIMES BESTSELLING AUTHOR

AMY HARMON

Copyright © 2015 by Amy Harmon
Editing by Karey White
Cover design by Hang Le
Formatting by JT Formatting

Library of Congress Cataloging-in-Publication Data

Harmon, Amy
The Song of David — 1st edition
ISBN-13: 978-1514185018 | ISBN-10: 1514185016

TO THE FIGHTERS,

CODY CLARK
STEPHENIE THOMAS
RICHARD STOWELL
AND NICOLE RASMUSSEN,

AND TO THOSE WHO FIGHT BESIDE THEM.

Will you forget me forever?
How long will you hide your face from me?
How long must I wrestle with my thoughts
and day after day have sorrow in my heart?
How long will my enemy triumph over me?
Look on me and answer.
Give light to my eyes
Or I will sleep in death
And my enemy will say, "I have overcome him."

Psalm 13 – The Song of David

Prologue

Moses

MILLIE CALLED ME yesterday morning. Tag is gone. He's gone, and Millie doesn't know where to look for him, even if that were possible. He knows she can't follow him, and that doesn't sound like Tag. He's not cruel. Never has been.

The first time I met Millie, I knew Tag had found someone who might keep him still, keep him unraveled. She would happily untangle his knots and force him to slow down, and in return he would love her the way only Tag loves. It seemed like destiny, even though I don't believe in that shit. You'd think that I would, seeing what I see, knowing what I know, but knowing that there's a whole lot we don't understand has made me reluctant to indulge in foreordination, destiny, or things that people say are "meant to be." Saying something is "meant to be" is a cop out. It's a way for people to deal when they screw up or when life hands them a bowl of shit stew. The things that are meant to be are the things we can't control, the things we don't cause, the things that happen regardless of who or what we are. Like sunsets and snow-fall and natural disasters. I've never believed hardship or suffering was meant to be. I've never believed relationships were meant to be. We choose. In large part, we choose. We create, we make mistakes, we burn bridges, we build new ones.

But Tag is different. Tag *is* meant to be. He just is. He's a whirlwind, a tornado you can't control. He just sucks you up and in, but unlike a natural disaster, he never lets up. He never lets you go. Yet suddenly, without warning, he has. He's let go.

Three years ago, Tag and I came back to Salt Lake City and we stayed. In the beginning I worried that Tag wouldn't be able to settle down, and that I would have to let him go. He's always been restless, driven, and easily bored. When you spend almost six years traveling all over the world, it gets in your blood. The movement, the speed, the freedom. It becomes hard to stay in one place for very long. But he had. We both had. We'd run away together as lost boys looking for Neverland and somehow managed to come full circle as men.

Tag had dug in and developed an entire city block, a world that provided a home for all the people he attracted and adopted along the way. I'd built my reputation, grown my clientele, almost gotten myself killed, eventually reconnected with Georgia, and managed to convince her to marry me. Our daughter, Kathleen, was born six months ago. Tag cried when he held her the first time, completely unconcerned with the fact that he was supposed to be a badass. He had seemed so happy. So whole.

And now, inexplicably, he has let go.

He's let Millie go. He's let Tag Team, his businesses, his plans for a title fight, all go. He's let me go. And none of it makes any sense. If there were signs I hadn't seen them. And I am the guy that is supposed to see what others can't. I'm Moses Wright—medium, artist, best friend—and I hadn't seen the signs.

One

Moses

TAG DIDN'T LEAVE a note and his place was clean. More than clean. Boxed up, cleared out, a realtor's sign in the window. Tag isn't an especially tidy person, something he would have had to change if Millie moved in. Obviously his housekeeper had been and gone, but when I called her, she didn't know anything. Nobody knows anything. Tag didn't tell anyone he was going. His place is for sale, his truck is gone. He is gone. And he hasn't left a forwarding address.

He'd left an envelope at the gym with Millie's name on it. Inside were a set of keys—one to her front door, one to the training facility, one to the bar, one to a filing cabinet in his office at the gym. It took us a while to match the keys to their locks, but we had. It didn't feel like Tag was taking us on a wild goose chase. That wasn't his style either. He just didn't want us to find him. And that scared the shit out of me.

In the very top drawer of the gray filing cabinet, was a shoebox filled with cassette tapes. They were labeled with Tag's name, a number, and a bumpy sticker. A little tape recorder, the kind with the buttons on the end and the speaker along the long top, the kind that looks a little like a grand piano, was in the box too.

When I asked Millie if she knew anything about them, she'd run her fingers over them in surprise and then nodded.

"My brother, Henry, must have given them to him. He's had this cassette player in his room forever. Henry used to pretend he was a sportscast-er and create his own play-by-plays. He'd watch my dad's games and speak into the recorder like he was Bob Costas or something. Before my mom died, she bought him a digital recorder. But Henry keeps everything. He must have given them to Tag."

Tag likes the things he can touch. He and Millie have that in common. She needs to touch to see. He needs to touch to feel connected. I could picture him sticking the tapes in and talking away, taking forever to get to the point. Telling stories and laughing like this was all just a big joke. I tried to feel angry, but I knew the real reason he'd left them was because it was the only way he could leave a message for Millie. The only way to allow her the privacy of hearing whatever he had to say without an audience.

"You know how to use this, right?" I asked.

She nodded.

"I think these are for you, Millie," I said.

"He's labeled the tapes," she whispered. "He's labeled them so I would know which one to listen to first."

"The sticker?"

She nodded again. "Yes. I have them on all my clothes and I keep a little box full of them in my bedroom. Numbers, letters, words. I guess he was paying attention when I showed him."

"Tag always pays attention. You don't think he does because he's restless. He fidgets. But he doesn't miss anything."

Millie's mouth started to tremble and tears leaked out beneath her lashes. I looked away, even though I didn't need to.

I heard her fumbling with a tape, heard her slide it home and push the play button. I listened until Tag's voice filled the silence, making me flinch and smile simultaneously, unable to decide whether I was pissed at him or scared for him. Regardless of which, I didn't think Tag wanted me to hear what he had to say to Millie, and I opened the door of the office, preparing to leave her alone. The tape clicked off immediately, interrupting Tag as he told Millie about his bar. I knew all about his businesses and didn't need to hear more. But Millie had other ideas.

"Moses? Please don't leave. I want you to listen with me. You know him best. You know him the way I want to know him. And you love him too. I need you to listen with me, so that I don't miss anything. And then I need you to help me find him."

2

I MET DAVID Taggert in a psych ward when I was eighteen years old. Montlake Psychiatric Hospital. I'd met his gaze for the first time across a counseling circle, seen his dead sister hovering at his shoulder, and asked him if he knew who Molly was. That was her name. Molly. His dead sister. He'd flown into a rage, flying across the space and knocking me onto the floor. He had his hands wrapped around my throat, demanding answers, before the psych techs could pull him off of me.

Not an especially promising beginning to a friendship.

We were there for different reasons. I'd been committed by people who were afraid of me, and Tag had been committed by people who loved him. I saw dead people, and he wanted to die. We were young, we were lonely, we were lost, and I didn't want to be found. I wanted to run to the ends of the earth and make the dead chase me.

Tag just wanted to figure the world out.

Maybe it was our youth. Maybe it was the fact that we were both in a psychiatric facility and neither of us especially wanted to leave. Or maybe it was just that Tag, with his exaggerated twang and his cowboy persona, was nothing like me. Whatever the reason, we fell into a sort of friendship. Maybe it was because he believed me. Without hesitation. Without reservation. Without judgment. He believed me. And he never stopped.

Tag and I had been put in isolation for three days due to the slug-fest in the counseling session, and neither of us were allowed out of our rooms. On the third day of isolation, Tag sprinted into my room and shut the door.

I'd stared at him balefully. I was kind of under the impression the door had been locked. I hadn't even checked to see, and I felt stupid for sitting in a room for three days behind an unlocked door.

"They stroll the hall every few minutes. But that's all. That was ridiculously easy. I should have come sooner," he had said, and sat down on my bed. "I'm David Taggert, by the way. But you can call me Tag." He didn't apologize for choking me, and he didn't act like he wanted to do it again, which was disappointing.

If he didn't want to fight, I wanted him to leave. I immediately went back to the picture I was working on. I felt his sister there, just beyond my sight, her image flickering through my walls, and I sighed heavily. I was weary of Molly, and I didn't like her brother. Both were incredibly stubborn and obnoxious.

"You're a crazy son-of-a-bitch," he stated without preamble.

I didn't even raise my head from the picture I was drawing with the nub of a grease pencil. I was trying to make my supplies last. I was going through them too fast.

"That's what people say, don't they? They say you're crazy. But I don't buy it, man. Not anymore. You're not crazy. You've got skills. Mad skills."

"Mad. Crazy. Don't they mean the same thing?" I murmured. Madness and genius were closely related. I wondered what skills he was talking about. He hadn't seen me paint.

"Nah, man," he said. "They aren't. Crazy people need to be in places like this. You don't belong here."

"I think I probably do."

He laughed, clearly surprised. "You think you're crazy?"

"I think I'm cracked."

Tag tilted his head quizzically, but when I didn't continue, he nodded. "Okay. Maybe we're all cracked. Or bent. I sure as hell am."

"Why are you bent?" I found myself asking. Molly was hovering and I drew faster, helplessly filling the page with her face.

"My sister's gone. And it's my fault. And until I know what happened to her, I'm never gonna be able to get straight. I'll be bent forever." His voice was so soft I wasn't sure he meant for me to hear the last part.

"Is this your sister?" I asked reluctantly. I held up my sketch pad.

Tag stared. Then he stood. Then he sat down again. And then he nodded.

"Yeah," he choked. "That's my sister."

And he told me everything.

David Taggert's father was a Texas oil man who'd always wanted to be a rancher. When Tag started getting in trouble and getting drunk every weekend, Tag's father purchased a fifty acre ranch in Sanpete County, Utah and moved the family there. He was sure if he could get Tag and his older sister, Molly, away from their old scene, he would be able to straighten them up.

But the kids hadn't thrived. They'd rebelled. Molly ran away and was never heard from again. Tag struggled to stay sober, but when he wasn't drinking, he was drowning in guilt and eventually tried to kill himself. Several times. Which landed him in the psych ward with me.

I listened, letting him talk. I didn't know how his sister had died any more than he did. That wasn't what the dead wanted to share. They wanted to show me their lives. Not their deaths. Not ever. When Tag finished talking he had looked at me with sorrow-filled eyes.

"She's dead, isn't she? You can see her, so that means she's dead."

I nodded, and he nodded too, accepting my answer without argument, his head lowering, my esteem for him rising. So I showed him the things Molly showed me, drawing the images that flitted through my mind whenever she was near.

Then Tag told his father about me. And for whatever reason—desperation, despondency, or maybe just a desire to placate his adamant son—David Taggert Sr. hired a man and his dogs to cover the area I had described. The dogs caught her scent quickly, and they found her remains. Just like that. In a shallow grave piled high with rocks and debris, fifty yards from where I'd once painted her smiling face on a highway overpass, the remains of Molly Taggert were uncovered.

Tag had cried when he told me. Big, wracking sobs that made his shoulders shake and my stomach tighten painfully. It was the first time I'd ever done something like that. Helped someone. Found someone. It was the first time my abilities, if that's what they were, made sense. But Tag just had more questions.

One night after lights out, he came and found me, creeping down the hall undetected, the way he always did, seeking answers that none of the staff could give him, answers he thought I had. Tag was usually quick to smile, quick to anger, quick to forgive, quick to pull the trigger. He didn't do anything in half measures, and I wondered sometimes if the facility wasn't the best place for him, just to keep him contained. But he had a maudlin side too.

"If I die, what will happen to me?" he'd asked me.

"Why do you think you're going to die?" I'd responded, sounding like one of our doctors.

"I'm here because I tried to kill myself several times, Moses," he confessed.

"Yeah. I know." I pointed at the long scar on his arm. It hadn't been a hard deduction. "And I'm here because I paint dead people and scare the livin' shit out of everyone I come in contact with."

He grinned. "Yeah. I know." He'd figured me out too. But his smile faded immediately. "When I'm not drinking, life just grinds me down until I can't see straight. It wasn't always that way. But it is now. Life sucks pretty bad, Moses."

"Do you still want to die?" I asked, changing the subject.

"Depends. What comes next?"

"More," I answered simply. "There's more. That's all I can tell you. It doesn't end."

"And you can see what comes next?"

"What do you mean?" I couldn't see the future, if that's what he meant.

"Can you see the other side?"

"No. I only see what they want me to see," I said.

"They? They who?"

"Whoever comes through." I shrugged.

"Do they whisper to you? Do they talk?" Tag was whispering too, as if the subject were sacred.

"No. They never say anything at all. They just show me things."

Tag shivered and rubbed the back of his neck, like he was trying to rub away the goose flesh that had crept up his back.

"Do you see everything? Their whole lives?"

"Sometimes it feels like that. It can be a flood of color and thought, and I can only pick up random things because it's coming at me so fast. And I can only really see what I understand. I'm sure they would like me to see more. But it isn't that easy. It's subjective. I usually see pieces and parts. Never the whole picture. But I've gotten better at filtering, and as I've gotten better, it feels more like remembering and less like being possessed." I smiled in spite of myself, and Tag shook his head in wonder.

"Moses?" Tag pulled me from my thoughts.

"Yeah?"

"Don't take this the wrong way . . . but, if, you know, there's more, and it's not bad, it's not scary, and it's not the zombie apocalypse. If it's not fire and brimstone . . . at least, not as far as you can tell, then why do you stay?" His voice was so quiet and filled with emotion, I wasn't sure if anything I said would help him. I wasn't sure I knew the answer. It took me a minute of thinking, but I finally had a response that felt true.

"Because I'll still be me," I answered. "And you'll still be you."

"What do you mean?"

"We can't escape ourselves, Tag. Here, there, half-way across the world, or in a psych ward in Salt Lake City. I'm Moses and you're Tag. And that part never changes. So either we figure it out here, or we figure it out there. But we still gotta deal. And death won't change that."

He'd nodded very slowly, staring at my hands as they created images neither of us really understood.

"That part never changes," he whispered, as if it resonated. "You're Moses and I'm Tag."

I nodded. "Yeah. As much as that can suck sometimes, there's comfort in it too. At least we know who we are."

He never asked about his own mortality again, and in the weeks that followed, he'd donned a confidence that I suspected he'd once had in spades. He seemed to be making plans for what came next. I still didn't have a clue.

"When you get out, where you gonna go?" Tag asked one night at dinner, his eyes on his food, his arms on the table. He could eat almost as much as I could, and I was pretty sure Montlake's kitchen staff would enjoy a little reprieve when we left.

I didn't want to talk about this with Tag. I really didn't want to talk about it with anyone. So I fixed my gaze to the left of Tag's head, out the window, letting him know I was ready for the conversation to end. But Tag persisted.

"You're almost nineteen. You are officially out of the system. So where you gonna go, Mo?" I don't know why he thought he could call me Mo. I hadn't given him permission. But he was like that. Worming his way into my space.

My eyes flickered back to Tag briefly, and then I shrugged as if it wasn't important.

I'd been here for months. Through Christmas, through New Year's, and into February. Three months in a mental institution. And I wished I could stay.

"Come with me," Tag said, tossing down his napkin and pushing his tray away.

I reared back, stunned. I remembered the sound of Tag crying, the wails that echoed down the hall as he was brought into the psych ward the

7

night he was admitted. He'd arrived almost a month after I had. I had lain in bed and listened to the attempts to subdue him. At the time, I hadn't realized it was him. I only put two and two together later when he told me about what brought him to Montlake. I thought about the way he'd come at me with his fists flying, rage in his eyes, almost out of his head with pain in the session where we'd met. Tag interrupted my train of thought when he continued speaking.

"My family has money. We don't have much else, but we have tons of money. And you don't have shit."

I held myself stiffly, waiting. It was true. I *didn't* have shit. Tag was my friend, the first real friend, other than Georgia, that I'd ever had. But I didn't want Tag's shit. The good or the bad, and Tag had plenty of both.

"I need someone to make sure I don't kill myself. I need someone who's big enough to restrain me if I decide I need to get smashed. I'll hire you to spend every waking minute with me until I figure out how to stay clean without wanting to slit my wrists."

I tipped my head to the side, confused. "You want me to restrain you?"

Tag laughed. "Yeah. Hit me in the face, throw me to the ground. Kick the crap out of me. Just make sure I stay clean and alive."

I wondered for a moment if I could do that to Tag. Hit him. Throw him to the ground. Hold him down until the need for drink or death passed. I was big. Strong. But Tag wasn't exactly small, not by a long shot. My doubt must have shown on my face because Tag was talking again.

"You need someone who believes you. I do. It's got to get old always having people thinking you're psychotic. I know you're not. You need somewhere to go, and I need someone to come with me. It's not a bad trade. You wanted to travel. And I've got nothing better to do. The only thing I'm good at is fighting, and I can fight anywhere." He smiled and shrugged. "Honestly, I don't trust myself to be alone just yet. And if I go back home to Dallas, I'll drink. Or I'll die. So I need you."

He'd said that so easily. "I need you." I'd wondered how it was possible that a tough kid like Tag, someone who fought for the fun of it, could admit that to anyone. Or believe it. I'd never needed anyone. Not really. And I'd never said those words to anyone. "I need you" felt like "I love you," and it scared me. It felt like breaking one of my laws. But at that moment, with our release looming large, with freedom at my fingertips, I'd admitted it to myself. I had needed Tag too.

We made an odd pair. A mixed-race delinquent who couldn't stop painting and a big Texan with too much attitude and shaggy hair. But Tag was right. We were both stuck. Lost. With nothing to hold us down and no direction. I just wanted my freedom, and Tag didn't want to be alone. I needed his money, and he needed my company, sad as it usually was. And so we went. We ran. We didn't look back.

"We'll just keep running, Moses. It's like you said. Here, there, on the other side of the world? We can't escape ourselves. So we stick together until we find ourselves, all right? Until we figure out how to deal." That's what he'd said. That's what we'd done. And Tag Taggert became my best friend. When I needed him most he held on to me, and he didn't let me go.

So now I have to find him.

The thing that scares me the most, is maybe he's found his answers. Maybe he knows exactly what he's doing. Exactly who he is. Maybe he's figured the world out. But we'd made a deal when we were eighteen. And as far as I'm concerned, a deal is a deal.

"I need someone to make sure I don't kill myself. I need someone who's big enough to restrain me if I decide I need to get shitfaced. Hit me in the face, throw me to the ground. Kick the shit out of me. Just make sure I stay clean and alive," he'd said. He'd wanted me to keep him alive.

I just hoped it wasn't too late.

TWO

MY BAR IS called Tag's because it's mine. Simple as that. When I bought it, I thought about the name for a couple of weeks, trying to think of something catchy, something intelligent, but in the end, I just slapped my name on it. Makes sense, doesn't it? When something is yours, you give it your name.

As a recovering alcoholic, owning a bar could be considered masochistic, but I don't own it for the booze. I own it because every time I walk in, look around, tend the bar or pour a drink, I feel powerful. I feel like I've conquered my demons, or at least beat them back. Plus, I'm a man, and the bar is a man cave to surpass all man caves. Flat screens hang on walls and in thick clusters overhead so that customers can keep an eye on several games at once, with sections of the bar dedicated to different sports. If you come in to watch a particular fight or a football game, there's a screen tuned in just for you. It smells like expensive cigars and leather, like pine needles and stacks of cash, all scents that make a man grateful for his testosterone. The décor consists of rock walls, dark wood, warm lighting, and pretty waitresses. And I'm extremely proud of it.

But I don't just own the bar. The whole block is mine. The bar on the corner, the small indoor arena where local fights take place every Tuesday night and once a month on Saturdays, the gym beyond that, and at the end of the block, a sporting goods store, filled with Tag Team gear and equipment with my label emblazoned across every surface. My own apartment and two others, occupied by people of my choosing, sit above the training gym. The city block is my whole world, a world of my creation. And it's all connected, each business playing off the others.

Even the bar and the fight arena are connected, and on the nights when there aren't fights, the arena seats are cordoned off by a wall of metal accordion doors, and the cage becomes a stage in a back room, a private alcove filled with a dozen small tables and booths, the bar easily accessible just around the corner, and waitresses keeping you comfortable and in your seats. Four nights a week, the little arena is home to a totally different kind of show, a completely different kind of sporting event. A pole is erected in the center of the cage and there are no fighters allowed inside, just one woman after another, spinning and writhing on the pole in time to the throbbing pulse of music that is muted throughout the rest of the establishment. I keep it classy—as classy as stripper poles and half-naked ladies can be. The girls dance, they don't strip, and they don't mingle beyond the cage. But it's just hot enough, just risqué enough, that I keep it separate from the rest of the establishment. It's the back room for negotiations—I do more business there than anywhere else—and the cherry on the top of an establishment that caters to hard-working men who feel appropriately sheepish and grateful just to be there.

Tag's opened two years ago, corresponding with the launch of the clothing line and my first big fight, the fight where I beat someone I had no business beating. I knocked him out cold and became a hot commodity. I timed it all, capitalizing on one success to launch another. I was a rich kid turned businessman, a cowboy more suited to riding a wave of adoration than riding a horse, and more interested in taking on the world of ultimate fighting and mixed martial arts than in taking over my father's holdings. I could have. It was a golden-paved path that stretched out before me, a road of privilege and entitlement. But it was a road I hadn't built, and I'm convinced you can't ever be completely happy walking on someone else's road. Someone else's path. The way to true happiness is to forge your own, even if your road isn't straight. Even if there are bridges to build and mountains to tunnel through. Nothing feels as good as paving your own way.

I'd come to Salt Lake City ready to start building roads three years before. I had money—some of it my own, money I'd earned with Moses, and some of it money I hadn't earned. I was a rich kid, but I wasn't a stupid kid. I knew I needed capital to build an empire. Sometimes it takes money to make money. So I took the money my dad gave me and promised myself that I would give it back before I died or before I turned thirty. Whichever came first.

At twenty-six, I didn't have much time or wiggle room. But I was on track, and the bar was doing extremely well. The evidence was all around me when I walked in the front door that Monday night—typically the slowest night of the week—to full stools and tables, to the happy thrum of relaxed customers. The place hummed and my heart warmed to the music. Two of my waitresses pranced by, dressed like ring girls in Tag Team booty shorts and halter tops, delivering rounds instead of announcing them. They sent identical smiles my way and tossed their hair, almost as if it were part of the job description. Maybe it should be . . . or maybe it was just common sense. You always smile at the boss.

I wasn't there to flirt, though I smiled automatically. Instead, I calculated the mood of the room, the number of men bellied up to the bar, the number of tables filled, the flow of the alcohol and the efficiency of the wait staff. When I approached the bar to touch base with Morgan, my manager, a pulsing beat began to throb from down the hall, from around the darkened corner where the girls danced and the music was louder.

"Who's dancing tonight?" I inquired, not really caring, but asking anyway.

"Justine. Lori. And the new girl." Morgan smirked like he had a secret, and I was immediately suspicious. He slid a Coke in front of me as I sat down and I took a long pull before I gave him a response.

"Oh yeah? Judging from that shit-eating grin, I'm guessing there's something you need to tell me about the new girl."

"Nah. Nothing. She's beautiful. Great dancer. Great body. She's been on the schedule for the last two weeks, though you've missed her every time. She's always on time, never says two words. She dances, doesn't drink, doesn't flirt. Just how you like 'em." Again with the smirk.

"Huh." I pushed my Coke away and stood, knowing I might as well go see what he was up to. Leave it to Morgan to dress up one of my Tag

Team fighters and put him in the cage in a bikini. He loved a practical joke. But he was a damn good bartender . . . even if he drove me crazy with the pranks.

I called out to a few customers, shook some hands, kissed Stormy's cheek as she delivered icy bottles of cold beer, and waved to Malcolm Short, who obviously hadn't taken the time to change after work and looked slightly ridiculous in his three piece suit and his Utah Jazz ball cap. But the Jazz were playing, and he was getting in the spirit, happy as a clam sitting on his stool, eyes fixed on the screen. He was one of my Tag Team sponsors and it was good seeing him happy.

I was almost as good at working the room as I was at working the octagon, though I'd rather be fighting any day. But my thoughts were on business as I strode across the room and through the arch that separated the dancing girls from the sports bar. My eyes went straight to the cage, expecting the worst. But it was Justine at the pole, finishing her number with a swivel of her hips and a final turn around the cage. Justine strode off, hips swaying arms waving, as if she'd just announced the next round, and the lights went dark.

When they came up again, the new girl was at the center of the octagon, hands on the pole, head down. As the music began to swell, she immediately swung into her routine, and I scowled in consternation. The girl was slim and lithe, smooth muscles moving beneath taut skin. Her straight, dark brown hair was silky under the lights, her oiled limbs glistening, and her barely-there shorts and bikini top no different from the girl who danced before her. I watched her for a moment, waiting for the punch line. There had to be one.

She was beautiful—delicate-featured with a small nose, a rosebud mouth, and a heart-shaped face, and I felt a sudden flash of fear that she was only fifteen or something equally alarming. I dismissed the thought immediately. Morgan was a prankster, not an idiot. Something like that would ruin the bar. Something like that would cost Morgan his job. And Morgan loved his job, even if he didn't always love me, even if I didn't always appreciate his sense of humor.

Nah. She was at least twenty-one. That was my rule. I pursed my lips and tipped my head, studying her. She worked the pole as well as any of the other girls, maybe even better, but her dancing was more acrobatic, more athletic, than it was overtly sexy. Her eyes were closed and she had a soft smile on her lips, which could be interpreted as sultry, especially considering that she was dancing for an audience of mostly men. Scratch that. An audience of all men. But her smile wasn't sultry. It was . . . dreamy, like she was imagining she was somewhere else, a tiny ballerina spinning in place inside a child's snow globe, endlessly dancing alone. Her small smile didn't change, and her eyes stayed closed, the heavy sweep of dark lashes creating half circles of shadow on her porcelain cheeks.

The lighting was strategic, hiding the viewers and displaying the dancer. Maybe the lights hurt her eyes. Or maybe she was a little shy. I chuckled. Um . . . no. The shy pole dancer was as big an oxymoron as the timid fighter. But someone should probably say something. The men in the audience loved to believe that the dancers were looking right at them, and though the dancers never mingled with the men, at least not in the bar, eye contact and subtle flirting were part of the job. I wondered if that was Morgan's joke. If so, Morgan was losing his touch.

I turned away as the song ended and the cage lights went black, indicating the end of the set. Three girls danced a fifteen minute set each hour, with another fifteen minutes between sets from nine to midnight. It was Utah, after all, not Vegas. The dancers were off two, sometimes three, nights a week for fight nights and club nights, when the octagon was needed for bouts or disassembled to create a dance floor. With four dancers, now five, on my payroll, it wasn't a full-time job by any means. Most of the girls had day jobs and grabbed extra hours and good pay announcing the rounds and bouts on fight nights.

"So whaddaya think, Boss?" Morgan grinned and slid a glass to a waiting patron as I rounded the bar and sat back on the same stool, my eyes shooting up to check the score, not giving Morgan the attention he wanted.

"'Bout what?"

"About the new girl."

"Pretty." He didn't need all the other adjectives that had run through my mind as I watched her dance.

"Yeah?" Morgan raised his eyebrows as if my one-word assessment was surprising.

"Yeah, Morg," I sighed. "You got something you wanna tell me? 'Cause I'm not gettin' it."

"No. No siree. Not a thing."

I shook my head and groaned. Morgan was definitely up to something.

"So how many weeks, Boss?"

"Eight." Eight weeks until I fought Bruno Santos. The fight that would give me a shot at a Vegas title fight. The fight that would catapult the Tag Team brand into living rooms across the US. Eight weeks of perfect focus—no distractions, and no decisions beyond one fight. After I won the fight, I would face what came next. After I won that fight the world could end, for all I cared. After I won.

"Hey, Boss. Lou called in sick tonight. He usually makes sure the girls get to their cars. You wanna fill in? Since you're here?"

All the women on my staff are escorted to their vehicles at the end of their shifts. Always. This part of town is changing, but it isn't there yet. Tag's is situated close to the old Grand Central train station in a refurbished district that is still caught somewhere between restoration and dilapidation. Two blocks north there is a row of mansions built in the early 1900s, two blocks south there's a strip mall complete with bars on all the windows. A high-end day spa takes up the corner of the block to the left and a homeless shelter is two blocks down on the right. The area is a conglomeration of everything, and there are some elements that aren't safe. I feel responsible for my employees, especially the girls. So I imposed some rules, even if it means I am sometimes accused of being overprotective, sexist, and old-fashioned.

"Yep. I can do that."

"Good. That was their last set. I'd do it, but the drinks won't fill themselves, ya know. Kelli's boyfriend came in and picked her up ten minutes ago, and Marci and Stormy are closing with me, so I'll walk them out. You've just got Justine and Lori and Amelie."

"Ah–muh–lee?" I parroted, eyebrows quirked.

"Yeah. The new dancer. Amelie. Didn't I say?"

"Nah. You didn't. What is she, French?"

"Something like that," Morg said, and I could see that he was trying not to laugh. "She lives close by and she walks, though. Lou complains about it, but it really is just around the block. I tell him it'll do his fat ass some good."

"Huh." So that was the funny part. I would be walking the new girl home, and it was starting to snow. The French girl. Fine with me. I was too antsy to sleep anyway. I was considering hitting the speed bag until I could wear myself out enough to shut down for a few hours.

On cue, Justine and Lori appeared in the entryway between the lounge and the bar, winter coats belted, duffle bags in hand.

"Where's Amelie?" Morgan asked, looking beyond them.

"She said she'd meet Lou out front," Justine answered.

"Lou's not in tonight. Tag is walking you out. Right, Boss?"

"Right, Morg." I tamped down my irritation as Morgan laughed again and winked at the girls.

I escorted Justine and Lori to their vehicles in the back parking lot, watched as they pulled away, and then walked around to the front the building, opting not to go through the bar, eager to avoid Morg for the rest of the night. As I rounded the building, I could see the new girl waiting on the sidewalk, face tilted up, letting the fat flakes land on her cheeks as if she enjoyed the sensation. She waited for me, as if she weren't in any hurry to get out of the cold, her hands wrapped around a long stick that, in the soft light spilling from the bar and the snow falling around her, made her look like a shepherdess in a Christmas pageant.

"Hello?" There was a question in her voice as I approached, and she slid her staff forward just a bit and nudged my foot as I halted. "Lou?"

"Lou's sick, so I'll be walking you home." I answered slowly, flooded with shocked realization as she turned her face toward me. Her eyes were wide and fixed, and I felt a surprising pang from somewhere behind my heart. She had beautiful eyes. They were large and luminous, fringed by black lashes that swept her cheeks when she closed her eyes. But they were vacant, and looking in them made me inexplicably sad. So I looked away, studying her mouth and the straight dark hair that framed her face and spilled over her shoulders. Then she smiled, and the pang in my heart sliced through my chest once more and took my breath.

"Ah, the long pause. I always get those. My mom always said I was beautiful," she said drily, "but just in case I'm not, will you promise to lie to me? I demand detailed lies regarding my appearance." She said all this good-naturedly. No bitterness. Just acceptance. "So you pulled blind girl duty, huh? You don't have to walk me home. I got here all by myself. But Morgan told me it's the rule with all the girls. He said the boss insists."

"He's right. It's a great neighborhood, but you and I both know it's still pretty rough around the edges," I responded, refusing to feel sheepish, refusing to apologize for staring.

She stuck out her hand and waited for me to grasp it.

"Well then, I'll introduce myself. I'm Amelie. And I'm blind." Her lips quirked, letting me know she was laughing as much at herself as at me. I reached out and wrapped her ungloved hand in my own. Her fingers were icy, and I didn't release them immediately. So she wasn't French, she was blind, and somehow Morg thought that was hysterically funny.

"Hello, Amelie. I'm David. And I'm not."

She smiled again, and I found myself smiling too, the pang of sympathy I'd felt for her easing considerably. I didn't know why I told her my name was David. No one called me David anymore. The name David always made me feel like I'd failed without even trying. It was my father's name. And *his* father's name. And *his* father before him. David Taggert was a name that carried weight. And I had felt that weight from an early age. Then my friends had started calling me Tag. Tag set me free. It allowed me to be young, free-spirited. Just the word itself brought to mind images of running away. *"I'm Tag . . . you can't catch me."*

"Your hands are calloused, David."

It was an odd thing to comment on when shaking hands with someone for the first time, but Amelie curled her fingers against my palm, feeling the rough ridges that lined the base of my fingers like she was reading braille.

"Exercise?" she guessed.

"Uh, yeah. I'm a fighter."

A slim eyebrow rose in question, but her fingers continued to trace my hand intimately. It felt good. And weird. The roof of my mouth started to tingle and my toes curled in my boots.

"The callouses are from the weights. Pull-ups. That sort of thing." I sounded like an idiot. Like a dumb, Rocky wannabe. I might as well yell, "Yo, Adrian!"

"Do you enjoy it?"

"Fighting?" I asked, trying to keep up. She didn't converse like the girls I knew. She was so direct. So blunt. But maybe she had to be. She didn't have the luxury of learning through observance.

"Yes. Fighting. Do you enjoy it?" she clarified.

"Yeah. I do."

"Why?" she asked.

"I'm big, strong, and angry," I said honestly, smirking.

17

She laughed, and I expelled all the air I'd been holding since she'd held out her hand in greeting. Her laughter wasn't girlish and high, tinkling and sweet. It was robust, healthy, the kind of laugh that came from her belly and had nothing to hide.

"You smell good, David."

I half-gasped, half-chuckled, surprised once more. But she kept right on talking.

"So I know you are big, strong, angry, and you smell nice. You're tall too, because your voice is coming from way over my head. You're also from Texas and you're still young."

"How do you know I'm young?"

"Old men don't fight. And your voice. You were singing Blake Shelton under your breath when you approached. If you were older you might sing Conway Twitty or Waylon Jennings."

"I sing them too."

"Excellent. You can sing while we walk." She flicked her stick with a practiced hand and it collapsed neatly into thirds. Then she tucked it under her left arm while reaching toward me with her right. Then she wrapped her hand around my bicep as if it were the most natural thing in the world. And we were off, walking slowly but steadily through the silent streets, the snow falling, the wet seeping into our shoes. I am a guy who can make conversation with the best of them, but I found myself at a complete loss.

Amelie seemed completely comfortable and didn't offer up conversation as we walked, arm and arm, like two lovers in an old movie. Men and women don't walk that way anymore. Not unless a father is walking his daughter down the aisle or a boy scout is helping an old lady across the road. But I discovered I liked it. I felt like a man of a bygone era, a time when men would escort women, not because women couldn't walk alone, but because men respected them more, because a woman is something to be cared for, to be careful with.

"There was a time when everything in the world was more beautiful." The words fell from my mouth, surprising me. I hadn't meant to think out loud.

"What do you mean?" She seemed pleased at my statement. So I went with it.

"Well, if you look at old pictures . . ." My voice drifted off awkwardly, realizing she couldn't actually look at old pictures.

She saved me, gracefully. "If I could look at old pictures, what would I see?"

"They had less. But they had more. It seems like people took more care with their possessions and their appearances. The women dressed up and the men wore suits. People wore hats and gloves and were well-groomed. The way they talked was different, more careful, more cultured. Same language, but totally different. Even the buildings and the furniture were beautiful—well-crafted with attention to detail. I don't know . . . The world had more class. Maybe that was it."

"Ah, the days when men didn't fight for a living and women didn't dance on poles," she said, a smile in her voice.

"Men have always fought. Women have always danced. We're as old-fashioned as it gets," I shot back. "We're timeless."

"Nice save," she giggled, and I laughed quietly.

We walked in companionable silence for several minutes when it occurred to me that I had no idea where we were going.

"Where do you live?"

"Don't worry, big guy. I know where we are. Turn right on the next corner. I'm the old house thirty paces in."

"You live in one of the old mansions?"

"Yes. I do. My great-great-grandfather built it, speaking of a time when the world was more beautiful. I'm guessing my house isn't quite as lovely as it once was. But everything looks amazing in my head. Perks of being a blind girl."

"You said thirty paces. What? Do you count steps?" I could hear the amazement in my voice and wondered if she could too.

"Usually. But I'm less observant when someone is walking with me. I know where the sidewalk ends, where the trees are, the potholes too."

"That's amazing."

"Well, I grew up here and I could see, once. I can still see it in my mind. It'd be harder if I had to start over in a whole new place."

"So what happened?"

"A rare disease with a fancy name you would probably forget as soon as I said it. We didn't realize what was happening until it was too late. And even if we had known sooner, there probably wouldn't have been anything anyone could do."

"How old were you?"

"Eleven."

I swallowed. My life had changed at eleven too. But in a totally different way. Before I could comment, Amelie came to a stop.

"This is me. This is it." She snapped her stick back out and tapped it in front of her, turning toward a little wrought iron fence and stopping as her stick rattled against it. She released my arm and stepped away, feeling for the latch on the gate and releasing it easily. The house was old, turn-of-the-century old, if not older, and it was still stately, though the smattering of snow and the darkness camouflaged the yard and the large, wrap-around porch that had seen better days. Light shone from the upstairs windows, and the walk and the steps were clear. Amelie seemed comfortable traversing them, so I stayed by the gate, waiting until she was safely inside. She stopped about half-way down the path and turned slightly.

"David?" she asked, raising her voice as if she wasn't sure I remained.

"Yeah?"

"Thank you for walking me home."

"You're welcome."

I waited until the front door closed behind her before I turned away. The snow had stopped and the world was so still I sang to keep myself company, closing my eyes now and then and counting my steps, wondering how it would be to not see at all, and wondering how a blind girl had ended up dancing in my club.

(End of Cassette)

Moses

MILLIE REACHED FOR the tape recorder, sliding her fingers along the buttons until she reached the one she wanted. Then she pressed it down and Tag's voice ceased. She sat gripping the player as if she were holding onto the memory. The room was filled with expectancy, with anticipation. I'd heard it in Tag's voice, felt it in the care with which he remembered the details, and felt his wonder as he retraced his steps. He'd pulled me in, and I'd forgotten for a moment where I was. But now I felt awkward, intrusive, and I wanted to put my hands over my ears.

"I couldn't stop thinking about him, and I couldn't get that Blake Shelton song out of my head," Millie said softly. "He was nice. And strong. I could feel his strength as he walked beside me. That night I actually dreamed about the way his arm felt against my hand. Right after I lost my sight I still dreamed in pictures. I loved it because I could see when I went to sleep. But as the years have gone by, my dreams have started to look more like my reality. I still dream in pictures sometimes, but more often than not, I dream in smells and feelings, in sounds and sensations."

Millie's voice was hushed like she was thinking out loud, like she'd forgotten I was there at all. I thought maybe I should speak up, before she told me something she would rather keep private, but she continued suddenly.

"I've gone on a few blind dates." She smiled in my general direction, letting me know that she was aware of me after all, and I laughed, which is probably what she intended.

"Blind, blind dates, I mean. And I've gone on a few dates with blind guys I actually knew beforehand. One guy I dated insisted on being called 'visually impaired.'" Amelie made finger quotes in the air. "I don't really understand that. To me it's like calling someone 'melanin deficient' instead of calling them white. People are so weird. I am a white, blind girl. I am a twenty-two-year old, white, blind girl. Can we just call it like it is?"

I laughed again, wondering where she was going with this, but happy to let her talk. I wondered briefly if she knew I was black. It was kind of an amazing feeling knowing that for once, it truly didn't matter.

"I've dated guys who can see too—you know, the visually unimpaired." She smiled at the label. "Not many of them. But a few. My cousin Robin usually sets me up. And I'm pretty sure every one of them has been extremely unattractive. Ugly, strange, warty, and generally rejected by other women. Which is okay. I can pretend they all look like a million bucks, and I'll never know any different. The image in my head is the only one that counts, right? But once Robin tried to set me up on a date with a deaf guy, and I put my foot down. It wasn't that he was deaf, exactly, but how did she think we were going to communicate? Robin sometimes thinks that because I'm disabled, I can only date guys with disabilities. Because, of course, no one else would want me, right?" Millie's voice caught, and she smiled immediately, laughing at herself. "Uh oh. Struck a nerve there."

"That isn't true," I challenged.

"It's true sometimes," she whispered, and I could tell she was wondering if the truth had gotten to be too much for Tag.

"I found myself hoping David wasn't a good looking guy. I hoped he wasn't good looking because it didn't matter to me, and it would make him less desirable to everyone else. I thought if he were homely, it would make him more open to someone like me." She let her breath out slowly, almost sadly.

"But I knew he was beautiful. It was in the way he carried himself, his confidence, his kindness. I thought about asking the girls at work about him. But I chickened out. I didn't want them to laugh at me or to feel sorry for me. I told myself maybe we could be friends. He seemed open to that."

I didn't know what to say. I was fascinated. But I didn't know what to say. Millie just sat, gripping the tape recorder between her forearms. Then, without further comment, she pushed play once more.

Three

THE STAGE BECAME an octagon on Tuesday for fight night, and on Wednesday Amelie wasn't on the schedule to dance, which Morgan informed me as soon as I walked in, smirking like he'd really pulled one over on me.

"What's with you, Morgan?" I asked, dumbfounded and just a little pissed. "You act like it's a big damn joke. What? You hire the blind girl as a prank? That's an asshole thing to do."

Morgan threw up his hands and protested, all the while laughing like that was exactly what he'd done. "She came in here with her stick, looking more like Helen Keller than Heidi Klum. No makeup, hair in a messy ponytail wearing a big coat and snow boots. Kinda frumpy, you know? She said she wanted to apply for the job. Vince was tending the bar that day, and he and I thought maybe you had put her up to it. Like you were punking us or something. So we said, sure. You know me. I'm always up for a good laugh. She waited for her audition with all the other girls, and amazingly enough, everyone was really nice to her. The girls kind of took her aside. Next thing we know, she's in the cage, wearing a little tiny pair of shorts and a skin-tight top, hair loose, working that pole like a pro."

23

Hearing Morgan describe Amelie's audition make me feel slightly sick to my stomach. It shouldn't have. If he'd been talking about Justine or Lori, or any of the other girls, I wouldn't have thought twice. But I didn't like thinking about Vince and Morg looking at Amelie, laughing and leering when she couldn't even see them doing it. Morgan continued, completely unaware of my discomfort.

"She was good enough that we knew you weren't messing with us. And she seemed pretty damn determined. Excited even. And, I admit, I thought it was funny."

"Hilarious."

"You gonna fire her, Boss?"

"Now, why would I do that?" Morgan was really getting on my nerves.

"She's not as popular as some of the girls. Couple of the guys complain that she doesn't look at them when she's dancing."

"Isn't it enough that they get to look at her?" I shot back, irritated.

"Hey!" Morg raised his hands in surrender again. "Don't shoot the messenger, Boss. She can't carry a round card on fight nights, so we're a little short there."

"We're not short there, Morg. We have four other girls totally capable of working fight nights," I replied. The girls who danced at Tag's also got to prance around the octagon, announcing the rounds.

"Okay. If you want to keep her, that's cool. She'll be back in on Thursday, just in case you wanted to have a talk with her about sexing it up a little. You know, maybe dancing with her eyes open." Morgan was laughing again.

"Morg?"

"Yeah, Boss?"

"Go home."

"Wh-what?" Morgan's chuckle skittered to a halt.

"I'll help Vince finish out the night. Go home."

Morgan pulled on the hand towel he always kept over one shoulder and rubbed his hands nervously.

"But—" Morg attempted to argue.

"You think it's funny to laugh at a blind girl. That kind of worries me, Morg. Makes me wonder about what kind of man I have managing my bar. See, there are two things I hate." I held up my thumb and my pointer finger and counted them off. "Bullies and bitches. I never knew you were a bully, Morg. Now, don't bitch, or I'll have two reasons to fire you. Go home. And if you want to come back, you will rethink your sense of humor. You got me?" My voice was mild, my posture relaxed, but I didn't break eye contact with my bartender, and I watched as Morgan dropped his eyes and shifted uncomfortably, as if waiting for me to change my mind. When I was silent, he threw down his towel and reached for his wallet and keys that he kept stashed beneath the bar.

"I'm old enough to be your father, Tag. Your dad was one of my best friends. You need to show me a little more respect," Morgan huffed, all joking clearly aside.

"You'll have to earn it, Morg. Bottom line, you're not my father, you're not my best friend, and I don't owe you shit. You can come back tomorrow if you're man enough to make some adjustments. If I don't see you tomorrow, I'll understand, and I'll be looking for your replacement."

Morgan started to argue once more, thought better of it, and shut his mouth. With his lips clamped into a hard line, his jaw clenched, and his fists tight, he walked out from behind the counter and through the bar, shoving his way out the front door, practically mowing down Amelie, who had just entered the establishment. Morg cursed and shot a look over his shoulder at me before disappearing into the darkness.

"Excuse me," Amelie gasped, her stick clattering to the floor as curious patrons turned to stare. She hesitated briefly and then squatted down, feeling for her stick before her fingers found it and she rose gracefully. Her cheeks were slightly pink, and I wondered if she could feel the stares of those watching. She moved forward slowly allowing the stick she held to guide her to the bar. I realized belatedly that I was on duty and hurried around the counter, pulling off my jacket and rolling up my sleeves. Amelie had climbed up on a stool and was waiting patiently to be greeted. I wondered what she did when people ignored her.

"Amelie, what can I do for ya?"

"David?" she asked, her head tilting in surprise.

"Impressive. You've got a good ear for voices."

"Thank you. Uh, where's Morgan? Are you working?" She kept herself very still on her stool, not slouching or rotating in her seat like most people did. She didn't even lean on the bar, as if she were fearful of upending something or invading someone's space. She couldn't know that the only other people at the bar sat at the far end, nursing beers and staring at the Spurs game above them.

"Yep. I'm filling in tonight." I didn't elaborate. "Can I get you something to drink?"

Amelie bit her lip and shook her head. "No. I don't drink. I'm already blind and drinking dulls my senses, the senses I have left. Instead of relaxing me, it scares me to death." She shrugged. "I probably sound like a little kid."

"Nah. I understand. I don't drink either."

Her brows rose doubtfully. "But you work in a bar."

"I don't drink because I've never been able to figure out how to do things in moderation. See, I don't drink. I get drunk. I'm all or nothing, all the time. Can't do all, so I gotta do nothing," I said conversationally, wondering at my need to reassure her. "You want something else? A soda, water, something non-alcoholic?" I changed the subject smoothly.

"I'd love a Diet Coke."

I hopped to it and within seconds set the drink on a coaster in front of her. "Diet coke at twelve o'clock."

She smiled at my instructions and thanked me, then eased her hand forward carefully, letting her fingers brush the cool glass, tiptoeing around it until she could grasp it and pull it toward her. She leaned over it, almost like she was smelling it, and I watched as she held her face, oddly suspended, over her drink, her nose so close to the fizzy liquid it would be submerged if she moved another inch.

"Is there a problem?" I asked.

She sat up and rubbed her nose with her right hand, still grasping the drink with her left. "No! I, um, I like the way it sounds and the way the bubbles feel against my face. I didn't realize you were still watching me." There was a little steel in her voice, letting me know that staring wasn't appreciated.

"I'll just be moving along then." I grinned, liking the bit of sass she threw back at me.

"Um, David," her voice rose, "I actually just came to get my check. Could you get that for me?"

"Absolutely. Give me a minute, and I'll be right with you. I won't be watching if you want to enjoy the bubbles a little longer."

The checks were in a lockbox beneath the bar, and it took me a few minutes to locate the spare key from Morg's office. Morgan had taken his set of keys when he walked out. I swore, thinking of the complications—like re-keying the whole damn place—that would arise if Morg decided his pride was more important than his job. I really hoped the man came back contrite in the morning. I really didn't want to find a new manager, and Morg did a good job when he wasn't being an ass.

When I slid the check labeled with her name across the counter, brushing the hand not gripping her drink so she knew it was there, she grabbed at it and then handed it back.

"Could you open it please and read me the total? I'll be able to deposit it at the ATM on the corner if I know the amount."

When I tore it open and looked at the amount I was stunned. I read the numbers back to her almost sheepishly, and she sighed.

"Morgan told me I would be making minimum wage until my probation period was over. Do you know when that ends?"

I felt the heat of outrage roil in my gut, but squelched it for her sake. I had to play along, not to protect Morg, but to protect her feelings. There was no probation period. Morgan had been playing games. Amelie had been hired as a joke, and a cheap joke, at that. But I couldn't tell her that.

"It's up. You'll be making the same as all the other dancers, and you'll receive the full amount you would have made in the first two weeks, minus the amount of this check."

"Really? That's great! Morgan didn't tell me that part."

I grimaced. Morgan was the one who was going to be on probation.

She repeated the total of the check, a slight question in her voice, and I read the numbers back once more.

"Got it. I'm going to go deposit it. What do I owe you for the drink?"

"Employee perk. No charge for Diet Cokes. Or bubbles." She smiled widely and I smiled back, her pleasure making it impossible not to, whether or not she could see my response.

She slid carefully from the stool and snapped her stick out, heading for the door, her check tucked in her broad coat pocket.

"Do you need any help? You want me to send someone with you?"

She shook her head without looking back. "Touch screens are obnoxious. I can't feel a touch screen. But the ATM on the corner has braille on the keypad, thank God! If the world is too flat, people like me will slide right off." She said this cheerfully, with humor, and I shook my head in amazement as she pushed out the front door into the darkness, the door swinging closed behind her, the night swallowing her up.

I fought the urge to follow her, to make sure she wasn't mugged at the ATM, her paltry check stolen, her stick used against her. The world was a scary place for most people. For Amelie, it was downright lethal. She was completely vulnerable. *If the world is too flat, people like me will slide right off.*

And yet she didn't hesitate at all.

I respected that, admired it, so I stayed behind the bar for several long seconds, a silent show of support, even though my heart was pounding and my palms grew slick. My sister's face flashed in my mind. She'd disappeared into the night once too. And I never saw her again.

"Vince?" I called out to the young bartender swapping stories with a couple of regulars down at the far end of the bar, completely unaware of the drama that had unfolded in the last ten minutes.

"Hey, Tag."

"You're going to be alone here for about a half hour. I'll be back to finish out the shift and help you close. Morgan had to leave. Will you be okay?"

"Yeah, boss. No big deal. It's been kinda slow all night."

I grabbed my jacket and was out the front door without another word, running down the street toward the ATM on the corner, catching up to Amelie before she'd made it half a block. She was surprised when I reached her, but shrugged easily when I referred back to the rules.

"But I didn't even work tonight," she protested.

"Humor me, okay?"

She shrugged again, and I stood back patiently, giving her privacy to make her deposit, which she did easily, her fingers gliding over the key pad with confidence.

When she was finished, I moved to her side and she linked our arms the way she'd done the night before. We walked in easy companionship, me humming softly, Amelie matching my stride like she trusted where I was taking her.

We were almost to her door when she stopped, her hand pulling against my arm with urgency.

"Listen!"

I searched the darkness with my narrowed eyes, suddenly nervous that we weren't as alone as it seemed.

"There it is," she said.

And then I caught the hollow whistle of a distant train and the clattering of wheels on a track.

"Ten pm. Right on time," Amelie breathed.

The sound thickened and deepened and the whistle came again, louder, bugling through the night with a warning that felt more like a song. I had always loved the sound of a train, but it had been a while since I'd stopped just to listen.

"Trains are like time machines. If you close your eyes—not that I have to—it's easy to imagine the world hasn't changed much in a hundred years. You hear that sound, and it could be 1914 instead of 2014."

"Or we could be getting ready to head to Hogwarts for the new school year," I teased.

She laughed again, and I liked the way she didn't hold back. "You aren't a Harry Potter fan. No way." She poked me in the side.

"Not really. But I know the basics."

"I love Harry Potter. And I love the sound of a train," she sighed. "It's one of my favorites."

"You have favorite sounds?"

"Yes. Lots of them. You?"

"I guess I never thought about it," I confessed.

"I collect them," she said breezily.

"How do you collect sounds?"

"The same way you collect memories." She tapped a finger to her temple.

I had no response to that, but she didn't seem to need one.

"Speaking of collections, would you mind saying hello to my little brother? He is a huge sports fan. He would love to meet an actual fighter. He's a little awkward, but he would be thrilled."

"Sure." I shrugged. I was curious to see the inside of the house, curious to see how she lived, curious about parents who let their blind daughter wander around the city and dance half-naked in a bar.

She fished a key from her coat pocket and felt her way to the lock. It didn't take her long and she didn't ask for help, so I was silent at her side.

The door groaned as she pushed it open into a foyer that was dark. The house smelled slightly of mildew and furniture polish, which was probably due to its age more than anything.

"Henry?" Amelie called, setting her stick aside and pulling off her coat, hanging it on an old-fashioned hat and coat-tree to the left of the door with only a hint of fumbling.

"Henry?" she called a little louder.

I heard a door open overhead, the sound of sports commentary spilling out and then cutting off again as the door was closed. Footsteps sounded above and a chandelier came to life, showering light from the top of the ornate staircase that the house had been built around.

A boy in his early teens appeared from around the corner, his hair an unruly mass of red curls. He'd either been asleep or combing his hair wasn't a priority. He wore a black, Chicago Bulls Jersey with a pair of flannel pajama pants, and he folded his thin arms across his chest when his eyes met mine, shifting from one foot to the other, clearly uncomfortable with the unexpected company.

"Henry?" Amelie had obviously heard his approach and subsequent halt. "Henry, this is David . . . um David, I forgot to ask your last name." She didn't wait for me to supply it before she added enthusiastically, the way a mother does with a child. "He's a real live fighter, Henry! I thought you might like to say hello."

Henry stayed frozen at the top of the stairs. I waved.

"Hi Henry. I'm David Taggert. But you can call me Tag," I offered. The boy seemed more nervous than impressed.

"Tag?" Amelie squeaked in alarm, turning toward me slightly. "Oh, my gosh. I didn't realize . . . I mean, you're Tag Taggert. You said your name was David! I just thought you were a bouncer at the bar who fought in his spare time! Like Lou! Oh, my gosh. You're my boss!" Amelie put her hands up to her cheeks and I tried not to laugh as she breathed in and out, clearly a little embarrassed by her earlier informality.

"Boxing became a legal sport in 1901!" Henry blurted.

"He's not a boxer, Henry," Amelie recovered quickly. "He's an MMA fighter, right Mr. Taggert?"

So now I was Mr. Taggert. I started to laugh. I couldn't help myself.

"It's kickboxing, wrestling, judo, grappling. It's a little of everything," I agreed, still chuckling.

"Float like a butterfly, sting like a bee," Henry said, and folded his arms even tighter.

"You like Mohammed Ali, huh?" I asked.

"The Greatest, The People's Champion, The Louisville Lip," Henry rattled out before turning and fleeing down the hall. A door banged closed, muting the radio, and leaving me and Amelie alone in the foyer once again.

"The next time he sees you, he'll know everything about you, your record, and everything about mixed martial arts. Henry has a phenomenal brain, but he's not great at small talk," Amelie said softly. She bit at her lower lip like she wanted to say more and then stiffened her back as if deciding against it.

I guessed it went a little deeper than not being great at small talk, but I said nothing.

"I didn't know who you were. I feel stupid now," she offered timidly.

"Why?"

"I treated you the way I treat Lou."

"What? Like a friend?"

"I flirted with you."

"Well, that's happened to me before. I think I can deal."

Her nose wrinkled and her brows curled. "Are you smiling?"

"Yes. I am."

"Okay. Well, that's good. I will try to be more professional in the future." With that she held her hand out in my general direction, obviously wanting to shake hands in a "professional" manner.

I clasped it briefly, fighting the urge to laugh again. She was funny, especially because she wasn't trying to be.

"If you think Henry would like it, bring him by the gym. It's two doors south of the bar, same side of the street. I have a whole team of fighters. Lou works out with us sometimes too. We spar and train from about ten to four most days. I can show him a few things, introduce him to the guys."

"Really?" she squeaked, and she squeezed my hand tightly, bringing her other hand up to envelope it between her two smaller ones. "I'll ask him. I actually think he might like that. He's really shy, and he doesn't like it when people touch him, but maybe he could just watch."

"I wasn't going to ask him to get in the octagon," I said wryly.

"Are you smiling again?" It was a strange sensation to think I could wear whatever expression I wished, and she would be totally unaware. I could make fun of her, roll my eyes, grimace, stick out my tongue. And she would never know.

"Yes. I guess I am."

"I thought so." Amelie smiled too, but her face was tilted away from me, her eyes fixed on nothing, almost excluding me. Her teeth were white and straight behind smiling pink lips, scrubbed free of the red lipstick she'd worn in the cage the night before. In fact, her face was completely devoid of make-up, and here under the bright lights of the chandelier, where I could really see her, she was young and lovely with her dark hair tucked behind her ears. The way she didn't make eye contact felt strangely coy, as if she were playing hard to get, though I knew better. She wasn't playing that game. She couldn't.

I released her hand and stepped back, my hand reaching for the door. She tilted her head toward the sound of me moving away. I knew she was the one at a disadvantage technically, but damned if I didn't feel like I was the butt of a private joke, the way her eyes never drank me in.

"Thank you for seeing me home, Mr. Taggert."

"You're welcome, Miss . . ."

"Anderson," she supplied, although I already knew her last name.

"Goodnight, Amelie Anderson."

I let myself out, pulling the door closed behind me.

(End of Cassette)

Moses

THE FIRST TAPE ended with the loud click of the play button releasing, and I exhaled deeply, as if I'd been released as well. I'd been holding my breath throughout, afraid to relax, worried I would miss the clues, that I wouldn't pick up on what Tag wasn't telling us. The problem was, he seemed to be baring his soul, leaving nothing out of their first encounters, even the details better left unsaid.

"I don't watch movies. I listen to them. I'm partial to great dialogue and awesome soundtracks, and romance is a must," Millie spoke up, as if she felt compelled to supply the behind-the-scenes details Tag hadn't shared. "A while back, my cousin Robin and I had an eighties movies marathon, complete with *Dirty Dancing* and *Flashdance,* and I did my best to follow along while Robin filled in the blanks. I put *Flashdance* on again when Robin went home. I listened to it over and over, and I imagined how it would feel to dance in front of an audience, to dance in front of people who didn't know I was blind. That's where I got the idea. I did a little research, hired a handy man, and within two weeks a sturdy stripper pole was keeping the water heater and the furnace company in our basement. The handyman asked me out, too. I declined."

"Smart girl," I said. I was impressed. She was full of life, and I felt a brief flash of happiness for my friend before I remembered that he'd let go.

"I took dancing and gymnastics when I was younger, and I was competitive all the way up to the time my sight started to fail. But being blind didn't take away my ability to tumble, or swing from a bar, or even balance on a beam. With the help of my mom and some patient coaches, I was able to continue with my gymnastics up until just a few years ago. I still work out at the training facility sometimes, but I've over-stayed my welcome. I've outgrown my pathetic appeal, and I feel like a burden more often than not, always having to have someone nearby, keeping an eye out for me.

"But in the basement with the pole, with the music pounding as loud as I want, I can put my dance and gymnastics training to good use. And no one has to help me. Nobody has to make sure I don't fall or hurt myself. When I dance, I can pretend like I'm the real thing, I can pretend I look as good as dancing makes me feel. I even got brave enough to show Robin. She told me I looked amazing. She was so excited for me. So I started creating routines, you know, dreaming a little.

"I even choreographed a routine to "Perfectly Blind" by Day 26. It's a sexy song and that's funny, admit it. I figured if I could laugh at myself, then it wouldn't bother me if other people laughed too. I wanted to dance. I dreamed about it. But I could just imagine the wave of new material available for stand-up comics. I would start a movement. Instead of blonde jokes, or Yo' Mama jokes, it would be blind stripper jokes."

"I can think of a few." I was teasing her, and she giggled.

"Yeah, me too. I have a million of 'em."

I didn't ask her to share, but I was curious. Her laughter faded quickly, and she smoothed her hair self-consciously.

"I make jokes, but I actually care about the way I look. I go to a lot of work to take care of my appearance. Robin's a beautician and that helps. I've been told I'm pretty often enough, and there's no reflection in the mirror to dispute it. So I choose to believe it. But dancing in front of people? That's a whole different story.

"A few months ago, Robin told me they were hiring dancers at the club on the corner of Broadway and Rio Grande. She thought I should apply. I wanted to. I really, really wanted to. I could laugh at myself with Henry and Robin, and I could dance around a pole in my basement, but could I actually dance anywhere else? Could I actually get paid to dance?"

"Tag apparently thought so," I interrupted.

Millie nodded but continued her narrative.

"Robin told me she would help me. And she would have. She would have had me looking like a million bucks. But in the end, I walked into the audition looking like a bag lady. A blind bag lady. Or at least what I imagined a bag lady looked like. I walked in off the street, prepared to be turned away, my clothes unflattering, my hair a mess. I did it on purpose. I wanted to give them every reason to turn me down. I wanted to provide them with an easy way out. But they didn't turn me down." Millie paused. "I guess now we know why."

I had no idea why Tag included that part of his story on the tapes. I'd watched Millie when Tag had recounted the scene with Morgan, and her face had fallen like a house of cards. I'd wanted to throw the tape recorder out the window and hunt my best friend down, so I could slap some sense into him.

But then, as Tag had continued talking, Millie's expression grew thoughtful and her stiff posture relaxed, and I realized suddenly why Tag was sharing the uncomfortable story. Tag confessed the details of Millie's hiring because he didn't want her hearing it from someone else and thinking that he was in on the joke. Tag clearly wanted Millie to know that the first time he'd seen her dancing, he'd had no idea she was blind. He'd thought she was beautiful.

"You heard what he said, Millie. He didn't know. You convinced him you were the real deal. He thought you were even better than the other dancers." My gut twisted again. If Tag were coming back, he wouldn't have felt the need to make that clear or insulate Millie from gossip.

"I know," she whispered and then stood. "I need to take a break, Moses. I need to go home and make sure Henry's okay."

I offered to give her a lift, but she refused, claiming she needed to stretch her legs. She had to dance at the club in a few hours too, and I was glad to hear it, even if she was only going through the motions. Going through the motions means you aren't sitting still. Sitting still is what kills you. And so far, everyone was keeping up appearances for Tag, everyone was showing up for work, doing their jobs at his gym, his bar, and his store on the corner. Tag may have abandoned his world, but if we all went through the motions, maybe we could keep it turning for him until he came back. I didn't let myself think any further than that.

Four

MORGAN DIDN'T COME back to work. I made sure I was at the bar at two the following afternoon, ready to meet him or fill in for him, whichever it was going to be. When five thirty rolled around with still no sign of my manager, I cursed and started flipping through options in my head. I had a big fight to get ready for, and I didn't want to be working late shifts at the bar every night. That's why I'd hired Morg. I wanted to come in, make my rounds, slap some skin, and work the back room. I didn't want to be working forty hours a week behind the bar managing the place. I already had too much on my plate. But I'd embarrassed Morgan. Hurt his pride. Still, I was surprised he hadn't shown.

I spent the evening making drinks, chatting up my regulars, and watching the door. I was sure Morgan would slink in eventually. He just didn't have that many options. Amelie came through the door at seven, using the front entrance instead of the back, which was customary for employees. Henry was with her, his riotous hair covered by a Giants ball cap, his eyes darting from one side of the bar to the other. It was interesting to see the siblings together, one so composed, one so uncomfortable.

I called a greeting to both of them, and Amelie smiled uncertainly, moving toward the bar with Henry in tow. She was on the schedule to dance, and I wondered what she was thinking, bringing her brother to work. Henry didn't act like he heard me at all. His eyes shot straight to the television over my head and he halted about three feet from the stools, stuffing his hands in his pockets, shutting out everything around him. His lip looked swollen and there was a bruise on the side of his face. I wondered if Amelie had any idea.

"Uh, hi David . . . Mr. Taggert," Amelie said, feeling for the edge of the bar.

"Amelie," I interrupted. "Please, for the love of Pete, stop calling me Mr. Taggert."

"Okay. Right." She smiled sheepishly, but continued, discomfort evident in her voice. "Could Henry sit in here and watch the Laker game? My neighbor usually comes over and house sits while I work, just so Henry has someone there at night. But she's not feeling well. He's old enough to be alone, obviously, I mean, I've left him home at night before. But never for very long. And he's had a rough day. Robin's coming to get him, but she won't be here for about twenty minutes . . ." Her voice faded off uncomfortably.

I wondered briefly about her parents and then decided it wasn't any of my business.

"Does he like bubbles too?" I teased. If Henry could sit quietly on a stool and watch the game until Robin arrived, I'd keep him in drinks and pretzels. He wasn't old enough to be in the bar, but as long as he wasn't drinking—which I could make sure of—and as long as it wasn't for very long, I wasn't too concerned about it.

"Sprite. He loves Sprite." She sounded so relieved I thought she was going to break into tears, but she turned to Henry instead, finding his arm and instructing him gently.

"Henry, did you hear that? Mr. Tag—um, Tag says you can watch the game with him." Henry slid onto a stool, his eyes not leaving the screen.

"Is he okay right here, David?" She just couldn't get comfortable with my name. I wondered why.

"That's fine. Go on. I'll keep an eye on him."

"Thank you. Thank you, I . . ." She stopped, squared her shoulders, took a deep breath, and smiled. "Thank you. I appreciate it," she said firmly. With her stick in hand, she tapped her way around the bar and disappeared down the long hallway that led to the restrooms and the employees' locker room.

I put a bowl of peanuts in front of Henry, along with a tall Sprite, thought better of it, and replaced the peanuts with pretzels. Henry seemed like he might be the type of kid who would be horribly allergic to peanuts. That was just what I needed tonight.

"Kobe Bryant leads the league in free throws." I had no idea if this was true. I just threw something out there to see if Henry would engage.

Henry's eyes snapped to mine and he shook his head, indicating my stat wasn't the case.

"He's the tallest man in the NBA?" I knew this wasn't true.

Henry started to smirk.

"He has the biggest feet?"

Henry shook his head.

"His best friend is named Shaq?" I asked.

Henry shook his head so vigorously I thought he was going to fall off his stool.

"Kobe Bryant is the youngest player in league history to reach 30,000 career points," Henry informed me. I gave myself a mental high five that he was talking at all.

"Oh, yeah?" I asked, nonchalant.

"He was also the youngest player to ever start in the NBA," he added.

"Big deal." I waved my hand. "Everybody knows that." I winked, letting him know I hadn't had a clue.

"Did you know he was named after Japanese beef?" Henry boasted, pulling his Sprite toward him and taking a long pull at the straw.

"No kidding!" I started to laugh. I moved away from him to take care of some customers a few stools down, and greeted Axel, my Swedish sparring partner, who slid onto a stool one over from Henry and said "tack"— thank you in Swedish—before guzzling back the beer I placed in front of him.

"Shaquille O'Neal and Kobe Bryant aren't friends," Henry said seriously, and placed a pretzel carefully on his tongue. He looked at his now empty glass despondently.

"No? Why not?" I asked, refilling his Sprite.

"Giants don't make good friends."

"Are you talking about Shaq or Kobe? They're both pretty big." I tried not to laugh because Henry wasn't laughing.

"Giants don't like when someone is bigger than they are."

"I don't know about that. Look at me and Axel. We're both pretty big."

"Who's the biggest?" Henry asked.

"I am," I said firmly, and at the same time Axel thumped his chest.

Henry looked at me owlishly, as if I had just proven his point. Axel started to laugh, and I laughed with him, but Henry didn't laugh at all. He just wrapped his swollen lips around his straw and drank his Sprite like he was dying of thirst. I waited until Axel turned his attention to Stormy, who had stopped to flirt as she waited tables.

"Henry? Are you having problems with a giant?" I touched my lip and looked pointedly at his mouth.

"The Giants won the World Series in 2012," he said softly. "In 2010 too. They're very popular right now."

I wasn't sure if there was a hidden message in the popularity of the Giants or if Henry just wanted to change the subject. I tried again, using a different approach.

"You know the story of David and Goliath, right? David's just a little guy, Goliath's a huge warrior. David ends up killing him with just a sling-shot and Goliath's own sword."

"Your name is David," Henry said, his eyes on the game.

"It is. Do you need me to slay a giant for you?"

"The Giants' bench is deep."

I narrowed my eyes at Henry. He didn't look away from the television. It was like conversing with Yoda. Or R2D2.

I sighed and refilled his drink again. "When all this Sprite catches up with you, the bathrooms are down the hall on the right."

I didn't want to upset Amelie, but when she checked to make sure Robin had come and retrieved Henry, covering her dancing "uniform" with a Tag Team T-shirt and leggings, I pulled her aside and stressed once more that she should bring Henry by the gym. It wouldn't hurt for the kid to learn how to take down a bully, or a giant, if that's what was going on.

AMELIE AND HENRY didn't come by the gym the next day. On Saturday, I thought I saw them once, beyond the wall of windows along the front of the gym, but when I looked again they were gone. I shrugged, deciding Henry must not have been as excited by the idea as Amelie thought he would be. A few minutes later I looked up to see them hovering near the speed bags, Amelie holding firmly to Henry's arm, Henry looking as if he was about to bolt like a runaway seeing-eye dog and drag his poor sister with him. They were garnering some strange looks—Henry with his crazy bedhead, his darting glances, and jittery hands and Amelie because she stood so still with her eyes fixed straight ahead.

I called a quick halt to my bout, escaping Axel, who was trying to pummel me into next week, and slid between the ropes that cordoned off one of the octagons.

"Amelie! Henry!" I called, noting how Amelie's face was immediately wreathed in a relieved smile, a smile so wide it spread to her eyes, giving the illusion of sparkle and life. But Henry started backing up, pulling his sister with him.

"Yo, Henry. Hold up, man." I stopped several feet from them and lowered my voice. "Did you know that Jack Dempsey versus Jess Willard was the very first fight to be broadcast over the radio?"

Henry stopped moving and his hands stilled.

"Do you know what year that was, Henry?"

"1919," Henry said in a whisper. "The first televised fight was in 1931. Benny Leonard vs. Mickey Walker."

"I didn't know that." Actually, I had only known about the Dempsey, Willard fight because I'd seen a biography on Dempsey on Netflix the night before. God bless Netflix. The mention of the radio had made me think of Henry and the sportscast blaring from his bedroom. "You wanna tell me more?"

"David 'Tag' Taggert, light heavyweight contender with a professional record of eighteen wins, two losses, ten knock outs."

"You checked up on me, huh?"

Henry's mouth twitched, and he looked away shyly.

"You did! What else did you find out? That all the ladies love me, that I'm the best looking fighter, pound for pound, in the universe?"

Henry looked confused for a second, and I realized he was searching his mind for that stat. I laughed. "Just kidding, buddy."

"Six-foot three, 215 pounds, most often compared to Forrest Griffin and Michael Bisping?" Henry's voice rose on the end, clearly seeking approval.

"I'm more charming than Bisping, and I have better ears than Forrest. But they could both probably kick my ass."

"He said ass, Amelie!" Henry whispered, half shocked.

"Yes he did, Henry. It's okay. That's how fighters talk," Amelie soothed.

"Can I say ass?" Henry whispered again, curiously.

"You can," I cut in, "after you learn how to fight."

"I don't like to fight." Henry started backing away.

"That's okay, Henry. There's a lot of different ways to fight. I can show you some stuff when you're ready. Some moves are just about protecting yourself. But right now, I'm gonna introduce you to my team."

"Tag Team?" Henry's voice lifted with excitement.

"That's right. We're missing a few people, but a bunch of my guys are here."

Henry had already met Axel, my Swedish sparring partner, at the bar, but Amelie shook his hand politely and Axel shot me a pointed look over the top of her head. He'd seen her dance, obviously. Mikey, with his powerful forearms and his missing lower left leg, greeted Henry and Amelie with a smile and a handshake. Mikey is always a gentleman in front of the ladies, but reverts to a foul-mouthed marine in front of the guys. He lost a leg in Iraq and works out his demons in the Tag Team facilities. He'd taught me a few things about hand-to-hand combat you can only learn from someone who has actually fought for his life more times than he can count.

I moved on to Paulo, a Brazilian, and a better grappler than all of us, and then to Cory, the youngest on the team. Cory Mangum was a wrestler, an NCAA heavyweight champion his junior year. But he threw it all away his senior year and ended up at Montlake Psychiatric Hospital after trying to escape his drug habit by jumping off a bridge. My old friend, Dr. Andelin, had sent him my way. So far, he'd managed to stay clean and pin me daily. I was learning a ton from him.

Beyond Axel, Mikey, Paulo and Cory, who provided training but didn't compete, I had a handful of MMA fighters in a bunch of different divisions who all fought under the Tag Team label, and they greeted Henry and Amelie politely, with side-long looks at Henry's crazy hair and

Amelie's blinding smile. I wondered if Amelie knew how appealing she was. Probably not. There were plenty of women in and out of our facility. Some came to see me or one of the guys, some came to work out with us. I had two female Tag Team fighters who were ranked in the UFC. Amelie was a novelty, though, and I was positive the guys had all noticed her sweet figure, her shiny hair and her pretty mouth. The thought bothered me. Just wait until Axel told them she danced around a pole several nights a week at the bar. That *really* bothered me.

"This part of the gym is for fight training. The rest of it—the weight room, the exercise equipment, and the classes—is for Tag Team fitness members. For fifteen bucks a month you have access to everything on that side of the facility. We have classes over here a few nights a week too, the classes that need the mats like judo and some of our self-defense classes, and those things are extra."

"Maybe you'd like to try out a judo class or a self-defense class, Henry," Amelie spoke up. "I took judo classes for a while. There's a division for blind athletes. Pretty cool. But my heart wasn't in it unless the music was blaring and I could do kicks and spins, which doesn't work in judo."

"Yeah. Not unless you're throwing someone while you're spinning."

"Would I have to punch a bad guy?" Henry asked doubtfully.

"Nah. Judo's all about throws. An MMA fighter uses a lot of throws and submissions, so judo is a pretty big deal around here," I said. Henry seemed overly worried about having to punch someone. Which meant I probably needed to teach him how.

"You don't have to punch anything. Except maybe that bag. Do you think you'd like to punch that bag over there?"

Henry halted and looked suspiciously at the punching bag a couple of feet to the left of where we were standing.

"You could punch the speed bag too. It's fun. And it doesn't hit back."

Amelie was still holding onto Henry's arm, her stick nowhere in sight. I reached out and gently grabbed her elbow, pulling her beside me so that Henry wouldn't hurt her if he attempted a jab. I was doubtful Henry had ever punched anything in his life. He was a small, skinny kid, and he clearly had developmental problems. He sounded a little robotic when he talked, and I wondered if he was autistic. On the one hand he could spit out sports trivia like he was a walking record book. On the other, the kid asked for permission to say ass. Not your average teenager.

Henry walked toward the long punching bag, eyeing it like it might transform into something deadly. His left hand darted out and slapped the bag, and he jumped a foot in the air.

Amelie clapped. "Was that you, Henry? I heard that!"

"Try again, Henry. You can kick it too," I instructed.

Henry's leg shot out as if he were kicking open a door, and the bag swung back and bumped his upraised leg, sending him sprawling.

"He got me, Tag," he groaned, and Amelie gasped. I guess I was wrong. Apparently the punching bag could hit back.

"Stand up, buddy. You kicked it hard. You gotta watch out for the swing, make sure you step back a little, time your kicks and your punches."

Henry rose to his feet as if the bag was going to take his legs out from under him at any minute. He jabbed at it, jabbed some more, kicked a time or two without falling, and then moved onto the speed bag while I threw out instructions. Amelie stayed quiet, listening intently, and I realized that I'd kept my hand on her elbow all along, clutching her to my side as I coached Henry. When Henry seemed to get a bit of a rhythm going on the speed bag, and began chortling happily to himself, she spoke up.

"David?"

I almost looked around to see who she was talking to and then remembered my own name. It sounded different on her lips.

"Yeah?"

"You're so nice. I didn't expect you to be so nice."

"Why?"

"Because all the girls at the bar are either in love with you, and they want to sleep with you, or they hate you, and they still want to sleep with you. I thought you were one of those bad-boy types."

"Oh, I'm plenty bad. I just try not to be an asshole to people who don't deserve it. I guess you could say I'm a nice bad guy."

"I don't think it works that way," she said softly.

"Trust me. It does. I'm good with people. But don't cross me. And don't cross the people I care about. Or you'll see my bad side."

"I'll remember that," Amelie said seriously, nodding as if she had been contemplating crossing me only seconds before. The thought of the dainty, blind brunette with the pearly skin and the sweet smile screwing me over was comical.

"You plotting something?" I asked, trying not to laugh.

"I was. But I thought better of it." She shivered dramatically. "Don't want to see bad Tag."

"Bad Tag and Silly Millie."

"Millie?"

"Doesn't anyone ever call you Millie for short?"

"No," she answered frankly.

"Henry and Amelie aren't names you hear every day. They sound kind of old-fashioned."

"That's because we were actually born in the late 1800s, when our names were more popular. We vampires don't age, you know. And my blindness is just a ruse to make people feel safe." Her lips twisted in a smirk.

"Is that right?" I drawled, "Well, I'll be damned. So you and Henry are forever gonna be, what, thirteen and twenty-two?"

"Fifteen. Henry's fifteen."

"But you're actually one hundred and twenty-two?"

"That's right. We'll still look this good in another hundred years." That was a sad thought for Henry, but for Amelie, not so much.

"You'll outlive us all."

Amelie's face fell a smidgeon and her smile slipped. If I hadn't been looking directly into her face I wouldn't have seen it. But I did, and I realized Amelie had already outlived someone she cared about.

"Are your parents among the undead too?" I asked lightly, wondering if she would abandon the banter.

"No. My dad isn't in the picture. Haven't talked to him in years. My mom died a while back." She shrugged, the fun completely ruined by reality.

"I'm sorry, sweetheart." It was an endearment that I used easily. I'd called more women sweetheart in my life than I could count, but Amelie's cheeks pinked and her chin dipped almost shyly. People must not call her sweetheart very often. "My dad didn't handle it very well when I went blind. Two kids with issues was one too many for him, apparently.

"So you take care of Henry . . . by yourself?" I was stunned and tried not to let it show, but she heard it anyway, from the set of her chin and the stiffening of her back.

"Do you really want to know, or are you doubting me?" She turned her face toward me, as if confronting my question head on, and when I stared down at her, I felt a quaking in my chest that was instantly familiar. It was a jumping-off-a-cliff kind of feeling, a heart-swelling, chest-bursting sensation, and I'd stumbled across it a few times in my life.

I felt it when I watched Moses hold his new baby girl for the first time. He and Georgia were so happy, so deserving, and the joy in his face had spilled over and filled my heart with wonder. I felt it two years ago when I came back in the fifth round to win my first big fight. I've actually felt it a lot of times over the last few years, seeing Moses at work, seeing people weep at his gift. But the first time that feeling took my breath away was in Venice. It was a year after I'd gotten out of Montlake, eight months since Moses and I had taken off across the globe. I'd been so sad and so lost for so long that I'd gotten used to not feeling anything else. But there, in a little boat in Venice, as I watched the sun set—a fiery, hellish, red ball turning the water and sky into shades of heaven—my eyes had filled up with tears at the violent beauty of it all. In that moment, I realized I wanted to live again. For the first time in a long time, I was glad to be alive.

Looking down into Amelie Anderson's heart-shaped face, her mouth set in a stubborn line, I had that feeling again. It rushed through me, taking my breath with it.

"I really want to know," I said, and it came out in a husky whisper.

"We take care of each other," she said simply. "He helps me with the stuff I have a hard time doing. He even cooks sometimes. I mean, not gourmet, but between the two of us, we get by. I may never truly know if my clothes match, or if the house is actually clean, or if there's a fly in my soup, but Henry takes as good a care of me as I take of him."

Right. It was pretty obvious who played parent and who played child. This girl was a surprise a minute.

"Henry and I are a team. You've got Tag Team, right? You understand. Everybody contributes something different."

"Oh yeah?"

"He's the eyes. I'm the heart. He's the hands, and I'm the head. That's what my mom used to say."

We were silent then, my mind reeling, Henry back to fighting an epic battle with the huge punching bag, and Amelie standing straight and still, listening, as if by doing so she could actually see her brother's attempt to take down an impossible opponent. What she didn't know, what she couldn't have known, was that she'd leveled me. I may have been standing next to her, but I was already falling.

(End of Cassette)

. ⠦ ⠂ ⠴ .⠦ ⠦

Moses

HE'S THE EYES. I'm the heart. He's the hands, and I'm the head. The words rang in my ears. Millie could have been describing me and Tag. I was the eyes and the hands—the artist who could see what others could not, what Tag could not. But he was the leader, the head and the heart, and his head and his heart had provided for my eyes and hands time and time again. Tag was all heart, and sometimes it got him in trouble, it got *us* in trouble, but more often than not, it led us in the right direction. He'd taken care of me. I don't know if I had taken care of him, though. I hadn't thought I needed to.

"Why did he leave, Moses? Where did he go? Nobody's seen him for two weeks. Nobody knows anything. If he was falling for me, like he says, then why did he leave like that?" Millie was close to tears and I had resorted to drawing, my fingers flying over a sketch pad so that I wouldn't go crazy listening to my best friend saying goodbye.

I'd called Tag's dad, who called his mom, who in turn called his two younger sisters who were away at school. Millie was right. Nobody knew anything. Nobody had seen or heard from him since he'd left.

"Did he say or do anything that seemed off? Anything that you can think of that might give us a clue where he went?" I asked helplessly. Listening to Tag had filled me with hopelessness. He was clearly telling a love story. And my experience with love led me to believe this story would not end well. Love stories tend to be tragic.

"No. I mean, he had seemed tired, which was unlike him," Millie answered, interrupting my depressing train of thought. "Tag never seems tired. Have you noticed that? He has more energy than anyone I've ever met. But he was tired. He'd been training so hard for the Santos fight. A couple of nights he fell asleep on the couch watching TV with Henry. Once, I woke him up at about midnight because our couch is small and he had to have been uncomfortable. He was disoriented and so out of it that he was slurring his words a little. If I didn't know better, I would have thought he was drunk. But he hadn't had anything to drink. He's never had so much as a beer the entire time I've known him. And he'd been asleep on the couch for three hours.

"I didn't want him to drive. I told him he was too sleepy to be driving. Even if it was just a few blocks. But he said he was fine. I walked him out to his truck, and he made a joke about the blind leading the blind." Her voice broke.

"Was that the last time you saw him?"

"No. The last night I saw him he . . . he and I . . ." Millie's voice trailed off and her cheeks grew suspiciously pink.

Son of a bitch. I didn't need any further explanation. Once again, I was at a complete loss. I excused myself to call Georgia, and she answered on the first ring, her voice sharp with hope and fear.

"What's the news?" she said, foregoing a greeting for the obvious. That's Georgia—take the bull by the horns. It was one of the things I loved most about her, one of the things that had saved us when our own love story took a few tragic turns.

The phrase awakened a memory and instead of answering I said, "Do you know that Tag actually grabbed a bull by the horns once? I saw him do it."

Georgia was silent for a heartbeat before she pressed me again.

"Moses? What are you talking about, baby? What's going on with Tag?"

"We were in Spain. In San Sebastian. It's Basque country, you know. Did you know there are blond Spaniards? I didn't. I kept seeing blond women and they all reminded me of you. I was in a horrible mood so Tag got this bright idea that we should go to Pamplona for the Running of the Bulls. He said a shot of adrenaline was just what I needed to cheer me up. Pamplona isn't that far from San Sebastian. Just an hour south by bus. I knew Tag had a death wish. At least he did at Montlake. And I knew he was a little crazy. But he actually waited for the bull to run past him. And then he chased the bull. When the bull turned on him, he grabbed it by its horns and did one of those twist and roll things that cowboys do at rodeos."

"Steer wrestling?" Georgia still sounded confused, but she was listening.

"Yeah. Steer wrestling. Tag tried to wrestle a bull. The bull won, but Tag got away without a scratch. I still don't know how. I was screaming so loud I was hoarse for a week. Which was fine. Because I didn't talk to Tag for two. That son-of-a-bitch. I thought he was going to die." I stopped talking, emotion choking off my ability to speak. But Georgia heard what I couldn't say.

"What's happening, Moses? Where's Tag?"

"I don't know, Georgia. But can you come? I need you. And I have a feeling that before this is all over, Millie's going to need you. There are certain things you can't talk about with a man. Even if he's your lover's best friend. Especially if he's your lover's best friend."

Five

I WAS PARKED in front of Amelie's house Monday morning, waiting for Henry to leave for school. I'd coaxed the information out of Robin when she came to pick up Henry from the bar, determined to figure out who had bruised up his face. Henry had gone to the bathroom to relieve himself of a bladder full of Sprite, and I'd grilled her. I hadn't said anything to Millie that night or even at the gym Saturday, but it wasn't okay to ignore it, and the thought of someone making Henry's life miserable, of someone putting their hands on him, gave me the itch to hurt people. Bullies and bitches. Hated 'em. So I took it upon myself to intervene, beyond just teaching him a few moves at the gym.

Robin said Henry walked to and from school most days. It was only a few blocks, and sometimes Millie walked with him. He went to regular classes in a regular high school and, according to Robin, he got decent grades. Apparently Millie was in frequent contact with his teachers and was on a first-name basis with the administration. I wondered how much he participated in his classes and how well he got on with the other kids. Robin said he didn't have any friends that she knew of. Judging from his lip, he was getting some attention from someone. I told Robin I would handle it. She seemed a little surprised and then shrugged.

Henry left the house at seven-thirty, and I was idling at the curb, my truck warm, two cups of coffee in the drink holders. I didn't know if Henry liked coffee, but I did. I felt like a creeper, waiting at the curb for a kid, but I rolled down my window and greeted him easily and asked if I could talk to him for a second.

"And I'll take you to school so you won't be late," I added when Henry looked at his watch.

He smiled widely, like my presence was welcome, and trotted around to the passenger door without protest. I made a note to talk with Henry about stranger danger and creepers. He shrugged his back-pack to the floor and took the coffee I handed to him with a grateful groan. I chuckled and we sat, doctoring our brew for a few minutes before I jumped into the conversation that needed to be had.

"Henry? You need to tell me what happened to you. Why was your lip swollen? And who put that bruise on your cheek?"

Henry blushed a deep crimson and choked a little on his coffee. He set it down and wiped the back of his hand across his lips uncomfortably. I felt my temperature rise a notch.

"You know, the reason I wanted Millie to bring you to the gym was so I could teach you how to defend yourself. But that's going to take a while. And in the meantime, I want to know if someone is giving you trouble at school."

Henry wouldn't look at me.

"Henry? Whose ass do I need to kick?"

"You can't."

"I can't what? Kick a giant's ass?" I said softly, remembering his cryptic talk of giants.

"Not a giant. A girl," Henry whispered.

"A girl?" I wouldn't have been more surprised if he told me Millie had punched him in the face.

"My friend."

I shook my head. "No. Not a friend. Friends don't smack you around."

Henry looked at me and raised his eyebrows doubtfully. Touché.

"Well, they don't smack you around unless you ask them to," I amended, thinking of all my friends at the gym who regularly slapped me around.

"What did you do?" I asked, trying to understand. "Did you say something that upset her? Or is she just a bully?"

"I told her she was like a sumo wrestler," Henry said softly.

"You said that to her?" I yelped. "Ah, Henry. Don't tell me you said that to her." It was all I could do not to laugh. I covered my mouth so Henry wouldn't see my lips twitching.

Henry looked crushed. "Sumo wrestlers are heroes in Japan," he insisted.

"Henry," I groaned. "Do you like this girl?"

Henry nodded.

"Cool. Why?"

"Sumo wrestlers are powerful," Henry said.

"Henry, come on, man. You don't like her because she's powerful," I insisted.

Henry looked confused.

"Wait. You do?" Now I was confused.

"The average sumo wrestler weighs over 400 pounds. They are huge."

"But she's not huge, is she?"

"No. Not huge."

"Does she look like a sumo wrestler?" I asked.

Henry shook his head.

"No. But she's big . . . maybe bigger than other girls?"

Henry nodded. Okay now we were getting somewhere.

"So she punched you when you told her she reminded you of a sumo wrestler."

Another nod.

"She blacked your cheekbone and split your lip."

Henry nodded again and smiled slightly, as if he was almost proud of her.

"Why did you say that, Henry? She obviously didn't like it." I couldn't think of a girl who would.

Henry gritted his jaw and fisted his hands in his hair, obviously frustrated.

"Sumo wrestlers are awesome!" he cried.

"Hey man, I get it. Talking to girls is hard. I said all kinds of stupid things the first time I walked Millie home. Luckily she didn't punch me."

"Amelie isn't a fighter!" Henry said, and laughed a little, releasing his hair and taking a deep breath.

"You're wrong about that, buddy. She's a fighter. She's just a different kind of fighter."

We were both quiet for a minute, mulling that over.

"I l-l-like her," Henry stuttered sadly, as if such a simple statement was so much harder than spitting out trivia. And maybe it was.

"Because she's powerful," I repeated, hoping he'd give me something more.

"Yes."

"And has she been nice to you? Before she hit you in the face, I mean."

"Yes." Henry nodded vigorously. "Like a bodyguard."

"She looks out for you?"

Henry nodded again.

I felt light-headed with relief and I started to laugh. "So nobody, no giants, no jocks, nobody is pushing you around?"

Henry shook his head slowly.

"I'm sorry," he whispered. "I messed up."

"And I'm going to help you fix it, man," I said suddenly, shifting my truck into drive and pulling away from the curb.

Henry pulled on his seatbelt as if he were about to go for a wild ride.

I slid into the parking lot in the front of the school, turned off the ignition and climbed out. Henry was staring at me, his eyes huge.

"Let's go, Henry. I'll help you smooth it over with your friend. Come on!"

Henry walked beside me, holding onto the straps of his back-pack like he was getting ready to parachute from a plane. His face was grim.

"You can do this, Henry," I encouraged. He nodded once, but his eyes stayed forward. A few people stared, but the hallways were thick with kids, and, for the most part, the only heads that turned were of the female variety. I would have felt flattered, except everybody looked like they were about fourteen, especially the guys. It was weird. I thought I was such a badass in high school. I thought I was a man. These kids looked like they still secretly sucked their thumbs.

Henry stopped suddenly, and I laid a hand on his shoulder. He was shaking so hard he was vibrating. He pointed toward a girl standing alone next to a row of red lockers.

"Is that her?" I asked.

Henry nodded, still staring. I choked, swallowing my laughter. She wasn't huge at all. But she *was* Japanese.

She was short and softly rounded, maybe a little bit chubby, but most of her weight was in her chest, which told me a lot about where Henry's attention had been. Henry continued toward her and then stopped next to her, his eyes darting between the lockers beside her head and my face. He looked desperate.

The Japanese girl stared at me and raised one eyebrow expectantly. She had a row of loops through that eyebrow, a tiny diamond in her nose, and two rings through her bottom lip. Her ears were practically bedazzled.

"I'm Tag Taggert." I stuck out my hand and gave her a smile of dimpled sincerity. It was my money grin.

"Ayumi Nagahara," she answered, extending her small hand. I almost laughed. Her voice was impossibly sweet and high.

I gave her hand a brisk shake and released it. Then I folded my arms and got serious. "Henry likes you. He thinks you're amazing. He's told me all about you." Both eyebrows shot up, and I had a feeling it had more to do with Henry confiding in me than the fact that he liked her.

She looked at Henry for a minute, her expression softening, and then looked back at me. Henry leaned his forehead against the lockers as if the whole conversation was making him dizzy.

"He's sorry, Ayumi. He wasn't trying to infer that you are like a sumo wrestler. He was trying to tell you he reveres you, the way the Japanese revere their wrestlers."

Henry started to nod, his head banging against the locker. I put my arm around his shoulders and pulled him back just a bit so he wouldn't knock himself out.

"However, he does think you're tough. You obviously know how to throw a punch." I looked pointedly at Henry's face and Ayumi blushed a deep, ruby red. I figured I didn't need to say anything more on that subject. I just hoped she'd think before popping poor Henry again. Because girl or not, she couldn't go around slugging people. Especially people like Henry. "And anytime you want to come and hang out with us at Tag Team, me and Henry, you can. A friend of Henry's is a friend of mine."

"Okay," she squeaked, and I tried to imagine her angry enough to double up her fists and swing. Henry must have really set her off.

The bell rang and Henry jumped. Lockers slammed, and kids started to clear the hall.

"See you at the gym after school Henry, okay?"

Henry nodded, his face relaxing into a smile. His color was returning to normal, and his grip on his back-pack had eased.

I tousled Henry's hair, giving him a one-armed man hug, and as I walked away, I heard him rattle off my record to his little friend.

"David 'Tag' Taggert, light heavyweight contender with a professional record of eighteen wins, two losses, ten knockouts."

"THERE'S NO WAY you can support Henry on a dancer's wage," I said. Even the wage I'd moved her up to. I was walking Millie home again, like I'd done every night she'd worked for the last two weeks. I still hadn't found a replacement for Morgan, and I was still working too many hours at the bar. But I hadn't minded it at all, and the reason walked beside me.

"No. There isn't. But lucky for us my mom planned well. She had a life insurance policy, a good one, and the house was hers, free and clear. It's been in her family forever. And my dad gave her a chunk of money—maybe you've heard of him. Andre Anderson? He played for the San Francisco Giants. He was a first baseman. I don't know what he's doing now."

"Well, I'll be damned," I said, surprised. "I do remember him."

Amelie nodded. "We think that's why Henry became so fixated on sports. He was only five when my dad split. You know how players study game film? Well, Henry does that. My mom had discs made up of all the video, all the recordings of my dad's games, as much as she could get her hands on. Henry would sit and watch, endlessly. He still does. He can quote entire innings. It's crazy."

"So why do you dance?" I hadn't meant to ask. It just came out, the way most things usually did. If I felt something, it eventually worked its way from my gut to my throat and out my lips.

"Why do you hit people?" she asked. I didn't bother to defend the sport. I did hit people. That was a big part of it, and it was silly to argue about it.

"I've spent my whole life fighting."

"Your whole life?" Amelie asked doubtfully.

"Since I was eleven," I amended. "I was the happy-go-lucky fat kid on the playground that was fun to laugh at and easy to mock. The kid that other kids taunted. And I would laugh it off, until one day I'd had enough, and my happy-go-lucky slipped and became happy-don't-likey."

Amelie giggled softly and I continued. "That day, I used my fists and the anger that had been building for five, long years since Lyle Coulson had said I was too fat to fit in the little kindergarten desks. It didn't matter that he was right. I *was* too fat to fit in the little desks, but that only made me angrier. The fight wasn't pretty. I only won because I laid on Lyle and trapped his skinny arms beneath me and wailed on his mean, red face. I got sent to the principal's office for the first time ever, and then I was suspended for fighting. But Lyle Coulson never bothered me again. I learned I like to fight. And I'm good at it."

"Well, there you go." She shrugged. "We're not so different. I like to dance. And I'm good at it."

"I don't like you dancing at the bar."

She laughed—a sudden, sparkling eruption that created a white plume in the frigid air and had me staring down at her upturned face, marveling, even though I knew I was about to take some heat. It was my bar, after all. I was her employer. It was my freaking pole, for hell's sake.

"What don't you like? David Taggert, are you a hypocrite? You aren't. I know you aren't." She was smiling, but not up at me, like other women did. She was smiling straight forward, at no one and nothing, and I felt an ache in my chest, a warning note. She would never smile at me like other women did. Was I okay with that? Because if I wasn't, I needed to back the hell off. I was getting personal.

"Nah. You know what I mean. Why do you dance in a smoky bar, spinning around a pole, wearing next to nothing, for money that isn't all that good? You're a classy girl, Amelie, and pole-dancing just isn't very classy." Backing off wasn't my style.

Her smile was gone, but she didn't look angry. She stopped walking, her stick extended like she was strolling with an imaginary pet. Then she pulled the stick upright and tapped it sharply on the sidewalk.

"See this stick?"

I nodded and then remembered she couldn't see me. "Yeah."

She pushed it toward me and it knocked against my shoulder. "Being blind comes with a stick. Not a cute golden retriever. A stick. But this stick means I can walk down the street by myself. I can make my way to the store. It means I can go to school, walk to work, go to the movies, go out to eat. All by myself. This stick represents freedom to me." She took a deep breath and I held mine.

"I guess I just replaced the stick with a pole—and when I dance, for a few hours, several nights a week, I'm living my dream. Even though it may not look that way to you. My mom wouldn't have liked it. You're right about that. But she isn't here. And I have to make my own choices."

Amelie stopped talking and waited, possibly to see if I was going to argue. When I didn't, she continued.

"I used to dance and do gymnastics. I used to leap and turn. I could do it all. And I didn't need a pole. Just like I used to walk down the street and chase my friends and live my life without my stick. But that isn't an option anymore. That pole means I can still dance. I don't need to see to dance in that cage. If that means I'm not a classy girl, so be it. It's a tiny piece of a dream that I had to give up. And I'd rather have a piece of a dream than no dream at all."

Well, shit. That made perfect sense. I felt myself nodding again, but punctuated it with words. "Okay. Okay, Millie. I sure as hell can't argue with that."

"So now I'm Millie?"

"Well, we've just established that you aren't a classy girl," I teased, and her laughter rang out again, echoing in the quiet street like a faraway church bell. "Amelie sounds like an aristocrat, Millie sounds a little more down home. A girl called Millie can be friends with a guy named Tag."

"David?"

"Yeah?"

"I have a new favorite sound."

"What's that?"

"The way you say Millie. It shot straight to the top of my list. Promise me you'll never call me Amelie again."

Damn if my heart wasn't pounding in my chest. She wasn't flirting, was she? I couldn't tell. All I knew was that I wanted to call her Millie again. And again. And again. Just because she asked me to.

"I promise . . . on one condition."

She waited for me to name my price, a small smile tiptoeing across her mouth.

"I'll keep calling you Millie if you call me Tag," I said. "You callin' me David makes me feel like you expect me to be someone I'm not. The people I care about the most call me Tag. That's what fits."

"I like calling you David. I think you're classier than you give your-self credit for. And everyone calls you Tag. I want to be . . . different," she admitted softly.

I felt a slice of pain and pleasure that had me holding back and leaning in simultaneously, but I pushed the feeling away with banter, the way I usually do.

"Oh, I'm very classy." She laughed with me, the way I wanted her to. "But you bein' special and different has nothing to do with what you call me, Millie. But you can call me any damn thing you want to."

"Any damn thing doesn't have the same ring as David, but okay," she quipped.

"You're a smart aleck, you know that, right?"

She nodded, grinning and gave my nickname a shot. "So, Tag."

"Yeah, Millie?"

"Tomorrow's Sunday. Do you go to church?"

"No. You?" I was guessing she did. Amelie was full of contradictions. It wouldn't surprise me at all if she was a pole-dancing church-goer.

"In a manner of speaking. Church is hard for Henry. I could go alone. He's fine at home by himself for a little while, obviously. But when I was younger, my mom would try and take us, and when Henry would get agi-tated or start making too much noise, she would take us out. That's when I discovered one of my favorite sounds. You want to hear it?"

"Now?"

"No. Tomorrow. Eleven a.m."

"At church?"

"At church."

Well, damn. Maybe I should go to church. Work on saving my soul. "Okay."

"Okay?" Her smile knocked me over, and I mentally kicked myself. I was spending too much time with her, and the more time I spent, the harder it was to keep my head on straight. Before I thought better of it I spoke. "We're just friends, you and I, right Millie?"

The smile wobbled and Millie reached out for her gate, feeling for the latch as if she needed something to hold onto while I kicked her in the stomach.

"Yeah. Why would I ever presume to be more?" she asked, her voice light. The gate swung open and without turning toward me again, she walked toward the front door, barely using her stick.

Six

FRIENDS OR NOT, I found myself in front of Amelie's door at a quarter to eleven. I knocked and waited, wondering if Millie had changed her mind. The friend comment had been insulting—I knew it as soon as it left my lips—but I had to make sure I wasn't leading her on until I knew where I was going. I was dressed in my navy blue suit jacket and a starched white shirt, but I'd left the tie at home and pressed my Wranglers instead of wearing slacks. I could dress up when I needed to, but I was hoping my pressed Wranglers and shiny boots were good enough. I'd slicked back my shaggy hair and told myself I didn't need a haircut. I'd never been attached to my hair, I just never got around to taking care of it. But it made me look a little unkempt, so I wetted it, threw some goop in it, and slicked it back. I looked like one of those shirtless guys in a kilt on the cover of a romance novel, the kind my mom used to read and collect. It didn't matter. Millie couldn't see my long hair or the way it curled well over my collar. She couldn't see my jeans for that matter, so I didn't know why I cared.

The front door swung open and Henry stood there with wide eyes and a baseball bat.

"Hey, Henry."

Henry stared. "You look weird, Tag."

Said the guy with the bat and the hair that looked like a burning bush.

"I'm dressed up, Henry."

"What did you do to your hair?" Henry hadn't moved back to let me in.

"I combed it. What did you do to yours?" I asked, smirking.

Henry reached up and patted it. "I didn't comb it."

"Yeah. I can tell. It looks like a broom, Henry."

We stared at each other for a few long seconds.

"They use brooms in the sport of curling," Henry said.

I bit my lip to control the bubble of laughter in my throat. "True. But I'm thinking you would look more like a baseball player with less hair. That's your favorite sport, right?"

Henry held up the bat in his hands, as if that were answer enough.

"I was thinking . . . I was thinking that you and I should maybe head over to my friend Leroy's and get a trim tomorrow. Leroy owns a barbershop. Whaddaya say? Leroy is nice and there's a smoothie shop next door. It'll be a man date. A date for men." I might as well kill two birds with one stone.

"A mandate?" Henry ran the words together.

"Yes. I am mandating that you get your hair cut. We'll go to the gym afterwards, and I'll show you some moves."

"Not Amelie?"

"Do you want Amelie to come?"

"She's not a man. It's a man date."

Amelie chose that moment to gently push Henry aside.

"I am definitely not a man, but Henry, you really should have invited Tag inside."

Amelie was wearing tan boots and a snug khaki colored skirt that came to her knees, along with a fitted red sweater and a fuzzy scarf that had streaks of red and black and gold in the weave. I wondered how in the world she coordinated it all. Judging from Henry's hair, he couldn't be much help.

"On February sixth, 1971, Alan Shepard hit a golf ball on the moon," Henry offered inexplicably, and moved aside.

"And today is February sixth, isn't it?" Millie said, clearly understanding Henry's thought processes a whole lot better than I did.

"That's right," I said. "So February sixth a golf ball was hit on the moon and on February seventh, 2014, Tag Taggert and Henry Anderson are going to get haircuts, right Henry?"

"Okay, Tag." Henry ducked his head and headed up the stairs.

"Call me if you need me, Henry," Millie called after him. She waited until she heard his door shut before she addressed me.

"Henry has an attachment disorder. He doesn't even like it when I cut *my* hair. If my mom had allowed it, he would be the biggest pack rat in the world. But hoarding and blindness don't mix. Everything has to be in its place or the house becomes a landmine. So he wears the same clothes until they're threadbare, won't cut his hair, still sleeps with his Dragon Ball Z sheets he got for his eighth birthday, and has every toy he has ever been given stored in plastic bins in the basement. I don't think he'll go through with the hair cut. He's only let Robin cut it twice since my mom died, and both times he cried the entire time, and she had to put the clippings in a Ziplock bag and let him keep them, just to get him to calm down."

I was slightly repulsed, and I was glad Millie couldn't see my expression. "So he has bags of hair in his room?"

"I'm assuming he does though he won't tell me where. I pay my next-door neighbor to come in and clean once a week, and she hasn't found it either."

"Well, Henry said okay. So I'm planning on it. But we won't be bringing any bags of hair back home."

Millie's brows furrowed and she looked as if she wanted to argue, but stepped toward me instead, felt for her walking stick that was leaning against the wall, and changed the subject. "Did you drive? Because I'm thinking we should walk. The church is around the corner."

I eyed my shiny red truck wistfully and then forgot it when Amelie slid her hand around my arm.

Other than a few scattered snow flurries that dumped in the mountains and frosted the valleys, Salt Lake City was enjoying the mildest winter we'd had in years, and though the temperatures plummeted here and there, in comparison to normal February temperatures, it was almost balmy.

We walked east towards the mountains that ringed the valley. The mountains were the first thing I noticed about Utah when my family moved from Dallas my junior year in high school. Dallas didn't have mountains. Salt Lake City had staggering, snow-covered mountains. I'd spent more than a few weekends in them skiing, though I was careful about how much skiing I did when I was training. Unfortunately, I always seemed to be training.

Amelie lifted her face as if to soak up the sun.

"Can you see anything at all?" I wondered if the question would offend her.

"Light. I can differentiate light from darkness. That's about it. I can tell where the windows are in the house, when the door is open, that sort of thing. Natural light is easier for me than artificial light. And the light doesn't illuminate anything else, so it's really only good for orienting me in a room with windows, if that."

"So if I danced around in front of a spotlight, you wouldn't be able to see my outline?"

"Nope. Why? You thinking about doing a little pole-dancing at the bar?" she said cheekily.

"Yes. Dammit! How did you know?" I exclaimed, and she tossed back her head and laughed. I admired the length of her throat and her smiling mouth before I caught myself and looked away. I stared at her way too often.

"You look nice, Millie," I said awkwardly, and felt like an idiot for the understatement.

"Thanks. I'd say the same thing to you, but, well, you know. You smell nice, though."

"Yeah? What do I smell like?" I asked.

"Wintergreen gum."

"It's my favorite."

"You also smell like a pine-based aftershave and soap—"

"New cologne called Sap," I joked.

"—with a hint of gasoline."

"I stopped to fill up on the way. Guess I didn't need to, since we're walking."

"We're walking because we're practically there." An old church that looked like it had been built around the same time as Millie's house rose from a circle of trees at the end of the block. "There's been talk that they are going to tear it down. Then I'll have to find somewhere else to go."

As we closed the distance, I could see that the church was a pale brick with a towering white spire and soaring windows on the tallest end. A

THE SONG OF DAVID

creek ran to the north of the building and Amelie and I crossed a sturdy bridge that ran adjacent to the road.

"No water in the creek?" She asked as if she already knew the answer.

"No."

"Soon. A couple of months and I'll be able to come hear two of my favorite sounds at once."

"You like the sound of the creek?"

"I do. When spring comes, I stand on this bridge and just listen. I've been doing it for years."

When I began to veer across the grass on the other side of the bridge, heading for the wide double doors that were clearly the entrance to the church, she pulled against my arm.

"Aren't we going in?" I asked.

"No. There's a rock wall. Do you see it?"

Ahead was a crumbling, twenty-foot wedge of piled rocks cemented into a divider that rimmed the side of the church, separating it from the grassy slope that led down to the dry creek bed. I led Millie to it, and she dropped my arm and felt her way down it a ways before she sat and patted the spot next to her.

"Are the windows open?" she asked

"It looks like one is, just a bit."

"Mr. Sheldon usually remembers. He leaves it cracked for me when the weather's good."

"Do you listen from out here?" I was incredulous. I could hear muted men's voices and then laughter, as if there was a meeting of sorts going on behind the windows.

"No. Not exactly." She listened for a second. "They've started earlier today. It fluctuates. Sometimes it's eleven-fifteen or eleven-thirty. They like to visit and are slow to begin sometimes. But I don't mind waiting. This is a nice spot, and when it's not too cold I'm happy to just sit on this wall and think. When it's warm Henry comes with me and we have a picnic. But he gets bored, and I don't enjoy it as much when he's here. Maybe because I can't relax."

The piano began playing and Millie sat up straighter, tipping her head in the direction of the music.

"Oh, I love this one."

I could only stare at her. This was one of her favorite sounds? Then voices were raised, and the sound seeped out the slim opening and floated down to the place where we sat, and I forgot about the fact that my suit coat was a little tight across the shoulders and my knuckles were sore from yesterday's sparring session. I forgot about all of it because Amelie's face was lit up by the sound of men's voices, singing in worship, mellow and smooth, lifting and lowering over the words. They weren't professional. It wasn't a barbershop quartet or the BeeGees. There were more voices than that, probably twenty or thirty male voices singing praises. And as I listened I felt it deep in my belly.

> "There is no end to glory;
> There is no end to love;
> There is no end to being;
> There is no death above.
> There is no end to glory;
> There is no end to love;
> There is no end to being;
> There is no death above."

When they finished, Amelie sat back and sighed. "I'm all about girl power, but there is nothing like men's voices. They knock me out every time. The sound makes my heart ache and my bones soft."

"Is it the words you love? It was a beautiful song." I was still thinking about the words.

"I love that particular one. But no. It wouldn't matter if I couldn't understand a word they were saying, and there have been days when Mr. Sheldon doesn't attend or he forgets to open the window, and the music is muffled, even more than it was today. And I still love it. I can't explain it. But love is like that, isn't it?"

"Yeah. It is."

"Did you like it? Now you've heard two of my favorite sounds."

"I liked it a lot. I wish I would have worn my sweats instead of this damn suit coat. But hey, at least I didn't have to actually go to church."

Amelie reached toward me, feeling along the lapels of my coat and up to my collar. "Yep. I got you good. I can't believe you agreed to come."

"You're wearing a skirt!"

"Yep. If I'd worn pants you would have known something was up."

I stood and pulled her up with me. "You're a smart aleck and a tease. I don't know if I like you, Silly Millie." I was smiling as I spoke, and she grinned with me before reaching for my lapel once more, as if asking me to wait.

"I want to feel you smile. I can hear when you're smiling. I love the way it sounds. But I want to feel it. Can I?" she asked sweetly.

I brought her hands to my cheeks and laid them there, dropping my hands to my sides.

"Are you smiling?" she asked.

I realized I wasn't, not anymore. But she was, her pink lips parted slightly over pearly teeth, her eyes on a distance she would never see. I smiled down into her face, accommodating her, and her hands immediately fluttered over my lips and her fingers traced the grooves in my cheeks. I'd always used those grooves to my full advantage. When her left thumb slid into the notch on my chin, her smile grew even wider.

"You have dimples in your cheeks and a cleft in your chin."

"My mother dropped me on my face as a child. I'm severely dented. What can I say?"

"Ah. I see." One hand flitted up and traced the bridge of my nose. "Is that what happened here, too?" she asked, tracing the bump that I'd earned over and over again.

"Nah. My mama's not to blame for that one. That's a product of my favorite pastime."

Her hands moved to cradle my face, melding to the shape of my cheekbones and my jaw. As she pulled her hands downward, the tips of her fingers touched the hair that brushed my neck on either side, and she paused in her exploration. She fingered the curls thoughtfully and a groove appeared between her dark brows.

"Haircuts with Henry tomorrow, huh? That's very sweet of you. But don't cut it all away, okay?"

"You like the Scottish highlander look?" I tried for a Scottish brogue, but didn't quite make it. My heart was pounding and I wanted to close my eyes and lean into her hands. Her explorations were erotic without meaning to be, sensual without sexual intention, but my body didn't seem to know the difference.

"I don't know. Maybe? I'm not sure what a Scottish highlander looks like. But I like your face. It's strong . . . full of character. And the hair suits you." She was staring up into my face, describing me, and yet she couldn't see me at all. I stared at her mouth and wondered what she would do if I pressed my lips against hers. Would it startle her or would she recognize the sensation immediately? Had she ever even been kissed? She wasn't shy and she was beautiful, and at twenty-two she should have had her fair share of boyfriends and kisses. But she was blind, she had a dependent brother, and she spent her free time listening to men's choirs and babbling brooks. Somehow I suspected she wasn't all that experienced with men. She dropped her hands and stepped back from me, almost as if she could hear my thoughts.

"Let's get some ice cream," she said, and I shook myself awake, pushing away thoughts of kisses and linking her arm back through mine.

(End of Cassette)

Moses

"I WANTED HIM to kiss me. But he didn't. And I was convinced that he didn't like me that way," Millie said sheepishly, her face flushed. I kept expecting her to turn off the tape recorder and ask us to leave. Hearing Tag's inner thoughts and feelings was downright embarrassing, and when I saw him again, I was going to punish him for making me sit through it.

We were at Millie's now, parked in her living room so that she would be there when Henry got home from school. It had been forty-eight hours since Millie had called me, forty-eight hours since my world had shrunk to one priority, everything else pushed aside or postponed.

"Tag went to church with you?" Georgia's voice was incredulous. Millie and I had brought Georgia up to date, and her presence calmed me, reminded me that regardless of the priority, regardless of my fear, she was with me. She was mine. That part of my world was intact. She'd arrived last night with baby Kathleen, and we'd rented a hotel room, unwilling to stay in Tag's apartment, though I had a key. There was a freaking "For

THE SONG OF DAVID

Sale" sign in the window, and I didn't want to be sleeping in Tag's bed only to have a realtor show up with buyers in tow.

The thought made me angry, even as Georgia's question made me laugh. Tag and church didn't really mix. The thought of him sitting in a suit coat, his hair slicked back, listening to hymns with Millie was almost too unbelievable to imagine.

"Moses?" Georgia's lips quivered, the seriousness of the situation making her hesitant to join in.

"I had to drag his ass into dozens of churches throughout Europe. I don't think he ever went willingly, and we were just looking at the ceilings and the sculptures, no singing involved."

"He loves music. Have you ever heard him sing? I love hearing him sing." Millie smiled and then her smile immediately fell, as if reality had slapped her back down and whisked away her joy.

"I'm still stuck on the fact that he volunteered to get a haircut," Georgia smirked, giggling in spite of her attempts to be appropriate.

"Well . . ." Millie hedged. "That didn't quite go according to plan."

Seven

HENRY CLIMBED INTO my truck and buckled his seatbelt with the grimmest expression I had ever seen. His hair stood out in every direction, and his hands shook.

"You okay, buddy?" I asked, trying to be gentle.

"Do you want to go see Robin instead? She'd be glad to cut it, Henry." Millie had followed him out, tapping her way down the sidewalk with a concerned frown between her dark brows. She now stood holding onto the passenger side door. I could tell she wanted to ride along, but Henry didn't seem to want her to.

"It's a man date, right Henry? Men go to the barber. Not the salon."

Henry tapped his fingertips together nervously and wouldn't look right or left.

"Kite flying is an official sport in Thailand!" Henry blurted.

Amelie bit her lip but stepped back from the passenger door.

"Bye, Millie. I'll bring him back. Don't worry," I called.

She nodded and tried to smile, and I pulled away from the curb. Henry's tapping became a cadence. Clack clack. Click click. It sounded like the rhythm Millie made with her stick when she walked.

"Henry?"

No response. Just clicking, all the way to the barbershop.

I pulled up to Leroy's shop and put my truck in park. I jumped out and came around to Henry's door. Henry made no move to disembark.

"Henry? Do you want to do this?"

Henry looked pointedly at my shaggy locks and clicked his fingers.

"I need a haircut, Henry. So do you. We're men. We can do this."

"Ben Askren, Roger Federer, Shaun White, Troy Polamalu, David Beckham, Triple H."

"Triple H?" I started to laugh. Henry was listing athletes with long hair. "You're getting desperate, Henry."

"Larry Fitzgerald? Tim Lincecum?"

"Tim Lincecum, huh? He plays for the Giants, doesn't he? Your favorite team, right?"

Henry didn't respond.

"Ah, shit. What the hell. I didn't want to cut my hair anyway. I kind of think your sister likes it."

The clicking slowed.

"You wanna go buy a kite? I hear it's an official sport in Thailand," I said.

Henry smiled the smallest ghost of a smile and nodded once.

WE WENT TO Toys R Us for the kites. They have the best selection of fun stuff, and we weren't messing around. Henry took his time considering and settled on a kite with LeBron James on it. I bought the only red one I could find, which was an Elmo kite, the happy red monster staring out at me, his furry face in the shape of a diamond. Henry thought it was hilarious, which made it even better.

"I like red!" I told him, laughing because he was laughing. "We should get Millie one too. What do you think she would pick?" I felt stupid immediately. I was constantly forgetting that she couldn't see and wouldn't care what it looked like.

But Henry didn't seem to think it was a stupid question and considered the kites all over again. He pulled a shimmery, bright pink one from a shelf and handed it to me.

"Referees in the National Rugby League wear pink jerseys," he said seriously.

"Okay, I don't know what the National Rugby League has to do with Millie. But good choice."

When we arrived back at the house, an hour after we left, Henry scooped up all of the kites and was out of my truck before I put it into park. He ran up the walk like he was five instead of fifteen, barreling through the door, while I followed him at a slower pace.

By the time I made it into the kitchen, Millie was running her hands over Henry's head with a furrowed brow. I lifted one of her hands and placed it against the back of my neck where my hair fell over my collar.

"You were right," I said simply. "We're too attached to our hair."

The furrow lifted but she didn't drop her hand. She curled her fingers against my scalp and tugged a little, testing its length, and I did my best not to start purring. Henry didn't. He dropped his head to her shoulder and closed his eyes, completely tamed.

"Don't fall asleep Henry. We have some kites to fly."

Millie threw back her head and laughed, her hands dropping to her sides.

"Oh, you didn't miss that not-so-subtle suggestion, huh?" she snickered.

"Nope. I got it loud and clear. We got you a pink one. Henry picked it out."

"He knows me well. Pink's my favorite color."

"Oh yeah? Why?"

"Because it has a smell. It has a flavor. Every time I taste something pink I can remember the color. It floods my memory for a second before I lose it again."

"Huh. I thought you were going to say it's because you love rugby."

"Ah, the pink jerseys?" Millie asked.

"Henry needs to get out more," I answered, laughing.

"Let's go!" Henry shouted, running for the door, as if taking my advice to heart.

The street was tree-lined, the front yard too small, and the traffic a little too steady to give us an open place to put our kites in the air. We piled back into my truck, Millie in the middle, straddling the gear shift, and Henry sitting by the door, practically bouncing with enthusiasm.

Moses hates my bench seat. He says it's irritating not to have an arm rest. But Mo isn't the smartest man, sometimes. I was never more grateful for the bench seat than I was at that moment with Millie pressed up against my side, my right tricep brushing against her breasts every time I shifted. She smelled like fruit. Strawberries or watermelon. She smelled . . . pink. The thought made me smile. She felt pink too. Pink and soft and sweet. Damn. I decided then and there that pink was my favorite color too.

I drove to Liberty Park, just south of downtown, and within minutes, Henry had his kite out and was urging LeBron James into the air.

"He's done this before," I said in surprise.

"Not in forever. I can't remember the last time, actually," Millie replied. "Is he doing it?"

"Listen," I said. "Can you hear it?" I listened with her, straining for a sound that would connect her to the visual. Then the kite dipped, caught the wind again, and lifted, making a soft, wop wop in the air, like laundry on a clothes line, flapping in the breeze.

"I hear it!"

"That's Henry's kite. He's a natural."

"Will you help me get mine in the air? I could take off running, but that might be dangerous. I don't want to run head first into the pond. There is a pond, isn't there?"

"Just run away from the sound of the ducks."

Before long I had our kites airborne, and LeBron James, Elmo, and Millie's bright pink triangle were dipping and darting, enlivening the pale afternoon sky.

"Give it some slack, Millie!" I hollered as her kite veered downward, tethered too close to the ground. "Let it fly!"

Millie squealed, panicked, but immediately followed my instructions, and her kite corrected itself, catching a draft and soaring higher.

"I can feel it climbing!" she shouted, ebullient. Henry wasn't the only one who was a natural. He was running back and forth, the kite streaming behind him, his hair falling in his eyes, his cheeks ruddy in the tepid February sunshine.

"If you could go anywhere, just holding onto the tail of that kite, where would it be?" I asked Millie, my eyes on the sky, thinking about the places I'd been. "Or is traveling kind of a scary thought?"

"No. It's not scary. Just unrealistic. There are lots of places I'd like to go even though I wouldn't be able to see them. I could still press my hands against the walls and soak them in. Buildings soak up history, you know. Rocks do too. Anything that's been around a while." Amelie paused as if waiting for me to snicker or argue. But my best friend can see dead people. I have no doubt that there is a lot we don't understand. And I can accept that. It's easier than trying to figure it all out.

"It's true!" Millie added, even though I hadn't argued at all. "My mom took me and Henry to the Alamo in San Antonio when I was thirteen. Apparently there are signs all around the Alamo that say 'Don't touch the building,' and it's cordoned off by rope so you can't do anything but look. Which is pretty unfair if you ask me. I look with my hands! So my mom got special permission. She was always finding a way to help me experience as much as I could, even if it meant finding someone to let us break the rules. I stood right next to the Alamo and laid my hands and face on the walls and just listened."

"And what did you hear?" I asked.

"I didn't hear anything. But I felt something. It's hard to describe. But it felt like a vibration, almost. The way your legs feel when you're waiting for a train to go by. That sensation . . . you know what I mean?"

"I know exactly," I said.

"Whenever we traveled, my mom would make sure we stayed in hotels that had some history. In San Antonio, there's a hotel called the Fairmount. Built in 1906. We walked in that place and I felt like I was on the Titanic. I felt my way all over that hotel. Remember how you said that the world was more beautiful, once upon a time?"

"Yeah." I'd felt stupid when I said it, but now I was glad I had.

"It's so true. There's still original furniture in the Fairmount, and the whole place just feels . . . ripe." She laughed at her word choice. "Ripe is the only word that fits. Like it's bursting at the seams with history and time and energy. There's so much beneath the surface, but *no one* can see it. Not just me. No one. And because no one else can see it either, it makes me feel privileged that at least I can feel it."

"I know that hotel. They relocated it in 1985. Actually picked the hotel up and moved it down the street. My grandma was one of those rich old ladies who was big on preserving the historical sites. A lot of the wealthy families are. She was on the committee to save it. That was before I was born, but there was a big gala at the Fairmount to mark its one hundred year anniversary that we all attended. It's a cool place."

"I loved it." Millie sighed. "Where else have you been?"

"I've been all over the world. I've seen more in twenty-six years than most people see in a lifetime. A lot more."

"Did your parents take you?" she asked.

"No."

She waited for me to elaborate, and I weighed what I should share. It wasn't a happy story. But I realized, much to my astonishment, that I wanted to tell her.

"I had never thought about traveling. It wasn't even my dream. I didn't really have any dreams. At eighteen, I was a lost, rich kid with no idea who I was or how to navigate the rest of my life."

Millie didn't respond. Considering she couldn't give a guy eye-contact, she was the best listener I'd ever met. She reminded me a little of Moses, the way she just soaked it all in and didn't miss anything. The difference was, Moses didn't hang on my every word. Millie did. And I wasn't sure how I felt about it. I didn't want her hanging on the wrong ones, hanging her hopes on something I hadn't meant, and holding me accountable for everything that came out of my mouth. I spoke the truth with a layer of bullshit thrown in for entertainment value. It was the Texas in me, part of the charm. But I couldn't be that way with Millie. I had to say what I meant, always. I didn't know how I knew it to be true. But it was. And I felt the responsibility in my gut.

"When I was sixteen, my sister, Molly, disappeared. She was kind of a party-girl. Same as I was. We were wild. But we were close. And we always looked out for each other. She was a couple years older than I was, but I was the man, you know? She up and disappeared on the Fourth of July and we didn't know what happened to her. Not for two years. And I blamed myself. I looked for her, but I couldn't find her. So I drowned my frustration with alcohol. Dad kept a well-stocked bar in the house, and I helped myself often. But by the time I was eighteen years old, the alcohol couldn't touch the itch beneath my skin or the restlessness in my blood. I'd lost my sister and I was strangely jealous that she couldn't be found." I considered how far to go, and ended up leaving a bunch of stuff out, not because I was ashamed, but because it was just too damn heavy for kite flying.

73

"And then I met Moses. Moses had nothing, but Moses knew every-thing. He painted away his pain. That was how he coped. And he let me hang around. He let me in. He helped me see. Neither of us had anywhere to go. But I had money. My parents were relieved to see me leave. They were tired. Grief-stricken. And they handed me a credit card and washed their hands of me."

"And you just went to Europe?" Her voice awe-struck.

"We went everywhere. We were barely legal. Kids, really. But he could paint. I could bullshit my way out of almost anything, so he painted his way across the world and I made sure people bought his stuff instead of throwing us in jail for vandalism. He wanted to see all the famous art. The Louvre, the Sistine Chapel, the architecture, the Wall of China. That was his dream. So that's what we did. And when I couldn't talk us out of trou-ble, we fought our way out of trouble. That was my goal, see. I wanted to get in a fist fight with someone from every country. I got my ass kicked by a big Swede. He now works at my gym, and I make it my mission to kick his ass every day."

Millie's laughter pealed out like a song, and I examined my words to make sure I'd told the truth at every turn. Satisfied that my account had been spot-on, I relaxed and laughed with her.

"Axel?" She ventured a guess as to the Swede's identity.

"Axel," I confirmed. "I met Andy in Ireland and Paulo in Brazil. When I opened the gym I tracked them all down and asked them to come work with me."

"So you collected people and Moses collected art?"

"Something like that."

"How long did you travel?"

"We kept traveling until we found ourselves."

"What does that mean?"

"Moses told me once that you can't escape yourself. You can run, hide, or die. But wherever you go, there you'll be. I was pretty empty for a long time. It took a while to figure out what fills me up."

"I understand that. Darkness is very empty. And I'm always alone in the dark."

Without thinking, I reached over and took her free hand, the gesture so instinctual that I was holding her hand before I realized what I was do-ing. I forgot about Elmo, about kite tails and excess string. And she must have too. For a minute we were wrapped up in past places and painful memories. She gripped my hand, but didn't continue speaking, obviously waiting for me to finish my story.

"We kicked around for more than five years. Just moving from one place to the next. We ended up here a few years ago and it finally felt like it was time to stay put. This was where we started our journey. And this is where it ended."

"And you found yourself?"

"I'm always looking. But there just isn't that much to me. I'm kind of a shallow fella."

She giggled, and I slid my hand from hers, worried that I'd given the wrong impression. She let me go easily, but something flickered across her pretty face, and I wondered if I was being completely honest after all.

Henry came bellowing across the grass, trying to warn me, but it was too late. Millie must have felt the lack of tension in her string because she squeaked and tried to recover, pulling away from me, winding and unwinding, hoping to get lucky and save the situation.

"Mayday!" Henry yelled. Seconds later the kites fell in a tangled pile to the earth.

My inattention to the task at hand caught up with me, and the little red monster above our heads got tangled up in Millie's tail and attacked from the air, swan diving downward, taking the pink kite down with him. I'd gotten too close, I'd gotten careless, and it cost us both.

(End of Cassette)

Moses

"WE WERE IN Ireland. Dublin," I said, when Millie made no move to change cassettes. "Tag can sniff out a fight. It's his secret power." That and his ability to get laid. I kept the last bit to myself. She wouldn't appreciate that ability, though I had a feeling Millie knew exactly who Tag was, warts and all. But maybe because she wasn't distracted by the way other women looked at him, she seemed to be able to really see Tag, and it was interesting to me that she insisted on calling him by his given name instead of the name he used to charm his way through life.

"But this time it was an actual boxing match between two fighters that Tag had heard of and wanted to see fight. Andy Gorman and Tommy Boyle. Tag had actually had a run-in with Andy, believe it or not, when I painted a portrait for Andy's mother. Andy's father had passed away the year before, and his mom was pretty desperate to make a connection. Andy thought I was a charlatan—that's what he called me—and he ran us off. Tag got mouthy in my defense, as usual, and Andy broke his nose. So when Tag told me he wanted to see this match, I wasn't very excited about the idea.

"Andy won, though. And he won big. He knocked Boyle out in the first round. Apparently people weren't very happy about that. Andy was supposed to win, but he was supposed to draw it out, keep it close. He owed some people some money. And when he didn't do as he was told, they cornered him in an alley behind the venue and beat him up. Guess who went running right into the middle of the fight?"

Millie smiled, but it wobbled on the edges.

"He just had a nose for it. Someone was fighting, and Tag was always getting in the thick of it. Tag went running in there as if Andy were his best friend and not the guy who broke his nose a couple of weeks before. We had to leave Ireland. That's how stupid it was. That's how dangerous the people were that Tag had pissed off. But Tag doesn't think about stuff like that. It isn't important to him. He just saw five against one and went in, fists flying. He and Andy Gorman were fighting back to back, and I had to wade in there too. I was afraid Tag was going to get himself killed.

"Long story short? Andy Gorman and every other guy in that gym owes Tag. Everyone is loyal to him, but it's only because he was loyal first, because he stuck his neck out for them. Not because they asked, but because they needed help. It kind of became Tag's purpose. I saw him change, saw him decide to live, to fight, to embrace life. I watched him find himself."

"And now he's lost again," Millie whispered.

"Something happened," I argued.

"He's saying goodbye, Moses. It feels like he's writing his memoirs or something."

Millie was right. It felt like a suicide note.

Eight

I FOUND SOMEONE to work at the bar part-time, and I started training Vince to manage. I still kept an eye out for Morg, but maybe he'd found a better situation. He baffled me. But it was his choice. I sent his check to the address I had on file and kept juggling. I trained for my fight four or five hours a day and was at the bar almost every night. And I kept walking Millie home.

She never wanted to drive. Neither did I. The nights were cold, but not too cold, and I looked forward to having her grab my arm, walk by my side, and talk to me. I made her laugh, and she made me laugh. She impressed me, and I didn't have to try and impress her.

I liked her so much.

It was a weird sensation, genuinely liking a girl that much and not trying to get in her pants. I know that's crude, but there's a reason men are wired the way we are. There's a reason women are put together the way they are. It's just biology. Basic biology. But I wasn't trying to sleep with Millie. I had no designs on Millie. I just liked her. And I pushed the rest of it away. I firmly ignored biology for the first time in my life.

I was relaxed with her. And I found myself continually telling her things that I didn't comfortably share with anyone. One night, I pulled on a vest to walk her home instead of my jacket, and my white dress sleeves were rolled to my elbows, which was how I always tended bar. For the very first time, my forearms were bare to the touch for the walk home, and when Millie wrapped her hand around my arm she felt my scar.

What's this, David?" Her fingertips traced the long puckered line on my right forearm that extended from my wrist to my elbow.

"There was a time when I didn't want to live very bad," I confessed easily. "It was a long time ago. I love myself now. Don't worry." I meant for her to laugh, but she didn't.

"You cut yourself?" Her voice sounded sad. Not accusing. Just sad.

"Yeah. I did."

"Was it hard?"

Her question surprised me. Most people asked why. They didn't ask if hurting yourself was hard.

"Living was harder," I said.

She didn't fill the silence with words, and I found myself needing to explain. Not impress. Just explain.

"The first time I tried to kill myself, I held a gun to my head and counted backwards from seventeen; one count for every year of my life. My mother walked in when I reached five. The guns were locked away and the combination on the safe changed. So I resorted to a pocket-knife. It was sharp and shiny. Clean. And I wasn't afraid. For the first time in a long time, I wasn't afraid at all."

Her fingers traced the line as we walked, smoothing, as if she could rub the scar away. So I told her the rest.

"But fate intervened again, and they found me before it was too late. They kept finding me, saving me. But I couldn't save my sister, see. And I felt helpless. Helpless and hopeless. After a week in the hospital I was transferred to a psych ward. My mother cried, my dad was stone-faced. They'd lost one child, and there I was, trying to take myself away too. They told me I was selfish. And I was. But I didn't know how to be any different. They gave me everything and everything was never enough. And that is terrifying. Emptiness is terrifying."

"That's where you met Moses." She remembered the conversation in the park.

"Yep. You'll have to meet him sometime. His wife Georgia too. They are my favorite people in the whole world."

"I'd like that."

"They have horses. Georgia actually works with kids kind of like Henry. Equine therapy, she calls it. Henry would probably eat it up." I found myself warming to the idea. Henry made everything easier. Henry made it okay to spend time with Millie beyond walking her home. He was a perfect buffer between biology and friendship.

Before I knew it, I'd set a date and I was bringing Millie to meet my best friend. And Henry too. Can't forget Henry.

MOSES AND GEORGIA had leveled his grandmother's old house and in its shoes built a sprawling, two-story with a huge wrap around porch and a private side entrance so Moses could paint and conduct his business without exposing his family or his clients to one another. It held no resemblance to the sad, little house with a tragic past that I'd first seen eighteen months before when Moses and I rolled into town looking for answers and trailing ghosts. Lots of ghosts. It hadn't taken me long before I'd figured out I didn't want to stay in Levan. It hadn't taken Moses long to decide he wasn't leaving. I wouldn't have stayed if I were him. I would have taken Georgia and found a place to start over. But sometimes history can be magnetic, and Moses and Georgia, their story, their history, was there in that town.

And Moses wasn't the only one who had a business to maintain. Georgia broke and trained horses and was an equine therapist, using her animals to connect with children and adults in a way that helped their bodies and their spirits. The land she'd grown up on butted up to Moses's grandmother's land, the land she'd left him, and I supposed it made a lot of sense to make it work. Moses always told me you can't escape yourself. I guess I just felt protective of my friend. I wanted him to be safe and happy and accepted, and I worried that the people in that small, Utah town had already written him off. But what did I know? My friend was happy. So I kept my fears to myself.

The day couldn't have been better. Utah was flirting shamelessly with spring, and it was sixty degrees out, even though it had no business being that warm. I'd told Moses and Georgia we were coming, and Georgia was ready for us. Before long we were in the round corral with Millie and Henry petting Georgia's Palomino, Sackett, and a horse named Lucky who was as black as Georgia was fair, and who followed Georgia with his eyes wherever she went. She'd told me once she'd tamed him right alongside Moses, though neither of them had known she was actively breaking them.

Moses still wasn't comfortable around most animals. He'd come a long way, but a life time of nervous energy was hard to corral, and animals, especially horses, tended to mirror his unease. He and I stayed out of the way, leaning against the fence, watching Georgia work her magic. I was holding baby Kathleen—who I insisted on calling Taglee just to bug her father—and making faces at her, trying to make her smile. When she started yawning widely, Moses reclaimed her and propped her on his shoulder where she promptly dozed off. We listened to her baby sighs in companionable silence until Moses eyed me over her downy head, his eyes narrowed, his hand stroking Kathleen's tiny back.

"Say your piece, Mo," I said, knowing it was coming.

When Georgia had greeted Millie with a hand shake and a sweet hello, she had smiled at me like she really wanted to tease me about my new "lady friend," but she contained herself. Moses didn't want to tease. He apparently wanted answers.

"What's going on, man?" Moses didn't mince words. He never had. You wanted to get to know Moses, you had to pay attention, because he didn't give you much. You had to force your way into his space and refuse to go when he pushed you away. That was what I had done. That was my gift. Push, fight, cling, grapple, wear you down. It was what Georgia had done too, and she'd paid a price. The price for Moses's love and devotion was a high one. But she'd paid it. And in return, Moses worshipped Georgia.

"What do you mean?" I scowled at my best friend.

"Millie's not like the girls you . . . date." Moses finished the sentence with a much milder word than the one we both mentally inserted into his long pause.

"That's because I'm not . . . dating . . . her."

"No?"

"Nah. She's an employee. A friend. She's funny. Interesting. And tough. I like that. I like Henry too. She's been bringing him by the gym.

I've been working with him a little. His dad split when he was little, and he just soaks it up."

"You rescuing people again, Tag?"

"I don't rescue people."

"Bullshit. You collect lost causes and charity cases like old, white women collect cats. You rescued me. You rescued Axel and Cory and even that piece of shit Morgan, who thinks he's doin' you a favor by managing your bar. You call it Tag Team, but you should call it rag tag team. You rescue everyone. You have an invisible cape. You've been wearing it your whole life."

"I never rescued you." I couldn't argue about the rest of it, though I'd never thought of it that way.

"Yeah, Tag. You did."

"We rescued each other."

"Nah. I would have let you drown, man. That's the difference between you and me. At least the Moses I used to be. I would have let you drown to keep my head above water. I was all about surviving. But not you. You would have died before you let me sink. Maybe it worked out for both of us in the end. But you saved us, Tag. Not me."

"What about all the people you help with your art?"

"I'm just a messenger. You? You're a savior. That's why you fight so hard. You don't know how to do anything else. But that girl doesn't want a savior. She wants a lover. Two completely different things. Georgia's more like you. That's why she and I work. But Millie? I'm thinking she's more like me. She just observes. Takes it in."

"Observes?" I questioned, my lips twisted wryly.

"Observes. You don't have to see to observe. I guarantee that girl already knows what kind of man you are. And she likes what she observes. But she doesn't want saving. I didn't want saving either, not from Georgia. I wanted submission."

Moses's eyes lingered on his wife, who was leading Henry and Millie around on horses she'd broken and trained with her own hands. Her back was straight, her voice steady. She was a tall, young woman with a lean, strong frame and sun-streaked blond hair that swung in a fat braid almost to her waist. Submission was not in her vocabulary. But then she glanced up, and I watched as her eyes skipped over me and rested on Moses, holding their sleeping child, and I understood what Moses meant. Sometimes submission meant releasing pride, letting someone else take the reins, trusting someone with your love and your life, even though they didn't deserve it. She'd done that.

"You want Millie? You're going to have to take off your cape at some point and give in, baby." Moses spoke again, his voice soft, his eyes softer. "Submit."

"Who says I want her?" I resisted.

"Give me a break, man. You're talking to an observer. I know you better than you know yourself. Don't try to pull that crap with me."

"So I have a best friend who sees it all and a girl—" I couldn't say girlfriend, "—a girl who sees nothing at all."

"She sees plenty. You're the blind one. You're blind because you're scared. And you're scared because you already know it's too late. And you should be scared, man. She won't be easy to love. She's a package deal. She and Henry. But hell, Tag. You've never been about loving the lovable. I'm about as unlovable as it gets. And you practically threw yourself at me. I couldn't shake you off. You like a challenge. Hell, you live for it!"

"I'm not there yet, Moses," I said firmly. "Don't push me."

"Says the man who told me to go hard and fast with Georgia."

"Turns out I was right, now wasn't I?" I laughed, loving that I had been right.

"You were. But so am I. You're not ready? Fair enough. But don't hurt her."

"Now why would I do that, Mo?" He pissed me off sometimes.

"Because you can be stupid." He smirked at me over his daughter's tiny head and I considered how and where I could punch him without causing him to drop her.

"Her mother's dead." It was a statement, not a question. Moses didn't ask. He didn't have to. His smirk was gone and his eyes had that look he got when he was seeing things.

"Yeah." I nodded. "A while back. Lung cancer. Their dad took off about a year after Millie lost her sight. Millie seems to think it's because he couldn't handle having an autistic son and a blind daughter. I don't know what the truth is. But they haven't had any contact with him, beyond money. At least he sends money."

"She's worried about her kids. She keeps showing me Amelie's walking stick and a book, a children's book. Something about a giant."

"They're doing all right. They look out for each other," I insisted.

"Hmm," Moses muttered, and something oily and dark twisted in my gut.

"She's not waiting on one of them, is she Moses?" Moses said spirits started to linger around their loved ones when they were about to die, as if waiting to greet them or take them home.

"Nah. It doesn't feel like that." Moses didn't offer anything else and I let it go, accustomed to Moses's quirks, to his abilities, accustomed to his reluctance to expound.

(End of Cassette)

Moses

"YOU SAW MY mother, Moses?" Millie asked me.

I nodded and then caught myself and answered out loud. "Yeah."

"What did she look like?" Millie asked, and I heard more wistfulness than doubt.

"You. She looks like you. Dark hair, blue eyes, good bone structure. I knew who she was the moment she came through. But you and Henry were right there in front of me. It wasn't hard to make the connection."

Millie shook her head briskly like she needed to rearrange her thoughts, rearrange everything she thought she knew. It was always like this. It took people time to process the improbable.

"The book—the book about giants. What is that?" I asked, giving her something tangible to focus on while her head and her heart found compromise.

"I don't know . . ." she stuttered, her hands fluttering to her cheeks.

"Giants playing hide and seek?" I prodded. The picture that filled my head was of a huge pair of feet sticking out from under a bed.

"Where do giants hide when playing hide and seek? I can't think of any place that will cover up their feet," Millie whispered.

"That's it," I said.

"They cannot wiggle under the bed, or cower in a closet. They cannot hide behind a tree or slip inside a pocket." This time it was Georgia who recited the lines, and I looked at my wife in surprise.

"It's called *When Giants Hide*. I used to read it to Eli. He loved it. We read it almost as often as we read *Calico the Wonder Horse*."

I felt the same slice to my gut I always felt when I thought about my son. And then I felt the answering peace, the knowledge that love lives on.

"I forgot all about that book! Henry used to love it—my mom and I would read it to him, over and over. I memorized it, actually, and even when my sight started to go and then left me altogether, Henry would turn the pages and I would pretend to read."

"They could hide behind a mountain, but climbing takes all day. They could hide beneath the ocean, but they might float away," Georgia recited.

"They could stretch their arms and grab the moon—" Millie said.

"And hide behind the clouds—" Georgia supplied the next line.

"They could tiptoe up behind you, but giants are too loud," Millie finished, smiling. "In the story, the giants are hiding in plain sight. They are everywhere you look, but they are camouflaged by trees and buildings. In one picture you think you're looking at a boat dock, and then you realize that it's a giant laying on the sand. In another picture the giant is shaped like a plane, laying on his back, his arm stretched out to form wings, his shoes pointing upward to make the tail. It's a look and find book. You know, *Where's Waldo*, but instead of tiny figures in red and white striped shirts, the giants are huge. But the artist drew them in such a way that they just blend in."

"There is a place where giants hide, but I'm not about to tell. If you want to find the giants, you'll have to search yourself," Georgia inserted. She was smiling, but her smile was pained, and I reached out and grabbed her hand.

"When I went blind and started using the stick, Henry was only four. He thought I was looking for giants. He thought my stick was a giant find-er. He'd walk around with his eyes closed, smacking things with it."

"So why do you think your mom wanted me to see that book?" I asked, remembering her insistence. "She kept showing me the pages, the pictures. She wanted to tell me something."

"My dad left," Millie pondered, as if she wasn't sure how to answer me, but was willing to explore the question out loud. "We stopped reading that book when my dad left. He played for San Francisco—so he was a 'Giant.'" She shrugged like she was trying to convince herself that it hadn't been that important. "We knew where every giant was hiding in the book. We'd found them hundreds of times. But we didn't know where one giant was. That giant disappeared altogether. I remember hearing my mom read it to Henry once, right after he left. And she started to cry."

I wanted to take it all back. I didn't want to talk about this anymore. But Millie continued.

"Then Henry started having nightmares, and the hiding giants were no longer whimsical and harmless. They were scary. He was sure our beds were really giants in disguise and they would take us away while we slept. He thought the refrigerator door was a giant's mouth, that the garbage truck was a loud, hungry giant who would eat everything in sight. It got ridiculous until my mom banned the book and that was it. The giants slowly became household appliances once again, and his bed was just a bed. He still doesn't like garbage trucks though." She smiled at that, and I chuckled. But it wasn't very funny. None of this was.

"It's strange," Millie added. "Henry asked me about a month ago if I knew the story of David and Goliath. And even though I told him that I did, he felt it important to inform me that David had killed Goliath. He seemed especially thrilled that we had our very own giant slayer."

Giant slayer or not, I wondered for the first time if Millie's mother had been trying to communicate her distrust of Tag. Maybe she'd known he was going to run, just like her husband had. Maybe she knew her kids deserved better.

Nine

HENRY FELL ASLEEP on Millie's shoulder five minutes into the drive home and succeeded in crowding her into my side, gobbling up more than his fair share of space on the bench seat for the ninety minutes it took to get back to Salt Lake. I liked it too much. I liked the press of her thigh against mine, my arm resting between her knees every time I touched the gearshift, the smell of her hair every time I glanced down at her face. The conversation with Moses taunted me, and I felt a flash of anger that he had called me out on my friendship with her, that he'd forced me to examine the relationship. I didn't want to examine it. I wanted to enjoy it.

We'd spent the afternoon in comfortable conversation and time with the animals. Henry had taken to the horses with very little fear, and I had a feeling we were going to be getting a whole slew of statistics and interesting facts about jockeys and horse races in the days to come. Georgia had told Henry he was exactly the size of most professional jockeys, which made him puff out his chest and walk a little taller. He was already asking when we could go back. I'd promised him soon and scowled at Georgia and Moses when they'd waggled their eyebrows and smirked. They weren't very subtle about their fascination with Millie, but it was impossible not to be fascinated. She hadn't shown any fear either, and I'd spent much of the day trying not to stare at her, trying not to feed my friends' curiosity.

"How did that feel, being on a horse?" I asked Millie, my eyes swinging from the road to her face and back again.

"Like having eyes. The horse knew where to go and I was just along for the ride, but it felt good."

"You weren't afraid, not even a little?"

"Sure I was. I'm afraid all the time. I was so afraid when I first lost my sight that for a while I just sat in my room and played my guitar. But after a while, I realized if I allowed myself to be too afraid to do anything, that I wouldn't just be blind, I might as well be dead. That scared me more. The only thing I can see is me, you know? The stuff going on inside of me. My thoughts, my feelings, my fears, my faults. They are the only things I see clearly. The rest is a guessing game. Being blind forces you to come to terms with yourself, I think."

"Perks of being a blind girl," I said, and she laughed.

"I say that a lot, don't I?"

"You do. And it's damn cool that you do."

"Well, I could list the sucks of being a blind girl, but that would take all day."

"The sucks?"

"Yep. All the many things that suck about not being able to see," she said matter-of-factly.

"Tell me one. The first thing that comes into your head," I insisted.

She started to speak and then shook her head, biting her lip. "Nah."

I bumped her with my shoulder, making her head bob a little. "Come on. Whine, baby. Whine."

Her cheeks grew rosy. "No."

"You were going to say something and you changed your mind. I saw that!"

"All right. That. That sucks."

"What?"

"I can't see what YOU are thinking. I can't look at *your* face and get some kind of clue as to what's going on in *your* head. It's so unfair. I would really love to see your face. Just once."

We were both silent for half a second before I broke the tension.

"Damn. That really does suck. I do have a beautiful face," I teased, but my chest felt tight and my throat ached a little. I gasped and laughed as she dug her sharp little elbow into my ribs.

"You know what else sucks?" she shot back, emboldened by my apparent lack of empathy.

"I told you you could only name one. We don't want to open the floodgates, Millie."

She growled and continued on as if I were driving her crazy.

"I can't drive. I can't run away. I can walk, but that's not the same thing as just getting behind the wheel and taking off. Instead, I've got to rely on meanies like you to take me places. I hate that more than anything," she huffed.

Without warning, I changed lanes and took the nearest exit at a pretty aggressive speed. It was an exit just past a little town called Mona, and I sped under the overpass and turned onto the frontage road and pulled to the side of the road with a screech of tires. Henry bobbed in his seat belt and changed positions without waking up, conveniently freeing Millie's shoulder.

"Whoa!" Millie cried, grabbing at my thigh. "What are you doing? We've got a ways to go, don't we?"

"I'm gonna let you drive."

"Wh-what?" she gasped, clutching at the dashboard.

I adjusted the wheel up to create a little more clearance, shoved the seat back as far as it would go, which wasn't much farther, considering my size, and pulled Millie up onto my lap, ignoring the warning light that was bleeping in my head. *Too close. Back away. Hot female in lap. Breach! Friend zone breach!*

"David!" She was pressed back against me, her hands clinging, as if I'd told her we were jumping from a cliff.

"Stop wiggling!" I laughed so I wouldn't moan, and she immediately froze.

"I've got you, Millie. I've got you. This is going to be fun. Just like riding a horse with Georgia holding the reins."

"Okay," she squeaked, nodding vigorously, her head bumping against my chin, and I chuckled, impressed all over again by her guts and her trust.

I placed her hands where I wanted them on the wheel and she ran her hands down and back up, as if she had never touched anything like it.

Maybe she hadn't. She turned the wheel this way and that and giggled nervously before she put them back where I'd placed them.

"You good?"

"Yeah. Okay. Good."

"Now, I'm going to be right here to tell you what to do, and I'll help you steer if you start running us off the road."

I revved the gas pedal and then placed her foot on it and let her do the same. I could tell she was trying not to bail off of my lap—her body was practically vibrating with nerves—but she didn't. She stayed, listening intently. I gave her basic instructions, and then I helped her ease onto the road, going about five miles per hour. She didn't move her hands from two and ten o'clock, and I had to tug at the wheel slightly to straighten us out. And then we picked up speed, just a bit.

"How does that feel?"

"Like falling," she whispered, her body rigid, her arms locked on the wheel.

"Relax. Falling is easier if you don't fight it."

"And driving?"

"That too. Everything is easier if you don't fight it."

"What if someone sees us?"

"Then I'll tell you when to wave."

She giggled and relaxed slightly against me. I kissed her temple where it rested against my cheek, and she was immediately stiff as a board once more.

Shit. I hadn't thought. I'd just reacted.

"I would have patted you on the back, but your forehead was closer," I drawled. "You're doin' it. You're drivin'."

"How fast are we going?" she said breathlessly. I hoped it was fear and not that kiss.

"Oh you're flyin', baby. Eight miles an hour. At this rate, we will reach Salt Lake in two days, my legs will be numb, and Henry will want a turn. Give it a little gas. Let's see if we can push it up to ten."

She pressed her foot down suddenly and we shot forward with a lurch.

"Whoa!" I cried, my arms shooting up to brace hers on the wheel. I saw Henry stir from the corner of my eye.

"Danika Patrick is the first female NASCAR driver to ever win a NASCAR Sprint Cup Series pole," he said woodenly, before slumping back down in his seat. I spared him a quick glance, only to see his eyes were closed once more.

Millie obviously heard him and she hooted and pressed the gas pedal down a little harder.

"Henry just compared you to Danika Patrick. And he obviously isn't alarmed that you're driving because he's already asleep again."

"That's because Henry knows I'm badass."

"Oh yeah. Badass, Silly Millie. 'Goin' ninety miles an hour down a dead-end street,'" I sang a little Bob Dylan, enjoying myself thoroughly.

"And Henry trusts you," Millie added, more to herself than to me, and I fought the urge not to kiss her temple again. I suddenly didn't feel like laughing or singing anymore. I kind of felt like crying.

(End of Cassette)

Moses

THERE WAS SOMETHING about the smell of the gym. Tag loved it. He said it smelled better than fresh cut hay, a woman's breasts, and steak combined. And those were his favorite things. Tag's gym smelled like sweat, bleach, and a hint of fabric softener. I hadn't decided why the fabric softener smell was so prominent until I realized that heat and sweat made the scent rise from clothing. It smelled wholesome—perspiration, soap and good intentions mixed with a healthy dose of testosterone and overconfidence. It smelled like Tag.

Tag kept music pumping all the time, but his choices were interesting —a little Merle Haggard, a little more Metallica, interspersed with songs by Michael Jackson, Neil Diamond, and The Killers, just to liven things up. He had eclectic tastes. That, and he had a short attention span.

Before Georgia had stepped onto that elevator eighteen months before and stepped back into my life, I'd lived in an apartment over the gym and worked out there with Tag almost every day. It was comfortable for me—

the people, the atmosphere, all of it—and when I walked in the front doors, I was greeted on all sides with enthusiasm and obvious curiosity, which was fairly normal for me.

I spotted Axel working with a group of fighters and saw that Andy was padded up, taking punches in the octagon. As I debated who I should interrupt first, my name rippled through the gym, and they were both excusing themselves and approaching me without me having to make a move. Mikey followed on Axel's heels, grabbing up his crutch and bearing down on me like he wanted answers too. Mikey rarely worked out with his prosthetic, and he was a one-legged wonder in more ways than one. A kid named Cory who'd been new to the team when I'd married Georgia wasn't too far behind them.

The question in their eyes and the worry in their expressions had the tension I'd been trying to tamp down flaring once more. I didn't have any answers. That's why I was here.

"Any word?" Mikey asked, foregoing a greeting altogether. I noticed the people around us were waiting to hear what I had to say, and I didn't want to discuss Millie and Tag in the middle of the gym. Axel caught my wary side glances and led the way to the little office I'd plundered two days before in an attempt to find Tag. Mikey, Cory, and Andy didn't ask permission to come along, and I didn't deny them. Maybe together we could figure something out. Axel didn't wait for me to start the impromptu meeting. He pointed at the wall, at a schedule for the next month that was all filled out.

"That's Tag's writing. He must have come in here at some point last week and filled it in. Nobody saw him, and I didn't think anything of it when we first talked, Moses. The schedule's always updated, always written out a month in advance. It didn't occur to me that he would have had to come in." Axel shrugged. "It made me feel a little better. At least he's not lying on the side of the road somewhere, you know?"

I nodded.

"Tell him about the papers, Axel," Andy insisted.

Axel went to the filing cabinet, the cabinet where Millie and I had found the tapes. He pulled out a sheaf of papers and handed them to me.

"I got these this morning. Certified. They're from Tag's attorney."

I scanned it as quickly as I could, and then looked at Tag's team in horror.

"Did everyone get a copy?" I asked.

"I got a copy," Cory said.

"Me too," Mikey and Andy volunteered.

The papers were legal documents detailing the transfer of ownership of the gym to Axel Karlsson, with Andrew Gorman, Michael Slade and Cory Mangum listed as Tag Team co-owners and shareholders with merchandising and licensing rights.

"Has this already gone into effect?" I gasped, searching the legal jargon for dates and details.

"No. It's a process. And I have to agree to the terms. We all do. But the groundwork is done," Axel answered, and his expression said it all. He wasn't euphoric about his windfall, if that's what it was. He was devastated.

"What the feck is goin' on?" Andy growled, his Irish so thick it changed the words but not the sentiment.

"Nobody's seen or heard from Tag?" I had to get that out of the way again.

"Leo saw him last, but that was almost three weeks ago now," Axel said. He'd told me as much already, but a recap wouldn't hurt.

"Leo took him to the hospital to get some stitches after he ousted a rowdy at the bar," I summarized. Leo also took him back home. Millie saw him after that. He spent the night there."

The guys exchanged looks.

"What?" I demanded.

"Nothin'," Andy said. "We just like Millie. We're happy for him."

I nodded. I liked her too. I was happy for him too. I bit back a curse and plunged back in.

"He spent the next night there too, according to Millie. She said he was in a good mood and seemed to feel fine. He wasn't overly bothered by the blow to the head, apparently."

"Not surprised. Nobody takes a punch like Tag," Cory spoke up, admiring. Wistful.

"He was gone before she woke up," I continued. "There was a text waiting for her. Told her not to worry about him, that he was heading out of town to see his folks. Said it'd been too long."

"You called his family?" Mikey asked.

"I did. He never showed up there, and he never told them he was coming in the first place, so they weren't expecting him."

"He was gonna drive to Dallas? That's a long drive. Two day trip, each way. At least. Lots of miles to cover. Have you called the highway patrol?" Mikey asked.

I shook my head. "I did. But I don't think he ever intended to go to Dallas. I think he was just buying himself time. That paperwork is dated six days ago."

"Buying some time to do what?" Axel asked no one in particular.

"Buying some time to get his shit organized. To make sure things were covered," I said grimly.

"Tag made Vince manager about three weeks ago, and Leo got promoted too. But Vince said Tag's name isn't anywhere on the bar schedule anymore. He thought it was just because Tag was tired of working so many hours. He was putting in a bunch with Morgan gone," Axel added.

Cory let loose with a series of expletives that had the others pointing at a water jug already brimming with quarters labeled HENRY on Tag's desk. It was the swear jar, obviously.

"Your whole paycheck is going in that thing, Mangum," Mikey sighed, though I had the feeling no one was going to be making him pay up.

"So no one has actually talked to him or seen him for at least two weeks, and Millie saw him last?" Axel reiterated, running his hands through his hair. His blond crew cut didn't budge.

"Looks to me like his lawyer saw him last," I said, still reeling from the papers I clutched in my hands.

"How is Millie?" Mikey asked. "What does she say about all of this?"

"She's a very composed mess," I answered honestly. "She isn't saying it, but I'm pretty sure she thinks she's the reason he split."

Cory repeated the same string of scalding words that he's said a minute before.

"No," Axel shook his head. "No. That doesn't make any sense. I saw his face when Henry came into the bar that night. It was around closing, and I was keeping Tag company and having a few. Henry comes flying through the door, his feet bare, not wearing a coat. He'd run all the way there, and he was freaking out."

"Why?" I asked. I hadn't heard this story yet.

"We didn't know. You know Henry. He speaks in sports trivia. It's damn hard to communicate with him. But he kept saying something about Millie, and something had obviously set him off. I've never seen Tag look like that. He left Henry with me and was out the door in about ten seconds. You don't leave a girl that inspires that kind of reaction. We all give Tag a bad time about his women. But Millie's different."

"Millie's different," Mikey agreed, nodding.

Cory just swore and pulled at his hair.

"What the feck is going on?" Andy asked again. But this time he didn't sound angry. He just sounded as lost as Tag was.

Ten

"MILLIE!" THE HOUSE was pitch black. No light on the porch, no glow from the windows. I couldn't get the damn gate to unlatch though I'd unlatched it without trouble before. I hurdled it and was up the walk in three flying steps, clearing the stairs in another one, bolting through the unlocked door, my heart playing a base drum, complete with bashing cymbals in my head.

It was so dark inside, and the darkness convinced me that when I found the light I would see something I didn't want to see.

"Millie!"

I felt for the light, and my hand brushed against Millie's stick, toppling it. If Millie's stick was here, propped in its regular place, she was here too. I found the switch and light flooded the foyer, illuminating the drops of blood that tiptoed across the entryway and headed up the stairs, missing a step only to collect in a heavier pattern on another.

I was up the stairs and banging down the hall without knowing where I was going. I'd never been in this part of the house. I pushed doors open, flipping on lights until I found a room that had to be Millie's. The walls were bare, the wooden floor neat—no strewn belongings or tossed clothing that Millie could trip over. There were drops of blood leading to a closed door across from her neatly made bed.

"Millie?" I said, but it came out a whisper. I couldn't shout anymore. I was too afraid. I crossed the room and pushed open the door, bracing myself for the worst, only to find the bathroom dark, just like the rest of the house. Light from the bedroom spilled into the small space, and I found myself staring at Millie, perched on the edge of the tub in a tank top and shorts, her hair piled on her head like she was preparing to bathe and didn't want to get it wet. Blood was smeared all over the sink and across the splash tiles in a macabre finger painting. I slid my hand along the wall beside the door and the light I switched on turned the burgundy blood into a cheery red.

Millie had ear buds stuck in her ears and her head bobbed like she was just chilling out instead of bleeding out. She had wrapped one set of fingers in a ratty washcloth and was gripping them tightly. Her eyes were opened, blankly staring, and she was completely unaware that I was there.

I yanked the earbuds from her ears and she yelped a little, clearly startled.

"Amelie," I growled.

"David?" she cried, but her voice carried more surprise than pain.

"What the hell are you doing?"

"What the hell are YOU doing?" she shot back, immediately matching my angry tone.

"The house is dark, there's a trail of blood up the stairs, this bathroom looks like you attempted suicide, and you're sitting here zoning out to your iPod—"

"I sliced my finger open. I don't think it's that bad. It's throbbing a little, but that's all. It was bleeding a lot, so I'm just trying to get it to stop enough to put a band aid on it."

"Let me see." I knelt in front of her and eased the washcloth away from her fingers. The blood immediately welled and spilled over, but not before I got a decent look at the injury on the fleshy pad of her pointer finger.

"It's pretty deep, but you could probably get away with a band aid if you aren't afraid of a little scar." I wrapped her finger back up tightly and instructed her to keep it raised. "Where are the bandages?"

"I thought there were some in my cabinet above the sink. I couldn't find any. But I didn't look very long. I was bleeding and wanted to get it stopped before I made a huge mess. Henry hates blood and I didn't want to wake him."

"Too late."

"What?"

"You scared him to death, Millie. Henry came into the bar in his pajamas, babbling about blood and the number of stitches on a baseball. He was completely freaked out. I thought something terrible had happened to you. I didn't know what I'd find." I suddenly felt the room swim around me and I sank down onto the toilet seat before I passed out and created a whole different emergency.

"Henry did?" she asked, dumbfounded. "I thought he was in bed! I didn't hear him. I was . . ."

"Listening to music?" I barked.

"Yes! It's not a crime, Tag. I'm in my own home! I don't have to explain myself to you! And my house is always dark when Henry's asleep! I'm blind, remember? I don't need the lights on!" Her lower lip trembled, and I groaned.

"Damn it, Amelie. Don't cry, sweetheart. I was scared. Okay?" Scared was putting it mildly. I stood and opened the mirrored medicine cabinet above the sink. I could see where Amelie had searched from the bloody fingerprints and the blood streaked items crowded on the little shelves. There were three loose band aids on the top shelf, and I pulled them down gratefully, shutting the cabinet with a mental promise to scrub it down when I was done doctoring Millie.

"Where's Henry now?" she asked quietly.

"Axel was at the bar. He likes Axel, so I left him there until I could see what had happened. You scared the hell out of me, Amelie." I punched a message into my phone, a quick text to Axel, letting him and Henry know that Millie was fine and I'd be back to get Henry in a little while.

"Are you calling me Amelie because you're mad? You're not my mother, Tag. I know it must look bad, but I'm completely capable of handling this situation. I've cut myself before and I'm sure I'll cut myself again."

"Shh, Millie. I'm not mad. I'm not mad. Just . . . come here." I pulled her up, and positioning her in front of the sink, bandaged her finger. There were streaks of blood down her arms and some on her legs as well. I rinsed out the washcloth she'd used to stem the blood flow, wringing it out until the hot water ran clear. Then I used it to gently blot the blood away from her hands, trying not to notice the way her skin goose-pimpled as I continued up her forearms, and then up farther, wiping away a spot from her left shoulder and a smudge on the tip of her chin. The bathroom was small, the act intimate, and the frustration and fear I'd felt disappeared with the blood stains. I kept rinsing the cloth so it was warm against her skin, and when I knelt to clean her feet, she laid her hands on my shoulders for balance as I lifted one foot and washed it and then moved to the next. I stopped to rinse and warm my cloth before I moved up one lean leg and down the other and felt her fingers curl into my T-shirt, making heat curl in my stomach. I continued until every inch of her bare skin was pink from the heat of the cloth and slightly damp from my ministrations, and when I was done I wished I wasn't. I couldn't do anything about the blood on her black tank top or the hot pink shorts that matched her toenail polish. I touched one toenail with the pad of my thumb.

"How do you do that?"

"What? Paint them?"

"Yeah."

"Practice."

"So did you match the shorts and the toes on purpose?" I looked up at her to see her response.

"Of course." She smiled, but her voice remained a whisper, almost as if she too was afraid to disturb the charged air that buzzed around us. I rose from my haunches, leaving only a few inches between our bodies.

"Why?" It seemed so unimportant, so insignificant for something that must take a lot of effort. And she couldn't even see the results.

"It's all about the little things . . . haven't you learned that, big guy?" She said *big guy* the way I said *sweetheart*.

"When did your mom die, Millie?" My voice was soft, even softer than my hands had been on her body.

"When I was eighteen. She'd been sick for about two years. She shouldn't have made it that long. But she knew she had to make it until then. I had to be a legal adult in order to be Henry's guardian."

"So who takes care of Millie?" I whispered.

"I don't need to be taken care of, Tag," she whispered back. "I've been trying to tell you that."

99

"Need and want are two different things." I swallowed once, trying to convince myself that I didn't want what I wanted very, very much. When I made no move to take it, Millie stepped into me and carefully slid her arms around my waist. My heart was pounding in my chest and she laid her cheek against it, listening. I couldn't hide from her. She was blind yet she saw every damn thing. Almost as carefully, I wrapped my arms around her too, loosely, gently, my big hands resting on her slim back.

"Can I ask you something, Tag?" Her voice was plaintive and small as if she were speaking to my heart which lay directly beneath her lips. Its galloping response should have been enough. Maybe it was, because she didn't wait for my lips to answer. "Are you afraid to kiss me?"

"Why would I be afraid?" I was so damn afraid.

"Because kissing a blind girl is like stealing from a beggar or lying to a priest, don't you know? Like hitting a child or drowning a kitten? It's one of those unpardonable sins."

I swore beneath my breath, half-tempted to laugh at her audacity, half-angry that she was so astute.

"Or maybe you think it's like pulling on that loose string only to un-ravel an entire sweater. One of those things that is innocent but has dire consequences."

"That's not it, Millie," I lied.

"That *is* it, Tag. And don't insult me by assuming that I need some sort of guarantee just because I can't see. If I were any other girl, you would have had my clothes on the floor by now. It's a kiss, Tag. Not a promise signed in blood. A kiss."

When I gently pushed her away from me, forcing her to lift her head from my chest, I could see the hurt slam across her face, and her eyelids fluttered closed as if to protect what was already lost. But she misunder-stood. I was creating space to move, not distance. I slid my fingers along the sides of her face, cradled her head in my hands, and laid my lips across hers. She clutched at my wrists, a small gasp escaping from her mouth be-fore I swallowed it up, adding it to the fear that still hummed in my chest.

Her lips were soft and her mouth was slightly sweet, and for a few se-conds I was hyper-aware of the smallest details, the rasp of my whiskered chin against her smooth cheek as my mouth whispered over hers, the silky heat of her breath hitching in anticipation, a strand of her hair tickling my face as I applied the gentlest of pressures to her lips. And then she leaned into me hungrily, demanding more, and the details blurred into the heady experience of wanting and being wanted.

My stomach dipped and my hands slid from her face to her waist before my arms wrapped around her slim form, gripping her tightly, trying desperately not to lose control, trying valiantly to maintain emotional indifference as my body waved the white flag. Then my thoughts were overpowered by sensation, and I didn't think at all.

Millie didn't just kiss me, she traced me, holding my face to her mouth as her fingertips curled into my skin, the brush of her fingers and her mouth peeling away my resistance, sinking into my flesh until I was panting against her lips, my tongue tangling with hers, her feet dangling above the floor as I lifted her off her feet. I urged her legs around me in an attempt to get closer than we already were, and she acquiesced, her legs encircling me as tightly as my arms embraced her. Then I was stumbling out of the bathroom, gripping her to me, cradling her like a child I was desperate to protect, kissing her like a woman I was suddenly hell-bent on having, and falling across her bed like my legs had been shot out from beneath me.

My hands slid beneath her tank top, palming the satiny skin of her abdomen before pushing her bloodied shirt past the swell of her breasts and over her head, tearing my mouth from hers to yank it free, pulling the pins from her hair as I went so that it fell in dark waves across her shoulders and around her head, an inky pool against the white comforter. And my breath caught in my chest. My hands stilled and my heart tripped, thudding heavily against my ribs.

I pushed myself up and off her, bracing myself above her so I could stare down at the girl beneath me. Dark hair, smooth skin, full breasts. I swallowed, throat closing with an emotion that felt more like love than lust. Her eyes were closed, her lips parted, waiting for me to come back. She didn't cover herself or reach for me. She just waited.

A door slammed downstairs.

"Tag!" Axel bellowed. Millie jerked, and I was across the room, yanking open drawers, looking for a clean shirt to cover what I'd just unwrapped. She was suddenly there beside me, gently pushing me aside as she found what I was looking for and slid it over her head without missing a beat.

"Tag!" Axel sounded desperate, and I wondered if he was trying to hold back a panicked Henry.

"Henry needs to see that you're okay, Millie." But she was already headed for the door, moving with such surety and purpose that I marveled for a moment before I shook myself awake and followed her out of the room.

Axel and Henry stood at the base of the stairs, Axel holding on to Henry, trying to comfort and contain him. When they saw me and Millie above them, Axel let Henry go, cursing in relieved Swedish. Henry raced up the stairs, barreling into his sister, who heard his flight and braced herself, wrapping her thin arms around him as he flung himself against her.

"I'm okay, Henry. I'm okay. I just cut my finger. You should have talked to me, Henry, before running out of the house so late at night! I didn't even know you were awake. You should have let me explain."

"A baseball has exactly 108 stitches," Henry whispered and buried his head in his sister's shoulder.

"I don't need stitches, Henry. I'm fine. I promise." She smoothed her hand over his messy hair and held him tightly.

"Everything okay then?" Axel shifted his weight and reached for the door handle, as if Henry's distress had worn him out. I descended the stairs and extended my hand to my friend.

"Yeah, Axel. Thanks. I owe you one, man."

Axel nodded and grasped my hand, the relief still evident in his quick smile. "I couldn't convince him everything was all right."

"It's okay. He's had it tough. He had no reason to expect good news, poor kid," I said, my voice low, meant only for his ears. Axel nodded again, and releasing my hand, slid out the door into the night, calling his goodbye to Henry, who lifted his hand but didn't lift his head from Millie's shoulder.

I left Henry in Millie's consoling hands and went in search of rags and disinfectant, determined to rid the house of blood stains and bad memories. I threw myself into wiping down the kitchen, unloading and reloading the dishwasher while I was at it. Then I followed the blood trail up the stairs, through Millie's room, and into the bathroom, trying not to think about what would have happened had Axel not arrived with Henry when he did. I could hear the sounds of Millie's voice mixed with ESPN commentary, seeping out from beneath Henry's door and sorted through my jumbled emotions by scrubbing the sink and taking an old toothbrush to the tiles on the bathroom floor. I removed the contents from the medicine cabinet, making careful note of how it was organized so I could return it to the same place, enabling Millie to locate everything when I was done. I finished up by cleaning the toilet and the shower for good measure.

"It smells like pine sol and sap in here." Millie stood in the door, smiling softly.

"Ah. My signature fragrance," I joked, though it fell flat. I'd left my good humor back at the bar, abandoned it when Henry staggered through the door in his pajamas, and I hadn't had a chance to retrieve it. I stood washing my hands, but I didn't turn around. My hands were red from cleaning, but my nerves were raw, and I didn't really trust myself with Millie right now.

"Henry okay?" I asked.

"Yeah. Henry's okay. Are you?" Her voice was timid. I didn't answer immediately, and she waited me out, listening to me wash my hands and turn off the water before I finally spoke.

"When my sister disappeared, I kept thinking I'd come home one day, and she'd be there. Just a misunderstanding. A bad dream." I found her reflection in the little oval mirror, my eyes clinging to her face before forcing myself to look away. Tonight had made me feel like the old Tag. The sixteen-year-old Tag who lost his sister and couldn't save her.

"I'm glad Henry's okay." I was glad Henry's sister was okay too. I was so glad. So ridiculously, tearfully, gratefully glad.

I felt Millie's hand brush my back tentatively, finding me, and then she slid her arms around my waist and laid her head against me.

"Thank you, David. I don't know why you are so good to us. But you are. And I'm not going to question it. I'm just going to be grateful." I felt the press of her body against my back as her arms tightened briefly. Then she stepped back, releasing me, and I bore down on the desire that whooshed through me like a blow torch, only to curse at the heat, turn on her, slam the door, and back Millie up against it.

"Damn it, Millie!" I groaned into her hair. "Why do you have to be so damn sweet?" My lips were on her forehead, on her cheeks, nuzzling her neck before I found her mouth and forgot to be gentle.

She matched my fervor, biting at my lower lip before I licked into her mouth and felt a tremor run down her body. I wanted to feel her naked skin on mine, to pull her to the floor and shove our clothes aside, but I braced my hands above her head instead, gripping the door so I wouldn't touch her, so I wouldn't start something I had no business finishing. And I would finish if I started. If I saw her laying beneath me again, her hair spread around her, her hands pulling me to her, I would finish. And I couldn't go there. Not yet. Maybe not ever. Because regardless of what Millie said, insult or not, Amelie Anderson—beautiful, brave, and freaking BLIND— wasn't the kind of girl you played. She wasn't the kind of girl you played *around* with. I'd flirted. I had. But I hadn't harmed. She said she didn't need guarantees, but she sure as hell did. She sure as hell deserved them. And I wasn't there yet. My body was. My body had been there and back multiple times. My body was running circles around my heart, raging at me, mocking me, begging me to get with the program.

But as ridiculously, gratefully, tearfully glad as I was that she was okay, I wasn't there yet.

I wrenched my mouth away and buried my face in her hair.

"Are you a virgin, Millie?" I asked, my voice hoarse, my hands still braced above her head.

She froze, the hands that were curled against my chest, suddenly falling to her sides.

"Are you?" she asked primly.

I half-laughed, half-groaned at her sass and kissed the top of her head. The laughter burst the ball of tension in my gut, and I exhaled the residue in a long sigh.

"No, Millie. I'm not. Not by a long shot. Are you?" I repeated the question.

"No."

"You're lying. You have a little groove between your eyebrows and you're biting your lip. Those are your tells."

"My tells?"

"Yep. Don't ever play poker, sweetheart." I stepped back, my arms falling to my sides, mimicking her posture. I pulled Millie forward so I could open the bathroom door she still leaned against. "It's got to be close to two a.m. I need to go before I get careless. I'll say goodnight to Henry and be on my way."

Millie's back stiffened and her chin lifted slightly, another tell, but she followed me out without a word. I'd embarrassed her, but there wasn't a damn thing I could do about it, so I held my tongue and kept my hands to myself. I stuck my head into Henry's room, only to discover him asleep, sprawled across his narrow bed, the highlight reel flickering across his face from the TV on the opposite wall.

"The San Francisco Giants have won the 2012 World Series! The Giants have taken it all!" the announcer crowed, and I realized he'd been watching a replay. Baseball season was long over. I wondered if Henry hoped to catch a glimpse of his dad, Giants alumni, one of baseball's brightest lights. Too bad he was an asshole. Too bad Henry still cared.

I closed the door softly and made my way down the stairs, suddenly weary, my muscles achy, my neck stiff, my mind troubled. "He's never called, never contacted you? Not even since your mom passed away?"

Millie knew who I was referring to, though I had asked the question without clarifying. She shrugged as if it meant very little to her. "No. His lawyer called once, verifying that Henry and I were still here. Verifying that I was Henry's guardian. After that, the money doubled. He just sends money. Month after month, we get a check. I'm sure it makes him feel better about himself. Some people can't handle it, you know. The disappointment, the baggage, the responsibility that comes with having children with disabilities. He couldn't." Millie's voice was cool and her posture was straight as a board.

"Huh." I leaned in and kissed her forehead. "Goodnight, Millie." I let myself out, and was halfway down the street before I realized Millie probably thought I was one of those people—the people who couldn't handle it.

Eleven

∴

Moses

I NEVER KNEW my dad. I never knew my mom, for that matter. I knew who she was though. I knew her name, her life, her family, her weaknesses. Her name was Jennifer Wright, a blond-haired, blue-eyed, white girl with a crack habit. She had me, she left me, and she died. We had a three day relationship that didn't include exchanging important information, and she was the only one who knew who my dad was. He was dark-skinned—I'd inherited that much—and that was all I had to go on.

I wondered about him sometimes. Where he was, who he was, how he was. I wondered if he had any clue he had a son. Wondered if he would like to be a grandfather. Wondered if he liked to paint. Wondered if he looked like me. I wondered. I guess it's just human nature.

Millie knew who her dad was. He knew who she was. He knew where she was. But he'd chosen to distance himself from her and from his son, and I wondered if that wasn't worse. Odds are, my father hadn't had a clue. Odds are, he hadn't chosen to abandon me. I could give him the benefit of the doubt. Henry and Millie didn't have that luxury.

I'd stepped out of the room when Tag had described running through the house, following a trail of blood. It made my palms itch and my neck hot, his descriptions and feelings too reminiscent of the time I'd walked through my own house to find tragedy had struck. Plus, I'd noticed the heat on Millie's skin and the way her finger hovered over the buttons on the tape recorder, as if readying herself to push stop when things got too personal. Georgia had followed me from the room, and though Millie must have heard us go, she didn't stop us.

Even Henry vacated the living room with us, trailing us into the kitchen. He hadn't said anything about Tag's absence, hadn't asked questions, and I wondered how much Millie was telling him. He wasn't listening to Tag's tapes. When he wasn't at school, he sat with earphones on his head, listening to podcasts, watching YouTube videos, or he was up in his room playing the Xbox, cocooning himself in his own activities.

"Researchers have found that saturated fat intake increases sixteen percent among sports fans after their team loses a big game," Henry said matter-of-factly, as he opened the freezer and eyed a huge tub of rocky road ice cream. I wasn't sure if he was just making conversation, making a larger statement about loss, or if he was just hungry.

"Do you need dinner? We could order a pizza or something," I volunteered.

Henry inclined his head toward the crock pot on the counter top, and I noticed belatedly that the kitchen smelled warm and spicy.

"Amelie made chili. Lots of chili. Major League Baseball fans consume approximately ten million chili dogs per year."

"Well, Kathleen is hungry, and chili dogs aren't on her menu," Georgia replied, putting Kathleen's seat on the counter and digging in the overflowing bag she lugged everywhere, looking for something to feed her. Kathleen let out a yowl of impatience.

Henry shut the freezer on the ice cream temptation and pulled a stack of bowls from the cupboard. We were clearly invited for dinner. He took crackers and sour cream and cheese from the fridge, setting things out, stealing looks at Kathleen as her complaining gained momentum.

"Kathleen doesn't look like you," Henry said suddenly, staring at me.

"Uh, no. She doesn't. Not really," I stammered, not knowing what else to say. Without another word, Henry turned and left the kitchen. I heard him run up the stairs and looked at Georgia who met my gaze with bafflement.

"Did you hear that, woman?" I asked Georgia. "Henry doesn't think Kathleen looks like me. You got something to tell me?"

Kathleen shrieked again. Georgia wasn't moving fast enough with the jar of bananas she'd produced.

Georgia smirked and stuck out her tongue at me, and Kathleen bellowed. Georgia hastily dipped the tiny spoon into the yellow goo and proceeded to feed our little beast, who wailed as she inhaled.

"She may not look like you, Moses. But she definitely has your sunny disposition," Georgia sassed, but she leaned into me when I dropped a kiss on her lips. It didn't hurt my feelings at all that my dimpled baby girl looked more like her mother.

I heard Henry thundering back down the stairs and pulled back from my wife's soft mouth as he strode through the kitchen seconds later. He stopped beside me.

"See?" He clutched a picture in his hand, and he waved it in front of my face. "I don't look like my dad either."

I took the photo from his hand and studied it. It was worn on the edges and it had lost its sheen, like Henry had held it often. The man in the picture was familiar to me in the way sports figures are familiar to many. Andre Anderson was fairly well-known and admired. He stood smiling at the camera with a very small Henry, maybe three years old, clutched in his arms. He looked happy and relaxed, and he and Henry wore matching Giants jerseys and ball caps.

"You're right. You and Millie look more like your mom," I said, handing the picture back. I didn't like pictures. Pictures rarely told the truth. They were like gold lacquer over Styrofoam, making things seem shiny and bright, disguising the fragility beneath. A picture may be worth a thousand words, but it still wasn't worth a whole hell of a lot.

"That's because we spent more time with her," Henry said seriously, as if it were common knowledge, as if resemblances were based on nurture instead of nature. It was true, to a point. Mannerisms, quirks, style. All those things could be learned and copied.

"So if I spend a lot of time with Kathleen, do you think she'll start to look like me?" I asked him, steering the focus away from his father.

Henry looked doubtfully from me to my grunting, banana-bearded child and back again.

"I hope so," he said.

Georgia snickered, and I hooted and held my hand in the air so Henry could give me five.

"You hear that, Georgia? Henry hopes so," I crowed. "I guess that means your baby daddy is a beautiful man."

Henry obviously didn't mean to be funny, and he totally left me hanging. Georgia reached up and slapped my hand and winked at me.

"If she looks like you, everyone will know you're her dad," Henry
said, his voice perfectly level, his eyes solemn. "And that will make her
happy."

I nodded, no longer smiling.

"That's why I go to the gym. I want to look like Tag," he added to no
one in particular. He set down the picture and proceeded to dish up four
bowls of chili, handing one to me and placing Georgia's beyond Kathleen's reach. Before he ate, he took the fourth bowl into the family room,
and we heard the tape pause and Millie thank her brother. Henry came
back into the kitchen sans chili, and without a word, dug into his dinner.
We were all silent as we heard Tag's voice resume his tale.

PEOPLE WHO CAN see constantly move their heads. It wasn't anything I
had noticed before, not until I spent time with Millie. But movement was
directly tied to sight, and where everyone else tossed and turned their
heads, their bodies following where their eyes went, Millie moved cau-
tiously, her spine straight, her chin level, her shoulders back, ready to soak
in every available clue. She didn't tip her head toward her feet when she
tied her shoes or tilt her head up when the bell of a shop rang overhead.
Moving her head didn't give her any more information, and as a result, she
was perfectly contained, and strangely impenetrable. It made her appear
regal, like a Japanese Geisha. But it was intimidating too.

I was restless, always had been, and her stillness beckoned me while
her concentration on the smallest things made me more aware of myself, of

my size and my tendency to break things. I had always been physical, more inclined to hug than hold back, as inclined to touch as talk, although I did both. I wondered if Millie would have been as controlled if she could see, or if her poise and patience were a byproduct of the loss of her sight. The only time she moved with abandon was when she was dancing, hands glued to the pole, head moving with the music, body pulsing with the rhythm.

I watched her dance every chance I could get. It wasn't her skimpy outfit or her graceful limbs, taut stomach, and shiny hair, though I was a man and I'd taken note of all those things immediately. But all the girls had beautiful, strong, slim bodies. All the girls danced well. But I watched Millie. I watched Millie because she fascinated me. She was a brand new species, an intoxicating mix of girl and enigma, familiar yet completely foreign. I'd never met anyone like her, yet I felt like I'd known her forever. And since the moment I'd looked down into her face and felt that jolt of ode-to-joy-and-holy-shit, I'd been falling, falling, falling, unable to stop myself, unable to look away, helpless to do the smart thing. And the smart thing, the kind thing would be to stay away. But no one had ever accused me of being particularly smart.

Now she stood perfectly still in the center of the crowded room, people swarming and slipping around her, her eyes open and unseeing. But open. Her stillness drew my gaze. Her straight dancer's posture unyielding, chin high, hands loose at her side. She was waiting for something. Or just absorbing it all. I didn't know, but I couldn't look away. Everyone hurried around her and almost no one seemed to see her at all, except for the few who tossed an exasperated look at her unsmiling face as they squeezed past her and then realized she wasn't "normal" and hurried away. Why was it that no one saw her, yet she was the first thing I saw? Her dress was blue. A pale, baby blue that made her eyes the same color. Her hair was gleaming, her lips red, and she held her walking stick like the stripper pole, swaying to the music as if she wanted to dance. She'd never come to the bar on club night before. I would have noticed her.

It'd been almost a week since the kiss. Millie had worked her shifts as usual and was her same smiling self, calm and collected, unassuming and independent. I thought for sure I was going to have some explaining to do. Some unruffling. But Millie seemed unaffected. Or maybe she just had me figured out. I didn't know, but I was simultaneously grateful and offended that there hadn't been any attempts to pin me down. Instead, I walked her home like I had a dozen times before, and we conversed like old friends, though I found myself looking longer, eyeing her mouth, and thinking of her when we weren't together. Being with Millie spoiled me a bit. I never had to guard my feelings or school my expression. I could look at her like a man looked at a lover, and she had no idea.

She had no idea I watched her now, although I hoped like hell she'd come here for me. I excused myself from the palms I'd just greased and moved toward her. From the way her chin rose and her nostrils flared slightly, she heard me coming, even though she didn't turn her head. I took her stick and set it aside. Then I laid my hand on her waist, and took her hand in mine. I was a rich kid, wasn't I? My mama had made me learn all the rich kid things. Dancing, good manners, all the things that made me as slick as could be. All the things that made people trust me and made me slightly sick to my stomach. But Millie wanted to dance, that was plain to see, and no one was asking. Thank God. I didn't know if I could handle watching her dance with someone else.

I pulled her in tight and felt her little intake of breath and couldn't help but catch my own. She was so composed, but she felt something. She felt the ode. I wouldn't lead her around the floor in a silly side to side shuffle. I knew how to dance and dance we would.

"You know how to waltz, sweetheart?"

She raised one eyebrow disdainfully. "Who's the dancer here, David?"

"Just makin' sure you can keep up with me, darlin'," I cracked. I was laying it on thick and it was all I could do not to laugh when she snorted, setting her left hand gracefully on my shoulder, signaling she was ready.

"Are we going to dance or are you just going to hang onto me?" She wriggled impatiently.

"By all means, let's dance." With that, I began to move, pulling her so close she stood on her toes, her breasts pressed against me, her legs scissoring mine. She slid into the movement effortlessly, matching my sway, my timing, my steps, and we flew around the room. One-two-three, one-two-three, one-two-three, we waltzed, and everyone watched. Nobody waltzed anymore. But we did. Millie's eyes were closed, her lips parted, her cheeks lightly flushed.

Ray LaMontagne sang about being saved by a woman.

And I believed him.

"She won't let me go," he moaned. "She won't let me go."

I sang with him, my lips against Millie's hair. She tipped her face up, listening as we moved together. Then one song became another—another song in three/four time—and then another. I made a note to tip my DJ. He knew what he was doing. And I knew every word of every song.

We'd drawn quite the audience, though Millie wouldn't know that. A group of women huddled at the edge of the floor, their heads together, their eyes on us, and I realized I'd slept with all of them, and I'd never danced with any of them. Kara, Brittney, Emma and Lauren. Good lord. They were friends? I didn't know they were *all* friends. They came into the bar and worked out at the gym. I winked when I caught Brittney's eye. We'd ended on good terms, and I didn't see any reason not to be friendly. In fact, I'd never been especially serious with any of them. Looking at their scowling faces, maybe I was remembering wrong.

Brittney broke away from the others and strolled across the floor like she was on a catwalk and I was a fashion photographer. I should have spun Millie away, but the floor was small, and Brittney looked determined.

"Tag! I want to cut in! Who knew you could dance, baby?" she cooed, all gooey syrup and vanilla perfume. She snuggled up to my side and hugged my bicep, as if I wasn't already dancing with another woman.

Millie stiffened and stepped back. I grabbed her hand.

"I'm dancing with Millie now. Next song. Okay?"

Brittney pouted in that way some women do when they really want to get ugly and are trying to stay cute, and she didn't release my arm.

"Come on, Tag. You're embarrassing me. Don't say no."

Millie pulled out of my arms. "Point me toward my stick and tell me how far it is. Ten feet? Twenty? I'll be fine. Don't worry about me." Her expression was blank, her shoulders thrown back.

"She'll be fine, Tag," Brittney crooned. She was obviously well aware that Millie was blind.

"I'm dancing with Millie right now, Britt," I said firmly, and I could hear the frost in my voice. I shot a look at the edge of the dance floor, at the women huddled together, watching the little drama unfold. There were grinning at me like it was all a big joke.

"Whatever." Brittney released my arm casually. She turned away slowly, her pout still in place and sauntered off.

The song ended and for the space of a heartbeat there was relative quiet. Then her voice rang out loud and clear.

"You're such a manwhore, Tag. It's almost embarrassing," she called over her shoulder, and a few people laughed. "Who will you sleep with next?"

"I never pretended to be anything else," I called after her, smiling widely at the women beyond her. The laughter grew and a guy next to me held up his hand for a high-five. But Millie wasn't laughing. Shit.

Her hand was still in mine, but our bodies were no longer aligned for dancing. I didn't want to leave the dance floor. I didn't want to act like Brittney's interruption meant anything. The DJ had done what he could, giving me three sultry songs in a row. Maybe he thought he was helping me again by putting Justin Timberlake on full tilt, *Sexy Back* making my teeth vibrate and urging a few more people to the floor, creating a bit of a visual buffer between Millie and me and our audience, although not much of one. I needed an excuse to pull Millie close again, and I wasn't sure she would be willing to engage in the kind of bump and grind JT demanded.

I stepped into her so our bodies touched, and I put my lips to her ears so she could hear me above the music.

"You still interested in dancing with a manwhore?"

"It depends. Are people watching?" her mouth brushed my cheek as she spoke.

I looked around us at the curious and the pitying. "Yeah. They are."

"Good. Let's dance." She looped her arms carefully around my neck and tipped her face up, smiling for me.

And I felt the ode again, so strong it made my legs weak.

I threw back my head and laughed, whooping a little. More people looked our way. Let 'em look.

"I really like you, Millie."

"That's because you're a manwhore!" she teased.

And then I forgot about talking as I tried to keep up with Millie on the dance floor. Holy hell, the girl could dance. She kept at least one hand on me at all times, keeping herself grounded, centered, anchored, and it was the hottest thing I'd seen in my whole life. The fact that she couldn't see me dancing was liberating and I forgot about everyone else. I even forgot myself.

We didn't stop dancing until we were both panting and strands of Millie's dark hair clung to her damp forehead and smooth cheeks. Her skin glowed and her smile flashed, and I couldn't catch my breath, though it had less to do with exertion than with Millie herself. Millie was insatiable, and I was captivated, and I suddenly wanted her all to myself.

I snagged two bottles of water from behind the bar, taking quick note that things were running smoothly and my new bartender seemed to have it all in hand.

Millie stood waiting for me, holding her stick, and I snagged her coat and we slipped out the back door, breathing in fresh, cold air, her hand tucked through my arm, the muted, thumping bass mimicking my pounding heart.

We guzzled in silence until Millie sighed, capping her bottle and setting it aside so she could lift her hair from her damp neck. She'd refused her coat, claiming the air felt good on her skin. She held her hair atop her head, her slim arms raised high, her head tilted forward, and I watched the lovely display, grateful once again that I didn't have to hide my admiring gaze.

"I'm sorry," I said.

"For what?

"I *am* a bit of a manwhore."

"I know."

"And that doesn't bother you?"

"It doesn't apply to me."

I gulped.

"Oh yeah? What makes you think it doesn't apply?"

"I seem to remember having to beg you to kiss me." Millie let her hair fall back down around her shoulders and hugged her arms across her chest. In another girl I might think the action was designed to draw my eyes to the swell of her breasts, which it did, but she couldn't know how perfectly they were framed or how the moon made her skin glow.

"And I remember happily accommodating you," I drawled softly.

She didn't answer, didn't smile, didn't argue with me, and I was at a loss.

"I'm sorry," I said again.

"For what?" she repeated.

"Brittney was rude. And she was rude because of who I am, not because of who you are. You understand that, right?"

"They all must be so confused."

"Who?"

"All the girls in your life."

I laughed at that. "Why?"

"Because you are spending time with me. You're dancing with me. You left with me. You walk me home almost every night."

I waited.

"I admit, I'm a little confused, David." Her voice was soft, but it wasn't timid. Millie wasn't timid, and I loved that about her.

"You always call me David. Why?" I side-stepped the question. I was just as confused as she was and wasn't ready to give her a response.

"Because David fits you so perfectly," she said easily, letting me change the subject.

"What's that supposed to mean?"

"Names mean something. Too many parents get caught up in how a name sounds or how it's spelled. I wonder how often they take the time to find out what a name means, or at the very least, what it means to them? Is it the name of a beloved family member? Is it the name of a place that brings back memories? What? Or is it just the name Ashley spelled A-S-C-H-L-E-I-G-H in an effort to be unique? Utahans, as religious as their population is, are great at giving out spirit-less, meaningless names with preposterous spellings."

"So that's why Moses and Georgia didn't want to name Kathleen Taglee. I was so hurt."

She giggled and groaned, which was what I intended.

"Okay. So you say David fits me perfectly. What does David mean?"

"Darling. Beloved."

"Darling? Beloved? You've got to be kidding me!" My voice was wry, twisting the words so I mocked them even as I spoke.

"You are everyone's darling. Everyone loves you."

"Hmm. So why don't you?" Damn. I had to stop doing that.

"Because my name means work," she replied saucily.

"Work?"

"Yes. That's what Amelie means. Work."

"Oh, that's rich," I drawled.

"Yes. And Henry means 'ruler of the home.' Which he loves and takes very seriously."

"He would," I chuckled.

"Speaking of Henry, I need to go." Amelie sighed.

"I'll drive you."

"Nah. You go inside. I want to walk."

"Amelie—" I protested because I didn't have time to walk with her and walk all the way back. I needed to get back inside, I needed to see and be seen. I had hands to shake and people to work, and I'd completely ignored my host duties for too long.

"It's just not safe, Amelie," I pressed.

"You are not responsible for me, David," she said gently. "I want to walk. I like to walk. I walked home before I met you, and I'll be walking after you're gone."

I bit back a curse.

"Will you call me or have Henry call me, and let me know you got home all right? Please?" I snapped.

"Sure." She nodded agreeably. She slid her arms into her coat and freed her hair from the collar, and I watched, my gut churning. I didn't like her walking home alone at eleven o'clock at night. She straightened her stick and held her empty water bottle out in front of her, obviously wanting me to take it. As I did, my hand brushed hers and we both jumped as if we hadn't just spent the last hour dancing with our bodies pressed together.

"You know, David. You were wrong."

"About what?"

"My tells."

"Your tells?" I was lost.

"There was someone, once," she said quietly.

I stared at her blankly before realization struck me a heavy blow. Her tells. The night I kissed her. The night I asked her if she was a virgin and told her she lied when she said she wasn't.

She walked away, stick tapping, calling her goodbyes over her shoulder.

I watched her walk down the street, a sway in her step, like she was still hearing Ray LaMontagne. I swore again and walked swiftly to my truck. She could walk if she wanted. But I was going to make sure she got home. I followed her at a distance, watched as she turned the corner to her street, crawled along until I saw her unlatch her gate, and then I flipped a U-Turn and floored the truck back to the bar. I was so pathetic.

Henry texted me seconds later, telling me she had arrived, just like Millie promised.

Henry: Amelie is home. Her face is sad. Mohammed Ali practiced abstinence up to six weeks before his fights.

I laughed and swore simultaneously. Apparently everyone thought I was a manwhore.

Twelve

SATURDAY AFTERNOON, HENRY showed up at the gym without Millie. It surprised me a little, as she'd always come with him before, but I shrugged it off, feeling a little twinge of disappointment in my stomach and studiously ignoring it. Her words shot through my mind. *There was someone once.* I found myself worrying that there was someone again, someone from the school she worked at on Tuesdays, or maybe Robin had set her up again. Millie claimed she hated that, but there was always the exception.

Maybe it was the disappointment or maybe it was habit, but I lingered a little longer in conversation with some of my female fighters, accepted a hug and a smile from Deanna, a cute redhead who I'd taken to dinner once or twice, and spotted a couple female clients on their chest presses, like any good athletic club owner would. Henry glowered at me from the corner mats, where Cory was showing him how to shoot a duck-under.

I wondered if he was just feeling neglected, and took Cory's place, shooting instructions at Henry and critiquing his form, which was terrible, every time he tried to perform the move. His jaw was tense, his movements jerky, and he seemed close to tears.

"Henry! What's up, man? We're just here to learn a few things and look good for the girls. Loosen up," I teased gently, ruffling his hair.

Henry shoved at my hand and swung on me suddenly, wildly, one fist connecting with my stomach, the other glancing off my jaw.

"Whoa!" I half-laughed, shooting a double-leg and scooping him up across my shoulders, WWE-style. I straightened and roared, like I was Hulk Hogan or The Undertaker, and I spun a thrashing Henry around in exaggerated circles until I realized he was pounding and kicking furiously, and not in a way that indicated he was messing around or having fun. I put him down immediately, my arms steadying his shoulders in case he was dizzy. I felt a little dizzy myself, and tried to clear my head. Henry didn't let up though.

His face was flushed and his arms were pin-wheeling. I put a hand on his forehead, the way my dad used to do when I was little, my hand palming his head like a basketball, keeping him at arm's length.

"Henry! Buddy, we're just playing. Relax."

If anything, he just doubled his efforts to take me out with his scrawny arms and sharp knees.

"Henry, I outweigh you by a hundred pounds. You can't fight me, kid!"

"Manute Bol was seven foot seven!" he yelled. People were starting to stare. Axel and Mikey had stopped grappling on the mats nearby and were watching, both of them breathing hard. Axel rose to his feet and started toward us.

"What the fu—" I cut myself off immediately. Every time I swore, Henry looked slightly stricken. I'd had to talk to the guys about the every-other-word-is-the-F-word language we all used without thought. We had a huge water jug in the office brimming with quarters from our slips.

"You're going to have to explain that one, Henry." I released my hand from his head and let him come at me again. When he started pummeling my chest, I wrapped my arms around him, pinning his arms to his sides. He immediately started head butting me, though the top of his head barely reached my chin. I nuzzled my head down, trapping his head between the side of my face and my shoulder, the way boxers do when they're trying to stall, trying to catch their breath, and I was trying to do both as I scrambled to figure out why Henry was so angry about a seven foot seven basketball player.

"Henry!" I spoke into his bushy hair. "Henry, I don't know what you're trying to tell me!"

"Manute Bol's grandfather had forty wives." His voice had dropped slightly, but the fervor was still there, and behind the fervor, tears threatened, and he still strained against me.

"Seriously?" I laughed, trying to snap him out of it. "Lucky guy."

Henry jerked viciously, pulling his head free, nailing me in the mouth.

I let him go, spitting blood and forbidden words. I think I owed the water jug ten dollars.

"Not lucky!" he roared. He turned away and stomped to the edge of the mat. He picked up his duffle bag and his sweatshirt and headed for the door. I could only watch, completely dumbfounded.

"He's pissed at you," Axel commented, as if I hadn't figured that much out.

"Yeah. He is. Did you know Manute Bol's grandfather had forty wives?" I almost started to laugh. Henry communicated in the most frustrating way.

"Who's Manute Bol?" Axel frowned.

"Basketball player—one of the tallest to ever play in the NBA. From Sudan, I think."

"Hmm. Maybe Henry doesn't like you having forty girlfriends, big guy." Axel's use of Millie's nickname gave me pause.

"What? I don't—"

"Yes, Tag. You do." Axel grinned at me like he was proud of me.

"Henry!" I tore across the gym, trying to catch Henry as he pushed through the front door. He didn't wait for me, and it took me half a block before I over took him.

"Henry, the girls at the gym and the girls at the bar aren't my girlfriends." Well, they were. But not the way Axel and Henry were thinking. I liked girls. They liked me. But none of it was serious or committed. They were my friends. And they were girls.

"Amelie?" he asked, still walking.

"Millie's not my girlfriend either," I said softly.

"Screw you, Tag," Henry said, so clearly, so simply, that I almost cheered at his direct, uncomplicated response. But the celebration died in my throat as I registered what he'd said and the finality with which he said it. Henry kept on walking toward home, and I watched him go.

I KNOCKED ON the Anderson's door at a little after seven on Sunday evening, but it took some persistence to get anyone to answer it. I'd almost given up when Henry pulled it open and hesitated, as if not sure whether to greet me or not.

"Hey buddy. What's up?"

He shrugged.

"Can I come inside?"

Henry moved aside and let me in, his eyes on the floor. He shut the door behind me, but he didn't make eye contact, and I could tell he was still pissed.

"Henry?" I nudged him softly with my fist, the softest punch I'd ever delivered. His fists balled immediately. Yep. Still mad.

"Prior to 1900, prize fights lasted up to one hundred rounds," Henry said woodenly.

"What round are we on, man? I don't think I can go a hundred rounds with you. I'm tapping out. You win."

"No tap-outs," Henry said, his jaw tight, repeating something I'd told him in the gym.

"No tap-outs. Except when you're wrong. And I was wrong. I'm sorry, Henry."

"Amelie?" he asked. I wanted to hug him. He didn't want apologies, he wanted answers, and I respected that.

"Amelie is special. She's not like other girls. She's not like any girl I've ever liked. And I like her, Henry. I like her a lot. But there's an extra responsibility that comes with loving someone who will need you in a different way, who will rely on you in a different way. I have to be sure I'm ready for the responsibility. Do you understand?"

"Pig's bladders were once used as rugby balls," Henry said softly.

"Are you calling me a pig, Henry?"

Henry started to grin, his eyes darting to mine before he gave in, making pig sounds and giggling.

"You are!" I laughed with him. "I think that's the first time I've ever heard you make a joke!" I went to sling my arm around his neck, but he did a duck-under and shot in on my legs, just like Cory had taught him. I whooped, leaning over him and wrapping my arms around his thin back and lifting his legs off the floor, his arms still wrapped around my thighs so he was hanging upside down.

"Pound for pound, the best fighter in the universe! Say it, Henry. Say, 'Tag, you're the best fighter in the universe!'" I demanded, laughing.

"Georges St. Pierre is the best fighter in the universe!" he squealed, releasing his grip on my thighs.

"St. Pierre!" I roared, and dangled him higher. "Say Tag Taggert is the best fighter in the universe."

"Chuck Liddell is the best fighter in the universe!" he cried, wheezing.

"What? He's old news!" I protested, though I'd do just about anything to get Liddell in my gym.

"Tag Taggert is the worst fighter in the universe!" Henry was laughing, a full-out belly laugh, and his face was as red as his hair. I flipped him upright and he swayed on his feet, still laughing. I steadied him and gave him a fake glare.

"The best. The best fighter in the universe. You hear?"

"Ronda Rousey is the best fighter in the universe," he gasped, still-giggling, not giving in.

I hooted, throwing up my hands. "You might have me there, kid. Speaking of gorgeous, badass females, where is Silly Millie?"

Henry froze, listening, and then pointed at the floor. Now that I wasn't making so much noise, I could hear the bass thumping faintly from the basement.

"Downstairs? Show me the way."

Henry turned and padded through the foyer, across the kitchen and dining room, and into a large laundry room. It was neat and organized, like the rest of the house, and I took note of Millie's Braille stickers on the laundry baskets—a big white one and a bigger red one. I'd never been in this part of the house, and when Henry pointed at a door and immediately retreated, I decided he wasn't interested in whatever Millie was doing downstairs.

The door opened above a narrow flight of stairs that immediately made me nervous and dizzy. I didn't like the idea of Millie navigating them, and images of her tumbling head over heels seared my brain before I forced them back. Millie had grown up in this house, she'd probably been up and down these stairs a million times, and she wouldn't appreciate me going all caveman over them. Still, I clung to the railing as I descended them gingerly, wondering at my sudden light-headedness. The music was so loud Millie wouldn't hear me coming, but as I reached the bottom of the stairs, the music ceased abruptly, and someone started clapping and whistling. I halted, surprised, still hidden around the corner.

"Do I look ridiculous?" I heard Millie ask. "Can I pull it off?"

"What are you talking about, Amelie?" A female voice answered, and I recognized Robin's voice from the night at the bar. She had that valley girl vibe to her voice that seemed to be prevalent among so many American women. I like, totally hated it. But Robin seemed nice enough.

"You are pulling it off! Like, several nights a week, in fact!"

"But I've never attempted this move. I can't tell how I look, how my body looks, when I do it. It feels like I'm doing it right, but . . ." Millie's voice trailed off.

I peeked around the corner, extremely curious. Amelie was facing me, leaning against a tall pole. She was wearing little, black Tag Team shorts and a tank top, her hair pulled high on her head, her feet bare. Robin's back was to me, thankfully, and I watched as she took Millie by the wrists and pulled her forward.

Robin moved Millie's hands up and down her own body matter-of-factly, allowing her to feel the softness at her waist and the roundness of her hips and her belly.

"That's more action than I've had in months. So pathetic," Robin said wryly, releasing Millie's hands, and I smiled, liking her a little more.

"Now feel your own body, Amelie" Robin insisted, stepping back, and Amelie obeyed, running her hands down her chest, over the swell of her breasts, past her flat stomach to rest on her slightly flared hips. Then she cupped her butt in her hands and snickered, "I didn't grab your ass, Robin. Come here."

"Ha, ha. Keep your hands to yourself, Grabby," Robin laughed. "I've got to draw the line somewhere. But you can feel the difference, can't you? I'm lumpy. You're curvy. I'm soft, and you're sleek. You look the way you feel, Amelie. You have an amazing body. And when you dance, no matter what move you're doing, if it feels right, I can guarantee it looks right, too."

Robin rose another notch in my estimation.

"Really?" Millie asked.

"Really," Robin answered.

Amelie swung herself around the bar a couple times, almost absent-mindedly, her ponytail swinging as she hoisted herself up, executing a perfect split before she wound both legs around the pole and dropped upside down. She handled being upside down a whole lot better than Henry did. She trailed her arms over her head, felt the concrete beneath her palms, and released the pole, scissoring her legs back to a standing position, like she could do back bends in her sleep.

"I wish I could touch Tag like that. I wish it was okay to ask for things like that. I mean, I've felt him smile . . . but I want to feel the rest of him." Millie blurted, as if confessing something that had been bubbling over.

I bit my tongue to keep from gasping and wondered how in the hell I was going to get out of this situation without embarrassing everyone involved.

"Amelie! You naughty girl!" Robin squealed.

"I'm not trying to be, Robin. I know he has strong arms. I know he has dimples in his cheeks and a cleft in his chin. I know he has a slightly crooked nose. I know his body is hard and his lips are soft. And I know he has big, calloused hands."

"Stop it! I'm getting turned on and depressed," Robin groaned. "Amelie . . . I think Tag Taggert might be the kind of guy who likes women. Period. You know? And you're beautiful . . . so obviously, he's going to like you. But . . . that's not the kind of guy who's going to make you happy in the long run."

"No." Amelie shook her head, rejecting Robin's opinion of me, as spot-on as it was. "No. There's more to him than that. He's special, and he makes me feel special. Sometimes I think there's something between us. I can feel it in my chest, the way I can't ever really catch my breath when he's around. I feel it in my stomach too, the way it flips when he says my name. And mostly, I feel it when he talks to Henry. He's gentle. And he's sweet."

Millie shrugged. "But then other times, I think he's just the kind of guy who is really good at taking care of people, and Henry and I are . . . needy."

We were facing each other, twenty feet apart, and Millie had no idea I was there, standing by the stairs at the shadowy end of the long basement, listening as she confessed her feelings for me. I considered sneaking back up the stairs, but the stairs were old, and I was guessing they creaked like an old man's joints. I was frozen between wanting to hear Millie's secrets and wanting to hide from them.

"I wonder if he enjoys touching as much as I do," Millie mused. "I want him to touch me, and I want to touch him. But I want him to actually like me, the way I like him, and not just the beautiful parts of me. All of me. Blind eyes, knobby knees, big ears, pointy chin. All of me. So that when he does touch me, and I touch him, it will be wonderful and not weird."

I wished more than anything that Robin was not standing between us at that moment. I wished I could walk over, wrap my arms around Millie and kiss that pointy chin and whisper assurances in the ears that *were* a little big, now that she mentioned it. I slid back around the corner and sat down on the bottom stair, resting my head in my hands.

She'd laid it out. And I'd been lucky enough, or unlucky enough, to hear it. I was lucky because Amelie Anderson was falling in love with me. I was unlucky because I couldn't pretend that I didn't know. I'd refused to listen to Moses when he'd called me out on Saturday. I'd refused to examine the kiss in the bathroom or the line I'd already crossed when I'd lain Millie across her white comforter, a comforter I still saw every time I closed my eyes.

But standing there, listening to Millie spell it out, I couldn't ignore it any more. I couldn't. I couldn't pretend that I had more time to decide. Time was up, and I had to choose.

I didn't question my feelings. The feelings had been there from day one. From day one. I'd seen her standing like a shepherdess in the night, her head tilted back, her tongue catching snowflakes, and I'd felt something shift. Three days in, and I'd looked down into her face and felt the ode, a feeling no other girl had ever inspired. And I'd known. Since that day, I had found myself saying things, feeling things, doing things that I'd never done before. Millie had become my favorite sight, my favorite smell, my favorite taste, my favorite sound. My favorite. But that was never what any of this was about.

It was about me.

Millie called it the night I'd cleaned the blood from her skin and kissed her silly. Silly Millie. She wasn't silly at all. She knew the score.

And she was waiting for me to decide if I was man enough to love a blind girl.

Kissing a blind girl is an unpardonable sin, she'd said, taunting me. But she was wrong about that. Kissing a blind girl wasn't unpardonable. Loving her wasn't unpardonable either. But loving her and letting her down . . . that was unpardonable to me. That was unforgiveable. That was the part I struggled with.

The music resumed, but this time the melody was slower, sadder—music for listening rather than dancing. It was a Damien Rice song called "The Blower's Daughter" and it pleased me that Millie knew it too, the discovery making me feel hopeful in an 'if-we-love-the-same-music-our-hearts-must-match' kind of way. I rose, grateful for the noise to cover my ascent, but Robin rounded the corner before I could take a single step.

When she saw me she squeaked and jumped a foot in the air. I held a finger to my lips, shaking my head vigorously. Millie didn't need to know what I'd heard.

I turned and climbed the stairs, hoping Robin was following me, hoping Millie wasn't.

I walked into the laundry room with Robin at my heels. I shut the door carefully behind her and shoved my hands into my front pockets, meeting her wide-eyed gaze.

"I want you to yell down the stairs. Tell her that I'm here. Tell her I'm coming down," I demanded.

"But . . . you . . . how long were you there?" she stuttered.

I waited, not answering, and Robin's face twisted into a scowl.

"You're right about me, you know," I said, giving her an indirect answer. "I do like women. I like them a lot. Especially beautiful women. And I've never been interested in having just one. I've never even had a girlfriend. There's never been a girl that's kept my attention. Until now."

Robin's scowl evaporated instantly, and her pursed lips slid into a smile. Without another word, she turned, opened the door, and bellowed down the stairs.

"Amelie! You've got company!"

I slid past Robin, winking as I headed back down the way I'd just come.

"Don't screw this up!" she hissed. "She's had too much shit in her life, and she doesn't need more, Tag Taggert. Sunshine. Roses. Kisses.

Adoration. That's your job! No shit allowed!"

I couldn't promise a future with no shit. I couldn't even promise I wouldn't cause some. I couldn't alter my DNA, and I was sure I had strands that were soaked in the stuff. But I was bound and determined to shelter Millie from as much as I could. I shot a look over my shoulder and nodded once at Millie's protective cousin, an acknowledgement that I'd heard her, and Robin closed the door, giving us the privacy I hadn't afforded them.

Millie stood waiting, obviously not sure who her company was. She'd pulled her ponytail free, and her hair tumbled around her shoulders in rumpled disarray, but she didn't smooth it down or tug at her clothes. She was regal and composed in her stillness, confident enough in herself that she didn't fuss over what she couldn't fix. Damien Rice was singing about not being able to "take his eyes off of you" and I could only nod in agreement as I approached her.

"David?" she ventured softly. The fact that she knew it was me made me light-headed all over again.

"Am I the only guy who makes that much noise coming down the steps?" I'd purposely made plenty of noise the second time around.

"Nah. You should hear Henry. You're just the . . . only guy," she admitted sweetly. Then her cheeks grew rosy and my chest got hot.

I felt a huge flood of relief. I was the only guy. Thank God.

I stopped a foot from her and reached out, taking one of her hands in mine. "Do you like this song?" I asked. Obviously she did and obviously I was stupid.

"I love this song."

"Me too," I whispered. I reached for her other hand.

"*Accidental Babies*."

"What?" I tugged her hands gently, and she took a step. I was so close now that the top of her head provided a shelf for my chin, and Damien's song was being drowned out by the sound of my heart.

"It's another one of his songs. . . and I think I love it even more," she whispered back.

"But that song is so sad," I breathed, and laid my cheek against her hair.

"That's what makes it beautiful. It's devastating. I love it when a song devastates me." Her voice was thready as if she was struggling to breathe.

"Ah, the sweet kind of suffering." I dropped her hands and wrapped my arms around her.

"The best kind." Her voice hitched as our bodies aligned.

"I've been suffering for a while now, Millie."

"You have?" she asked, clearly amazed.

"Since the moment I saw you. It devastated me. And I love when a girl devastates me." I was using her definition of the word, but the truth was, my sister was the only girl who had ever devastated me, and it hadn't been sweet agony.

"I've never devastated anyone before," Millie said faintly, shock and pleasure coloring her words. She still stood with her arms at her sides, almost like she couldn't believe what was happening. But her lips hovered close to my jaw, as if she was enjoying the tension between almost and not quite.

"I'm guessing you've left a wake of destruction," I whispered. "You just don't know."

"Can't see my own mess. Perks of being a blind girl." I could hear the smile in her voice. But I couldn't laugh now. I was on fire, and the flames were growing uncomfortable.

Finally, as if she couldn't resist any longer, she raised her hands to my waist. Trembling fingers and flat palms slid across my abdomen, up my chest, past my shoulders, progressing slowly as if she memorized as she moved. Then she touched my face and her thumbs found the cleft in my chin, the way they'd done the first time she'd traced my smile. Hesitantly, she urged my face down toward hers. A heartbeat before our mouths touched she spoke, and the soft words fluttered against my lips.

"Are you going to devastate me, David?" she asked.

"God, I hope not," I prayed aloud.

Anticipation dissolved the lingering space between us, and I pressed needy lips to her seeking mouth. And then we melded together, hands clinging, bodies surging, music moaning, dancing in the wreckage. Sweet, sweet, devastation.

"Too late . . ." I thought I heard her whisper.

Thirteen

Moses

I SAT OUT on Millie's front porch with Kathleen and rocked in a wrought iron swing that had probably been there since the house was built more than a century before. I had abandoned listening to the cassettes altogether. Tag wasn't holding anything back. Every detail, every thought, every feeling hanging out. Naked. And I didn't like naked men. So I was letting Georgia listen with Millie, and Kathleen and I were bonding on the porch, Kathleen bundled up in a fuzzy hat and a fuzzier blanket, asleep on my chest, a buffer against the cool spring air, soaking up some daddy time so that she would grow to look like me and know she was mine, just like Henry said.

Henry had retreated to his room. It was late, and we were all tired. But Millie couldn't stop listening, and I couldn't blame her. The drum beat was quickening, and as much as I wanted to just skip ahead, just stick the last tape in the player, I had no right. And knowing Tag, it wouldn't be that easy.

And then Georgia opened a window, the window nearest my head, as if the emotions in the room had become stifling, and suddenly sitting there on the front porch, I could hear every word once more, and I listened as my friend struggled to put into words that which I could only ever describe with paint.

I'd told Georgia once that if I could paint her I would use every color.

Blues and golds and whites and reds. Peach and cream and bronze and black. Black for me, because I wanted to leave my mark on her. My stamp on her. And I had, though not ever in the way I intended. My mind drifted to my son—who had looked a great deal like me, though I wouldn't tell Henry. I hadn't spent a single day of his life with him. And still, he looked like me.

"Hey, little man," I whispered, wondering if he could hear me. "I miss you." I tasted the same bittersweet tang on my tongue that always came with saying his name, but I said it all the same. "Keep an eye out for Tag, Eli. He acts tough, but I'm guessing he's running scared."

"I don't want to leave." Tag's voice rang out behind me.

I jerked and cursed loudly, making Kathleen whimper in my arms.

Then I realized with a start that Millie had changed the cassette. It was just Tag's voice coming through the window, nothing more, and I cursed again.

"I DON'T WANT to leave," I moaned. We were standing on the front porch and it was cold, but I wasn't ready to go home. I didn't know if I'd ever be ready.

"Then don't," Millie said firmly. We'd been wrapped around each other all night, and it was messing with my willpower. I had the Santos fight in ten days, and fighting was the last thing on my mind. I needed to go home. I needed to sleep. I needed to get up early and hit the gym. But I didn't want to leave.

"I'm afraid of the dark, so I guess I'll have to wait until morning," I whispered. I was trying to make her laugh, but somehow the words rang true and I winced, grateful that she couldn't see me do so. But she was too attuned to the nuances in a person's voice to miss it. She stiffened a little. I felt it, just a tremor that traveled through her arms and down to her hands resting on my chest.

"Are you really afraid of the dark?" she asked, and I allowed myself to get sidetracked once more.

"No, not really. It's more tight spaces. Dark, tight spaces. I had asthma when I was a kid. I guess it's the feeling of not being able to breathe, of feeling helpless. Being trapped."

"I see. I won't make you sleep with me in my coffin then."

"That's right . . . you're a vampire. I forgot." I smiled, and she heard the grin in my voice because she smiled with me.

"The darkness is huge, though. You don't need to be afraid of the dark. Whenever you start feeling trapped or helpless, just close your eyes, and you have more space than you'll ever need."

I nodded and kissed her forehead because she was so earnest and sweet.

"Close your eyes. Come on, close your eyes," she commanded.

I did, but immediately felt dizzy, disoriented, and I reached for her. My balance had been off lately, and I blamed it on lust.

"Don't be scared." I could hear the smile in her voice. "I'm right here. I'm touching you, and you are safe." She was enjoying this game.

"Go down."

"What?" she asked.

"Your hands are on my chest," I said.

"Yeah, they are."

"Keep moving them down. I'll tell you when to stop," I demanded.

She burst out laughing, understanding dawning. "You have no idea how often I've used my blindness to "accidentally" feel someone up."

"Really?" My voice rose in surprise.

"No. Not really. Now shhh!" she commanded. "I need to look at you a little."

I swallowed as her hands slid across my chest and down my torso, her fingers brushing against the swells and valleys that made up my well-muscled abdomen. If it was possible, I felt more naked, more vulnerable than I'd ever felt with a woman, even though I wasn't naked at all. The fact that she couldn't see me made me more aware of the attention she paid to every detail. She slid her hands beneath my shirt, and I smiled into her hair. I was both ticklish and turned on.

"Your skin is smooth. But it's bumpy too. I adore bumps, you know."

I chuckled, thinking of all the braille, the "bumps" in her house that helped her order her world, and I tried not to moan as she ran her fingers up the swell of my lats and rested her head against my chest, pulling me close. I leaned down and kissed the top of her head, the silk of her hair welcome against my lips.

"I am going to touch you a lot," she said sincerely.

"I'm okay with that," I said magnanimously.

"But the things I can't touch, you'll have to describe."

"Okay."

"Your eyes . . . what color are they?" she asked.

"Green."

"Like the grass?"

"Yeah, maybe a little paler."

"And your hair?"

"Dark and light. A mixture of both. Yours is chocolate, mine is . . ." I thought for a moment, trying to come up with a description. "Do I really have to describe it? You can feel it." She ran her fingers through it, and I tried not to purr.

She reached for my hands and brought them to her face.

"Now, look at me the way I look at you."

I ran my fingers over her cheek bones, closing my eyes so I could see the way Millie did.

"Your cheekbones are high and pronounced, and your face is slightly heart-shaped," I declared, though her face was in my mind as my hands traced the features I described.

"I have a big forehead," she interrupted.

"And a pointy chin," I added.

I felt the silk of her hair and pushed her hair behind her ears.

"And big ears," she said.

I traced them with my fingertips. "You have pretty ears," I said. And they were. Between my fingertips they felt dainty and detailed, little whorls of soft skin in the shape of a question mark, always waiting for answers.

"What's your favorite thing about my face?" Millie said after I'd explored a little more.

I touched her mouth, pressing the pads of my thumbs against the full-est part of her bottom lip and then sliding them upwards to rest in the crease so I could part them slightly.

"This. This is my favorite part."

"Because you can kiss me?" Ah, my girl knew how to flirt. I liked that.

"Yes," I said. And I did. I kissed her softly and then sweetly. And then I kissed her again. And again, over and over, for several long minutes, until our lips were sore and I knew I should stop, but found myself sinking in again, licking between her smooth teeth and sliding my tongue against hers because the friction felt so good, and her flavor lit a fire in the pit of my stomach.

"I don't want to leave," I said again. I didn't know if I would ever be ready.

MILLIE TRIED TO take me to church again, but I had a surprise for her. We lived in a city that boasted one of the most famed choirs in the world, and we were going to hear them sing. I twisted some arms and made some calls and got permission to sit in on a rehearsal. I didn't want to share the experience with a crowd, and Millie would be completely surprised if I just led her in, right down to the front row of the tabernacle, and sat her down. If there was a crowd she would be expecting a performance. No crowd, and the surprise would be complete.

She was excited, her cheeks pink and her smile wide, and she held on-to me, squeezing my arm like an anxious child.

"Are we in a church?" she whispered theatrically.

"Kind of."

"It doesn't feel like there are lots of people here. Are there other peo-ple here?"

"Kind of."

Her eyebrows rose and she pinched my arm. "How can there 'kind of' be other people here? Either there are or there aren't."

"There are other people here . . . but they aren't attending church."

"Okaaaay," Millie said doubtfully, but I could tell she was dancing in her skin.

The entire back wall was a pipe organ, something I'd never seen before, and when the organist began to play, I felt the vibrations in my back teeth and the hair stood up on my neck. Millie gasped beside me and I reached for her hand and closed my eyes so that I could experience it the way she was experiencing it. Then the choir started to sing. A wall of sound washed over us, taking us both by surprise, the power and precision seeping into our pores and spilling down our spines, sinking into the soles of our feet.

I forgot my goal to keep my eyes closed and found myself staring at Millie instead, who had lifted her chin and was basking in the sound as if it were sunlight warming her skin. Her eyes were closed and her lips were parted, and she looked as if she were waiting for a kiss. It was an Easter hymn, the choir proclaiming joyfully that He had risen, followed by jubilant hallelujahs in triumphant harmony.

"That's what heaven sounds like. Don't you think?" Millie breathed, but I stayed silent, not wanting to ruin the moment with my own opinions about what heaven sounded like. In my limited experience, heaven was silence, a silence so pervasive and complete that it had mass. It had weight. And in that silence there was sadness and guilt, regret and remorse, and loss. Loss of what could have been, loss of what never would be, loss of love, loss of life, loss of choice. I'd felt all those things when I'd swallowed that bottle of aspirin and slit my wrists for good measure. I'd lost consciousness only to become more conscious, more aware. And the silence had been deafening. It wasn't dark. It was light. So light you had no choice but to see yourself, all of yourself. I hadn't liked it.

Though I'd wailed and protested being yanked back to the ground, yanked out of heaven—or hell, whatever it was—I'd been grateful too. And my gratitude had filled me with guilt. It wasn't until I'd met Moses that heaven had become something different. Moses saw people, people who had died and gone on. Heaven wasn't silent for Moses. It was filled with memories and moments, filled with color. He brought the dead back to life. He painted them. Moses hadn't wanted to see any of it, but he didn't have a choice. He had to come to terms with it. And as he had, I had gone along, persistent in my devotion, if only because Moses saw a sister I would never see again, and Moses had answers nobody else did. Even if those answers sometimes made death more alluring. At least death wasn't the end. Of that, I was sure.

Maybe for Millie, heaven was a place that sounded like angelic choirs and pipe organs, because that was where she felt alive. It was all about sound for Millie, not sight. Not colors, like it was for Moses. But for me, heaven would be something else. It would sound like the bell at the beginning of a round, it would taste like adrenaline, it would burn like sweat in my eyes and fire in my belly. It would look like screaming crowds and an opponent who wanted my blood. For me, heaven was the octagon.

"You know my fight against Santos is Tuesday night. Right?" Talking about this now, while we still sat in the tabernacle, wasn't probably the best time. The hairs on my arm had been standing at full attention for the last half hour while we listened to one song after another. The choir was singing "Beautiful Savior," and I was looking down at Millie's face, thinking what a beautiful savior she'd turned out to be. If heaven was the octagon then Millie was my angel at the center of it all. The girl with the power to take me down and lift me up again. The girl I wanted to fight for, the girl I wanted to claim.

"Yes?" Her lips were turned into my ear so our conversation wouldn't interrupt the rehearsal taking place. I didn't answer immediately, waiting as the stirring rendition came to a close. The director waved the organ and the choir into silence, and I grabbed Millie's hand and we slipped out the way we'd come, mouthing a thank you toward the friend in the Tabernacle Choir who had made it happen. He gave me a wink and a thumbs up, and Millie clung to my arm until we were out in the open sunshine. She loosened her grip and tipped her face up, soaking in the warmth and giving me a perfect view of her lovely throat.

"I don't want you in the audience on Tuesday, Millie," I said abruptly.

"You don't?" Her chin dropped, sunshine forgotten.

"I don't, baby," I said gently.

"Why?" Her tone was plaintive.

"I won't be able to focus on what I have to do. I'll be worried about you."

She sighed, a gusty swoosh that lifted the dark strands of her hair closest to her mouth.

"As soon as I win, I'm coming to you," I promised.

"You're that sure you're going to win?"

"Yep. I'm gonna win, I'm gonna raise my arms over my head, and I'm gonna say, Yo Millie, we did it!"

"How very Rocky Balboa of you." She smirked.

"That's right. And then I'm gonna go running through the crowd, out the doors, three blocks down, two blocks over, and I'll bang at your door, and you can congratulate me in any way you see fit. Make sure Henry's with Robin."

She laughed, but I could tell she didn't want to laugh. Silence settled between us, and we started to walk, meandering in the general direction of where I'd parked. The grounds around the tabernacle were perfectly maintained and ideal for walking, even if Millie couldn't enjoy the landscaping.

"I'm not made of glass, David," she said softly.

"I know."

"Really? Because I'm guessing if I could see, you would want me at your fight."

"Maybe," I admitted, nodding to myself. "But you can't see. And having you out there in the crowd, being bumped and pushed, hearing the fight going down, and not knowing if I'm winning or losing, that seems unnecessarily cruel. And I don't want that. You'll be afraid for me, and I'll be afraid for you, and if I'm worrying about you, my mind won't be where it needs to be."

"But Tag, that's kind of how it works. I care about you, you care about me. It's called a relationship." There was frustration in her voice, and I noticed she called me Tag whenever she was a little irked at me.

"I protect you, you protect me," I insisted. "That's how it works. You protect me by being safe and secure while I fight, so I'm not distracted. And I protect you by insisting on it."

She sighed again, and I stopped walking and turned her to face me. Gently, with the pads of my fingertips, I smoothed her forehead, traced the scowl between her eyes, and then touched her unsmiling lips, pushing the edges up, forcing her to smile.

She grabbed at my hands and nipped at my fingertips, biting a little harder than was playful, showing me her frustration.

"It'll be broadcast on FightNet. FOX sports will be there too, but I don't think it'll air until later. But on FightNet you can watch it in real time. You can log in and watch it at home. Mikey does the play-by-play for Tag Team fights. He's good at it, Millie, and I'll make sure he knows you're listening so he gives a little more detail than usual. That way you will know exactly what is happening, when it happens."

She shook her head as if she didn't like it at all.

"Please, Millie?" I whispered.

"I don't want you to feel alone. It feels wrong not to be there," she protested.

"Everyone fights alone, Millie. That's not something you can help me do."

"Okay," she whispered.

"Okay?" I asked.

"Okay," she acquiesced.

I kissed her gratefully, almost desperately, and she kissed me back. But I sensed the hurt and tasted her reservations.

When I dropped her off at home, I didn't come inside and she didn't sulk or simper. I was buzzing with pent-up energy, nerves, and anticipation. I had forty-eight hours to mentally prepare for the fight, and I needed a clear head and no distractions. Even beautiful ones.

"You'll come here Tuesday night, no matter what time it is?" she asked, her hand on the door handle, her stick at the ready.

"I will," I promised. Bloodied, bruised, beaten, I would be there.

"I'll be listening, I'll be cheering, and I'll be waiting," she said simply. She pushed the truck door open, slid to the ground, and I watched as she made her way inside and carefully shut the door.

(End of Cassette)

Moses

MILLIE *HADN'T* BEEN at the fight. I realized that now. At the time I was too amped on the energy of the crowd and the hype of the big event to notice a missing female, especially when she wasn't *my* female.

Georgia hadn't gone either. She'd kissed me and told me that babies and brawling didn't mix so I should go without her. She said she and Kathleen would stay home and do girl stuff. I knew that 'girl stuff' basically meant that Georgia would feed and bathe Kathleen, rock her to sleep, and go to bed early herself, but I let her talk me into it.

So I was running solo, sitting on the very front row with a few Tag Team members who weren't working Tag's corner, when Tag strutted into the arena to a Waylon Jennings song about cowboys being hard to love and harder to hold. The crowd cheered and joined in on the chorus, and Tag egged them on. It made me laugh. I was so nervous for him I was practically seeing double, and he was acting like a big gorilla, monkeying it up to the packed house, his smile wide, his muscles bulging. He didn't seem nervous at all, and when he caught my eye he smirked and pounded his chest.

Bruno Santos, on the other hand, entered the arena cloaked in a shimmery white robe with a hood so deep the only thing visible was the tip of his chin. His song of choice was something so bass heavy I couldn't make out the lyrics, though I caught the words "destruction" and "annihilation." He was hopping on the balls of his feet, shrugging his shoulders and tossing his neck, and I suddenly wished I'd stayed home with Georgia. Caring about people was a pain in my ass. Watching Tag fight was a bigger pain in my ass. My stomach turned over, and I glared at my friend, willing him to put me out of my misery as soon as possible.

Of course he didn't. But he battled. He battled hard and ugly, taking as many blows as he dished out, and as usual, he seemed to fight better after he'd taken a couple swipes to the face. Like the song said, he was hard to hold onto. But he definitely wasn't hard to love. The crowd was solidly on his side, and when he came back from a close call in the fourth round, escaping a near arm-bar that had made my stomach shake and my eyes water, the crowd was in a frenzy.

And then, when it looked like it would end in a decision, a decision that wouldn't favor the challenger—they so rarely did—Tag caught Santos in the temple with a booming roundhouse that wowed the crowd and rocked his opponent. Santos stumbled, and Tag was all over him, his fists flying, Santos covering his head, not returning the blows. And then it was over. TKO for Taggert. I was out of my seat, screaming and jumping with the rest of the team, delirious with relief and overjoyed with the upset.

Funny, it never even occurred to me that Millie wasn't there, but I'd definitely noticed that Tag didn't stick around when it was all over. He was all business at the end, interviews and congratulations, hand-grabbing and palm-greasing. But he left when I left—I walked him to his truck—and the party went on without us. I went home to my wife, and clearly, he went home to Millie.

Fourteen

IT TOOK ME about two hours after the fight ended to keep my promise. I had an interview, a shower, a deep muscle rub-down, and another series of interviews before I could separate myself from the celebratory atmosphere and head for Millie's. I was sore, and I'd popped a couple ibuprofens, but the adrenaline was still pumping, and I wanted to see my girl.

They must have been watching for me, because Henry shot out the front door and was buzzing around me before I was all the way out of my truck. Millie had her stick and was on the porch, waiting for me, just like she'd promised.

"Tag!" Henry was clicking his fingers again, obviously thrilled to see me. "Forty percent of Light Heavyweight fights end in TKO's or KO's," he recited. It was nice to see he had the lingo down. I put my arm around his shoulders and pulled him back toward the house.

"Amelie cried the whole fight. Then I told her your nose was bleeding, and she covered her ears."

"Henry," Amelie sighed, rebuking him. But she reached out her hand for me, and I took it, releasing Henry and pulling her toward me, tucking her against my body, under my right arm as we all entered the foyer and shut the door behind us.

"The referee stopped the fight! Did he stop the fight because you were going to kill Santos? Did it make you mad when he made your nose bleed?" Henry shadow boxed around the foyer.

"Nah, it just made me fight harder." I laughed at Henry's wild-eyed recap.

"Everyone was yelling Tag Team! I started yelling it too! The whole crowd had on Tag Team shirts!" Henry was so animated he was practically levitating. I remembered the shirt that was still clutched in my right hand.

"That reminds me! Here, I got you one." I tossed it to Henry, and he caught it and pulled it on, right over the Kobe Bryant jersey he was wearing. The shirt silenced him momentarily, and he admired himself in the ornate mirror hanging to the right of the staircase.

"I brought you one too, Millie," I murmured, "But I left it in my truck. It's your favorite color."

"Does it say, 'My boyfriend fought Santos, and all I got was this lousy T-shirt?'" she said drily, a smile playing around her lips.

"Oh man, that's cold!" I drawled, but I leaned in and touched my mouth to hers, wrapping both of my arms around her. She returned my embrace and held on tight, her face buried in my chest.

"I forgive you," she whispered. "But I'm never staying home again. That was the single most agonizing experience of my life."

"I told you I would win. And then I'd come here. And here I am," I said, nuzzling her hair.

"Will you marry us, Tag?" Henry asked intently, inserting himself back in the conversation.

"What?" I wasn't sure I had heard him right.

"Will you marry Millie and be my brother?" he repeated, his expression completely serious. He wasn't messing around. "We want to be part of Tag Team."

I laughed and looked down at Millie. Her face was frozen. Her back had stiffened the moment the words left Henry's mouth, and she pulled free of my arms. She reached for the stick she'd set aside, as if she needed something besides me to hold onto.

"Statistically, athletes with solid family units have better stamina, more purpose, better mental health, and overall improved performance than athletes who are either divorced or unmarried," Henry rambled off robotically, and I tore my gaze from Millie's stunned face.

"Did you make that up, Henry?" I grinned.

Henry looked confused, as if making up sports trivia to support his arguments was impossible. Maybe it was. Maybe in Henry's world, where lines and facts were clearly drawn, lying wasn't even feasible.

"You're already part of Tag Team, Henry," I said gently. "You've got the shirt to prove it. I'll get you as many as you want, in every color, and you can be in my corner any time."

Henry tilted his head to the side, considering my offer, but the disappointment was evident in his expression. Millie turned around and, fumbling for the front door, exited the house in a rush.

"Millie!" I called after her, but she didn't hesitate, and I could hear her stick clicking and clacking down the sidewalk in front of the house.

"Ah, Henry. You've gone and done it now." I laughed, and my laughter surprised me. So did my relative non-reaction to the 'M' word. When girls started dropping hints about any type of commitment, it was always the last time I asked them out. Always. I was great at playing tag. No one ever caught me.

I guess I'd always thought I would marry someday. When I was eighty. Yet Henry was proposing, and it didn't alarm me in the slightest. In fact, the thought of marrying Millie made my pulse quicken. It made my palms tingle. It made my heart smile so big I could feel the edges of the grin poking me in the ribs. That, or I was starting to feel the hurt from the Santos fight.

"Because they both lost so many players to WWII military service, the Pittsburgh Steelers and Philadelphia Eagles combined to become the Steagles during the 1943 season," Henry recited.

"What? The Steagles?" My eyes were on Henry, but I needed to chase Millie down.

Henry nodded, straight-faced. "We could do that. We could combine. We could be the Taggersons."

"That's a very interesting idea, Henry." I nodded, biting my lip so I wouldn't laugh. "But I need to convince Millie. I'm not sure she wants to be a Taggerson just yet."

"Andert?" Henry offered another combination, wrinkling his nose, and then shaking his head, as if it didn't have the same ring.

"Give me a minute to see what Millie thinks. Okay?"

Henry gave me a solemn thumbs up and sat down on the bottom stair to wait for the verdict.

I ran out the door and down the walk to the street, looking right and left down the sidewalk, hoping Millie hadn't gone beyond where I could easily find her. I spotted her about half a block down.

"Millie!" She looked like she was headed for the church, and I loped to catch up, calling after her, feeling every single blow I'd taken that night as I chased her down.

"Millie! Wait, sweetheart. You're killing me." She stopped but didn't turn around. She held herself stiffly, holding her stick vertically the way she'd held it the very first time I saw her outside the bar, the silent shepherdess once more.

"Millie." I slowed to a walk and approached her, wrapping my hands around hers so we both clung to her stick, like two people on a subway, sharing the same pole. Then I pulled gently, taking the stick from her hands, so she would hold onto me instead.

"Why you runnin' away?"

"The question is, why aren't you?" she asked, biting her lip.

"Do you want to be a Taggerson, Millie?" I whispered, freeing her lip with my teeth and kissing it better.

"A what?" she breathed.

"Or maybe an Andert?" I brushed my mouth over hers again, and her lips opened slightly, waiting for me to apply a little pressure.

"Henry seems to think we should merge our names," I explained.

Millie groaned, and I could feel the embarrassment coming off her in waves.

"Henry really needs to quit asking grown men to marry him," she complained.

"Yeah . . . he's a little young for that kind of commitment." I pressed another kiss on her upper lip, then one on her lower lip, soothing her, reassuring her, and for several long minutes there was no conversation at all.

"David?" she whispered when I finally let her breathe.

"Yeah?" I sank back into her, not able to help myself. She tasted like cold water and warm wishes, and I was drowning and basking, my fight forgotten, the swelling on my cheekbone and the tenderness in my ribs completely non-existent.

"I'm in love with you," Millie confessed softly. I felt her words on my lips and the shape of them in my head, and we both stood completely still, letting them whirl around us. The air was suddenly blooming, alive, a riotous explosion of color and sound. The world was magic, and I was king.

"I'm in love with you too," I said, no hesitation whatsoever. The words slid out of my mouth with the absolute ease of total truth.

Holy shit.

I was in love with Amelie Anderson. I was in love with a blind girl, and everything was in sharp focus.

Millie drew back and smiled, a big, dazzling grin that had me smiling too.

"Does this mean you'll wear my T-shirt?" I asked.

"Proudly," she answered.

Standing in the middle of the sidewalk, the streetlight creating a pool of soft white around us, I kissed Millie with every intention of never letting her go. Ever.

I walked her back home and there was no more talk of Taggersons or Anderts that night. Millie sternly informed Henry that he was too young for marriage, and he would just have to be happy with the T-shirt. He'd seemed a bit irritated by that, and I shrugged at him, like it wasn't my decision. I made sure he had a T-shirt for every day of the week, and one for Ayumi too, and that seemed to appease him slightly.

But the seed had been planted.

I'd only known Millie for two months, yet I was surer of her than I'd ever been of anything in my life. I was halfway down the aisle and just waiting for her to catch up with me.

IN THE DAYS that followed the Santos fight, things got more hectic, not less, and the frenzy had me running on empty. I was tired for the first time in my life. It was kind of a strange sensation. I found that I really just wanted to be with Millie and Henry, and I spent more time at their place than my own. In fact, it started to feel like home. So much so that I fell asleep on the couch one night watching a game with Henry, and woke up to music.

Millie sat on the floor in the middle of the living room, her back to me, and her guitar cradled in the well of her folded legs. The game was clearly over, and Henry had obviously given up on me and gone to bed. I would have to make it up to him, though I didn't mind missing the game. I'd never been much of a spectator anyway. I preferred to play.

I watched Millie pick her way through a couple songs, her head tilted toward the guitar like she liked the way the strings squeaked. She held the guitar upright, the neck almost vertical, and I listened, not commenting, letting her think I was still sleeping. She was always surprising me. I knew she could play, but she was pretty damn good.

"Why haven't you ever played for me before?" I asked quietly, my voice drowsy and content.

"You're awake," she said, and I could hear the smile in her voice.

"I'm awake, you're beautiful, and you need to come here."

She ignored me, her fingers finding their way across the strings. "If you were a chord, David, what chord would you be?" she mused, playing one chord after another.

I listened as she experimented.

"Oh, here's a good, sad one," she said, strumming softly.

"You think I'm sad?" I asked.

"Nah. Definitely not. That's not your chord. No minor chords for you."

"Absolutely not. I'm a major chord all the way. A major chord and a major stud." She laughed and I sighed. I didn't know what time it was, but the golden glow of the nearby lamp and the warm strings made my eyes heavy and my heart light.

"This is Henry's chord." Millie played something dissonant and curious, and I laughed out loud because it made total sense. "But you would be something deeper," she added.

"Because I'm a sexy man," I drawled.

"Yep. Because you're a sexy man. And we would want something with a little twang to it."

"Because I'm a sexy Texan."

"A sexy Utah Texan." She tried a few more, laughing and scrunching up her nose as she tried to find just the right chord. "And we need something sweet."

"Sweet and violent?" I asked.

"Sexy, twangy, sweet and violent. This might be more difficult than I thought," she said, still giggling.

She strummed something full and throaty, picking over each string and then strumming them together. "There it is, hear that? That's Tag."

"I like it," I said, pleased.

She stretched her hand, her pinky finger clinging to the bottom string and the chord changed subtly, another layer, a slightly different sound, like the chord wasn't quite yet resolved. "And that's David."

I sat down behind her on the floor and grabbed her folded thighs, pulling her back into me so that I cradled her the way she cradled the guitar. She leaned back against my chest, tucked her head to one side of my chin, and continued fingering the chords she'd named after me.

"Let me hear your song, Millie."

"You mean my chord?"

"Nah. Your song. You're a woman. Women don't have just one chord."

She laughed softly and bopped me in the head with the neck of the guitar. "I'm glad you know that, but I'm kind of wishing you didn't know quite so much about women. Makes me wonder how you gained all that knowledge. And I get a little jealous."

"I grew up with three sisters and one very opinionated, feisty mother. I learned early."

"Good answer, big guy."

"It's the truth, sweetheart. So play it. Play your song."

"I haven't written it yet."

"Will you put my chord in your song?"

"Why does that sound so suggestive?" She was smiling, but there was something wistful in her voice.

"Because I'm a sexy man."

"I'll put your chord in my song. Both of them, Tag and David. And I'll put Henry's in it too."

"What about your mom? Did she have a chord?"

Millie moved her hand immediately and played something warm and soft, something happy yet plaintive. "That's my mom, that chord there. Do you recognize it?"

I thought for a minute. "Is it part of her song?"

"It's part of an old country song. It's the very first chord of 'Blue Eyes Crying in the Rain.'"

I sang a couple bars of the song. I knew it well.

"That's it. I love that song. My mom had blue eyes, just like me and Henry. And she didn't spend a lot of time crying, thank goodness. She spent a lot of time loving. But there was longing in her too. She wanted to protect us. She wanted to save us from hurt. She wanted to give us back the things that had been taken from us or denied us. She longed for it. And she couldn't do it. No matter how much she loved us, she couldn't do it."

"I guess none of us can."

"No. None of us can. She told me something before she died, and I think about it sometimes when I'm having a hard time. She said that all her life she just wanted to save us from suffering. That was her job as a mom —save us from suffering, but we suffered anyway." Millie paused as if she were remembering the conversation, and I wanted to kiss her mouth, kiss that lower lip that trembled just a bit with the emotional memory. I pressed my lips to the curve of her cheek instead, afraid that if I kissed her mouth I'd never hear the end of her story.

"And then she said, 'I wanted to save you and Henry from suffering, but I've come to realize that your suffering has made you better people.' She was dying, and she was watching us come to terms with the fact that we were going to lose her."

"And what do you think? Does suffering make us better people?" I asked.

"It all depends on the person, I suppose," she mused.

"Maybe it depends on the amount of suffering too," I added, stroking a hand over her hair.

"And whether you have people holding your hand along the way, sharing the burdens, shouldering some of the pain." She leaned into my hand.

"Did you have that, Millie?" I asked quietly.

"I did. My mom may not have been able to keep me from suffering, and I certainly couldn't keep her from suffering, or Henry, for that matter. But we loved each other, and that made the suffering bearable."

"I want to be that for you, Millie. I want to carry you. I want you to give it all to me," I said, and then sang a little Rolling Stones in her ear, changing the lyrics just a bit.

"Let me be your beast of burden, my back is broad to ease your hurtin,'" I sang, kissing her earlobe. I would love her and keep her safe, and I swore to myself then that I would do the impossible. There would be no more suffering for Amelie Anderson. I would be the one shouldering all the shit.

She let me nuzzle her neck for a minute, humming happily.

"There are some other words in that song, David. He asks if he's enough. If he's enough for her. So I am asking you, Tag. Am I enough? Because I'm not too blind to see."

The bridge of the song she quoted cartwheeled through my mind and I shook my head, amazed. I'd forgotten the line about being too blind.

"Am I tough enough? Am I hard enough?" I sang, more than a little turned on.

"So are you going to give it all to me too, big guy? The good, the bad, and the ugly? Because I want it all." I smiled at her earnest delivery, her heartfelt declaration, and tried not to laugh at the sexual innuendo. She had no idea. So I wouldn't crack up.

I pulled the guitar from her hands and laid it on the floor.

"You're more than enough, Silly Millie."

She turned in my arms and found my face with her hands before she let her lips touch mine. I kissed her as Mick Jagger crooned the line about drawing the curtains and making sweet love somewhere in the back of my mind.

(End of Cassette)

Moses

"HELLO, DOC? IT'S Moses Wright."

"Moses! It's so good to hear from you." Dr. Andelin's voice was deep and butter warm, the way it always was, and I marveled at his ability to make people feel instantly safer, better, heard. He'd been a squeaky new psychologist when I first met him at Montlake—maybe twenty-six or twenty-seven years old—but he had that way about him that made you feel like his soul had lived a million lives. He was wise and kind, and Tag and I were both pretty fond of him. But I pushed through the niceties that Tag was so much better at, interrupting Noah Andelin even though I knew it was rude and he would think I'd lost all the ground I'd gained since being a surly eighteen-year-old in his care at Montlake.

"Doctor Andelin, I know Tag's seen you on a fairly regular basis since we came back to Utah. And I know you can't tell me what you talked about. I get that. Doctor-patient confidentiality and all that stuff. I don't need to know what Tag's said to you or what you've said to him. But he's gone, Doctor Andelin. He just split suddenly. He's in love with a great girl who loves him back, but I keep seeing his sister. I keep seeing his sister, Doc, and I don't have to tell you why that scares me to death."

I wasn't connecting my thoughts very well, but the swift intake of breath on the end of the line confirmed that Noah Andelin was keeping up with me.

"In your professional opinion, would he hurt himself? I mean. He's not suicidal," I stopped suddenly, because I realized I didn't know if that was true. Listening to Tag, I had no idea if he was emotionally back in the corridors of Montlake, wanting to escape himself. I amended my statement. "I mean, he's not suicidal like he was. In some ways, Tag is the healthiest guy I know. But he has a crazy streak, and he's great at saving everyone else and not always very good at taking care of himself. He just took off so suddenly. Where do you think he'd go? Do you have any advice that could help me find him?"

Dr. Andelin didn't answer immediately, and I could picture him with his hand against his face, his head tilted, just thinking.

"How do you know he isn't just . . . taking a break?" Dr. Andelin finished inanely, as if trying to come up with a viable alternative.

"He's left us some cassettes. The girl he's been seeing is blind. So he's recorded himself, talking to her, basically."

"Amelie," Dr. Andelin supplied, and I realized Tag had consulted with him on something.

"So you know about her."

"Yes. I saw him a month ago. He was—" Dr. Andelin stopped, as if trying to carefully negotiate confidentiality. "He was happier than I have ever seen him. This is . . . unexpected."

"Would it help you to hear the tapes?" I was desperate. I hoped Millie wouldn't object.

"Has he given you any reason to believe there is anything you can do?" Dr. Andelin asked quietly.

"What?" I felt the anger surge through my veins, and I wanted to throw my phone against the wall.

"How long has it been since anyone has seen him?" Dr. Andelin's voice was unbearably gentle.

"More than two weeks," I whispered.

Fifteen

"TAG?" LISA LOOKED a little harried, her eyes wide, her hands shaking. "Uh, I think we've got a problem. Morgan . . . Morgan is in the lounge. He's been drinking for the last few hours, and he's starting to get abusive. I didn't want to get him in trouble. Morg's my friend. I don't know what happened with his job, but, well—" I was around the bar, tossing instructions at Vince and moving down the hall and into the lounge with Lisa trotting after me, making all kinds of excuses for Morgan.

The music was thumping—something guttural and earthy, and Amelie was in the octagon, twirling and swaying around the tall pole, a determined smile pinned to her face. But unlike the first time I'd seen her dance, and every time I'd watched her dance since, her eyes were open, and her movements seemed stiff. She clearly wasn't enjoying herself.

"I'm not liking what I see!" a voice bellowed out. "Are you liking what you see, princess?" Laughter. "Get Danielle back out here!"

The other patrons had stopped watching Amelie and were peering, hands over their eyes in the direction of the corner booth. The dim lighting made it hard to make him out, and the loud bass camouflaged his taunts, but Morgan was doing his best to be heard, and the charged atmosphere in the room had nothing to do with sexual tension or the scantily clad dancer performing a seductive routine under a spotlight.

He was so intent on heckling Amelie, he didn't see me coming. So when I reached over the back of the booth and grabbed him around the ears and yanked upward, he came to his feet with a yelp of pain and surprise.

Lady Gaga was singing about having a poker face and Amelie was trying to take her advice, dancing like a wind-up doll, unable to see the cause of the drama unfolding in front of her. I was extremely grateful for that. Lisa squealed and Morgan roared as I dragged him across his table, sending empty bottles crashing and upending two chairs at another, thankfully unoccupied, table.

A few customers clapped and whistled as I locked my arm around Morgan's head and headed for the emergency exit. I pushed through the door as the final bars of Amelie's number played out. I didn't hang around to see the spotlight on the cage dim to black or the lounge lights softly rise, which was customary as a new dancer took her place in the cage. I wanted Morgan out of sight and out of ear-shot before I beat the hell out of him. But as we barreled through the doors and out into the cold night, both breathing hard, both angry, Morgan, off balance and clinging to my forearm around his neck with one hand, swung at me with his other. It was a Hail Mary, a desperation shot, but there happened to be a beer bottle in his hand, and that beer bottle connected with my forehead with a resounding crack.

The blow stunned me, and I went down to one knee, pulling Morgan with me. Blood filled my eyes, and rage filled my head.

"You gonna tell me what that was about, Morg? You gonna tell me why you decided to come back?"

I swiped at the blood on my forehead with one arm and ground Morgan's head into the ground with the other.

"I want my job . . . I want my job back," he wailed, pushing on my hand. "I just thought I'd have a drink or two first, to get my courage up to ask for it back. I watched Danielle and Crysti dance. Then I had a few more. Then *she* came out. It just made me mad that she still had a job and I didn't. Where's your loyalty, Tag? I don't get it, man."

My vision was starting to swim and my head had started to pound like Morg had taken Thor's hammer to it, instead of a bottle of Bud. Someone burst through the exit doors and I stood, releasing Morgan and swaying on my feet. I wasn't going to go down. Losing consciousness meant a concussion in the fight world. Concussion meant mandatory down time and testing. I didn't have time for that. Vince and Leo were suddenly at my sides, looking down at Morgan who still lay on the ground in front of me, as if he didn't know what to do with himself. His eyes were wide as he took in the blood pouring from the wound he'd inflicted. I pulled off my black T-shirt, mopped the blood from my eyes, and pressed it to the gash in my head. It felt like the Grand Canyon beneath my fingers and my stomach roiled and shifted.

"Don't come back, Morg. I'm all about second chances. But that? In there? That was it. That was your second chance, and you repeated all your mistakes. You've shown your colors, and I don't like the way you look in them. I don't want you around."

A trip to the ER was just where I wanted to spend my evening. They had to dig glass fragments out of my forehead, and that hurt worse than the actual blow to my head. The shot of Novocain wasn't a picnic either. But I kept my eyes open and my mouth moving as the emergency room doctor stitched me up.

"You're going to look a little like Frankenstein," the doctor said good-naturedly. "You've got thirty stitches holding your forehead together. It's right at your hairline though, and I'm guessing the scar will be pretty well hidden. I'm more worried about concussion. Your head is extremely swollen, your pupils still haven't returned to normal, and I know you think you're fooling me, but your speech is wobbly and so are your knees. I think we need to order an MRI just to be safe. In fact, I'm going to insist on it."

"That's my drawl, Doc. That's just how I sound, and I'm tired. I've been up for eighteen hours and an MRI isn't quick, right?" I'd had an MRI in high school when a bull I attempted to stay on for eight seconds, a bull named Ginger, sent me careening into a fence a few seconds after my butt hit his back. Less than eight seconds to warrant a test that had taken forever. I had learned I was claustrophobic and that I didn't especially want to ride bulls anymore.

Plus, I was feeling fine, and I wanted to see Amelie. She would be wondering where I was. Leo had run me to the hospital and Vince had gone back inside, while the new guy, Chuck, made sure Morgan went home. Everyone had been firmly instructed to keep their mouths shut. Millie didn't need to be worrying about me getting my head bashed in. For all she knew, she'd had a heckler, and he'd been removed. I told my employees as much. I would tell her an abbreviated version of events and leave Morgan's name out altogether. But her shift had ended hours ago, and I hadn't been there to walk her home for the first time since we'd met. I'd texted her and told her I'd come when I could—she had an app on her phone that announced her messages and read them aloud when she tapped the screen. I purposely made my texts ridiculous because it was so funny to hear the canned voice relay my messages. She'd responded with song lyrics about waking her up, and I responded with a demand that she go to sleep.

"I'll let you go home as soon as you're done. This will give us another hour of observation too. Humor me, Tag. In your line of work, sparring day in and day out, you can't mess around with a head injury."

I grumbled and resisted, but the doctor was adamant, and I finally decided it would be easier to give in than to keep arguing.

In the end, the ER doc got pulled out on an emergency, a tech wheeled me in, and I spent a grueling forty-five minutes trying to stay calm inside a tube while pictures were taken of my brain. It was three a.m. before I walked out of the hospital, the tech promising that a radiologist would read the results, talk to the doctor who'd ordered the test, and someone would be calling me. I waved it all off. Other than the dull ache in my forehead and a desperate need for a shower, I felt absolutely fine. The nurse who handled my discharge asked if I had someone who could stay with me and wake me up every so often, just to be safe.

Leo had fallen asleep in the waiting room, and I didn't want to put him out any more than I already had. Plus, Millie was the only one I was interested in spending the night with, even the few hours of the night remaining. Leo dropped me off at home and I took a bath, carefully washing the blood out of my hair, and made it to Millie's at about four a.m.

Maybe I shouldn't have been driving, but I felt fine and I didn't want to stay away any longer. I knew where the spare key to Millie's front door was stashed, the key Henry had shown me with all the seriousness of a man with a highly important secret. He kept it tucked inside a latticework curlicue, directly across from the door, and I felt for it in the darkness, finding it easily and mentally thanking Henry for entrusting me with the keys to the house.

I opened the door and put the key back in Henry's spot before I slid into the dark foyer and tiptoed up the staircase.

I turned on the light in her room, a definite perk of loving a blind girl, and found her sprawled across her bed, her phone by her head, her arms wrapped around a pillow like she didn't want to be alone. I flipped the light back off, pulled off my shoes, and padded to her side in the darkness. I laid down beside her, pulled the spare pillow from her arms and stuck it beneath my head, and rolled her into me, settling her on my chest to compensate for the theft of her pillow.

"Hey," she said sleepily, but the pleasure in her voice warmed me.

"Hey. Go back to sleep. I didn't want to wake you. I just wanted to see you."

"I want to see you too," she mumbled, and her hands immediately began exploring, making me feel immediately less sleepy. This was a first for us, sleeping side by side, and that was as far as it was going to go, though her sleepy sighs and roving hands had me considering options. I should have known she would discover my bandage immediately.

"What's this?" she asked, her fingers cradling my head.

"That's a few stitches I got when a drunk heckler decided to smack me in the forehead with his beer bottle."

She sat up immediately.

"*My* drunk heckler?" she asked, incredulous.

I didn't answer.

"So that's where you were? The hospital? Why didn't anyone tell me? Why didn't you tell me?"

"I didn't want you to worry."

"But . . . but . . . I'm your girl, right? So that's my job. That's what people do when they care about each other. They worry!" Her voice rose, and I shushed her immediately, smoothing her hair. We'd had this argument before.

"People that care about each other don't cause unnecessary worry. I'm fine. I'm here. And I'm going to have an awesome scar for you to trace when it's all healed up."

Millie pushed my hand away and rose from the bed, retreating to the bathroom without a word. She shut the door a little harder than necessary, and I tried not to laugh. Millie was a typical female when it came to showing her displeasure. She wasn't happy I'd kept her in the dark. I heard her

155

flush the toilet and listened as she slammed around for several minutes. When she finally clomped out of the bathroom and laid down beside me once more, I feigned sleep just to see what she would do. She lay stiffly beside me for several minutes and then turned into me, wrapping her arm around my waist.

"I know you're not asleep," she whispered.

"How can you tell?"

"You're too still and you're listening too hard."

"You can hear me listening?"

"People take very shallow breaths or they don't breathe at all when they are really listening."

"I'm trying to hear your thoughts."

"I'm mad."

"You must not be too mad. You brushed your teeth even though you didn't need to. Which means you want to kiss me. Which means you are planning on forgiving me."

"I'm mad because I really like you. And I want to kiss you because I really like you."

"You're mad because you like me?

"I'm mad because I love you," she confessed with a sigh. "And you didn't let me know you were hurt."

"Well, I love you too, Millie. And I'm always going to try to protect you. That's who I am. That's what I do. If you knew I was getting a few stitches in my head, you wouldn't have been laying here fast asleep, so sweet and so soft I could eat you. You would have been chewing on this lip, worrying, instead of dreaming about me." I leaned in and tugged on her lower lip with my teeth, gently mimicking her tendency to bite her lip when she was concerned. I kissed her pouting mouth and felt her anger slip away as I slid my tongue beneath her lips.

Our breaths grew short and our bodies restless, and it was Millie who pulled away first, clearly not quite ready to extend this night of firsts. I closed my eyes and willed my heart to still as she stroked my head, her fingers slipping through my hair and easing the dull ache still lurking behind my eyes.

"David?" she whispered.

"Yeah?"

"Sing me a song."

"What kind of song, baby?"

"A love song."

"Millie, Millie, You're so silly. I'm so glad your name's not Willy," I sang in my best country twang.

"Willy?"

"Let me rephrase." I cleared my throat and began again. "Millie, Millie, you're so silly, I'm sure glad you don't have a willy."

"That's not a love song," she giggled.

"Okay. How about this? I love your legs. I love your chest, but this spot here, I love the best." I tickled her smooth stomach and she squirmed against me.

"Keep singing!" she demanded, swatting my hand away.

"I love your chin and your funny grin, I love your hair and that spot there." I tickled her beneath her right rib and she grabbed my fingers, laughing.

"I love it! Second verse, please."

"I love the way you shake your booty, I love the way you smell so fruity! I love the way you call me David, and . . . . la la la nothing rhymes with David."

"That was beautiful," she giggled. "What's it called?"

"It's called 'Nothing Rhymes with David.'"

"Nothing rhymes with David?" Her voice was disbelieving, and she was quiet for several seconds, as if trying to find a word that rhymed to prove me wrong. Then she stroked the side of my face, her fingers tracing my jawline, and when she spoke again her voice was as earnest as her touch.

"It makes me feel close to you, listening to you."

"Is that why you always want me to sing? I thought it was my honeyed tones." I joked, but my throat was suddenly tight, too tight to sing.

"It's more than that. You can't see a song. You feel a song, you hear a song, you move to it. Just like I can't see you, but I feel you, and I move toward you. When you're with me, I feel like I glimpse a David nobody else knows is there. It's the Song of David, and nobody else can hear it but me."

My heart shuddered and then grew twice its size, a Hulk-like shredding and popping sensation filling my chest, and I wrapped her in my arms and buried my face in her neck.

"Nah. That's not me. That's the ode, Millie. I feel it too, every single time you're close to me."

"The ode, huh? That's what you call it?"

"That's what I call it."

"I think I'll stick with the Song of David. It's my favorite," she said, speaking the words against my cheek.

"If I sing, you have to dance," I whispered, and my mouth found hers, and the music between us became an urgent hum, a rhythmic pulse, and we danced around the fires between us until sleep slowed our steps and muted our song and softly pulled us under.

(End of cassette)

Moses

MILLIE STOOD AND with no warning, lifted the tape recorder above her head and threw it to the ground as if she couldn't bear to hear another word. The back of the tape recorder sprang off when it hit the ground, and the fat D batteries rolled out like wounded soldiers, their tank disabled, their weapons depleted.

Georgia and I stood watching, unable to form a coherent response. Millie was shaking with fury, and her eyes were bright with tears.

"I don't know what to think, anymore. I don't know what to do! We're sitting here listening to him tell us a story that I wholeheartedly believed two weeks ago. But he's gone. I'm actually . . . embarrassed. I've called you, interrupted your lives, and made a big deal about the fact that he's gone. But he obviously chose to leave!" Millie took several ragged breaths, but then her chin hit her chest, and the rage seemed to leave her as quickly as it had come.

"The worst part is . . . I actually hope it's just that he doesn't know how to tell me he changed his mind. I actually hope he woke up and realized he wasn't in love with me after all. I hope that's it. Because I can't think of an alternative that isn't a hundred times worse. And I'd rather lose him than lose him."

I knew exactly what she meant.

My phone pealed out mercifully, and Georgia knelt to put the batteries back in the tape recorder as I excused myself to take the call.

"Mikey," I greeted, slipping out the front door.

"Moses," he said in reply. "I've got news."

My heart did a belly flop.

"Tag is fighting in Vegas tomorrow. At the MGM. Cory caught the weigh-in on ESPN this morning. Apparently he's a last minute substitution. It's a big fight, Moses. A huge fight. It's the Terry Shaw versus Jordan Jones match-up. But now it's Terry Shaw versus Tag Taggert."

My mouth fell open, and I actually pulled the phone away from my ear and looked at it, as if Mikey wasn't really Mikey and my phone wasn't really a phone.

"Son-of-a-bitch," I hissed, and pressed the phone against my ear once more.

"That's what I said. We're all reeling. We don't know what to think, man. He's fighting, and none of us knew. We're his team. What the hell is he doing, Moses?"

"I have no idea, Mikey," I breathed. I felt lightheaded with relief that we'd found him, and sick with dread about what was coming next.

"Should we go? Should we drive to Vegas and just confront him?"

I could tell Mikey was pissed. And confused.

"How hard is it to get close to a fighter at the MGM if you don't have a pass, if you don't have clearance?" I asked doubtfully.

Mikey swore, and I nodded to myself. That wasn't going to work. If Tag didn't want his team there, they weren't going to get to him.

"Is everyone there, Mikey, all the guys?" I asked.

"Yeah, everybody but Paulo. But the rest of us are here, Moses."

"Hang tight. I'll be there in five."

I called into the house, letting Georgia know I was heading out for a minute. I wasn't ready to tell Millie what I'd just learned. I needed to know more. Judging from her attempt to smash the tape recorder, she had reached an emotional peak. Even still, the tape recorder was back on, clearly none the worse for wear. I could hear Tag speaking like he'd never left, and my anger spiked again.

I walked through the doors of the training gym four minutes later and headed for the office. As Mikey had promised, all the guys were assembled, and the footage was cued. It was a media zoo, just like all weigh-ins. The scale was center stage and one by one, each fighter took his position.

I watched as Tag stripped down with none of his usual smirk and swag. He was hard-faced and serious. No flashing dimples, no chest pounding, no nonsense. He stepped onto the scale in nothing but a Tag Team ball cap and a matching pair of fitted nylon shorts with Tag Team emblazoned in yellow across the butt. He stood as his weight was announced and then flexed his arms for the pictures. He looked lean and cut —thin—though that could be from cutting weight to hit the required 205.

"He looks skinny." Axel confirmed what I was thinking, although skinny was relative. Tag was big and muscular, ridiculously so, but there was something gaunt and hollowed out about his cheeks and hip bones. "His walking-around weight is easily 220 and he's at 203. What's he thinking, sucking off an extra two pounds?"

"He hasn't been in the gym for three weeks, that's why!" Cory exclaimed.

"And he's fighting freakin' Terry Shaw. This could be a bloodbath," Mikey moaned as we watched Shotgun Terry Shaw step onto the scale, looking surly and sour and cocky as hell. He shot Tag a look of disdain. Tag just ignored him altogether.

"No." Andy shook his head stubbornly. "Tag knows what he's doing." He folded his arms and stared us all down. "*We* just don't know what he's doin'. But I know one thing. I'm goin' to Vegas."

"Me too," Cory said.

"Count me in," Mikey agreed.

"I'll drive." Axel took out his phone as if the decision was made and reservations were in order.

"I gotta tell Millie," I sighed.

"What you gonna tell her, Moses?" Andy asked.

"Maybe we should go, see what's up, before you say anything," Axel suggested. His face was creased with concern and his big arms were folded across his chest. I had noticed that Axel was pretty protective of Millie, and Henry too, and I was pretty sure all the guys were thinking what I was thinking. Tag had run out on Millie. For whatever reason, he'd split, and now I had to tell her.

I shook my head slowly. "No, I can't do that. I have to tell her we found him."

Axel shook his head adamantly, like he couldn't believe any of it, and the rest of the guys kept their eyes trained on the floor.

My phone bleeped, indicating a text message, and I glanced down at it.

Georgia: Call me.

"Give me a second, guys," I said, excusing myself. Georgia picked up on the first ring.

"Moses?" Georgia's voice was tight.

"Yeah?"

"I think we know why he left. Come back to Millie's. You need to hear this for yourself."

Sixteen

I AWOKE TO a killer headache and a sense of well-being that completely belied the pain. Millie had let me sleep, though she'd gotten up with Henry for school and had been awake for hours, just waiting for me to roll out of bed. I liked the way it felt, coming awake in Millie's bed, listening for her in the house. I thought of the ring in my glove box and wondered if today wasn't as good a day as any to extend an official invitation to join Tag Team.

I staggered into her bathroom, considering how I would pop the question. One look at my reflection—both eyes black, my head swollen and ugly, the stitches across my forehead garish and spikey—and I decided it could wait until I felt a little better.

After a few kisses, a couple of pain killers, and a pile of fluffy eggs that Millie had expertly prepared, I was finally ready to start my workday, though it was almost noon. Millie had a full day too, and we parted at her front door, Millie going one way, me going another. She didn't want me to drive her to the blind center. She wanted to walk. Surprise, surprise. So I watched her walk away, enjoying the view enormously.

Millie didn't drag her stick from side to side when she walked. She tapped it, rapping it against the concrete, left foot forward, stick goes right. Right foot forward, stick goes left. Click, clack, click, clack. Maybe it was the dancer in her, but she liked creating a rhythm when she walked. Sometimes she bobbed her head, and wiggled her hips, even though anyone looking on would probably wonder at the blind girl shaking her butt to the rhythm of her walking stick. But she said she couldn't see them staring, she couldn't see them laughing, so she didn't care. Perks of being a blind girl.

"Hey, Silly Millie!" I called after her.

She stopped and turned around.

"Yeah, big guy?"

"What song you dancin' to?"

"It's a new one. Maybe you've heard it. It's called 'Nothing Rhymes with David.'"

I threw back my head, laughing at her quick wit and bellowing the song I'd composed the night before as she continued on her way. "I love the way you smell so fruity, I love the way you shake your booty!"

"That's the song!" she called out and wiggled a little more as she waved and continued down the sidewalk. My phone vibrated in my back pocket, and I answered it, still laughing at my girl.

"Mr. Taggert, this is Doctor Stein at LDS hospital. I had a chance to look over your MRI test results with radiology."

"Don't tell me. My brain is abnormally small," I teased, my mind not really on the conversation at all, but on Millie's retreating form. She made it hard for me to concentrate on anything else.

The doctor didn't laugh. That should have been my first clue. That and the fact that I'd left the hospital less than eight hours before and he was calling me himself. But in that moment, the moment before the news left the doctor's lips and my eyes left Millie, I was completely, perfectly happy. Life isn't perfect, people aren't perfect, but there are moments that are. And that was one of them. That moment was a bright red balloon filled with anticipation of what life would bring, of Millie and me and a million tomorrows. And then it ended. It popped with a loud crack, and the rubbery remnants of my perfect moment lay at my feet.

"I would like you to come back in. I want to run another test, focusing on the area of concern. There are some abnormalities, a shadow that needs some further investigation. This is not my area of expertise, so I've consulted a specialist, and he is actually available this afternoon. Could you come in an hour?"

I KNEW I was a little claustrophobic. I was claustrophobic for the same reason I was afraid of the dark. I had always attributed it to the asthma I'd had as a kid. Waking up in the middle of the night gasping for air, the feeling of being closed in, of not being able to take a deep breath. Of knowing you had to breathe or you would die, and not being able to. Claustrophobia was just another word for helplessness. I hated feeling helpless.

They told me not to move and I didn't, but I didn't breathe either, and they aborted the first attempt until I got my shit together.

"Is there someone we could call, Mr. Taggert? Someone you would like to be here?"

I shook my head. No. I didn't want a soul knowing I was here. They all thought I was okay. I had insisted I was okay. What was it Millie said about her blindness? The image in my head is the only one that matters? I was adopting that attitude. I was okay. And my opinion was the only one that mattered.

"Nah. It's good. I'm fine. Let's just do this." I found myself winking at the pretty nurse, putting on a show the way I always did. Distracting myself. She winked back. I knew she liked me. I could always tell when a girl found me attractive. The way their lips pursed, the way their eyebrows raised, the way their eyes darted. All the little clues and signals that I'd never gotten from Millie. And yet Millie loved me. Millie loved me, and I loved her.

"Whenever you start feeling trapped or helpless, just close your eyes, and you have more space than you'll ever need."

That's what Millie had told me. I tried to take her advice, closing my eyes and allowing the huge darkness to help me breathe. I had to be okay because if I wasn't, Millie was going to get hurt. And I had tried so hard to take it slow, to not rush her, to not rush us. To be absolutely sure I knew what I was doing. I had been careful for the first time in my life. I had been so careful. So cautious. And I was still going to hurt her. I felt panic rise in my chest and heard a voice telling me to breathe, to calm down.

"You're doing just fine, Mr. Taggert. You're almost there. You're almost done, Mr. Taggert."

"God? Oh God," I prayed. "I don't want to be done. Please don't let me be done. Please don't let me be done." I prayed like this all the time. It was my upbringing. Talking to God felt a little like having a conversation with myself, the inner me. I'd always believed God created that inner me, so talking to him was a bit like having a heart to heart with myself. No, I don't have a God complex. I just think most people make too big a deal about God, fighting wars to defend him or staging protests to deny him. He just seems like a good guy to me. I like talking to him.

I don't usually kneel when I pray, though I had when Moses almost died. I'd made all kinds of deals too. And I don't make deals with God—I know myself too well. I just ask him for stuff and thank him for stuff—no strings, no promises in return—so that I don't ring up a huge tab that I have to pay off at some point. I figure if He helps me, gives me what I need, it's because He thought I deserved it or wanted to give it to me. So I don't owe him anything. But I'd broken my rule for Moses. I guess that's what you did for the people you loved. You broke your rules. Moses had done it with Georgia. He'd smashed all his stupid laws. And I had broken mine. Not just with Moses, but with Millie. I had finally settled on one woman, and I was breaking my rules again now, begging God to forgive the tab. I'd made a deal for Moses, and I hadn't fulfilled my end of the bargain. Maybe God was calling it in.

"THERE'S A GIANT mass on your frontal lobe."

The doc didn't beat around the bush. He just pointed at pictures of my brain and spoke, very matter-of-factly. I could see the black mass he was outlining as clear as day. He turned to look at me.

"You haven't had trouble with your handwriting, trouble with speech . . . maybe weakness in your right side. It's off to the left side of your brain, which will always affect the opposite side of the body. You haven't had any symptoms?"

I wanted to say no, but the symptoms had been there. I just always rationalized them away. "I've been seeing spots when I'm tired, and I have noticed more muscle fatigue on the right side. My left hand has always been my dominant hand, so maybe that's why it didn't affect me as much. I've been training hard. I thought it was dehydration. Thought it was stress."

"You took a blow to the head in an altercation?"

"Yeah, to the forehead. It didn't even hurt, but it stunned me a little. It was a good thing he stopped swinging because I couldn't see a damn thing for about ten seconds. I just stood there while he laid on the ground, covering his head. My vision cleared once I mopped the blood off my face, and I could see again. I guess it was a good thing the guy was drunk and stupid."

"Guess so." His lips quirked, and I was glad he wasn't going to lecture me on the seriousness of the moment. I got it—the seriousness hadn't escaped me.

"So what do we need to do?" I asked.

"We have to get in there, see what the mass is, and remove as much of it as we can." He didn't call it a tumor. He called it a mass. But I wasn't stupid.

"Get in there?"

"Craniotomy. We put you out, drill a hole into your head, remove as much of the tumor as we can, take a section for biopsy, and stitch you up. It sounds a bit Frankenstein, but you can actually go home in a day or two. It's not something that requires a lot of recovery time."

"So it's no big deal?"

"I wouldn't go that far. We are talking about your brain, after all."

"And what are the risks? What if I don't want you drilling into my head?"

"The risk of leaving it there, of not determining whether it's cancer or not, could be fatal. If it is cancer and you don't treat it, it *will* be fatal. And then there are the risks that come with any type of surgery that involves the brain. Loss of memory, sight, motor functions . . . We're talking about the brain," he repeated.

I don't know what to do. I don't know what to do. I don't know what to do.

Idon'tknowwhattodoIdon'tknowwhattodo. The words became blurred and blended, and yet I couldn't shake them from my brain. The doctor urged me to move quickly. He said time was "of the utmost importance." He said we needed to act . . . And all I could do was shake my head.

"No," I'd said. "No."

"David. It's the only way we can move forward. We have to operate as soon as possible."

Millie was the only one who called me David.

"Tag. Call me Tag," I insisted numbly.

"Tag," he nodded agreeably. "Talk to your loved ones. Tell them what's happening. You need some support. And then we need to see what we're dealing with."

"What are the odds?"

"What do you mean?"

"This kind of mass—it's a tumor, isn't it?

"Yes. It is. We don't know if it's cancerous, but even benign tumors need to be removed."

"What are the odds?"

"That it's cancer?"

"Yes."

"I would be lying if I told you I believed it was benign."

"Have you ever seen a tumor in the brain that wasn't cancer?"

"Not personally. No"

No. No. No. No. There was an odd echoing in my ears and I couldn't sit still.

I stood and headed for the door.

"Tag?"

"I need to think, Doc."

"Please. Please don't think too long, Mr. Taggert. You have my number."

I jerked my head in a semblance of a nod and pushed out of his office and into the long, sterile hallway beyond.

I don't remember walking out of the hospital. I don't remember walking across the grounds or whether the sun was shining or whether rain fell. I remember pulling my seatbelt on and staring at the buckle in my hand and clicking it home carefully, as if it would protect me from the news I'd just received. I stuck the key in the ignition and backed out of the lot as my phone rang. I couldn't talk. I wouldn't be able to hide my agitation, but I clicked the speaker anyway almost desperate to avoid myself. I didn't look at the display, didn't know who was calling, but it delayed what came next.

"This is Tag," I barked, and then winced at the volume of my voice.

The echoing remained and I rubbed at my temple as if I could adjust the reverb in my head.

"Tag. It's Moses." With his voice on speaker it was like he was sitting beside me in my truck. I wished he was and was grateful he wasn't.

"'Sup, man?" I shot back and winced once more, this time because I was such a fake.

"You okay?" It was an I-demand-to-know question, not a polite how-are-you, and it shook me. It made me defensive too. How the hell did he know I wasn't okay?

"Yeah. Yeah. Why you askin'?" I pushed back.

"I saw Molly." Moses sucked at polite conversation.

My mind tripped over itself again.

"What?"

"I haven't seen Molly in years . . . not since Montlake. Last night I ended up painting a mural of David and Goliath, like something from a Sunday School story, instead of painting the picture I'd been commissioned to paint. Now I'm behind. And I blame you."

"Me?" I was only half listening as I backed out of the parking lot and began to drive. I didn't know where I was going.

"Yeah. You. The David in my mural looks suspiciously like you. So your dead sister is obviously trying to tell me something. That, or she doesn't like your chosen profession."

"David kicked Goliath's ass, remember? Nothing to worry about." I was conducting the conversation from a very mechanical, detached side of my brain, and I observed myself talking to Moses even as my thoughts were bouncing in a million different directions.

"I don't think Goliath's ass was involved," Moses growled. "If I remember right, it was his head. Goliath took a blow between the eyes."

"Yeah . . . right. That must be it. I got cracked between the eyes with a bottle of beer last night." Was it just last night? "Guy laid my head open. I have a few stitches. I'm impressed, Mo. So now you're a psychic too?"

"You okay?" There it was again. The demand to tell him everything.

"Yeah. All stitched up. Doesn't even hurt." I wasn't lying. It didn't hurt. But I was skirting the truth. I wasn't okay. Not at all.

"Well, that's not surprising. You have the hardest head of anyone I know. What happened?"

"Just someone heckling Millie while she was dancing. I grabbed him to throw him out, and he nailed me in the head." I didn't want Mo saying I told you so. He'd never liked Morgan. So I left Morgan's name out of it.

"Millie?" he asked.

"Millie," I answered.

He was quiet for a heartbeat, and I waited, wondering what he was stewing over.

"You there yet, Tag?" he asked.

"Where?"

A huge sigh seeped through the phone's speaker.

"Are you there yet?" he said again, louder, slower, so damn pushy.

"Yeah. I'm there. I love her. Is that what you want me to say?" My hands started to shake, and suddenly I couldn't see the road. A horn blared behind me, and I realized I had drifted out of my lane.

I swerved and swiped at my eyes, trying not to kill myself, at least not yet.

"I don't care what you say. I already knew. I'm happy for you, man. She's kind of a miracle."

"Yeah. She is." The tears were streaming down my cheeks, and I gripped the wheel with both hands.

"I wasn't sure you'd get one . . . or even that you needed one. But you did. We both did. How the hell did that happen?" He had relaxed with my confession, and I could hear the smile in his voice.

"You believe in miracles, Mo?" I wasn't smiling. I was searching.

"I got no choice. I've seen too much."

"You think I'll get more than one?" It was all I could do to spit the words out.

"More than one miracle? Why? Millie's not enough?" He laughed at me, but I heard the surprise too.

Millie was more than enough. I wasn't greedy. I just wanted to be around to enjoy my miracle.

Seventeen

⠿

Moses

TAG HAD ENDED that phone call too quickly. I should have realized something was wrong. But I could tell he was driving and had let him go without protest. I had thought he sounded off, but he'd had me on speaker, and everything sounds a little distorted when you're hearing someone that way. I thought that was all it was. I told myself that was all it was. I don't know when I started believing my own lies.

I had grown complacent with the dead. I painted them in pretty pictures, and they no longer hounded me like they once had. They weren't portends of destruction. They didn't look like zombies or haunt the halls of my house. They had become manageable. Life had become sweet and soft. Georgia had done that for me. She'd settled me and smoothed out my edges, and with the loss of those edges I guess I wasn't as sharp as I used to be.

So when I saw Molly Taggert, a soft mirage from the corner of my eye, I refused to be suspicious. Eight years, almost nine? It'd been a long time since she'd demanded my attention. I was in the middle of something, communing with the dead of a wealthy client. His dead were not particularly interested in keeping in touch, and I was pushing, opening myself up wider, trying to find inspiration, something worthy of a paint brush, something I could work with. So far, they were giving me the middle finger, and I didn't think that would please my client.

I told myself seeing Molly was nothing more than happenstance, that I'd simply opened myself up wide and attracted an old ghost who knew how to slip around my walls. She had flooded my mind with color, streaks of red fear and blue despair shot with purple-hued passion and green regret, all washed in white and dipped in black. Before I knew it, I was painting something completely irrational, completely at odds with the girl we'd laid to rest, years before.

Two hours later, I stepped back from the canvas and stared, dumbfounded, at the picture I'd created. It looked like something from one of my Grandma Kathleen's books, the ones she'd taken from the church library because they were a tad too erotic and disturbing for the people in the pews. It was David and Goliath in violent detail, and the details were troubling, the details were specific, and I'd let myself miss them.

So I'd called him. And I'd let him tell me what I wanted to hear. What I needed to hear. He said he'd taken a blow to the head. Such a clean, simple truth that left out all the pertinent details. All the violent details. The details were troubling, the details were specific, and I'd let myself miss them.

As Georgia requested, I came straight home from the gym, walked in the house, and without a word, my wife had cued the cassette tape. Then I listened to my conversation with my friend, I listened to all the things he hadn't told me. Now the fear was twisting in my gut, and I was pacing. Millie was standing when I arrived, as if Tag's revelation had lifted her out of her seat. Her face was petrified rock—layers of shock imprinted in her expression. By the time we reached the end of the tape and Tag's voice had broken, Millie broke with him, and she'd bowed her head, fumbled for her chair, and collapsed into it. Henry sat nearby, and for the first time, he seemed to be aware that something was very, very wrong.

"He came looking for you that night, Moses. Remember? You weren't home, and he didn't stay very long." Georgia's voice shook, and she held Kathleen to her chest, rocking and swaying, something she did even when she wasn't holding the baby. It had become a habit that I teased her about. Keep moving and the baby won't cry. Keep moving and the baby won't wake. I wanted her to hold me too. I wanted her to move with me in her arms so that I wouldn't wake up, so I wouldn't cry. If I was asleep then none of this was real. But there was more. And it was all too real.

I KEPT DRIVING. The weather was clear, the sun shining, the sky blue, the air crisp and cool, so I drove and I thought. I pulled into Moses and Georgia's driveway late in the afternoon, and the sky was so radiant over the crouching hills west of town that I stopped for a minute as I stepped out of my truck and just let the view settle on me. But the beauty just made me ache. *What am I gonna do? What am I gonna do? What am I gonna do?* The chorus started up in my head again.

No one answered the door, and I ended up walking around back to see if anyone was in the pasture beyond. Moses was becoming more and more comfortable around animals, though it was Georgia who was the horse-woman. She was working on her man, and had coaxed Moses into the saddle enough times that he had actually started to enjoy it, though he grumbled and scowled whenever I asked him about it.

Georgia was in the round corral, dead center, running a glossy sorrel around in circles. The sorrel seemed to be cooperating, and Georgia's attention was glued on the animal, talking, reassuring, applying pressure and then releasing it to draw him to her. She was nothing like Moses. And she was perfect for him. I'd known it the moment she'd opened her mouth, the moment she looked in my eyes and stuck out her hand.

"Hey George." I called her George because Moses hated it.

"Hey Tag! What's happenin' handsome?" Georgia's face lit up in a smile so big the ache in my chest spread to my gut and made my insides twist. I missed her already. I didn't want to miss her. *What am I gonna do? What the hell am I gonna do?* She strode to the fence, stepped up on the bottom rung and reached for me, pulling me into a fierce hug.

I needed that hug. I needed it so badly. But I knew if I gave in to the

THE SONG OF DAVID

need to hold onto her longer than I usually did, she would sense my tur-
moil, and she would know something was up. So I squeezed her tight and
let her go, and put a smile on my lips that felt like a lie and called on my
God-given ability to bullshit. It was a talent that had served me well in my
life.

"Hey baby. Where's Mo?" Yep. I still had it. My voice was smooth
and my hands were steady as I pulled the hat off her head and perched it on
my own. Always the flirt, even with my best friend's wife, even when I
was hanging by an emotional thread. It was just my way. And Georgia
knew it. She grabbed her hat back and ducked under the fence to join me
on the other side. The horse she'd been working with whinnied at the loss
of attention, and Georgia looked back and laughed.

"Oh, now you want me around, Sis? You were running from me a minute ago!"

"Ah, but the chase is the best part, George. You know that," I said,
laughing with her, my eyes on the disappointed sorrel. "The moment you
turn away is the moment she'll beg you to come back."

"Ain't that the truth," Georgia laughed. "But it's my turn to play hard
to get. Speaking of hard to get, you just missed Moses. He had a session
tonight in Salt Lake. I think he was going to drop by and see you, actually.
But you're here. So that's not going to work. You didn't bring Millie?"

I winced. I didn't mean to. But I couldn't think about Millie. Not right
now.

"Tag?" Georgia hadn't missed the wince, and she studied me, a troubled groove between her eyes.

"Nah. I didn't bring her. It was a spur of the moment trip. Moses
called me, said he'd painted me into a picture last night, and I was curious.
That's all. Plus, I miss my God-baby. I want to hold her. Where is little
Taglee?"

"My mom's got her." Georgia pursed her lips and narrowed her eyes.
"Moses didn't tell me about the painting. Let's go snoop, shall we?"

I didn't really care about the painting—it was just the first thing that
had popped into my mind—but I trailed after Georgia agreeably and kept a
steady stream of bullshit coming so that she wouldn't get too close.

It was David and Goliath, but lusty and lush, with bold colors and
barely covered bodies, as if the biblical confrontation between a shepherd
and a soldier had taken place in the Garden of Eden instead of on a battle-

field.

Moses's David was small and young. A boy really, ten or eleven, younger than I imagined he had actually been. And in the boyish face, I saw my own. The shaggy hair, the green eyes, the strong stance. I hadn't looked like that at eleven. I'd been rounder, softer. And I'd been big for my age. My size had made me a target, the way physical difference always does.

Goliath was huge, towering over the boy like they belonged to two different species. His biceps and thighs bulged, his calves were unnaturally large, and his shoulders were as wide as the boy was tall. His head was thrown back, and his mouth was gaping, as if he roared like the beast he resembled. The fists clenched at his sides were bigger than the boys head, and young David stood stoically looking up at Goliath, his sling hanging from his hand, his eyes solemn. I leaned in closer, noting the detail, the lack of fear on the boy's face. I looked at Goliath again, comparing and contrasting, and then my breath caught in my throat. I didn't just see my face reflected in David. I saw myself in Goliath too.

David was me. And Goliath was me. They both had my face. I was the boy, and I was the giant. I stepped back, distancing myself from the suddenly disturbing image.

"Georgia? Am I seeing things, or did Moses put my face on David *and* Goliath?"

"Well I'll be damned." She was surprised. But she saw it too. It wasn't just me.

"What do you think it means?" I pressed.

"Hell if I know, Tag. I don't understand half of what Moses paints. *He* doesn't understand it. It's intuitive. You know that."

"But it always means something." And he'd seen Molly. Molly had inspired the painting.

"Maybe it means you are your own worst enemy," Georgia said cheerfully and winked at me. I swallowed and looked back at the picture.

"So which one are you? David or Goliath?"

"Neither," I said quietly, a memory resurfacing so swift and so sharp that it swept me away.

"Fight, fight, fight, fight!" The chant rose up around my head, the fact that they were children's voices didn't dull the roaring sound or the intim-

idating taunts. It didn't ease the pressure I felt to swing my fist or give in to the curiosity to see what it would feel like. I'd never wanted to hit anyone so badly. "Fight, fight, fight, fight!"

"He's a chicken! He's a baby. You're a baby, aren't you baby Cammie?"

Cameron Keller huddled in a ball, his knees tucked into his chest. Cameron and I were friends. Cameron was small and sickly, where I was tall and heavy-set. Cameron was quiet, and I was the class clown. But we were both outcasts, teetering on the far edges of the spectrum, and normal and acceptable lay somewhere between us. I pushed my way into the circle, my size making it easier than it otherwise would have been. And people parted, more out of surprise than anything. I hadn't ever gotten physical with anyone before.

Lyle Coulson leaned over Cameron's shaking form and gathering the spit in his mouth, let it hang from his lips, dribbling in a long, phlegm-thickened strand, before it landed in Cameron's hair.

With a roar, I shoved Lyle Coulson to the ground and pressed his sneering face into the dirt.

Someone pushed at my back, toppling me off to the side before Lyle was up, swinging and cursing. Someone else grabbed at my arms, trying to prevent me from slugging Lyle before Lyle could punch me. There was a roaring in my ears. Maybe it was my heart working overtime, maybe it was adrenaline dulling my senses, but whatever it was, I liked it. The roaring in my ears made the rage echo in my belly. It was the sound of finally fighting back. I took a hard punch in the back, or was that a kick? I turned, swinging wildly, arms pumping like pistons, landing a few, taking a few more, until suddenly kids were running away, scattering like wildebeest on the African savannah—just like the show on the National Geographic channel that I had watched with Molly on Sunday. This time, I was the lion. I was the predator. But Cameron didn't run. Cameron stayed huddled like the wounded calf he'd always been.

"Cameron?" I knelt beside my friend. "You okay, buddy?"

Cameron peeked out from beneath the arm that covered his head. "Tag? Are they gone?"

"Yeah, buddy. They all ran away." My chest filled with pride. I looked at my hands in amazement. I'd used my fists. One knuckle was bloody and torn and the pain was sweet.

"You made them run, Tag?" Cameron was as surprised as I was. I *had never fought back. I was a fat kid who tried to make everyone laugh. I didn't fight.*

"Yeah, Cam. I did. I beat the shit out of 'em."

My first fist fight. It had probably looked more like a squirming wrestling match between fat puppies, but I had come out the victor for the first time ever. I had been David then. And I had been Goliath too, I supposed. The boy who fought back, and the giant who made everyone run in fear. Now? Now I didn't know if David still existed or if Goliath ever had, and the picture troubled me. It had obviously troubled Moses too, or he wouldn't have called.

"Is everything okay, Tag?" Georgia asked softly. I turned away from the painting and met her serious gaze.

I nodded once, just a brief jerk of my head, and Georgia pressed harder.

"Are you going to tell me about Millie? Moses seems to think she's special. Is she?"

"She's special."

"Is she special enough to tame the wild man?" Georgia was teasing me, trying to shake me out of the mood she obviously sensed I was in. Or maybe she was just a girl digging for romantic gossip. My sisters were like that too, or they used to be, when I knew them.

I slung my arm around her shoulders and turned us both away from the biblical standoff.

"Some things are born to be wild. Some horses can't be broken," I said in my best Clint Eastwood.

"All right. Well then I guess the question should be, are you special enough to let a blind girl break you?"

"It's already happened. I just don't want to break her." My voice caught, and I pulled my arm from Georgia's shoulders and shoved them into my pockets, striding away so she wouldn't see the trembling around my mouth and the panic that I could feel oozing out of my pores. I was so glad Moses wasn't here. I don't know what I'd been thinking trying to find him. I wasn't ready for Moses yet.

"I gotta go, George. Give Taglee a kiss for me. Give Moses a kiss too. He loves my kisses." Georgia laughed, but the laughter didn't lift the worry from her voice. I was acting a little strange, and I knew she was wondering what the hell was up.

"Don't be a stranger, Tag. We've missed you." Georgia called behind me as I strode to my truck.

"I'll miss you too, George. Every damn day."

MAYBE IT WAS Moses talking about Molly, but I found myself pulling off the freeway fifteen minutes after I left Levan, exiting at the truck stop in Nephi near the spot where they found my sister's remains. The dogs found my sister's body. The dogs found her when I could not. I'd looked. I'd looked so hard and so desperately that I'd almost convinced myself she couldn't be found. If she couldn't be found then I hadn't failed. Not exactly.

Her grave was just a hole in the earth, marked by tumbleweeds and ringed by sagebrush. Almost two years we'd looked, and she'd been waiting in a litter-strewn field near an obscure overpass outside a little town everyone mispronounced. A town that meant nothing to the girl who was forced to make it her final resting place. Nephi. NEE FIGH. When I had first heard it pronounced I'd thought of the giant in Jack and the Beanstalk, yelling from his castle in the heavens, "FEE, FI, FO, FUM, I smell the blood of an Englishman." FEE FI rhymes with NEPHI.

NEE PHI FO FUM, I smell the blood of your missing ones.

The dogs could smell her. But there was no blood. Not then. When they found her only bones and bits of fabric and several long blonde hairs remained. Some drug paraphernalia was buried with her, labeling her an addict, deserving of her fate. Suddenly she was no longer missing. But she was still gone. And for years we didn't know who took her.

NEE PHI FO FUM, I smell the blood of your missing ones.

They say that most murders are committed by the family members. By the loved ones. But the man who killed my sister didn't know her at all. And he didn't love her. It turned out, he'd killed lots of girls. So many girls over so many years. All of them missing. All of them gone.

NEE PHI FO FUM, ready or not, here I come. And come he had. I'd put a bullet in the man's head, avenging the blood of the missing ones, *all* the missing ones.

NEE PHI FO FUM, pull the trigger, now you're done.

NEE PHI FO FUM, pull the trigger, now you're done.

Oh, God. I didn't want to be done. I sat in my truck and thought of Molly, staring into the field where they found her body. And I talked to her for a while. I asked her what the hell I was supposed to do. And I wondered if she was coming through to Moses because my time was up, if she was suddenly hanging around because she was waiting on me. If my time was up, I could deal. The truth of that settled on me. It surprised me. But I could deal. I could handle it. Moses had told me once that you can't escape yourself. I'd wanted to once. Not anymore. I had come to terms with myself. I liked myself. I liked my life. Hell, I loved my life.

But I wasn't going to spend whatever time I had left being sick.

I'd never been good at in-betweens. All or nothing. That's who I was. All or nothing, dead or alive. Not dying. Not sick. Dead or alive, all or nothing.

Having made my decision, I called the doctor. I actually heard relief in his voice when I told him I was ready to go ahead with what came next, and his relief terrified me. He cleared his schedule and just like that, the craniotomy was set for the following day.

I pulled back onto the highway and left my sister's shadow in the rearview mirror. I headed back home, back to Millie, suddenly desperate to see her.

Eighteen

MILLIE OPENED THE door to greet me, a smile on her lips, my name on her tongue, but I didn't wait for her to release it. I wanted her to keep it, savor it, and never let it go. I needed my name to stay inside her so that I wouldn't float away like a word that's already been spoken. So I pressed my lips to hers and swung her up in my arms like a man in a movie, and my name became a cry that only I heard.

I felt slightly crazed, and my kiss was frantic as I barreled up the stairs with Millie in my arms. My legs didn't shake and my mind was clear, as if in its health my body was rebelling too. I wanted to roar and hit my chest. I wanted to shake my fists at the heavens, but more than anything I wanted Millie. I didn't want to waste another second with Millie.

Then we were in her room, the white comforter pristine and smooth, like Millie's skin in the moonlight, and I laid her across it, falling down beside her. I was anxious. Needy. I wanted the safety of her skin, the absolution of her flesh, and the promise that came with it. I wanted to take. I wanted to cement myself in her memory and leave my mark. I needed that. I needed her. She matched my fervor like she understood. She didn't understand. She couldn't. But she didn't slow me down or beg me for reassurance.

My hands were in her hair and tracing her eyes, fingering her mouth, pausing in the hollow of her throat. I wanted to touch every single part of her. But even as I lost myself in the silk of her skin and the sway of her movements against me, I felt the horror rise up inside of me and shimmer beneath my skin. It wouldn't be enough. It wouldn't be enough, and I knew it, even as I closed my eyes and tried to make it be enough. I couldn't breathe and my heart raced, and for a moment I thought I would tell her everything.

She must have mistaken my fear for hesitation, the cessation of my breath for something else, because she cradled my face in her hands and pressed her forehead to mine. And then she whispered my name.

"David, David, David." It sounded like a song when she said it. And she kissed my lips softly.

"David, David, David." She chanted my name, like she couldn't believe it was true, like she liked the way it felt in her mouth.

"I love the way you call me David," I said, and remembered the line from my silly song, the line that had no rhyme.

"I love that you are mine," she breathed, and the fear left me for a time. It tiptoed away and love took its place, love and belonging and time that can't be stolen. Millie said she had to feel to see, and she saw all of me. Her fingers traced the contours of my back like she was reading a map, following a river to the sea across a long expanse, over valleys and hills. She was thorough and attentive, her lips and cheeks following her fingers, her tongue testing the textures that needed more attention. When Millie made love she actually *made* love. She created it, drew it, coaxed it into being. I'd always hated that term and preferred a little baser description, maybe because it felt more honest. But with Millie, nothing else fit. And she didn't just make love, she made *me* love. She made me listen. She made me feel. She made me pay attention. I didn't hurry or take. I didn't rush or push. I closed my eyes and loved the same way she did, with the tips of my fingers and the palms of my hands, and I saw her so clearly that my eyes burned behind my closed lids.

She was confident in a way she shouldn't have been, confident in a way that is born from knowing you are loved, and I reveled in that. She wasn't the girl in sexy lingerie, wondering if she should pose her body this way or that. She was a woman deeply in love and completely lost in the experience. She didn't ask me what I liked or what I wanted. She didn't hesitate or hold back. She didn't plead for pretty words or reassurance.

But I gave them anyway.

I gave them because they fell from my mouth, and I pressed them to her ears, needing her to know how much I loved her, how perfect I found her, how precious the moment was. And she whispered back, matching each expression with affection, gifting words with caresses, until the effort to speak became too great and the words felt inadequate. When she reached the peak she pulled me over the edge with her, and I wished we could just keep on falling and never stop. Falling would feel like flying if you never hit the ground. But the landing was soft and our breathing slowed, and I pulled her in tight as the world righted itself. Or wronged me. I wasn't sure which. Millie was pliant and sleepy in my arms, and I felt her drifting off.

"I love you, Millie. Do you know that?" I said.

"Yes." She said the word on a long, satisfied sigh, as if the knowledge was wonderful.

"You have your favorite sounds, and now, so do I. I love it when my back is turned, and I hear you coming. I love the sound your stick makes. When I hear it, it makes me smile. I love your voice and the way you laugh from your chest. It's one of the first things I noticed about you. That laugh." I felt her smile, her lips moving softly against my throat.

"I love that little breath, the little gasp in your throat when I touch you here." I pressed my hand to her lower back and pulled her tightly against me. Her breath hitched on cue. "That's it. That's the sound."

Millie kissed my chest but didn't speak. I counted to sixty slowly, and then I continued, whispering so softly and so unhurriedly she was sure to fall asleep.

"And you hum. You hum when you're happy. You hum when you run your fingers through my hair and when you're falling asleep. You are almost humming now."

There was silence in the room, and I knew she'd slid under the downy blanket of slumber. It was what I'd intended. I'd waited until she was gone.

"I want to hear that sound every night of my life." I felt the panic rise up in my throat, not knowing how many nights I would have and not wanting to think about that when I was holding her. With the panic came tears, and they leaked out the corners of my eyes and dripped into my ears.

"I love you, Millie. And it's the most amazing feeling, the most incredible thing I've ever felt. I can't hold it in my chest, that feeling. So it spills out of me whenever you're around. It spills out of my mouth and my eyes and my ears. It spills out of my fingertips and makes me walk faster and talk louder and feel more alive. Do you feel like that, Millie? Do I make you feel more alive?"

Her deep, soft breaths were my only response, and I kissed the top of her head.

"How can I possibly be dying when I feel more alive than I've ever felt before?"

I CREPT INTO Henry's room at about dawn. I wanted to see him, just in case. Just in case the news was bad and I didn't come back. I wanted to say goodbye, even if it was temporary, even if he couldn't hear me. He looked big in the small bed, his long feet and knobby knees sticking out from beneath the covers. He needed a new bed. I made a note to tell Millie and then stopped myself. What had Millie said? She'd been taking care of herself before she met me, and she'd be taking care of herself, and Henry, after I was gone. They'd been taking care of each other.

I didn't want to wake him, and I moved to go, my eyes skimming over his desk, over the book about giants that had once scared him. Moses had mentioned Millie's dead mother and that book, and it had gnawed at me for a week as I tried to figure out how to approach the subject without upsetting anyone. I had shared Moses's abilities with Millie in broad strokes, but knowing someone could see the dead and having someone see *your* dead were two different things. I knew that first hand. But it bothered me enough that I finally asked Henry about it.

"You wouldn't have a book about giants, would you Henry?" I inquired hesitantly. It wasn't very subtle, but apparently, Henry didn't need subtlety. He'd known immediately what book I was referring to. He also knew where to find it. He had clattered down the stairs to the storage bins that were neatly stacked and labeled, and within a few minutes, returned with a handful of old treasures, including a book that was well-worn and obviously well-read. It was called *When Giants Hide*. Henry had shown me the pictures and made me find each giant before turning to the next page.

"My dad's name is Andre," he'd said abruptly.

"Yeah. I know."

"Like Andre the Giant," he added.

I nodded. One Andre was a giant, one Andre played for the Giants. Interesting. I hadn't made the connection, but Henry obviously had.

"Andre the Giant was over seven feet tall and weighed five hundred pounds," Henry continued as we turned the page, our eyes resting on a giant who blended into the trees, his hair a huge, leafy afro, his skin weathered and brown.

"He was a professional wrestler. I used to watch old highlight videos of him wrestling Hulk Hogan," I said.

"Who won?" he asked, looking up from the book.

I laughed. "You know what? I don't remember. I just remember thinking how big Andre was, and how much I wanted long hair and a big gold belt like Hulk Hogan."

"This book used to scare me."

"Not anymore?"

Henry shook his head. "No. But I still look for giants sometimes."

"Giants . . . or just one giant?" I asked quietly. I thought maybe I'd figured out why Millie's mother had shown Moses the book.

"Andre the Giant died," he said soberly. "I'm not looking for him anymore."

I had sensed Henry knew exactly who I was referring to, but I let the subject drop.

Now, looking down at the book on Henry's desk, the doctor's words rang in my head.

"You have a giant mass on your frontal lobe."

A hiding giant no one had seen. Until now.

"Giants don't make good friends."

Henry was right. Giants were something to be afraid of.

"When Giants Hide," I read the title again, and Henry tossed a little, murmuring in his sleep. I placed the book back down and noticed the old tape recorder Henry had unearthed along with the book. There was a shoebox of tapes too, some used, some new. Apparently, Henry had once used them to record his own sportscasts. He had a digital recorder now, but he'd been excited by the discovery of his old collection.

The tapes and the recorder gave me an idea, and I felt a little sliver of relief, a tiny lifeline. I would use the tapes to leave Millie a message. I lifted them carefully from the desk, treading quietly as I eased back out of the room with my hands now full. I would give it all back, I promised Henry silently.

(End of Cassette)

⠠⠉⠀⠄⠀⠠⠊⠠⠉

Moses

WE LEFT FOR Vegas early the next morning. Georgia stayed behind with Kathleen, but Millie refused to be left behind. She apologized for insisting yet insisted anyway. And Henry couldn't stay home alone. So it was the three of us in the cab of my truck, heading to Vegas with our stomachs in knots and our thoughts turned inward. It could have been awkward, but it wasn't. We'd passed awkward a long time ago and were well on our way to being friends.

Tag's team left at about the same time, but we had no plans to meet up. It was divide and conquer. That was the plan, though the plan lacked specifics. My goal was just to get to Vegas and get into the fight. I'd worry about the rest later.

There wasn't a cassette player in my truck. They didn't make them that way anymore. But Millie brought the tape player and the box of tapes, and she sat with them in her lap as if she couldn't bear to part with them. They were a lifeline. A Tagline. Since the day before, when Tag revealed the results of his MRI, Millie hadn't shared the contents of the remaining tapes with me or Georgia, and I hadn't asked to listen. I didn't want to listen. The conversation had grown too personal, the love story too ripe, the feelings too raw, and the story was for Millie's ears alone. I wasn't sure if she had continued listening after we parted, but I was guessing from the way she held them, she'd done little else.

About halfway into our trip, she pulled out a cassette and put in some earphones. I was impressed that the tape recorder even worked with earphones. She turned away slightly, drawing her knees to her chest, and lost herself in Tag's voice.

It wasn't until a half hour later that she started to cry. She'd been so resilient. So composed. But now—now she wasn't. Something on the cassette had set her off. Tears dripped down her face, and her lids were tightly closed, clearly an attempt to hold them in.

I needed Georgia. I didn't know what to do. And Henry sure as hell didn't know what to do. He caught sight of his sister's tears and immediately started fidgeting and pulling at his seatbelt, reaching for Millie and then turning away from her.

"Lou Gehrig, Jimmie Foxx, Hank Greenberg, Eddie Murray, Buck Leonard . . ." Henry started muttering and rocking, "Mark McGwire, Harmon Killebrew, Roger Connor, Jeff Bagwell . . ."

"Millie!" I raised my voice in an effort to be heard over the earphones that covered her ears.

Millie yanked the earbuds from her ears and immediately tuned into Henry.

She slid the cassette player to the floor and climbed over the seat without hesitation. She swiped at her wet face with one hand as she pulled Henry into her arms.

"I'm sorry, Henry. I'm okay."

"Cap Anson, Bill Terry, Johnny Mize," Henry mumbled.

"Baseball players?" I asked, recognizing a few.

"First basemen," Millie supplied. Her lips were tight, and I could see she was still trying to force back the grief that had gotten to her in the first place. Henry's forehead rested on her shoulder, his eyes hidden from her tear-stained face, giving her a moment to pull it together.

"Andre Anderson," Henry added, but didn't continue listing names.

It took me a minute to put it all together. Baseball. First basemen. Andre Anderson. Henry and Millie's dad.

"Rookie of the Year, Gold Glove, Silver Slugger." Henry pulled out of Millie's arms and touched her cheek. I was getting dizzy watching the road and watching my rear view mirror and the drama in the backseat.

"Rookie of the Year, Gold Glove, Silver Slugger, lousy father," Millie said firmly. "I am not crying over dad, Henry."

"Tag Taggert, light heavyweight contender, nineteen wins, two losses, eleven knockouts, lousy boyfriend?" Henry asked.

I wanted to laugh. I wanted to cry. I did neither. But my throat ached from the effort of doing nothing. Millie laughed, but a quick glance in my rearview confirmed that tears streamed down her cheeks once more. It was tragically funny.

"No, Henry. It's not the same. It's not the same at all. Tag didn't leave *us*. This isn't about *us*, Henry. This is about Tag."

I felt a rush of awe for Millie Anderson. People didn't impress me very easily. I could count on one hand the people who had exceeded my expectations, but Millie had just joined the ranks.

"He's still gone," Henry insisted, making me flinch. Millie said nothing. I just continued to drive.

Nineteen

Moses

THE ARENA WAS bright flashes and swinging strobe lights, and the seats I'd garnered were just to the right of the announcer's table on the left side of the octagon. I had it on good authority that we would be able to see Tag's corner and he should be able to see us if I could get his attention. I would have to sell one of my lungs to recoup the cost of the tickets, but we were in. Axel, Mikey, and the rest of the guys had managed to come up with seats as well, but they were somewhere else in the arena, and I hadn't spotted them yet.

Henry's face was blank, but his eyes swung wildly, soaking in the celebrity sightings, the electric energy, the announcers, the ring girls, the music. Millie had her game face on, and she held Henry's hand tightly so he could guide her through the crowd, but I was afraid the two of them were going to be swept away, so I reached down and held her other hand, the three of us linked like a line of kindergarteners in a crosswalk.

The crush of people made *me* nervous, and *I* could see. I couldn't imagine what it felt like for Millie, bumping through the crowd in total darkness, senses on overload, unable to get her bearings. She gripped my hand and flashed me a smile as we wound our way to our seats. Tag's fight wasn't the main event, but he was the last fight before the final, and there were two fights lined up before his.

He still wasn't answering his phone. In fact, calling his number resulted in a message that the user's mailbox was full. We had tracked him down the best we could, and now we had to wait.

Millie had been subdued on the trip to Vegas, her face shadowed and shuttered, looking after Henry and making quiet conversation with me, and beyond the tears that had leaked out when she had listened to one of Tag's tapes, she'd kept her emotions close to her chest. Me? I was angry. If Tag didn't get his ass kicked in his fight, I was going to kick it afterwards. The anger kept me from being afraid. I had enough self-awareness to know that. But I didn't understand what Tag was thinking. Not really. I didn't understand just cutting us off and leaving. I'd seen a documentary once about how old Native Americans left their tribes when they were ready to die. But Tag was twenty-six. And he wasn't Native American. And I refused to believe he was dying. The rage built in my chest again, and I mentally changed the subject.

Henry was tuned into the announcer's table, more interested in the commentators than the fights themselves, and his interest drew my own. They were talking about Tag, and I felt Millie stiffen next to me.

"For our viewers who are just tuning in, Tag Taggert was not scheduled to fight tonight. But when Jordan Jones pulled out at the last minute due to a shoulder injury, fight commissioner Cliff Cordova called Tag Taggert, definitely a rising star in ultimate fighting, and asked him if he wanted to step in. Tag defeated Bruno Santos by technical knock-out in the fifth round only a month ago, which is the second time he has completely obliterated his underdog status and beaten a highly-favored opponent.

And now, David Taggert is entering the arena wearing his signature Tag Team gear. But he's completely alone. He has two arena security guards with him. That's it. No corner help, no coaches, no team whatsoever. I don't think I've ever seen that before. For a guy who has been building the Tag Team brand so aggressively, that's a little odd."

"Tag! Tag!" Henry was screaming and jumping up and down, trying to draw Tag's attention, and Millie was shaking so hard I gritted my own teeth to help her stop. Tag saw Henry, saw me, and then he saw Millie. His jaw clenched, his eyes widened, and he slowed, almost stopping, before he seemed to remember where he was. He actually stepped toward us, and Henry yelled his name once more and waved theatrically. Tag's eyes shot to mine again and he pointed at me and then pointed at Millie, as if to say "take care of her." I could only stare back.

Then, after a nudge from security, he continued on to the edge of the octagon, pulled off the Tag Team warm-ups, stepped out of his shoes, stuck a mouth guard over his teeth, and waited for the official to call him forward. He didn't look toward us again, and I recognized the set of his shoulders and the jut of his chin. I'd seen this Tag more times than I could count. It was game time, and sadly, this wasn't a game.

"What's happening, Moses?" Millie asked, the fear in her voice cutting through the roar of the crowd around us. I leaned down and put my head next to hers. I didn't have enough air in my lungs to shout.

"He's going to do it. He's going to fight."

"I hate that I can't see him." Her face was white and her mouth trembled. I marveled for the millionth time at her courage. How would it feel to go through life in perpetual darkness, putting yourself out there and hoping the world could see you, even if you couldn't see it? I saw more than I wanted to see, and for much of my life I'd hated it. I'd hated what I could see. But it was better than seeing nothing at all.

"He saw you, Millie. He knows you're here. He knows we're here."

"How does he look?"

"He looks ready." It was the only thing I could say.

"Why is he doing this?" The question was almost a sob, and I took her hand again. I didn't have an answer.

The announcer began his build-up, introducing Tag first, and Henry mouthed his sequence almost word for word, the wins and losses, the nick-names and finally David "Tag" Taggert, as the crowd roared and my conscience screamed. Tag was such an idiot. It was David and Goliath, and I could only look on helplessly as Terry "Shotgun" Shaw was announced and the referee called the two fighters to the center of the octagon. Henry knew Shotgun's stats as well.

Millie's attention was once again riveted on the television play-by-play, the two co-hosts chatting excitedly, giving her information that she couldn't see. I listened to them launch into an introduction of the upcoming fight as the referee stood in the center of the octagon and talked to the two fighters who stood chest to chest, eye to eye, trying to take each other apart before the buzzer sounded. Tag had told me once that those few seconds of intimidation were invaluable.

"Shotgun's camp wasn't very happy about the match-up. They don't think Taggert has earned the right to be in the octagon with Shotgun. They really wanted the fight with Jones, but Jordan Jones was out, and after Taggert's big win against Santos last month, he was the obvious choice in my opinion. He's a rising star, popular with the fans, popular with other fighters, just an all-around great ambassador for the sport. He's a solid striker, solid grappler, and his wrestling skills have improved immensely. He was a bull-rider in high school, so he's definitely an adrenaline junky, though he claims a few broken bones was all it took to convince him to leave the bulls alone. But more than anything else, the man just enjoys the sport. He loves getting in the octagon, battling it out, and he claims that's the reason he's any good. He loves to fight, and he has a hell of a chin."

The buzzer sounded and the announcers grew silent for all of five seconds. Tag and Shotgun circled each other, and the broadcasters couldn't help themselves. They had to jump back into the fray.

"That's right, Joe. In his recent fight against Bruno Santos, there were a few times where everyone thought he was going down. Bruno landed some brutal shots, and Taggert just kept coming. He just kind of wore Bruno out, and in the end, caught Santos just right and sent him to the canvas, absolutely stunning the fight world. Santos was the clear favorite, just like Shotgun is the favorite here today. But don't count Tag Taggert out. Don't count him out, because he just might surprise you."

My heart bounced like a ball in my chest and the sweat trickled down my back. Tag attempted a take down and caught a flurry of fists instead.

"Oh, Shotgun lands a solid combination to Taggert's body! And out comes the smile from Tag Taggert! He is grinning from ear to ear.
"Is it part of his game plan? Smile through the pain?"
"You know, it might be, but I've watched several of his fights, and I honestly think he just loves the battle. He starts smiling when the fists start flying, and he doesn't stop."

I had to tune the announcers out. They were making me nervous. But they were right. The harder Shotgun came at him, the bigger Tag's smile grew. With his dimples flashing, the women in the crowd were all solidly in his corner after the second round. I'd seen it before. Tag smiling as blood dripped out his nose and from his mouth. The man was a lunatic.

But he didn't look sick, and he didn't act sick, and I felt a sliver of relief that Tag wasn't trying to die. Not yet. Shotgun's fist glanced off Tag's forehead at the end of the first round and for a minute, Tag's legs stiffened. Shotgun saw that Tag was temporarily rocked and flew at him, fists flying, only to have his confidence and momentum used against him. Tag lunged into a perfect double leg, wrapping his arms around Shotgun's knees, and toppled Shotgun cleanly to his back.

The crowd went crazy, the announcers went wild, and Millie strained to hear their commentary, her hand in mine, her other hand resting on Henry.

"Tag took him down," I yelled downward, giving her the play-by-play I knew she needed, but my eyes stayed locked on Tag's back as he struggled to grind his way past Shotgun's guard.

"Ground and pound!" Henry shrieked.

But the round ended, and Tag was forced to let Shotgun up. Tag stood easily and walked to his empty corner, but he didn't sit on the stool that was placed there for him, nor did he lean against the ropes, giving the crowd his back. Instead, he grabbed a towel, shot his mouth with water, spit it out again, took another drink and found Millie in the crowd. He stood, fingers clinging to the cage that surrounded the octagon, and he didn't look at me or anyone else. He kept his eyes on her long enough that the announcers were turning their heads, trying to see who or what held his attention.

"I've got this, Millie!" he roared suddenly. "I got this! I got this, baby!"

"Did you hear him, Millie?" I yelled down at her, my eyes never leaving Tag as his eyes stayed planted on Millie's face. She nodded vigorously. "He wants you to know he's okay."

Everyone was staring at her now, and the announcers were wide-eyed and openly speculative as the buzzer sounded and Tag turned away.

It continued on that way through the next four rounds. When the buzzer sounded, Tag would find his corner, find Millie, and reassure her, always in the same way. "I got this, Millie. I got this."

And the crowd started to believe him. They started to chant for him, a chant that began with Henry.

"Tag Team! Tag Team! Tag Team!" he'd yelled continually, and before too long, the people around us picked up the chant, and it spread through the crowd in pockets and in power, until Shotgun caught Tag on the forehead again, staggering him, causing him to go down on one knee only to surge up and catch Shotgun beneath the chin, knocking his head back with a whip-lash inducing crack.

Shotgun crumpled.

For half a second there was a collective intake of breath, a shared, stunned heartbeat that silenced the crowd before pandemonium broke out and the referee practically slid to Shotgun's inert form, frantically waving his arms over his head, indicating the fight was over. Tag had won.

"It's over!" I screamed. "He did it!"

"Tag!" Henry howled in wild delight. "Tag!"

But Millie just stood, shaking, her eyes dry, her palms drenched. Or maybe that was my hand. We clutched each other, and Henry hung on too, the three of us caught up in the surge and swell that raged around us. The crowd was hollering, people clapping, jumping up and down, jostling us, patting us on the back, congratulating us. Everyone had watched as Tag zeroed in on Millie throughout the fight, and they were zeroing in on her now.

Tag approached his corner again, this time with his hands raised above his head. But as he found Millie once more, his eyes narrowing on her face, his right leg buckled and his hands came down, relinquishing celebration for something to hold onto. He swayed wildly, the crowd gasped, and I lunged forward, letting go of Millie's hand, my arms out-stretched as if I could catch him.

His fingers tangled in the netting, his eyes rolled, and his body jerked, collapsing into a shuddering heap on the octagon floor. And he continued to convulse.

I was up and over the cage wall before anyone could stop me.

The crowd grew silent beyond the octagon, and strangely enough, no one challenged me. I knelt beside him, trying to hold onto him, not knowing what to do, and the referee was immediately at my side, as well as someone from Shotgun's corner.

"He's seizing!" the referee said sharply, and someone shoved a mouth guard back between Tag's teeth to keep him from biting his tongue. I slid my arm beneath his head to prevent it from knocking against the floor.

Shotgun was sitting up blearily, and the medical personnel who had come immediately to his aid abandoned him for the new emergency. From the corner of my eye I thought I saw Molly. Blond hair, blue eyes, silently waiting. And I bit back a curse and slammed down my walls, refusing to acknowledge her.

THE TELEVISION IN the emergency waiting room was tuned into a local station, and Millie, Henry and I sat in numb silence, listening to a Vegas reporter sharing the news of the day. Axel, Mikey, Cory, Andy and Paulo were there too, looking as grim and gutted as I felt, and they raised their eyes to the screen when Tag's name was mentioned. The reporter stood outside of the MGM, where people were still streaming in and out of the venue, her hand clutching a fuzzy blue microphone, her expression both serious and exultant, telling us what we already knew about Tag's fight and none of the stuff we wanted to know.

It was fight night at the MGM this evening, the main event one many had been waiting a long time to see, but it was an undercard fight featuring a last-minute fill-in that has been the subject among fight fans here tonight. David Taggert was called up only three days ago to fill the slot vacated by Jordan Jones. Jones had been scheduled to fight long-time UFC favorite and former Light Heavyweight champion, Terry Shaw, when he sustained an injury that left him unable to fight.

David Taggert, after a stunning upset in April against Bruno Santos, was called in to take his place. Fight fans definitely got their money's worth when Taggert and Shaw went a full four rounds before Taggert knocked Shaw out cold. However, that's not where the story ends. The controversy is over an apparent seizure Taggert had after the fight ended. Shaw was out cold. The fight was over. The referee raised Taggert's hand, Tag Taggert turned toward the crowd, raised his hands, took a few steps, and collapsed.

He was taken to an area hospital in critical condition, and we are now hearing reports that shortly following the April fight where Tag Taggert

defeated Bruno Santos, he had a run-in at his Salt Lake City bar with a
former employee. Taggert was struck across the forehead in the altercation
and sustained a fairly serious head wound. Word is that he was treated and
released that night, but has kept a very low profile in the weeks following
the altercation. Speculation is now running rampant. We will keep you
posted about his condition and any developments that may shed more light
on this stunning series of events.

Tag went into surgery about an hour after arriving in the emergency room. He actually regained consciousness briefly in the ambulance, or so we were told. He asked about the fight, was told he had a seizure, and he went under again. He had the gall to make sure he really won before losing consciousness again. It almost made me laugh. I would have laughed if I wasn't so angry.

According to the doctor who came and talked to us about three hours after we arrived in the hospital waiting room, Tag's brain had started to bleed and swell, most likely during the fight. I thought of the blow he took to the forehead at the end of the first round, when his legs had wobbled and we all thought he was going down. He'd fought for three more rounds before he took another blow to the same spot right before the fight ended. The swelling created pressure which had then caused the seizure, which in turn helped them discover the bleed. Apparently, people who undergo a craniotomy and have tumors removed from their brains shouldn't enter the octagon less than three weeks post-surgery.

I wasn't able to ride in the ambulance with Tag. I'd had to stay with Millie and Henry. We'd fought our way through the crowd as quickly as we could, which hadn't been easy, and then sped to the hospital, arriving a good twenty minutes after Tag had been rushed through the emergency room doors. I'd told the nurse at the desk everything I knew, everything Tag had confessed in his tapes, and asked her to please relay it to those caring for my friend. She'd given me a look like she thought I was high and dangerous, peering at me over the tops of her little glasses and pressing her fat chin into her chest in bafflement. She listened and then stood, exiting through swishing doors where Millie and Henry and I weren't allowed to follow.

I could just imagine the stunned reactions of the nurses and doctors when they got Tag in there and started pulling up his medical history and running him through the MRI. He'd pulled his shaggy hair into a tail at the back of his head for the fight, completely covering up the shaved lines crisscrossing his skull, evidence of the craniotomy, but those things don't stay hidden. His hair was coming loose from the band and falling around his face when I held him in my arms in the octagon. I'd seen the evidence, and so would they.

When the fat desk clerk had finally come back to her post, she was shaking her head, and she kept looking at us like we'd escaped from a freak show. I'd been looked at that way a time or two, so I just stared back with all the insolence I felt, and Millie was obviously unaware that she was the focus of such suspicious attention. Henry was a jittery, trivia-spouting mess, but Millie just held his hand, stroked his hair, and commented on his inane trivia as if he was the smartest kid in the universe. Before long, he was eating peanut M&Ms and guzzling Sprite from the vending machines with relative calm, whispering a stat to himself every once in a while.

"He's out of surgery. We were able to stop the bleed," the doctor said solemnly. He looked from me to Millie. His eyes widened and he looked back at me again, obviously realizing that he could only make eye contact with one of us. To his credit, he went right on talking, hardly pausing.

"He's unconscious, and we'd like to keep him that way at this point, but we think when the swelling eases in the next twelve hours or so, he'll come around. We need to watch him over the next few days, but he should be fine. Brain activity looks good, vitals are good. I have consulted with Dr. Stein and Dr. Shumway at LDS hospital. Dr. Shumway performed the craniotomy on your friend, and I can't tell you much more, but Mr. Taggert's got some big decisions to make. I think having you here, having people call him on what he did, and on what he needs to do, is important. What he did tonight was incredibly foolish. He's lucky to be alive."

Twenty

⠞

Moses

TAG WOKE UP just as the doctor predicted, but they didn't let us see him until they moved him out of the ICU, which didn't happen for a full twenty-four hours after he regained consciousness. We'd gone back and forth from the hospital to a nearby hotel, running on terror and little sleep, until, two days after we'd begun our vigil, we went back to the hotel to shower and change, and Henry climbed into bed and refused to get out again. Millie didn't dare leave Henry alone at the hotel for hours on end, so she stayed behind and I went back to the hospital.

I was surprised to find Tag sitting up in his bed, his eyes heavily circled, his jaw rough with several days' worth of beard, his shaggy hair hanging lank around his face. The bald patches and staple marks were extremely visible now, and he scratched at his skull as if the bare skin were driving him crazy.

"It's been almost three weeks. It's mostly healed, and it itches," he complained with a smile, as if it were just road rash—nothing serious.

"I think I've convinced one of the nurses to help me shave it all off. We'll be twins, Mo," he said, referring to the fact that my hair had never been much longer than stubble.

I couldn't respond. I didn't do small talk and bullshit as well as Tag did. In fact, I didn't really do it at all. I just stared at my friend and shoved my hands in my pockets to repress my urge to paint . . . or kill him.

"I think Millie will dig a smooth head—" He stopped abruptly and rubbed at his jaw, clearly agitated. "Is she here, Mo? With you?"

"She's at the hotel with Henry. He was exhausted, and she didn't dare leave him alone."

Tag nodded and closed his eyes, as if he too were exhausted. "Good. That's good."

A nurse bustled in, saw me, and hesitated slightly. I almost laughed. She probably wanted Tag all to herself while she fussed over him. Typical female. He probably had the entire nursing staff at his beck and call. He'd be the most well-cared for patient in the history of the hospital.

I watched as she carefully covered him with a sheet and gently started removing his hair with an electric razor, one long clump at a time, until he sat before me, smooth-headed and scarred, looking so different and defeated, so changed, that I unclenched my hands, releasing some of my rage.

The nurse exclaimed that he "must feel so much better now," and whisked away the shorn hair and the sheet that covered him. Then she helped him maneuver out of his hospital gown—avoiding his IV and the various monitors—and assisted him in donning a new one. I caught Tag's eye as she carefully tied the strings at his back. I raised an eyebrow, and he gave me a smirk that let me know that he hadn't changed all *that* much.

Still, when she left the room, he closed his eyes briefly, resting momentarily, and I felt the fear swell in my chest once more.

"You look like shit, Tag," I said.

"So do you, Mo," he shot back, not even opening his eyes.

"It's your fault," I said.

He sighed and then murmured, "I know."

I didn't comment, thinking he needed to sleep. But after several long breaths he opened his eyes again and met my gaze.

"I'm sorry, Moses."

"You shouldn't have left like that. You've put us all through hell." I guess we were going to go there, after all.

"I didn't see a better solution."

"I can think of one," I snapped, and when he didn't respond immediately, I exhaled heavily and pressed my palms into my tired eyes.

"Sometimes I feel like death is the only thing I haven't done," he said eventually. "Hell, and I've even attempted *that* a couple of times. The problem with death is that it's exclusive, like sex and child-birth. Once you've done it, there is no going back."

His thoughts were clearly rhetorical, and I waited him out again.

"The thing is, Mo. I'm okay with it. If I've learned anything from being your best friend, from watching you commune with the dead, it's that death isn't anything I need to be afraid of. I'm not a perfect man. But I think I'm a good man. I've lived a hell of a life, even with all the heartache. Millie told me once that the ability to devastate is what makes a song beautiful. Maybe that's what makes life beautiful too. The ability to devastate. Maybe that's how we know we've lived. How we know we've truly loved."

"The ability to devastate," I repeated. And my voice broke. If that wasn't a perfect description of the agony of love, I didn't know what was. I had felt that devastation. I had survived it, but I didn't want to survive it again.

"I love her so much, Mo. I love her so damn much. That's the thing that sucks the most. I can deal with the cancer. I can deal with death. But I'm going to miss Millie. I miss her already." He swallowed, his throat working overtime against the emotion that choked us both. "I would miss you too, Mo, but you can see dead people, so I can haunt you."

I laughed, but it came out a groan, and I stood, needing to escape, hating the sorrow, raging against the futility of grief, yet feeling it anyway. Tag watched me pace and when I finally sat back down, indicating I was ready, he spoke again.

"I'm okay with death, Mo. I'm good with it," Tag said quietly. "But dying . . . dying is different. I'm afraid of dying. I'm afraid of not being strong for the people who love me. I'm afraid of the suffering I will cause. I'm afraid of the helplessness I'll feel when I can't make it all better. I don't want to sit in a hospital bed, day after day, dying. I don't want Millie trying to take care of me. I don't want Henry watching me fade from giant to shadow. Can you understand that, Mo?"

I nodded slowly, though doing so made me feel sick, like I was condoning what he'd done, leaving like he had.

"I laid in bed all night after they told me what I was facing. They gave me all the risks, the time frames, best case scenarios, worst case scenarios. By morning, I knew it wasn't for me. I told my doctor, thank you very much, but I'm gonna go now."

"And you weren't going to tell anyone?"

"No." Tag shook his head, his eyes on mine. "No."

"But . . ." I didn't understand. I wasn't following.

"I got my affairs in order. I met with my attorney, got things figured out. Drew up the will, liquidated a bunch of stuff. The only thing that was bothering me was the money I still owed my dad. I could sell it all—the bar, the gym, the clothing line. If I did, I'd have more than enough, but I don't want to sell. I want to leave the gym to the guys. I want to leave the bar to Millie and Henry so Millie can dance around that damn pole until she's eighty-two and no one can tell her no, and so that Henry can have a place where he can talk sports and someone will listen. He loves the bar. I wanted to leave you something too, but I knew you would hate that."

He got that right. He was messed up about everything else. But he got that right.

"But even with the sale of the apartments, the liquidation of every-thing but my truck, I still owe my dad fifty grand," Tag continued.

"Wasn't that an inheritance?"

"I didn't want an inheritance. I wanted to build my own road," Tag argued. "I told him I would pay it all back by the time I was thirty. Thirty ain't gonna happen, Mo. So I needed to find a way to pay it back sooner."

"The fight."

"Yeah." Tag nodded. "The fight. It just so happens I got offered a title fight that would pay me fifty Gs if I won. And I had absolutely nothing to lose."

"And after the fight?"

"I was going to take a trip to Dallas, see my mom and my sisters and pay my dad back. I haven't seen them in a while. Then . . . take a hike up into the hills above that overpass in Nephi."

"The one where Molly was buried?"

"The one where Molly was buried," he confirmed. "Hike up into the hills. Take a pill. Watch the sun-set as I went to sleep."

"That's it?" I asked, reining in my temper.

"That's it," he answered, with no temper at all.

I felt the rage surge in my chest and pop in my ears, but I kept my voice level. Apparently, he hadn't thought he needed to say goodbye to me.

"So you left the tapes. Why?"

"It was my way of saying goodbye. I wanted Millie to know how I felt. Every step of the way. Falling in love with her. I never wanted her to have a reason to doubt me. I wanted her to know it was real, that is was perfect, that it was the best gift I've ever received."

"And you repay her by taking that gift and tossing it?"

Tag was silent, staring at me, his face a study in compassion. Love lined his face and leaked from the corners of his eyes.

"I love you, Mo. You know that, don't you?" he said gently. And I knew he did. I had no doubt whatsoever. But he had a hell of a way of showing it.

"Fuck you, Tag!" I hissed. "I know what you want from me. I know you want me to tell you I support your decision. But I'm not that selfless. I'm not that friend. I don't want you to suffer. I really don't. I would share that burden if I could. I'd spell you on the worst days if I could, because I know you'd do that for me in a heartbeat. But I'd rather see you suffer than say goodbye. Sorry. If that makes me an asshole, then I'll change my name. Just put it on a nametag, and I'll wear it. I don't give a shit. When did you start being afraid of a little pain?"

"That's not it, Mo."

"Bull-shit!" I roared. "You owe it to the people who love you to battle. You owe us!"

"It's not my pain I'm worried about, man," he said it so softly I barely heard him.

"Where is your rage? Where is the green-eyed monster who wanted to kill me just for breathing his sister's name? Where's the guy that grabbed the bull by the horns in Spain just to see if he could? Where's the guy who shot a man to protect me, who threw himself in the line of fire? Let me get this straight, Tag. You would die to save my life, but you won't even fight to save your own?"

"Not if I have to put people through hell to do it."

"Take off the cape, bro. Take it off! Or I'm going to beat the hell out of you, put you in a strait-jacket, and start pumping you full of chemo myself. You watch me."

"I love you, Mo."

"Stop saying that, Tag!"

"I love you, Mo."

I felt a splintering sensation inside my chest, and I knew I had to get out before I lost it. I rarely cried, but I had a tendency to store up the grief, tucking it away in hidden compartments, boxing it up, building partitions. I hoarded my grief. But now I was bursting at the seams, unable to escape the towering feelings that had been threatening to bury me since Millie called and told me Tag was gone. I was falling apart. And I had to go.

IT TOOK ME several days to make the tapes. It had started out as a way to say goodbye, a way to express my feelings, my love for Millie in my own words. And as I told our story, I realized what a miracle it was. Moses was right. I got a miracle. And with every word, every tape, I became more convinced of it. The problem was, I didn't know how to stop. I didn't want the tapes to end. I couldn't say goodbye.

When I got the call about the fight, I put the tapes I'd completed, along with the tape recorder I'd borrowed from Henry, in the filing cabinet in the office at the gym, and left the key in an envelope for Millie. But I still had so much to say. I would remember something else, something I'd missed, something I wanted to tell her, and I would want to call her and talk to her. Then I'd remind myself of what the doctor said—stage four glioblastoma—and I would consider all the terrible things I'd read and re-searched about my diagnosis. I'd think about the pictures I'd seen, recite the survival rates. I'd think about the way I would die, the way I would suffer, the way those closest to me would suffer. And I wouldn't let myself call her. Instead, I went searching for a tape recorder of my own so I could make more tapes.

I ended up spending the next day, when I should have been on the road to Vegas, going from pawn shop to pawn shop looking for one. I hit pay dirt at the fifth shop I tried when an old woman sold me a dusty hand-held tape recorder from her back room, along with an unopened package of empty cassettes, all for a hundred bucks. She'd told me, straight-faced, that I was getting a deal. She was probably right. I would have paid two hundred.

The results of my biopsy had come back fairly quickly. I was only in the hospital for two days after my craniotomy. Not very long, considering they drilled into my head and took a big chunk of tissue off my brain. They were able to remove ninety-five percent of the tumor, which was great news. They also got the biopsy results back much sooner than they anticipated. They thought it would take six days post-op to get results. I got lucky. It only took them four. Lucky, lucky me.

When I went in for the craniotomy, I made a deal with myself. If the results came back negative, no cancer, I would call Moses and I would call Millie, and I would tell them about the little scare I'd had. I'd tell them I hadn't wanted to worry them, and hey, no big deal. I was fine. I would let Millie get mad at me and huff, and then I would kiss it all away, and I would make her marry me. Why wait? What had I said? When you love something you give it your name. I'd done that with my bar, I was going to do it with my girl. Hell, if Henry wanted my name, I'd adopt him too. I didn't see why it couldn't be done. We'd all be Taggerts. That's the deal I'd made with myself.

And if the news wasn't positive? If I had a terminal diagnosis? If the news wasn't positive, I wouldn't be calling anyone.

And that's what I did. I called a cab to come and get me after the craniotomy. The nurse had insisted on calling someone, and I'd insisted right back that I could take care of myself. I felt fine. My head ached, which made sense. But other than that, I felt fine. I kept saying that because it was true. My body felt fine. It was my heart that hurt. My heart felt like shit. But I felt fine. I went home and slept for two days, waking up to drink water, go to the bathroom, and go back to sleep. Then I got the word that the results were in, and I drove myself to the hospital to find out I had anywhere from six months to a year to live.

I drove myself back home again.

I still didn't call Moses, and I didn't call Millie. I didn't call Axel or bother Mikey. Instead, I let everyone believe I had gone to Dallas to see my family, and I called my lawyer. Then I started putting things in motion. During that time, I ignored my phone calls. I didn't read my texts. I couldn't. I couldn't and remain strong. But I was in the middle of making Millie a tape when the phone started ringing, interrupting my flow, and I'd grabbed at it to silence it, only to see Cliff Cordova's name lighting up the display. I'd answered it on instinct.

He had a fight for me. Saturday night in Vegas—six days away—against Terry Shaw. Fifty thousand dollars if I won, ten thousand just for showing up. I told him I'd only do it for fifty thousand, regardless if I won or not, but I promised him I would win. He agreed and told me if I won, Tag Team would get another twenty-thousand dollars, and he told me to be in Vegas in forty-eight hours.

It would mess up my plan. My team would find out. They would be hurt that I'd fought alone. Word would wind itself to Millie. She would be hurt too. Moses would find me in the afterlife and kick my ass. But what a hell of a way to go out.

I thought I would be strong. I thought I would take one for the team. I thought I was going to go out in a blaze of glory. Fight and die. Strong. But they found me first. And when I'd seen Millie, standing there in the crowd, Henry at her side, Moses holding her hand and looking at me like he wanted to strangle me, my resolve shook and my legs got weak.

And it had pissed me off.

I wasn't going to dissolve in a puddle for Terry Shaw to wipe up in one round. I was not going to have all my sacrifice and all my plans shot to hell because my girl was in the audience and my best friend was pissed. I was not going to let the dull throb in my head that hadn't gone away since I'd woken up with twenty staples in my skull make me sloppy and slow. I was not going to let cancer win. Not this round, at least.

I fought harder than I've ever fought before. Everything hurt, my energy was spotty, my two weeks out of the gym more of a factor than the surgery. I'd jogged three miles the day Cordova called. I ran five the next. The day before the fight I'd hit a Vegas Gold's gym and worked up a good sweat punching and kicking the hell out a bag, smelling the last of the anesthesia on my skin, feeling pretty damn strong, reminding myself I had nothing to lose. I wasn't even nervous. It was bizarre.

That feeling had continued until I'd seen Millie. Then the nerves had hit me like a fire hose and I'd been terrified that I would let her down, worse that I would get my trash kicked and she would have to stand there and witness it happening. I'd seen her face after that first round. She was miserable. And I'd called out to her. I couldn't help myself. I had to reassure her. I'd done it again after the next round. And again. And then I'd won. Her face had worn the most beautiful smile, and Henry was screaming my name. Moses still looked pissed.

Then the room spun. One screaming face blurred into another, as if I was on a carousel. The octagon was revolving. I didn't know that was possible. Must be a new feature. Then I realized it was me. I was the one spinning. And then I was falling, and my body bounced off the floor, my head connecting half a beat later, the dot on the 'i', the point on the exclamation mark. And the crowd roared. I didn't lift my hands to catch myself or cover my face. The fight was over, wasn't it? The bell had rung. Instead my eyes focused blearily on Moses, his smeared face further obscured by the crisscrossing web of the cage. Moses didn't look angry anymore. He looked stunned, and I saw him run toward me. Up over the side of the octagon, he came. I felt like I was in a fog and I couldn't control my right arm. My muscles were suddenly twitching, jerking, trying to jump out of my skin. And then the roaring began. It sounded like a big rig bearing down on me. Like I stood on the side of the road. Like I stood beneath the overpass not far from where they found my sister's body.

"Tag, can you hear me? Damn it. I think he's having a seizure!

It was Moses talking to me, but he sounded odd, far off. Like his voice came from far across the field where Molly was buried. Across the field and past the truck stop that paid a negligent vigil on a dead girl. The roaring of the trucks continued, one after the other, a typhoon of semis flying past me.

"He's biting the shit out of his tongue! Put the mouth guard back in his mouth! Tag! Tag, come on, baby!"

The pain in my head was suddenly so enormous there was no way I could open my eyes. Maybe I was the one with a bullet in my brain. Maybe my sister's killer had killed me too. No. That wasn't right. Molly's killer was dead. I killed him. I found him and killed him. And the dogs found Molly.

"Mr. Taggert, if you can hear me, can you try to open your eyes?"

I tried. I tried to open my eyes. The pain ricocheted in my head again, the sound of a gunshot reverberating from my memory into my present. Nah. That wasn't it. There wasn't a bullet in my brain. There was another problem with my brain.

Once, my sister Molly had dared me to eat two handfuls of sand. She'd said I couldn't do it. So of course I had. It hadn't even been wet sand. It had been gritty and sharp, and so dry that it got stuck in my throat and I'd coughed sand for three days afterward. My mouth felt like that again. I couldn't swallow and my tongue was fat and foreign behind my cracked lips. My throat was on fire.

Maybe I was back on the beach with Molly, the sky a never-ending blue, interrupted only by a low-flying plane pulling a streamer about car insurance behind it. But the buzzing and the light didn't come from the bright sky above a long stretch of beach, and my throat wasn't filled with sand. Bright lights circled my head instead of bi-planes, and the buzzing morphed into beeping machines and worried voices.

"Mr. Taggert?"

"Call me Tag," I rasped.

"Tag, do you know where you are?"

"Montlake Psychiatric Hospital," I whispered. I could even smell the bleach.

"Mr. Taggert?" Moses didn't call me Mr. Taggert. No one at Montlake called me Mr. Taggert. Not even Dr. Andelin. Maybe I wasn't at Montlake. But I was in a hospital. I was sure of it.

"You were in a fight, Mr. Taggert. Do you remember the fight?"

"Did I win?" I whispered, trying to lift my hands to see my knuckles. If I was in the hospital because of a fight, then I probably hadn't won. My dad would be so disappointed. I shut my eyes against the light and the voices, trying to remember how I lost.

"I'm proud of you, David." My father hadn't ever said that to me. Eleven years old, and he'd never said he was proud. But he was proud now.

"You are?" My voice cracked in amazement.

"Yeah. Sometimes we have to get mean in life to get some respect. There's nothing wrong with defending yourself. It's not a popular thing in this day and age. People think it's enlightened to be weak. It isn't. There's a time for words and a time for action."

I nodded. I liked words. But action had felt amazing.

"Words work much better if the person you're talking to knows you got something to back it up if words fail. How long you been tryin' to be friends with that kid?" My dad looked over at me and then back at the road.

"A long time."

"I thought so."

"I think I broke his nose." I tried not to sound as pleased as I felt.

"Yeah. You probably did. But now that he knows you can, he won't be quite as quick to start a fight, now will he?"

"Nope." I was silent for several minutes, until I forced myself to confess. "Dad?"

"Yeah, son?"

"I liked it. I like fighting. I want to do it again."

"I want a rematch. I thought I won. I thought I had that guy beat. The bell rang." I tried to form the words but they were slurred and sloppy and I wasn't sure anyone would understand. It was the sand in my mouth. The sand and my sore tongue. Damn my mouth hurt.

"You won the fight. It was over. But you had a seizure, Mr. Taggert. We need to find out why."

And then my eyes closed and the world went dark, darker than the world had ever been. That was the last thing I remember. And now I was here. Now I was in a hospital, the one place I'd sworn I wouldn't return to. And there would be no more running away. So what did I do now? Where did I go from here? I didn't know.

Idon'tknowwhattodo Idon'tknowwhattodo Idon'tknowwhattodo—the old refrain was back in my head, an ear worm that refused to morph into a solution. So I was talking to the tape recorder. Again.

Someone on Cordova's payroll had delivered my truck to the hospital, as well as all my things. I got a nurse to help me up—I was shaky and dizzy, but I could get around well enough—and I positioned the player by my head on the flattened out hospital bed, talking into it so I wouldn't have to hold it up to my face. They wouldn't keep me here much longer. We would be heading back to Utah in a day or two. Axel would be driving my truck home. When I said I could do it, Millie had cut me off immediately and the nurse had laughed.

I hadn't been alone with Millie. Not once. She'd stayed close, her hand on my arm, always touching me, but we hadn't had any time to ourselves. I didn't want a repeat of the scene with Moses, and I had no idea what to say to her. The seizure had left me exhausted and sleep was a relief. When I was awake and she was nearby I could only stare at her, cling to her hand, and try to imagine what she was thinking. What she was feeling. I think I knew, and her agony only made me want to sleep again. I'd tried once to tell her how sorry I was, and she just nodded and said, "I know, big guy. I know." But her eyes had filled up with tears, and she'd laid her forehead down on my chest to hide them from me. I'd smoothed her hair until sleep pulled me under.

The guys—Axel, Cory, Mikey, Paulo and Andy—were in and out. They refused to head back home without me. I got the feeling they were taking turns guarding me, like I would slip away again. None of us talked about why I was here. We tiptoed around that elephant like talking about it would make us all fall apart. So for now, we pretended it was the fight that landed me here. A fight I had won in fairly glorious fashion. It gave us something to talk about.

Moses hadn't come back. Moses had never been capable of pretending. He delivered Millie and Henry and picked them up again when Henry got restless and needed to head back to the hotel. I could tell Millie wanted to stay. But duty called, and she left without protest, a squeeze to my hand, her arm looped through Henry's, and none of the things that needed to be said were discussed.

It was late. The guys had all finally left, heading back to their hotel for the night, after making a big show of tearing up the contracts my lawyer had sent them, saying the gym was mine and they weren't going to sign anything. They were gone, but I was pretty sure someone had stayed behind to sit outside my hospital room door.

I was finally alone, talking to a tape recorder that was easily as old as I was, telling my story in hopes I would figure out an ending that wouldn't devastate the people I love.

Twenty-One

THE NEXT MORNING, Henry arrived at my hospital room first. I almost didn't recognize him. His hair was gone, just like mine, and only a shadow of stubble remained.

"Henry! Is that you, man?"

"It's me," he whispered, nodding. He looked troubled. Obviously, Millie or Moses had explained a few things to him. I wished they hadn't, but I guess there was no way around it. I had hoped they would let him believe I was only here because of the fight. I didn't want him worrying about the rest of it.

"Where's Millie?" I asked as the silence stretched between us.

"On the phone, in the hall."

"And Moses?"

"He went to get some breakfast for us, in the cafeteria."

I nodded, grateful. Moses was taking care of them. Good. Andy, Cory, Axel and Mikey had been looking out for them too, but they were on their way home now.

"What'd you do to your hair, Henry?" I asked when he refused to come closer than the foot of my bed.

Henry rubbed his smooth head with both hands, obviously aggravated. His face looked so different without all the hair, and for the first time I could see the resemblance between Millie and her brother. It was in the eyes. Millie's eyes would look just like Henry's if she could see. As it was, the shape, the pale color, the thick black lashes were the same, but Henry's eyes were wide with questions.

Henry sat down at the end of my bed abruptly, and when he looked at me again, his eyes were glassy, and his lips trembled.

"Brian Piccolo was a running back for the Chicago Bears."

I stared at him, puzzled. I had to think about that one for a minute. Then I understood.

"Yeah. He was." He was. And Brian Piccolo died of cancer at age twenty-six. Same age as me. I had made Moses watch *Brian's Song* with me, cried during the whole damn thing, even though I'd seen it a dozen times before, and then called him Billy Dee for a month afterwards. It was more fun than calling him Gale, after Gale Sayers, Piccolo's best friend. Moses didn't appreciate the nickname, but the dynamic between James Caan and Billy Dee Williams in the movie was pretty spot-on to Moses and me. I guess it was my own, Henry-esque way of communicating to Moses that I loved him without telling him. Apparently, I reminded Henry of Brian Piccolo too. I was honored. And I was terrified.

"Did you shave your head for me, Henry?"

Henry nodded and rubbed his head nervously once more. "Moses took me to a barber."

"Did he really?" My heart ached at the thought of my friend. "Feels pretty good, doesn't it?"

Henry nodded again. "Shaquille O'Neal, Michael Jordan, Brian Urlacher, Matt Hasselbeck, Mark Messier, Andre Agassi . . ."

"We're twins," I commented, interrupting his nervous recitation of bald athletes.

"I know," Henry answered. "I want to look like you."

The ache in my heart spread. Henry was irresistible sometimes.

"Can I rub your head?" I just wanted to get him to come closer. I needed to hold onto him for a minute.

Henry stood and moved until he was standing beside me. I tugged his hand and he sat next to me, his head bowed, eyes on the floor.

I placed my left hand on his head and rubbed in gentle circles, wanting to comfort him, hating that I was helpless to do so.

With a sudden sob, he fell against my chest, and I wrapped my arms around him, stroking his shorn head. He cried for a minute, soaking my hospital gown, clinging to me like he was afraid to lose his grip. Then he started to speak.

"David 'Tag' Taggert, light heavyweight contender with a professional record of twenty wins, two losses, twelve knock outs." Henry sounded like a fight announcer who had been on the sauce, all hiccups and slurred words, his voice muffled against me, and I noticed he had added my recent wins to the bio.

"Not a bad record, huh?"

"You're a fighter," he cried.

"Yeah. I am," I said.

"You love to fight," he insisted.

"I do."

"You're a fighter!" Henry's voice rose, and I realized what he was saying.

"This is a different kind of fight, Henry." I kept stroking his head.

"Same."

"Nah. Not the same at all."

"You're a fighter!"

"Henry—"

"Millie fights!" Henry insisted, interrupting me.

"She sure as hell does. Every damn day."

"Mikey fights," he lifted his head from my chest.

I could only nod.

"Moses fights," he said.

My throat closed.

"Henry fights?" This time it was more a question than a statement.

"You do," I whispered.

"My dad didn't fight." His eyes met mine, the pleading in them so heartfelt, so determined, so beloved, that I couldn't answer. Son of a bitch. He was killing me.

"Tag Taggert is the best fighter in the universe," he implored. "The best fighter in the universe."

I don't know how I ever thought Henry wasn't a good communicator.

"I NEED YOU to pull over, Mo," I insisted, my hand on the door handle. I was sitting in the back with Millie, and Henry was in the passenger seat beside Moses. We were on our way home from Las Vegas, and the trip couldn't have been more miserable if they'd tied me to the roof like Aunt Edna in National Lampoon's Vacation. I was trapped. I couldn't disappear again. I was on anti-seizure medication, and I was informed that it was illegal to "operate a motor vehicle for three months in the state of Utah after suffering a seizure." Some states, like Colorado, never allowed you to drive again. Legalize pot but don't let someone like me ever drive again. Made no sense to me.

Mo's eyes found mine in the rearview mirror. He had only spoken to me in grunts and single syllables since our heated conversation at the hospital, and I could feel his anger and frustration battling my own.

"Pull over," I barked. He could pull over or he could clean up my puke in his back seat.

He ground to a halt, gravel and debris kicking up as his tires dug into the asphalt on the side of the road.

I pushed the door open, climbed out, took several steps, and threw up all over Mo's rear right tire. He was going to be so pleased. I should have known better. Pain pills always made me sick. Now I was shuddering, braced against the truck, dizzy and weak, and it all just pissed me off. I was a badass. I had worked hard to become one. I was tough, I was powerful, and all I could do was sway and cling, begging the world to hold still so I wouldn't fall down.

We were north of Cedar City, south of a town called Beaver, which left nothing but open space and endless room for contemplation. The fields dotted with purple flowers on either side of the highway rolled serenely as the mountains looked on like indulgent parents. It was all so tranquil and benign it made me furious. It was such a lie. All of it.

"Do you need to pee, Tag?" Henry called from the interior of the truck. "Does he need to pee, Amelie? Can I pee too?"

Millie climbed out and gingerly felt along the side of the truck, her hands out-stretched until her fingers brushed my back. I heard Henry ask Moses if he could get out too, and Moses asked him to wait for just a minute. I appreciated that. I loved Henry, but I didn't want an audience. The fact that Millie couldn't see me was comforting. *She* was comforting.

She handed me a bottle of water without comment, and I took it gratefully, swishing my mouth and spitting a few times. I felt better and took a few careful breaths, filling my lungs to see if the nausea was gone.

"Better?" she asked softly.

"Yeah."

"You can lean on me, you know. Rest your head in my lap. It will make the rest of the ride easier if you sleep."

I had held myself stiffly the first few hours of the trip, keeping distance between us. She hadn't touched me, and I hadn't reached for her. There was so much to say, and so far, no chance to say it. Guilt and confusion and sorrow had been warring in me, especially in the last few days. I had had a plan—a shitty, terrible one—but still a plan. But it had been shot to hell, and now I couldn't see my way forward.

I realized I'd said the last words out loud and turned to look at Millie, whose up-turned face was suddenly close enough to kiss. We hadn't been this close since the night before my craniotomy, the night when we'd made love. I was such an asshole. I'd made love to Millie and then I'd run. Guilt sliced through me. Guilt and remorse and desire, and the nausea returned.

"I can't see my way forward," I repeated, giving her my back, willing the churning in my gut and the swaying in my head to ease.

"I can't either," Millie said softly. "But it hasn't stopped me yet."

I couldn't reply. I couldn't do anything but breathe and brace myself until my stomach settled. Eventually, Millie and I climbed back in the backseat, Henry took his turn outside the truck, and we resumed our journey.

Millie reached for my hand, and when she found it, she tugged, urging me toward her. I was a big man, and it was a bit of a press, but she cradled my head in her lap and pulled my coat up over my shoulders. I pressed my fists against my eyes like a child, holding back the helpless tears that wanted to fall. I kept them there until I fell asleep to Millie's hands stroking and soothing, forgiving me, even though I didn't deserve it.

(End of Cassette)

⠐⠉⠀⠄⠀⠐⠑⠀⠄⠐⠉

Moses

I DIDN'T KNOW what to do with my passengers. I didn't dare take them back to Salt Lake. Tag's apartment and the apartment above it were under contract—he had a buyer all lined up before he left for Vegas. Plus, he shouldn't be alone. He wasn't well, and I didn't trust him not to do something ridiculous. Again. I could take Millie and Henry home to Salt Lake and insist Tag come home to Levan with me, but I knew Millie wouldn't want that. I didn't think she and Tag had had a chance to air things out. And they needed to. Tag needed to make it right, if that was even possible. I'd watched them in the rearview mirror, Tag finally giving in and letting Millie hold onto him for the last stretch of the trip. She would forgive him, if she hadn't already, but I didn't know if he would let her. The whole thing was seriously messed up. All of it, and I felt the anguish boil up in me again. I had no idea what to do.

Tag had an appointment with his oncologist in Salt Lake in one week. I'd made him call Dr. Shumway in my presence, and he put the doctor on speaker. Dr. Shumway had been briefed by the Vegas medical team on Tag's fight, on the hemorrhage and swelling that had caused the seizure, and on Tag's present condition, which was surprisingly good, considering. Apparently, after a craniotomy, it's typical to wait at least a month to let the patient heal before embarking on a course of treatment, in other words, radiation and chemotherapy. It had been three weeks, so Tag's treatment hadn't been delayed by his decision to bolt, but Dr. Shumway informed Tag that it was unlikely, with the injury he'd "suffered"—Dr. Shumway was remarkably diplomatic—that treatment for the cancer would begin next week.

Tag would need more time to heal now, and the knowledge made me angry all over again. I wanted the cancer on blast. I didn't want Tag waiting any longer. He didn't seem upset by the delay whatsoever. Just subdued. Troubled. Unsure of himself. He watched Millie with such hunger

213

and regret that it was hard to stay angry with him. But I managed.

"You're all coming home with me. At least for the next few days," I insisted, arriving at the only solution I could come up with. We were nearing the Levan/Mills exit, an exit that boasted a few abandoned vehicles, several stray cows, and a man-made reservoir that wasn't much to look at. The freeway bypassed Levan completely, and the one exit, several miles from the town, was the only way to access it without backtracking from Nephi. Funny, Levan was just a blip on the map, a speck, but Georgia and Kathleen were there, and suddenly I was incredibly homesick for the town I once hated.

I caught Tag's gaze in my rear-view mirror, and he stared back at me steadily. He'd lifted his head from Millie's lap and straightened to a sitting position.

"You're all coming home with me," I repeated firmly.

He broke eye contact and turned to Millie, but she was already nodding.

"Okay," she said easily, and I released the breath I didn't know I was holding.

Henry was the only one smiling. "Did you know the average jockey weighs between 108 and 118 pounds?" he asked. Apparently, he was looking forward to riding again. "But a jockey has to be strong," he added. "Because the average racehorse weighs twelve hundred pounds and can run forty miles per hour."

I pressed the pedal down, flying toward home, leaving the average racehorse in the dust.

Twenty-Two

I SPENT THE first three days at Moses and Georgia's house holed up in my room. Georgia brought me food that I didn't want to eat, and I slept as much as I could. But on the fourth day, I was restless, irritatingly restored, and I couldn't hide in the room over Mo's studio forever. Even though I wanted to. They'd put Henry in the single bed in the baby's room—Kathleen still slept in a cradle in her parents' room—and Millie took the guest room on the main floor. It was a big house, a nice house, and I loved the people in it, but I had purposely avoided them.

Moses had stomped in that morning with the painting he'd done of David and Goliath and set it down on an easel facing my bed. Then he plunked down a huge bible, just tossed it in front of me, and opened it to a section that he had highlighted in red pencil.

"David kills giants. Giants don't kill David," he barked, slapping the book. "Read it." He stomped back out again.

I picked up the book, liking the heft in my hand, the silkiness of the pages. It had gold lettering engraved on the cover—Kathleen Wright—Moses's great-grandmother, the grandmother his daughter was named for. From the looks of it, her bible had been a trusted friend. It surprised me that Moses read it, but he obviously had, at least long enough to find the passage of scripture he wanted me to read. I turned back to the opened page and read the highlighted sections.

And it came to pass, when Goliath arose, and came, and drew nigh to meet David that David hastened, and ran toward the army to meet Goliath. And David put his hand in his bag, and took thence a stone, and slang it, and smote Goliath in his forehead that the stone sunk into his forehead; and he fell upon his face to the earth. So David prevailed over Goliath with a sling and with a stone, and smote Goliath, and slew him; but there was no sword in the hand of David. Therefore David ran, and stood upon Goliath, and took his sword, and drew it out of the sheath thereof, and cut off his head therewith.

Moses had underlined the part where David ran to meet Goliath. Eager little beaver, that David. The biblical David apparently enjoyed fighting too. I sighed and shut the book. I wasn't terribly inspired. I knew what Moses wanted, but deep down, I wasn't convinced, and I wished he would hear me out. Moses was all about seeing, but he could stand to listen every once in a while.

I could hear Georgia and Henry outside my bedroom window. The room overlooked the round corral, and Georgia was walking Sackett in slow circles, Henry perched happily on his back, chatting away like talking was his favorite thing and not something he struggled with at all. Georgia was damn good at what she did, and I marveled at the little miracle that Henry was here, enjoying the benefits of my friendship with Georgia and Moses. If nothing else, that was something I could hold onto. I hadn't messed everything up. It wasn't all bad.

It was just mostly bad. Including the way I smelled. I desperately needed a shower. In addition to the bed, Moses had a huge sink and a toilet tucked away above his work space, but no shower. I would have to brave the rest of the house for that, and it couldn't be put off any longer.

When I slipped into the house through the garage entrance, I stopped to listen. I could hear someone upstairs—Moses, by the sound of the footfalls—but nobody seemed to be downstairs. The big guest bathroom on the main floor was connected to the room Millie had slept in, but the bed was neatly made and Millie was nowhere to be seen. I released my breath and ducked into the bathroom, locking the door and making use of the shower.

But Millie was waiting for me when I came out. She sat primly on the bed, her hands folded in her lap, just waiting.

"You smell good, David," she said with a smile, and I felt a pang at the memory those words invoked. She stuck out her hand toward me, like she'd done the night we met, as if waiting for me to shake it.

"Hi. I'm Amelie. And I'm blind."

I couldn't deny her. I stepped forward and took her hand in mine and said my line.

"Hi. I'm David. And I'm not." I didn't release her, and she didn't pull it away. I ran my thumb over the silkiness of her skin, my eyes riveted to our joined hands. God, I loved her so much! I wanted to shut the door, lock it, and push her back onto the bed and just let it all go. Just for a while. I wanted that so badly.

"Now that we've introduced ourselves again, maybe you'll talk to me," she suggested gently.

"I don't want to talk, Millie," I whispered.

She tilted her head sideways, catching the heat in my voice. The ode. The freaking ode that was still thrumming between us, the song on constant repeat.

She stood up slowly, and she was so close that her body brushed mine. I felt her breath at my throat, a little flutter of the melody that I couldn't get out of my head, out of my heart. I brought one hand to her face and tipped her chin up, until her lips were directly beneath mine. And then I kissed her. So lightly. So gently. Trying desperately not to turn the song into a symphony, the ode into a cymbal-crashing orchestral arrangement.

She responded, but she didn't increase the tempo. Our lips met, merged, and retreated only to meet again and repeat the motion. When I urged her lips apart and tasted the wet sweetness of her mouth, it was all I could do not to moan in defeat. And then we were tumbling back onto the bed, her hips in my hands, my shirt clutched in her fists, and the kiss roared to an inevitable, if sudden, crescendo.

And that's when she pushed me away.

"David. Stop," she whispered, her mouth seeking me even as she asked me to quit. I pressed my forehead to hers to rein myself in and bit back a curse when my still-tender flesh protested the contact. She took my cheeks in her hands, and ran her fingers over my face, as if trying to read my expression.

"We don't have to talk. But you can't kiss me and then leave again. You can't do that to me, David." There was steel in her voice, though it was wrapped in velvet, and I knew she meant it.

"I may not be able to control whether I leave or not," I said, rolling away from her and staring up at the ceiling.

"That's not what I mean, big guy. And you know it." She sat up and folded her legs beneath her. She kept a hand on my arm the way she always did when we were close, the contact important to her. Yeah. I knew what she meant. I'd taken myself away. Removed myself. And she was asking me if I was going to do it again.

"People don't survive what I've got. They just don't," I whispered.

She immediately shook her head. Resisting. Her resistance made me harsh.

"It might seem romantic, Millie. Taking care of me. But it isn't romantic. It'll be ugly and painful. And I won't be the man you're in love with. I'll be the man trying not to die and dying anyway," I pressed. She stiffened and her hand tightened on my shirt. Good. She was listening.

"I'll feel like shit, I'll probably be mean as hell, and you'll wonder what you're doing. I'll lose my bumps. You're all about the bumps, remember? I've already lost my hair. I'll lose my ability to be strong for you. And for Henry. And when you've lost all that, when you've been through hell, I'll die anyway! I'll die anyway, Millie, and you won't have anything left. No David, no Tag. You won't have my song. You'll just have a belly full of sorrow," I argued, impassioned. But she was ready for me.

"Some people are worth suffering for. I'm strong. I've been training for this, you know. Instead of feeling bad that I've had my trials, be grateful that I'm strong. I've got this. I've got you. Don't take that away from me, David."

"I don't want our last days together to be with me in a vegetative state. I don't want you to feed me and hold my hand! I don't want to forget your name. I don't want you to watch me suffer!"

"Ah, but I won't. Perks of being a blind girl," she shot back, and there was anger in her voice. "I won't have to see you suffer at all, will I?"

I swore and stood, shaking her off. I didn't want to argue with her. I headed for the door. I now understood Millie's need to walk everywhere she went. Walking beat being trapped. And I was trapped.

"When are you going to start believing that you are worthy to be loved?" Her voice rang out behind me, clear and controlled, but there was a barely restrained fury that made her words wobble.

I paused and faced her once more. She was trying to follow me, and I had no doubt that if I walked out of the house, she would grab her stick, and I would be forced to play a game of Marco Polo down the streets of Levan so she wouldn't lose me. I needed her to let me go and she obviously wasn't going to do that.

"Millie—"

"No!" she cried. "You don't think you are worthy of love if you aren't Tag, if you aren't the 'sexy man!'" Millie did air quotes and mocked me, mocked the conversation we'd had when she'd played my chords. "You don't think you are worthy of love if you are sick. You don't think you are worthy of love if you can't be the strong one all the damn time! If you can't take care of me twenty-four seven, you must not be worthy of love."

"That's not it!" I protested, shaking my head, denying everything.

"That *is* it, dammit!" she cried, stamping her foot. She stepped toward the decorative vanity where she'd carefully placed her things and, with a rare show of temper, pushed everything to the floor. Toiletries, a blow dryer, a pile of folded laundry—all of it tumbled off the edges, and Millie kept pushing, just like she was pushing me.

"Millie, cut it out, dammit! You're going to hurt yourself, baby!"

"NO!" she shouted. "This is *not* about me! If I want to throw a few things, I will. I'm not an invalid. I'm not a princess. I'm a grown woman. And I can throw a fit if I feel like it!" She threw her hand out in my direction, pointing her finger at me and wagging it fiercely. "And I don't expect *you* to clean it up when I'm done!"

I didn't know what to say, so I said nothing as I watched her come unglued. At me.

"Do you know when I lost my sight I felt guilty for a long time? I felt guilty for the pain I put my parents through. Then my dad left. And my guilt grew tenfold. I felt guilty when my mom had to change her whole life to accommodate my blindness. Henry was just a little kid, and he had his own set of issues. And I made everything worse! I made everything fall apart. That's what I told myself for a long, long time."

I knew exactly how that felt. Guilt. I'd been consumed with it when

Molly disappeared. Eaten alive by it. And I was racked with it now. But Millie wasn't waiting for me to contribute to the conversation. She was shaking with anger, and I stayed silent.

"I don't know when things started to change. Maybe it was gymnastics. Maybe it was music and dancing. Maybe it was when my mother got sick, and someone started to depend on *me* for once. And I handled it, David. I handled it! I was strong. And I was worthy of love. I had been worthy all along! I just didn't see it." Millie thumped her chest emphatically and repeated. "I am worthy to be loved. Blind eyes and all."

The lump in my throat was so wide and hard that I groaned a little, trying to breathe around it. Millie's sightless eyes were filled with tears that spilled over and slid down her cheeks. She brushed at them impatiently.

"Even still. I would never have asked you to love me, David. I asked for a kiss because I wanted it so badly. But I would never have asked you to love me. My pride would not allow it. My self-respect would not stand for it. But you gave it. You offered it. You fell in love with me anyway! And I am worthy of that love," she repeated, her voice rising again.

"Yeah. I did. And you are," My heart was in my throat and I walked toward her. She heard me coming and stepped away, her arm extended stiffly, palm toward me, warding me off.

"No. Not yet," she told me firmly, though she was no longer yelling. "I understand guilt, David, I do. But love can't be one-sided. One person can't always give and the other person can't always take. If you truly love me, you have to trust me."

I couldn't think of someone I trusted more, not even Moses.

"I do trust you, Millie."

"No. You don't. You don't trust me. And you don't think *you* are worthy of love."

I couldn't breathe. I couldn't breathe and I couldn't move. So I listened.

"You don't think you are worthy of my love if you can't be strong all the time," she repeated firmly. "And you don't think that I'm strong enough to be there for you when you aren't. You don't trust me."

"This has nothing to do with my faith in you. I know who you are, Millie." I stumbled over my response, trying to express myself, trying to say what I meant and mean what I said. "I know you would see me through. You say give miracles a chance, but I feel like I already got mine. You're my miracle! The fact that you and I came together, that we met, that I found the love of my life. That's a miracle, Millie! I'm so grateful for that. So many people don't get that. We did. It's a miracle I was awake enough not to miss it. And it's a miracle you loved me back."

Her face crumpled and she reached for me. At last she reached for me. Entreating me. I went to her immediately, but she pressed both hands against my chest, framing my heart, keeping me from pulling her into me. Then she ran her hands down my arms and found my hands. She cradled one of my hands in both of hers and brought my palm to her lips. She kissed it softly, sweetly, pressing her lips to the center as if she could ease my pain and her own by kissing it all away. Then she moved my palm from her lips and let me cup her cheek. She leaned into it briefly, holding it there, as if she drew strength from me, despite what she'd said. Then she slid my hand down her neck, past the fine bones at her collar, and pressed my palm against her breast, covering her completely.

"Most people think the most intimate thing in the world is sex," she said softly.

I shuddered at the sense of belonging I felt, touching her like that, where no one else touched her, but I didn't curl my fingers against her, didn't caress the crest of her breast with my thumb or reach up and cradle her other breast in the hand that still hung at my side. I just waited, feeling the pounding of her heart against the tips of my fingers, and she rewarded me by continuing.

"I thought when I made love with you, when I let you see all of me and when you let me know all of you, every private inch, when we made that promise with our bodies and our lips, I thought that would be the most intimate thing we would ever do."

"Millie?" I whispered. I didn't know where she was going with this, but there was sorrow in her words, and finality, like she'd reached a conclusion about me, about us.

"But it wasn't. Sex is not the most intimate thing two lovers can do. Even when the sex is beautiful. Even when it's perfect." Millie drew a deep breath as if she remembered how perfect it had truly been. "The most intimate thing we can do is to allow the people we love most to see us at our worst. At our lowest. At our weakest. True intimacy happens when *nothing* is perfect. And I don't think you're ready to be intimate with me, David."

She stopped talking, letting her words ring in the air, and my hand curled against her breast, kneading her and needing her, and not knowing how to give her what she wanted. Her breath caught and her head fell into my chest as if the pleasure warred with the pain.

"I don't know how," I confessed, and I pulled my hand away so I wouldn't hurt her in my frustration.

She grabbed my hand and brought it back, this time pressing it to her heart.

"I'm telling you how. You hold onto me. You trust me. You use me. You lean on me. You rely on me. You let me shelter you. You let me love you. All of you. Cancer. Fear. Sickness. Health. Better. Worse. All of you. And you'll have all of me."

"I don't know if I can beat it, Millie." I choked on the words and suddenly I was crying. My first instinct was to be grateful she couldn't see me, and then I felt her hands on my cheeks, feeling the tears, and I braced myself. But I didn't pull away. She stood on tiptoe and pulled my face to hers, pressing her trembling lips to mine, comforting, quieting, and acknowledging my fear. And it wasn't just fear, it was my deepest fear. If I fought, I didn't know if I could win. In fact, I was pretty sure I wouldn't. I tasted Millie's tears, and I knew she tasted mine. And then she spoke against my lips.

"You don't have to beat it, David. You don't have to beat it. You just have to let us fight with you."

I wrapped my arms around her and held on for a moment, unable to speak. When I found my voice I still didn't let her go.

"No tap outs," I whispered.

"No guilt," Millie said gently.

"Amelie means work." I don't know why that came to my mind, but it did. As she held me up, I thought of her strength.

"That's right." She smiled tremulously. "So are you going to work for me or not?"

Twenty-Three

Moses

I HEARD A crash downstairs, and I paused, concerned and a little irritated. Kathleen was asleep, and I really didn't want her waking up. She had a couple new teeth coming in, and she was ornery and more than a little miserable. Then I heard Millie's voice, raised, angry even, and I froze, listening. I heard the rumble of Tag's voice too, and Millie came right back at him, even angrier. I walked to the top of the stairs and caught bits and pieces of what Millie was saying. She wasn't taking a breath, and she was laying it all out. And then the door to the bedroom was closed, and the voices were obscured. I started down the stairs, more hopeful than I'd been all week. I don't know how she'd done it, but Tag was in Millie's room, and things were finally coming to a head.

Henry came bursting into the house, Millie's name on his lips, and I raced down the remaining stairs, intercepting him.

"Henry, wait!"

Henry jumped and turned, startled at the vehemence in my voice. There was no way I was letting anything interrupt what was going on behind that door.

"Don't go in there. Millie's with Tag. And we need to leave them alone for a while."

Henry looked at the closed door and looked back at me. He nodded his head slowly. I got us both a cold can of Coke from the fridge and handing one to him, put my arm around his shoulders and steered him back out of the house. We sat out on the deck, putting our feet up on the railing so we could watch Georgia work while we downed our drinks. I loved watching Georgia work.

"Axel has never ridden a horse," Henry remarked, clearly thinking about the evening before, when Axel and Mikey had delivered Tag's truck, uncertain of where to stow it in Salt Lake, with everything up in the air like it was.

"Nope. Did you show him how it's done?" I knew Henry had shown off a little, but I wanted to give him a chance to talk about it. Tag hadn't come down when the guys arrived. It was a miracle he was talking to Millie now.

"Yep. I show him things, he shows me things," Henry said, nodding. "I'm part of the team."

It was my turn to nod. Tag had assembled an amazing group of guys. And the coolest thing about them was how they all treated Henry.

"There is no 'i' in team," Henry said suddenly, seriously, as if repeating something he'd heard at a school pep rally. Or maybe he'd heard it in the gym.

"Nope."

"There is no 'i' in Tag Team either," he added.

"Nope. There isn't," I agreed.

"Are we Tag's team?" he asked.

I started to explain what Tag Team was, the label, the fighters, the gym. And then I stopped myself. "Yeah. We are. We're Tag's team."

"Because we love him?"

"Yeah," I said, getting choked up all over again. I was so tired of being overcome with emotion. But Henry had a way of sneaking up on me and saying the obvious, and saying it in such a way that it seemed profound. In Vegas, Millie had explained Tag's condition to him the best she could, and he had come to me asking to go to a barber so he could get his hair cut like Tag's. I hadn't really known why he'd wanted to. I'd just thought it was just a case of hero worship. But Millie had been stunned by Henry's desire to cut his hair. Apparently it wasn't something that came easily to him. I realized now that it was his way of lending moral support, of being part of Tag Team. I watched as Georgia climbed over the fence and started toward us, grateful that I'd have her moral support momentarily.

"There *is* an 'i' in David, though," Henry said simply, as if that negated the whole "I in team," argument.

I laughed—a loud bark of relief that had him tipping his head toward me in curiosity. "You were doing so well, kid. I thought you were going to inspire me," I snorted, still laughing, and relieved to be doing so.

"There isn't an 'i' in Henry," he said blandly.

"Or Moses," I added, unable to stop chuckling. "We're the selfless ones," I explained.

"There's an 'i' in Georgia," Henry said, as Georgia joined us on the deck.

"Yep. And don't I know it. Me, me, me. All the time," I said, pulling on Georgia's hand and bringing her in close to me. She wrapped her arms around my neck and kissed my lips gently.

"Where's Millie?" she asked, not taking my bait.

"She's with Tag," Henry volunteered. "And we're leaving them alone."

Georgia's eyes shot to mine and her eyebrows rose.

"Oh yeah?" There was hope in her voice.

"Yeah. And Millie wasn't being gentle," I added softly. But Henry still heard.

"There's no such thing as a timid fighter," Henry parroted. "That's what Tag says. And he says Amelie fights every damn day."

"Hallelujah and praise the Lord for that," Georgia said, sounding just like my great-grandma Kathleen. They were both small-town Levan girls who had spent a good deal of their lives as neighbors. So I guess it wasn't surprising.

"Amen," I agreed.

"Muhammad Amelie," Georgia joked. "Floats like a butterfly . . ."

"Stings like a bee," Henry and I finished.

"I'm going to go check on Kathleen," Georgia said, easing away from us. I knew she was going to eavesdrop at the guest bedroom door on her way to Kathleen, but I didn't call her on it, hoping she'd report back. Henry stood too and wandered back out to the corral to commune with Sackett, who walked to the fence to greet him.

From the corner of my eye I saw a pulse, a shimmer, like the air above the black top on a sweltering day. My neck got hot, and instead of resisting, I opened myself up to the summoning flicker, curious instead of afraid. It wasn't Molly this time.

I recognized her, though I'd only seen her once before. She showed me lace. Just lace. A billowing swath, and then she was gone. But I understood, and for the first time since Tag disappeared, the vise around my heart eased slightly.

I TRADED ONE room for another, holing up in different parts of my best friend's house. But this time, I wasn't hiding. I was healing. Or hoping. Maybe that was it. Maybe I was allowing myself to hope.

No one came knocking. No one brought food or slid notes under the door. Even Henry. He was taken care of, and Millie and I both knew it. So we stayed locked away, together.

Darkness descended outside, and the stars came out. Millie couldn't see them, but I told her they were there, fat and bright in the sky outside the big bay window in the guest room. I told her how I'd lain beneath those stars as a boy, sleeping out on the trampoline in my backyard in Dallas. I told her how, ten years later, Moses and I had stretched out on the deck of a boat going down the Nile River in Africa. I'd looked up at that never-ending expanse, and I'd recognized that old feeling. The very same feeling I'd had as a kid. I didn't feel insignificant under the stars. I felt huge, like the heavens revolved around me. I was bigger than the stars. I was bigger and brighter, and the world was mine. I was so enormous I could hold up my thumb and completely blot one out, hold up my hand and obliterate a whole section of the sky. Such power. Such size. I wasn't David, I was Goliath.

As I laid in that bed with Millie, the drapes pushed aside, staring out at the winking stars over a tiny town I'd never called home, that feeling surged inside me once again. I was relevant. I was significant. I had wanted to disappear, if only so the cancer could disappear with me. But the stars whispered that there was no such thing. You don't ever disappear. You just change. You leave. You move on. But you never disappear. Even when you think you want to.

Millie didn't laugh. She didn't tease me about feeling God-like. She just listened to me talk, my fingers climbing up and down the smooth skin of her back, tracing the curve of her hip and the length of her leg that was thrown across mine. And then I pulled her into me, my hand at the base of her spine, and she caught her breath and said my name, and I felt God-like all over again.

I DON'T KNOW what time it was when we finally spoke again. We had slept for hours and awoke with growling bellies and dry throats, but stuck our faces beneath the bathroom tap and guzzled water to ease our thirst, just so we wouldn't have to leave the room. Then Millie's mouth found mine, her lips wet and cold, water clinging to her chin and sliding down her breasts, and we began again. Sometime before dawn, I attempted to slide out of bed, untangling myself from my sleeping beauty only to have her come fully awake and sit up, reaching for me, panicked.

Her fear made me sad because I had created it.

"Shhh, Millie. I'm not going anywhere. I promise. I'll be right back," I whispered, kissing her forehead and smoothing her hair. "Lay back down. I promise you I won't leave again. Not on purpose. Not ever again."

She nodded and sank back against the pillows as I pulled on my jeans, but when I came back several minutes later, her eyes were open and she was waiting, listening for me, the sheets pulled up over her body, one arm curled under her head.

"Where'd you go?" she asked.

"Your mighty hunter has brought meat. And bread. And cheese," I grunted in my best caveman voice.

"And Miracle Whip?" she interrupted.

"Gross."

"You know I like Miracle Whip."

"And Miracle Whip," I said, handing her a sandwich on a plate, complete with Miracle Whip, just the way she liked it.

I scarfed down three sandwiches in the time it took her to eat one and cracked the top on a can of soda, listening to the bubbles for just a second in quiet appreciation of Millie's favorite sounds.

When we were done, I padded back to the kitchen and set our plates in the sink, put the sandwich fixings back in the fridge, and closed the tie on the bread bag. That's when I spied the keys to my truck on the counter and paused, considering. I swept them up and was out the front door, inside my truck, and then back in the house in less than a minute, grateful that the house was still quiet and Millie hadn't chased me down.

Millie was brushing her teeth and her hair at the same time, wearing my discarded T-shirt and looking like salvation, even in the dark. I sat on the bed and watched her, enjoying her, but she'd heard me come in, even over the running water. She knew I was there.

She climbed back into bed, snuggling down, and I thought about tugging my T-shirt over her head and kicking off my jeans, but some things required pants and I kind of felt like this was one of them. I crawled up behind her and wrapped myself around her, pulling her back against my chest. Then I whispered into her hair.

"Will you marry me, Millie?"

"What?" she gasped.

"Will you marry me and let me be Henry's brother? I want you to be part of Tag Team." I was parroting Henry's proposal, trying to be cute, but my heart was in my throat and my hands felt slick against my T-shirt. I was glad I hadn't pulled it off her. I pressed on. "Statistically, athletes with families have more purpose, better mental health, more stamina and overall improved performance than athletes who aren't married." If it wasn't word for word what Henry had spouted off to me, it was close. But she was silent, and I couldn't see her face.

"I was gonna ask you a month ago. I bought a ring. It was still in the glove box in my truck," I explained, rushing over the words. And now it was in my pocket, in my jeans, waiting for her to give me an answer.

"I know. You told me," she whispered.

"The tapes?" I asked, realizing I had indeed told her.

"Yes."

"If none of this had happened, if I'd asked you two weeks ago, before all this went down, what would you have said?" I asked, my heart fat in my chest.

"No. I would have said no," Millie said quietly.

My stomach lurched a little, and I pulled her closer even though I wanted to let go. My heart was pounding.

"Why, Millie?"

"Because I thought you needed more time," she said.

"You thought *I* needed more time?" I asked, incredulous.

She nodded, one quick jerk of her head, and her hair tickled my lips. I waited for several seconds, processing.

"And now?" I asked.

"Now, I want to marry you so badly that I don't care if you need more time," she confessed.

I laughed, suddenly glad I was lying down. I felt lightheaded with relief. And then something else occurred to me.

"Have you changed your mind because I don't have any more time?" I probed, and my voice cracked.

I felt a tremor run down her body.

"No. I've changed my mind because I don't want anyone keeping us apart. I don't want someone telling me I can't be by your side. I want to be a Taggert. Or a Taggerson." I felt her effort to smile, but I don't think she succeeded. "I want to be yours. I want you to be mine. Hospital beds, my bed, your bed. I don't care. I just want to be with you."

"You want to take care of me," I said flatly.

She ignored my statement and made one of her own. "If I wasn't blind, I would have said yes. A month ago, I would have said yes."

I waited.

"But because I'm blind, I would have wanted to give you lots of time to know what you were getting into."

"I wouldn't have changed my mind, sweetheart."

"I'm always going to be blind, David."

"Most likely . . . yeah," I agreed.

"And a month ago, you wanted to marry me anyway?" she asked, clearly knowing the answer.

"Yeah. I did."

"You wanted to marry me in spite of my blindness, and I want to marry you in spite of your cancer. Is that so hard to understand?"

"No," I whispered. Because it wasn't. Not when she put it that way.

We lay in silence, listening to each other breathing, thinking, considering. But I'd made my decision the moment I submitted. Moses had warned me that's what it would take, hadn't he?

"All or nothing, Millie?" I asked, my mouth pressed against her temple.

"All," she answered back.

"Me too," I whispered. All or nothing. That's who I was. And if I was going to fight, if I was going to stay, I was going to have it all for as long as I could have it. I reached in my pocket and took out the ring.

Twenty-Four

Moses

I GOT UP before the sun rose. I was restless and moody, even more than usual, and I decided to paint for a while. But painting hadn't eased the prickle under my skin or the knots in my belly, and when the sun rose I made a pot of coffee and decided to spend a little time outside seeing the day break before the rest of the house woke up and made contemplation impossible.

"You look like your thoughts weigh a thousand pounds," Tag said, his voice rough with sleep, and the French doors to my left closed quietly. He eased down into the deck chair next to mine and faced the sluggish sunrise, his eyes trained forward. He held a cup of my coffee in a mug between his big hands and sipped at it like heaven came in mouthfuls of caffeine.

"Well, well, well," I said, and I felt my lips twist up in a smirk. I had told myself I wasn't going to give him any grief about being holed up with Millie for a solid sixteen hours. And here I was, giving him grief the moment he set foot on my deck.

He didn't smirk back or tell me to shut up. He looked tired. But he looked good. Amazingly enough, he looked good. Content even. I still wasn't used to his buzzed hair. It looked a little too skinhead for my taste, but Tag worked it. He had the jawline to pull it off, irritating as that was.

"You look like shit, Tag," I lied, just because it was our way with each other.

"So do you, Mo," he said amiably.

"It's your fault," I said, just like I had in the hospital. I immediately felt bad and wished I could take it back. It *was* his fault. But it wasn't his fault.

He didn't respond and took another long draw from his coffee.

"Do you ever think about Montlake?" I asked him, sipping the surface of the coffee, not going too deep. Kinda the way I was doing now, dipping my toe into a conversation that felt a little like a cauldron.

"All the time," Tag answered, tipping his mug again.

"I do too. All the time. Especially lately," I said.

We sat like two old men, sipping away, time slipping away, yet not in any hurry to fight it. Funny how that was. Old folks knew their days were numbered, and yet they rarely rushed to fill them.

"Those were some dark days, Mo," Tag said softly.

"They *were* dark. But we had nothing to lose," I said.

"And now, we've got everything to lose," he said.

"Now we've got everything to lose," I repeated.

"I dreamed about Dr. Andelin's wife," Tag said suddenly, inexplicably, and I was distracted from where I was leading the conversation.

"What?" I gasped.

"Remember that counseling session when you saw her?" Tag insisted, his green eyes sharp. "When we met?"

"That time you wanted to kill me?" I tried to laugh, but couldn't gather enough mirth. My laugh just sounded like I'd been punched in the stomach, which was strangely fitting, because Tag had done just that. I'd asked him about Molly, and he'd punched me in the stomach, slapped me across the face, and knocked me to the floor. And I'd welcomed it and fought back.

"How did you know?" Tag said, his eyes on mine. The din around us quieted slightly. "How did you know about my sister?" The orderlies pulled us off the floor and let us sit, but Dr. Andelin pressed me to answer.

"Moses, do you want to explain to Tag what you meant when you asked if anyone knew a girl named Molly?"

"I didn't know she was his sister. I don't know him. But I've been seeing a girl named Molly off and on for almost five months," I said.

They all stared at me.

"Seeing her? Do you mean you have a relationship with Molly?" Dr. Andelin asked.

"I mean, she's dead, and I know she's dead because for the last five months I've been able to see her," I repeated patiently.

Tag's face was almost comical in its fury.

"See her how?" Dr. Andelin's voice was flat and his eyes were cold.

I matched his tone and leveled my own flat gaze in his direction. "The same way I can see your dead wife, Doctor. She keeps showing me a car visor and snow and pebbles at the bottom of a river. I don't know why. But you can probably tell me."

Dr. Andelin's jaw went slack and his complexion greyed.

"What are you talking about?" he gasped. I'd been waiting to use this on him. Now was as good a time as any. Maybe his wife would go away and I could focus on getting rid of Molly once and for all.

"She follows you around the joint. You miss her too much. And she worries about you. She's fine . . . but you're not. I know she's your wife because she shows you waiting for her at the end of the aisle. Your wedding day. Your tuxedo is a little too short in the sleeves."

I tried to be flippant, to force him out of his role as psychologist. I dug around in his life to keep him from digging around in my head. But the savage grief that slammed across his face slowed me down and softened my voice. I couldn't maintain my attitude against his pain. I felt momentarily shamed and looked down at my hands. Then Dr. Andelin spoke.

"My wife, Cora, was driving home from work. They think she was blinded—temporarily—by the sun reflecting off the snow. It's like that sometimes up here on the bench, you know. She drifted into the guardrail. Her car landed upside down in the creek bed. She . . . drowned."

He supplied the information so matter-of-factly, but his hands shook as he stroked his beard.

Somewhere during the tragic recount, Tag lost his fury. He stared from me to Dr. Andelin in confusion and compassion. But Cora Andelin wasn't done—it was like she knew I had the doctor's attention and she wasn't wasting any time.

"Peanut butter, Downey fabric softener, Harry Connick, Jr., umbrellas . . ." I paused because the next image was so intimate. But then I said it anyway. "Your beard. She loved the way it felt, when you . . ." I had to stop. They were making love and I didn't want to see this man's wife na-

ked. I didn't want to see him *naked. And I could see him through her eyes.*

But Dr. Andelin was dialed in, his blue eyes intense and full of his own memories, and something else too. Gratitude. His eyes were full of gratitude.

"Those were some of her favorite things. She walked down the aisle on our wedding day to a Harry Connick song. And yeah. My tux was a smidge too short. She always laughed about that and said it was just like me. And her umbrella collection was out of control." His voice broke, and he looked down at his hands.

The room was so heavy with compassion and thick with intimacy that if the five others present were able to see what I could see, they would have looked away to give the lovers a moment alone. But I was the only one to witness Noah Andelin's wife reach out and run a hand over her husband's bowed head before the soft lines of her inconsistent form melded into the flickering light of the fading afternoon.

Strange. I hadn't thought about Cora Andelin since I'd left Montlake. And I hadn't seen her since that day, just as I'd predicted. But the memory was so sharp and specific that I felt a sense of déjà vu, like Tag wasn't the only one who'd dreamed about her. Dr. Andelin's face, when I'd told him I could see his wife, was burned into the backs of my eyes. I'd thrown all his precious details, details of her life, of their life together, in his face, simply because I had needed to distract him from looking too hard at my own. I was my own special brand of asshole in those days.

"Remember how you said that she was fine, but Doc wasn't?" Tag asked.

I nodded, incredulous. *"She follows you around the joint. You miss her too much. And she worries about you. She's fine . . . but you're not."*

"So that's why she was hanging around. She was worried about him," he said.

"I can't believe you remember that," I exclaimed in disbelief.

"Some things you don't forget, Mo." Tag swore. "I won't *ever* forget it." He shook his head like the images still haunted him. "Do you think the reason you saw Molly—and don't lie to me, Mo. I know you've seen her a few times now. Do you think it's because she's just worried about me?" There was a wistful note in his voice that made hope flicker in my heart.

"It very well could be," I answered softly, coaxing the flicker to a flame.

He nodded and set his empty mug down at his feet. But I wasn't ready to let Montlake go, not yet.

"Before we left Montlake, you asked me to keep you alive. You told me to knock you down, restrain you, whatever it took. Do you remember that?" I asked, not looking at him. I couldn't look at him and keep my emotions in check.

"Yeah. I remember," he said.

"I told you I would." I had to stop talking for a minute. I took a few deep breaths and a huge gulp of coffee to soothe my burning throat and ease the ache in my chest. "And I intend to keep that promise," I said, my voice cracking on the last word.

When he didn't respond, I braced myself and turned toward him.

Tag's throat was working even though his coffee was gone. He rubbed at his jaw, passing a hand over trembling lips, and I could tell he was fighting for control, just like I was.

"I can't cure cancer, Tag. And I sure as hell can't stop the people I love from leaving me. I couldn't save Gi. I didn't save Eli. But I've got some pull on the other side. And they're all gonna have to go through me if they want you."

He was nodding. "All right," he whispered. "All right. But Mo, if that's not enough. In the end, if that's not enough, I need you to take care of Millie and Henry. Millie won't want to let you. She's stubborn like that. But make sure she doesn't stop dancing. I hate it, but she loves it. And that's the important thing. Make sure she's doin' the things she loves. Don't let her grieve too long. Don't let her grieve like Dr. Andelin did, making his dead wife follow him around because he couldn't let her go. Help her let me go, Mo. Tell her I'm happy. Make shit up."

I choked, laughter and tears warring for supremacy.

"Tell her I'm fighting with legends in heaven, that I am running through meadows of flowers, that I'm being fed grapes . . . scratch that. She wouldn't like that. Just tell her I'm eating grapes."

I laughed harder and wiped at my eyes.

"I'll fight this thing, Mo. I'll fight as hard as I can until the bell rings. But if the bell rings sooner rather than later, then you gotta promise me that you'll take care of my girl. We gotta deal?"

"Deal," I whispered. And we were both quiet for a time, battling grief and gratitude and the irony that there is no sorrow without the sweet.

I heard the door this time and ducked my head, not ready for an audience, but it was just Millie, and Millie couldn't see my tears. Her face was shiny and pink, like she'd just washed it, and her dark hair was smooth and heavy around her shoulders. She had coffee in one hand—my pot was definitely gone—and she reached forward with the other.

"Where are you, David?" she asked, and she said David like an endearment.

"I'm here, baby." Tag stood and reached for her hand, guiding her forward and onto his lap. He took her coffee and stole a sip as she dropped a kiss on his whiskery head. Her left arm was wrapped around his neck, and I noticed the ring on her finger. My heart swelled in my chest, and for a moment there was only the sweet, even if I wasn't surprised. It reminded me of the images I'd been shown the day before.

"I saw your mom again, Millie," I said gently. Tag turned to stare at me, his eyes blazing in his tired face. Millie turned too, as if opening her mind to the impossibility.

"I saw her yesterday, just for a minute. I think she wants you to wear her veil."

MILLIE CALLED ME. Her voice was scared and apologetic, and it was so reminiscent of the call she'd made six weeks before, looking for Tag, that I was immediately taken back, immediately seized by fear and dread.

I'd just seen them at their wedding a week ago, and I'd been so hopeful. I'd been so sure that they were going to beat the odds. Not just the cancer, but the odds. They were crazy about each other, and their beauty and devotion was tangible, a rosy-hued pulse that I had itched to paint. They were moving fast, which was Tag's style, but it wasn't rushed. It was right. The impromptu wedding and celebration at Tag's bar made me wish I could marry Georgia all over again, and we'd gotten a sitter and danced together for the first time since our own wedding.

"Moses?"

"What's wrong, Millie?"

"We were supposed to start chemotherapy tomorrow. But Tag has been running a fever all day. He's sick, Moses, really sick, and I want him to go to the hospital. He says we should just wait until tomorrow, since we have an appointment anyway. But I don't want to wait. I could call Axel or Mikey. But he's their boss. And they tend to do what he says, even if he's being an idiot."

"I'm on my way."

Tag didn't argue very much, actually. By the time I arrived an hour and a half later, he was too sick to put up much of a fight, although he winked at me and insisted on sitting in the back seat with Millie so he could hold her hand. They hadn't gotten much of a honeymoon, though Millie said she didn't care. She was more interested in having her husband. Honeymoons could wait, chemotherapy could not. Henry didn't want to go back to the hospital again. I didn't blame him—I didn't want to go back either—so he stayed with Robin, who wasn't hiding her fear very well. None of us were.

"I'll be back, Henry," Tag promised. "Record the fights for me, okay? I ordered them on pay-per-view. I want the run-down when I get home," he warned.

Tag's white count was elevated, but his platelets were still high enough for the first round of chemotherapy to be administered, according to the doctor. They admitted him for observation, but couldn't find any infection or any reason for the fever, and finally concluded, twenty-four hours later, that the fever was just his body's attempt to fight the cancer on its own.

With the fever under control and no reason to hold off any longer, they administered the first round of chemotherapy there in the hospital. Tag was resting comfortably, Millie by his side—he even had them convinced that he could go home as soon as he was done.

Then the shaking began. Tag shook so hard the bed shook with him, and he went from resting comfortably to courting death in a very short time. I ran for a nurse who could do nothing for him, and she paged the doctor. The shaking continued. It was like the seizure all over again, but Tag was perfectly aware and racked with pain that seemed never-ending.

"Don't let them s-s-sa-save me-e, Millie. I d-d-don't want to be p-plugged in t-t-to anyth-thing someone will e-e-eventually have, have, have t-t-to unplug. I d-don't want that." Tag stuttered, grinding his jaw with the effort to form the words. "P-p-promise m-me you'll l-le-let m-me g-g-go."

"Okay, David. Okay, I promise. I promise," Millie crooned, but her eyes were wide open, as if she were straining to see him, as if she were focusing all of her energy on him, as if she refused to have any barrier between them, even her closed eyes. He had turned onto his side, and his forehead was pressed against her chest. She struggled to hold onto him, the rigors shaking her off and making her teeth vibrate with his. But she didn't let go. He asked for something to bite down on at one point, after his mouth started to bleed from him biting his tongue. But he managed to keep his head pressed into her chest while his body bucked on the narrow bed.

"We see this sometimes," the doctor said helplessly, when he finally responded. "The chemotherapy is attacking the cancer. There's a battle going on right now, and his body is just reacting to it."

What the doctor wouldn't say was whether or not Tag would win the battle. And for four long hours, none of us knew. I had to step out of the room at one point and get control of myself, call Georgia, and reinforce my walls. If my best friend was going to die, I didn't want to know. I didn't want to see his dead sister at his shoulder, his great-grandmother waiting patiently for him to cross over. I didn't want any of it. I didn't want to know. I refused to know, because hope was vital. Hope was precious. And I would not take that from my friend or the girl who loved him.

At one point toward the end of the night, when the shaking started to slow and the very worst was over, Millie stepped into the bathroom, and I took her place beside Tag. He looked at me and said, "Do you see them, Moses? Is Molly waiting for me? If she's waiting for me, then we both know what that means."

"No. She's not waiting, man. It's just us—you, me and Millie. We're the only ones here. It isn't time yet, Tag." It wasn't a lie. I just refused to believe anything else.

He breathed deeply and grabbed my hand.

"I love you, Mo."

"I love you too." It was the first time I'd ever told Tag I loved him, the first time I'd ever said something like that to anyone but Georgia, and the words hurt. When I told Georgia I loved her it didn't hurt. But this? This was excruciating.

"I knew you did," he whispered. And with a reassured sigh, Tag slid into sleep, and I clung to my friend, determined to keep my promise to keep him earth-bound.

Twenty-Five

IT'S WEIRD. I started Tag Team because I knew, in the ring, in the octagon, no one really fights alone. You're standing there, battling an opponent, but the fight really takes place in the weeks and months, sometimes years, that come before a fight. It's in the preparation, it's in the team you assemble that helps you prepare. See, a fighter always has a team.

Because you have a team, and that team is counting on you, no one wants to tap out. In MMA, tapping out is worse than losing a fight. If you battle to the end and you lose the fight, you haven't really lost. But if you go into a fight and you have to tap out? That's hard on a fighter. That's hard on his team. That's tough on morale. That means you didn't take your opponent seriously, you didn't do your homework, you didn't prepare, your team didn't help you prepare, and you got caught with your pants down. Or it means you got scared and you didn't trust your training. You didn't trust yourself. You didn't trust your team. So you tapped out. And that's hard to come back from.

No one fights alone. That was my motto for Tag Team, yet it was my motto for everyone else. It was my motto for my teammates, but I never believed it myself. I *was* the team, I wanted to *be* the team for everyone else. I'd told Millie before the Santos fight that everyone fights alone. And I guess, deep down, I didn't want anyone to have to fight for me. Stupid? Obvious? Maybe. But that's who I am. Or who I was.

My goal now? No tap outs. Stick around. Stay in it. Fight. And like I told Moses, when the bell rings, it rings. And so far, my team is getting me through. My whole team.

The guys all came to my wedding in Tag Team shirts. In fact, every single person in attendance was wearing a Tag Team shirt with a suit or a skirt. Even my parents and my two sisters, who surprised me with their presence, were wearing them. Henry wore his shirt with a tuxedo jacket and a bow tie. Moses wore all black, as usual, but he added a pair of shades that he didn't remove even once, even though the ceremony was inside Millie's favorite old church. The shades hid his eyes, and I knew he was crying. I cried too, but I didn't feel compelled to hide it. The room was filled with people I cared about, people who cared about me, and it was easily the best day of my life—proof that even with a cancer diagnosis, you can still have a best day. You can still have lots of best days.

Henry walked Millie down the aisle, and she wore her mother's veil and a white lace dress that seemed more suited to another era—maybe the era I'd described when we first met. Watching her walk toward me in that dress made me believe in destiny and all the crap Moses and I had always said we didn't believe in. Or maybe it wasn't about the dress at all, maybe *she* was just beautiful. Looking at her made me happy to be alive. But then again, she'd always had that effect on me.

We had a reception at the bar that was more after-party than anything, and Millie and I danced until we were breathless, but left when it was still in full swing. I wasn't supposed to drive, so Mikey played chauffeur and drove us to our hotel, dragging boxing gloves and cans and a pair of Axel's size 16 shoes from the bumper, blaring "Accidental Babies"—Millie's request—as we made out in the backseat.

Speaking of accidental babies, we found out Millie was pregnant exactly a month after the wedding. It wasn't really accidental at all. Millie had willed it to happen, I think. Once chemotherapy and radiation started, there wouldn't be any little Taggerts until it was over—whatever 'over' meant. So she made sure it happened before. She was strengthening the team, calling in new recruits, making sure I had every reason to dig deep. We kept the all or nothing mindset. And we celebrated the news and refused to see the giants lurking in the shadows, making us fearful of what was to come.

I was just glad she wouldn't be able to dance around that damn pole for much longer. I hadn't wanted to show my inner caveman—and let's be honest, my inner caveman is an outtie—but I wasn't crazy about other men looking at my wife dancing around a pole. I suggested she should play her guitar a couple of nights a week at the bar instead, but she seemed content to keep the dancing in the basement and add some pre-natal yoga classes to the Tag Team fitness schedule, and actually pulled in quite a few new memberships.

Moses did his best to keep death away, and I let him believe I thought he could. I'd come close enough with that first round of chemo to know better. Nobody could stave it off when it finally came. And I watched it come for many suffering around me at the same treatment center. I was grateful Millie couldn't see them. In some ways, it was a small mercy.

I'd been referred to the Huntsman Cancer Institute and upon further analysis, my tumor had been downgraded from a stage four glioblastoma to a stage three anaplastic astrocytoma. That was good news. Gigantic news. It changed a terminal diagnosis into a diagnosis threaded with hope. But the good news was cut off at the knees when the tendrils of the tumor I'd had removed refused to die, and month after month my MRI results hardly varied.

But bad news or good news, we still celebrated. We laughed. We loved. I kept singing and Millie kept dancing—if only for each other. She said as long as I kept singing she wouldn't lose me. And it seemed to be working. Her belly grew, my businesses did too, and Henry grew most of all. He shot up over the summer and started packing on muscle with continued guidance at the gym. With his short hair and changed body, he was hardly recognizable when he started his junior year in high school.

Henry had stopped looking for giants around every corner. Instead of giants, we were looking for miracles. It's strange, the more we looked the more we found, and Henry kept an ongoing, detailed log of our finds and recited them every day.

⠠⠹⠀⠄⠒⠀⠫

MILLIE'S LABOR LASTED a long time. Too long. But we made it. We *all* made it. Millie handled it like a champ, which wasn't surprising; she was good at almost everything she tried. He was a big boy—nine pounds, eight ounces, twenty-two inches long and he looked so much like me I could only laugh . . . and cry. He was completely bald, which made him look even more like me. I'd lost all my hair with the radiation, and had kept it short ever since. Henry just nodded sagely like our resemblance was a given.

Millie thought we should let Henry name him, and I braced myself for a son named after Japanese beef or something equally exotic that would sound ridiculous on a little white boy. Instead he thought carefully and pronounced him David Moses, which worked for me. Interestingly enough though, Millie, who'd never warmed up to my nickname, called him Mo. She said I was her David, and the little guy needed his own identity in the house. She was certain Moses wouldn't mind sharing his nickname, and when Moses heard the news, he said little Mo could have it, he didn't want it. He hated it when I called him Mo. But I knew he was secretly thrilled.

Little Mo might have been a big baby, but he was still so small we held him for three days straight for fear we would lose him if we laid him down. Millie broke down a few days before he was born, telling me how afraid she was that she wouldn't be able to take care of him, but I never doubted her. She was a natural. What she didn't know, she figured out, and she figured it out quick. She approached motherhood with the same attitude she approached everything, and she'd been mothering Henry for a long time. She wasn't exactly new to the job.

I wondered how many blind mothers there were in the world. I knew there were some, even if there weren't many. She demanded that I describe every minute detail as she ran her hands over his tiny body and traced his miniature features—his button nose, and his bow-shaped lips, his little ears, and his paper-thin eyelids. His fingers, his toes, the bumps of his spine, the slope of his belly. I'd caught her lovingly exploring him many times since his birth, as if she was determined not to miss a thing. It made me ache for her that she couldn't see him, that she would never see her son's face. She would never see my face, for that matter. But Millie was convinced that if she could see, she would know us immediately. Maybe she was right. Maybe she actually saw us better because she took the time to touch us, to feel us, to find us, to know us.

Millie was asleep now, and in the soft moonlight streaming through the window in our room, I could see the pale length of her arm and the dark pool of her hair against the white pillow. She was a worker, my Amelie, very well-named. She'd been true to her word, and had matched me stride for stride and taken care of me easily as much or more than I'd taken care of her.

I sat watching my wife sleep, holding my two-week old son against my chest, my hand on his tiny back, feeling the rise and fall of his little body as he pulled life into his lungs and let it go again. His fat cheek lay against the opening of the V in my shirt, and I could feel that he'd drooled on me, or drizzled. He'd fallen asleep while nursing, and I'd eased him out of Millie's arms to burp him so that she could rest, and so I could hold him. He ate constantly, and I was convinced it was just because he liked where the milk was coming from. What was it with boys and boobs? He would cry when we forced him to detach, and I had started saying "Mo wants mo', which had inspired the Mo wants Mo' slogan I was now going to market with my Tag Team clothing line. Maybe there would even be a kid's line—Mo & Co or a maternity line, Millie & Mo. I liked that even better.

"Mo always wants mo', don't you, big guy?" I whispered, kissing his soft head. He smelled like boobs. In other words, he smelled like heaven. He sounded like heaven too, even when he cried. Millie declared his lusty cry one of her favorite sounds the moment he came into the world, bellowing like his life was over instead of just beginning.

"Daddy wants mo' too. More, and more, and more," I murmured, still watching his mother.

I had started making him tapes. I could have moved on to a digital recorder. But the tapes worked for me. I liked how tangible they were. Millie said she was going to take them all and have the contents transferred onto discs, and I said that was just fine. But I kept making the tapes, and I had a big stack of them, a verbal journaling of the last year, the days of my life, the days of our life together. Now I was making them for little Mo.

"David?" Millie asked drowsily. She carefully patted the space beside her.

"I've got him. Go back to sleep, Silly Millie."

I thought she had, she was quiet for so long. We were both tired. Exhausted. The last year had been heaven and hell. Music and misery. It had not been an easy battle, and I still wasn't cancer free. But I wasn't losing the battle either. I might lose the war. Eventually, I might lose. But we didn't think about that.

"Now I've got that song stuck in my head," she said suddenly, startling me. I jerked and Mo stuck out his lips and let out the saddest cry known to man.

Millie and I sighed together, a synchronized, "awwww," that lifted on the end and conveyed our shared sentiment that he was the cutest thing in the universe. The cry turned into panicked suckling, his little head bobbing over my chest, his mouth wide in search of something I couldn't help him with, and I had to turn him back over to his mother.

Millie heard me coming and reached for him, snuggling him down next to her, giving him what he always wanted.

"So spoiled," I whispered, laying down beside them, watching them because they were too beautiful to look away.

"He's not spoiled, he's a baby," Millie whispered, a smile playing around her mouth.

"I wasn't talking about him. I was talking about me," I whispered back.

I kissed her softly and she started to sing.

"I love your legs. I love your chest, but this spot here, I love the best," she crooned.

"Is that the song that's stuck in your head?" I chuckled quietly.

"Yes," she complained in a whisper. "And I need a different verse because nothing rhymes with David."

I laughed again.

"I love you more each passing day, I'll love you when you're old and grey," I rhymed.

"Oh, that's better," she sighed.

"I love you morning, noon and night," I sang.

"I love you even when we fight," she made up the next line.

"I love to fight," I teased.

"I know," she answered, and her voice was tender. "And that's the thing I love the most."

I kissed her again and forgot about the song. I kissed her until her eyes grew heavy and Mo started to wiggle between us. I took him out of her arms once more and let her sleep while I held my boy and told him about my very first fight. It seemed to sooth him and it soothed me too, remembering the adrenaline, the way it felt to right a wrong, to settle a score, to come out the victor.

Mo snored softly in my arms, and I smiled down at him, acknowledging that my battles weren't of very much interest to him. He only liked boobs. I couldn't blame him, but I hoped to be around long enough to help him discover a few other pleasures. I needed to show him how to throw a punch and how to take one too. I wanted to show him how to fall and how to come back when you were losing. In my life there weren't many fights I hadn't won. But the truth was, I didn't know if I was going to win this one. I just didn't know.

My story might not end in a miracle. But I'm not eager for an ending, so I'll take the miracles along the way and avoid the ending all together. I've discovered I don't have to see what's in front of me to keep going. Millie taught me that.

Perks of loving a blind girl.

Epilogue

Moses

WE ALL DIE. Eventually, that is how the story ends for all of us. There is no variance. There is no exception. We all die. Young, old, strong, weak. We all go sooner or later. I've come to accept that, maybe even better than most, though I don't think I'll ever embrace it.

When the weather permits, I like to walk to the cemetery on the rise overlooking the valley south of Levan. There isn't much to see—a few houses on the edge of town, fields, a highway, and distant hills. In fact, the view has hardly changed at all these past forty years. I had lots of family buried here. My great-grandmother was buried here. My mother too. My little son who I'd never known in life was buried here as well.

Eli's grave was the one I visited most. I liked to leave things for him on his stone. Shiny rocks and arrowheads, a new paintbrush and a little plastic horse. As the years passed, the gifts never changed, because he never changed. In my mind he was always the little boy, the little boy who never aged and waited somewhere for me to join him. I knew he didn't need the things I left. I knew he didn't even want them. I left them because I needed to, because I needed him. Still. Even though I got along without him, and even though my life was filled with loved ones, nothing filled the space where he should have been.

I had other spaces like that—little scarred alcoves that never looked or felt the same. Inhospitable places that I couldn't fill, where nothing would grow, where the walls echoed and silence reigned. And I could match each space to a stone in that cemetery.

The Levan cemetery had grown over the years. When I'd first come back to Levan as a young man, looking for Georgia, looking for my life, there had still been rows and rows of unused plots, stretches of green grass waiting for loved ones lost. But those rows were filled now, new rows had been added, and the cemetery wasn't so little anymore.

Georgia's parents had both passed away and she'd lost a brother a few years ago too. Axel was killed in an automobile accident five years after Millie and Tag were married. We'd all been devastated by his loss, and when his family in Sweden never came forward or responded to our repeated attempts to contact them, we brought him here, to Levan, and buried him among family, for that's what he'd become. I'd seen him a time or two, as big and blond and brawny in death as he'd been in life. He always smiled and showed me things, memories of time in the gym, time with Tag and the team, and bits and pieces of things I didn't always understand but never failed to paint. They were his precious things—his greats—and I didn't have to understand them.

Life had not been easy on the team, but life isn't easy on anyone. A few years back, Mikey's wife had lost her fight with breast cancer and after that, Mikey had gone down-hill fast. Their kids were raised and Mikey was tired. He was a veteran, but he didn't want a military send-off. He lost his leg in Iraq, but found a home in Tag Team. He expressed a desire to be buried here, next to his wife, and we buried them six months apart, not far from Axel.

When Cory's youngest son died of leukemia a decade ago, they'd brought him here too, wanting him surrounded in death by people who would have loved him in life, had they lived, had he lived. His little monument was engraved with a tree, and we buried him close to Eli, though the spot right next to Eli was already taken with a stone that bore my name. Georgia's name too, with the years of our births, a dash, and an empty space, a date that death would someday provide.

I had grandkids now, several of them. Georgia and I had welcomed two more daughters—no sons after Eli—and all our girls were married and gone, raising kids of their own. Tag's boy Mo went into the marines and eventually got into politics. He looked just like his dad, big and green-eyed with his dimpled smile and a helluva chin. But he listened like his mother, worked like her too, and thanks to Henry had a brain like an encyclopedia when it came to the details. Senator David Moses Taggert was a force to be reckoned with, and people had started throwing his name around as a possible presidential candidate. I just shook my head at that and hoped nobody would come sniffing around Levan, trying to dig up dirt on his family and friends. I liked the quiet.

I breathed in deep, filling my lungs with the silence and the sweet air, and stooped to pull a weed, clearing the intruder from my precious cluster of stones. When I straightened, I caught movement from the corner of my eye and turned to find Tag striding toward me, his shoulders as broad as ever, his back as straight, his smile as wide. His name rose to my lips and my heart lifted in greeting, welcoming my old friend. It had been a while, and I had missed him.

Acknowledgements

I SAY THIS with every book, so it must be the truth. Each book is harder than the last. I never feel like the words flow and the characters take me away. I never feel confident, never feel sure of myself. I can never predict what someone is going to like or dislike. I never know if the book will be embraced by my loyal readers. I never, ever know. With that being said, I am proud of this book. I am proud of the sweat and the tears. I'm glad that it isn't easy. If it were easy, than it wouldn't be so rewarding to finish. The difficulty of a task makes the task mean something. And when I write, it means something to me. I hope it means something to you. This book is dedicated to the following people:

To Cody Clark, who passed away last January after a four year battle with cancer. You and I never met, but I was inspired by you anyway. Thank you for fighting so hard and for never failing to say I love you. I promise to keep an eye on your mom.

To Stephenie Thomas, your grace and strength are inspiring. Thank you for sharing your cancer journey with me so graciously. The world needs more women like you. May you never leave us.

To Nicole Rasmussen, a blind mother with four beautiful children and a devoted husband. Thank you for letting me learn from you, for sharing your life with me, and for being such an example of determination and grit.

To Richard Stowell and lovely Ann. Thank you for your goodness, your love for each other and for those you come in contact with. Thank you for reminding me that all storms pass.

Heartfelt thanks must also be given to:

My assistant, Tamara Debbaut, who is loyal, steadfast, smart and efficient, and who suffers with me. That is a true friend. To my children and husband, you make me better. Without you, I would never come up for air. You bless my life and remind me of the important things every day. Thank you for loving me. I want to extend the deepest gratitude to my parents and siblings who always let me know they love me and are proud of me. They are my biggest cheerleaders. To Tina Kleuker for sharing your talents with me, and Mandy Lawler for believing in my writing and helping me find my way through the publicity maze. To Karey White, author and editor extraordinaire, thank you for your good work and for your support. Hang Le – thank you for the beautiful cover! I am so grateful to have your genius on my projects. To Julie Titus of JT Formatting, you know I would be lost without you. To Adam Legas and Riven Athletics, thank you for answering my questions about the world of MMA. To the team at Dystel and Goderich, thank you for looking out for me. And finally, to the readers and bloggers who have supported me through thick and thin, and who believe in me and my stories—you make it all possible. I can't name you all, as I will surely miss someone who deserves my thanks. But thank you. You make me cry happy tears daily.

AMY HARMON IS a USA Today and New York Times Bestselling author. Amy knew at an early age that writing was something she wanted to do, and she divided her time between writing songs and stories as she grew. Having grown up in the middle of wheat fields without a television, with only her books and her siblings to entertain her, she developed a strong sense of what made a good story. Her books are now being published in seven countries, truly a dream come true for a little country girl from Levan, Utah. Amy Harmon has written eight novels—the USA Today Bestsellers, *Making Faces* and *Running Barefoot*, as well as *The Law of Moses, Infinity + One*, *Slow Dance in Purgatory*, *Prom Night in Purgatory*, and the New York Times Bestseller, *A Different Blue*.

Website:
http://www.authoramyharmon.com/

Pinterest:
https://www.pinterest.com/authoramyharmon/

Twitter:
https://twitter.com/aharmon_author

Facebook:
https://www.facebook.com/authoramyharmon?ref=br_rs

Other Titles by Amy Harmon

Running Barefoot
Slow Dance in Purgatory
Prom Night in Purgatory
A Different Blue
Making Faces
Infinity + One
The Law of Moses

Made in the USA
Las Vegas, NV
21 January 2023

66011999R00144